A Thousand and One First Nights

A Thousand and One First Nights

by
Leslie Yeo

Mosaic Press
Oakville, ON - Buffalo, NY

The Academy of the Shaw Festival
Niagara-on-the-Lake, ON

Canadian Theatre History Series #2
General Editor: Denis Johnston

Canadian Cataloguing in Publication Data

Yeo, Leslie, 1915-
A thousand and one first nights
(Canadian theatre history series; 2)
Includes index.
ISBN 0-9699478-1-X (Academy of the Shaw Festival)
ISBN 0-88962-648-0 (Mosaic Press)

1. Yeo, Leslie 1915- 2. Theatrical producers and directors-Canada-Biogra-
phy. 3. Actors-Canada-Biography. I. Johnston, Denis William, 1950-
II. Academy of the Shaw Festival. III. Title. IV. Series.
PN2308.Y46A3 1998   792'.023'092   C97-901125-6

MOSAIC PRESS, in Canada:
1252 Speers Road, Units #1&2,
Oakville, Ontario, L6L 5N9
Phone / Fax: (905) 825-2130
E-mail:
cp507@freenet.toronto.on.ca

MOSAIC PRESS, in the USA:
85 River Rock Drive, Suite 202,
Buffalo, N.Y., 14207
Phone / Fax: 1-800-387-8992
E-mail:
cp507@freenet.toronto.on.ca

MOSAIC PRESS in the UK and Europe:
DRAKE INTERNATIONAL SERVICES
Market House, Market Place,
Deddington, Oxford. OX15 OSF

Co-published by Mosaic Press and the Academy of the Shaw Festival,
Box 774, Niagara-on-the-Lake, Ontario, L0S 1J0, Tel. (905) 468-2153,
Fax (905) 468-5438.

Mosaic Press acknowledges the assistance of the Canada Council, the Ontario
Arts Council and the Department of Canadian Heritage, Government of
Canada, for their support of our publishing programme.

Cover design and photo layout by Scott McKowen
Edited by Denis Johnston and Michael Power
Printed and bound in Canada

For

Hilary and Oliver and George

*and the ninety-eight actors
and actresses who were part of
the great adventure that was the
London Theatre Company*

Knowledge acquired in one's youth arrests the damage of old age, and if you understand that old age has wisdom for its sustenance, you will so conduct yourself in youth that your old age will not lack nourishment.

Leonardo da Vinci

Editor's Notes
by Denis Johnston

Almost three years ago Christopher Newton, the Shaw Festival's long-time artistic director, came up with the idea of a new publications series devoted to Canadian theatre history. We had a manuscript in hand – *Also in the Cast*, Tony van Bridge's memoir of an extraordinary career in the theatre. We had an editor on staff – me. To create a series, we hoped, all we needed was a little money, a little advice, and more manuscripts. While Christopher's contacts soon yielded the necessary money and advice, Tony and I proceeded with the book, which has now delighted many hundreds of theatre buffs.

Early on, Christopher and I decided that the series ought to focus on stories that might not otherwise get told. This relieved us of the temptation to pursue famous Canadian actors (are there famous Canadian actors?) for new memoirs. Nor were we anxious to hijack potential clients away from more prestigious publishers. We took pride instead in a modest goal: to do something to preserve our theatrical heritage, a thing of which Canadians seem lamentably careless. We hoped that bringing one manuscript into print might attract others.

Apparently it did. The same week we received our first copies of *Also in the Cast* from the printer, I got a letter from Leslie Yeo describing a book he was writing entitled (then as now) *A Thousand and One First Nights*. Although I had never met Leslie, Christopher had worked with him several times in the 1970s; indeed, Leslie Yeo was Christopher's last predecessor as artistic director of the Shaw Festival.

Leslie's manuscript surprised me in several ways. First, it was extremely well written. Second, it sometimes made me laugh out loud. (Manuscripts very rarely do this for me, and when they do I treasure them forever.) But most importantly, it unfolded a story of Canadian theatre which was entirely new to me. Now, if I am a bit vain about my knowledge of Canadian theatre history, I am especially so regarding the new professional theatre companies that sprang up in Canada in the late 1940s and early '50s. They have become a bit of a hobby, as well as an academic specialty. I enjoy telling Canadian theatre people about their roots in such companies as Vancouver's Totem Theatre, Toronto's Crest, or Ottawa's Canadian Repertory Theatre. But here in Leslie's manuscript was another of these companies, one of which I had never heard. And its story was told with a combination of openness and passion that is very rare in theatre memoirs of any period.

From the moment I read the manuscript, I knew I wanted *A Thousand and One First Nights* to be our next book. And although it is entirely Leslie's achievement, I would like to thank a number of people who have helped to bring it into print. For his artistic leadership, Christopher Newton. For their financial support, Honor de Pencier and Clare and Earl Darlington. For the index, and especially for his help in the final stages of editing and production, Michael Power. For his cover design and photo layout, Scott McKowen. For supplementing Leslie's own photo collection, Lisa Brant at the Stratford Festival Archives and Bernard Katz at the University of Guelph Archives.

Now all of you, find a comfy chair, get a glass or mug of your favourite beverage and have a little read.

one

I can only assume that my earliest carryings-on were best forgotten, since my memory flatly refuses to yield a solitary titbit that was pre-Grandpa Stride. I remember him because he used to fart a lot. And every time he let one rip, he'd say, "Hullo, there's somebody talking behind me." As his backside habitually hogged the fire, he was constantly cooking one up, so he said it often. I don't think he meant it to be funny. He might have done once, but by this time it came out quite automatically as if he'd been programmed. He heard the note and he said it, like an opera singer picking up a music cue from the bassoon.

Grandfather Yeo had a weakness too. He liked to put his hand inside ladies' blouses. My mother was well into her eighties when she let slip that little goodie. I think she'd been into the sherry, but she swore to me that "the old bugger" had always made a beeline for her bra the moment my father left the room during their courting days.

I don't remember my grandmothers at all so they must have died young, one presumably from perforated eardrums and the other from exhaustion. But before they set sail for the land of eternal relief, they each saw to it that I was provided with a mother, a father, a good slew of uncles and a fine flutter of aunts. Matrimony multiplied their number by two and cousins began to sprout with a regularity that was almost indecent. I mean, we weren't even Catholics. Mind you, we were a bit High Church, so perhaps it was the incense that turned them on.

It does seem a waste after all that thrashing about, but I can't remember a thing about any of my fifty-odd first cousins except that one of the boys had buck teeth. It was easy enough to forget the Strides because they all lived in Silly Sussex on the other side of England, but I should have remembered some of the Yeo tribe because we all grew up in the same town. But their parents always looked upon my mother

1

as a bit of a foreigner, or perhaps it was the other way about, and we never became very close.

When you come into the world with a name like Yeo, you can bet your bootees they'll call you Yo-Yo the minute you show your face in kindergarten. And they'll do the same in the wolf cubs, the boy scouts, Sunday school, elementary school, secondary school and all through the never-finishing school of life.

The second thing you can be certain of is that your guests will frequently arrive expecting to come face to face with a Chinese fellow. Such peasantry can, of course, be quickly dismissed as lightly travelled and sparsely read or they'd have known that there is a river Yeo in Devon, a town called Yeovil in Somerset, the Yeomen of England, the Yeomen of the Guard and Salvation Yeo the gunner in Charles Kingsley's *Westward Ho!* and none of them had ever been near a crispy noodle.

Down in Devon to this day it is pure Yeo country and there are telephone books by the ton to prove it. The Yeos outnumber the Smiths in all of them, and the only reason they don't do the same in telephone directories everywhere is because most of them have never seen a particularly good reason for leaving Devonshire and they have a point because it's very beautiful. So, in 1877 when Daniel Joseph Yeo – he with the friendly hands – upped and migrated to Swindon, a full two hundred miles north, they practically thought he was a second Christopher Columbus.

Swindon is a market town, sixty miles from London as a crow clocks it, much further by car in the days before the motorways. If you didn't fancy the place and kept on going, you'd find yourself flanked by the giant ferns of Savernake Forest, or racing neck and neck with one of the historic white horses carved on the distant chalk hillsides of the Wiltshire Downs. Half an hour further on still would have put you in the awesome shadow of the giant bluestones of Stonehenge. When I was a boy, we would picnic inside the Druid's Circle using one of the bluestones as a backrest. Today a burly policeman and a hundred yards of turf stand between you and four thousand years of history thanks to a contribution by the twentieth century from a bunch of morons armed with aerosol paint cans. A visit to Stonehenge will never be the same.

Swindon didn't contribute a great deal to the beauty of Wiltshire, but it had a hell of an impact on its economy. In the days of steam, the better part of the town's entire labour force would stream through the gates of the locomotive works in time to beat the eight o'clock hooter and toil fifty-two hours a week, forging brass and sculpting steel into the giant juggernauts of the Great Western Railway: the Castle class, the King Class and the likes of the Cheltenham Flyer, which led the world with its daily sixty-mile nonstop run from Swindon to the heart of London in sixty minutes flat.

Swindon had one other claim to fame: it gave birth to Diana Dors, Britain's answer to Marilyn Monroe. After she and fame had found each other, she was invited back to receive the keys of the city. Her real name was Diana Fluck, and 'twas said that the mayor, who was to introduce her at a civic luncheon, was so nervous of making a mistake that he paced the corridor all through the main course muttering over and over to himself, "Diana Fluck, Diana Fluck, Diana Fluck", then strode to the microphone and introduced her as Diana Clunt.

Once ensconced in Swindon, Grandfather Yeo chose a house in the Old Town and set about founding the Wiltshire branch of the family. Perhaps it would be truer to say that the house chose him, for it went with the job of general manager of the cattle market which was just over the back garden wall. I used to think how lucky grandfather was because the market was such an exciting place to be on market day. To stand beside the sale ring was like going to the circus without having to pay. And if you kept a fast eye out for an opening and wriggled hard you could even end up in the front row. Every Wednesday, the auctioneer would mount his uncovered dais at one end of the ring, come rain, hail, snow or sleet, for nothing halted the market except foot-and-mouth disease.

The star of the show was, without question, the stubby little stockman who was as good as any ringmaster. Although his silk hat was but a cloth cap and his elegant carriage whip just a good stout stick, he ushered each animal in and out of the ring as if it were an international act. Best of all was when a cow came moving in accompanied by a calf and he'd shove his hand right up between the animal's back legs and shout out to the auctioneer "Bull calf, sir" or "Cow calf, sir" according to the kind of handful he ended up with.

The ringsiders were mostly regulars – butchers and farmers with chunks of chiselled granite for faces and complexions that spoke eloquently of an ongoing battle with the elements and rough cider. All were decked out in their Sunday best, and they jostled and joshed each other with great good humour during the breaks in the action. But it only needed a cough from the auctioneer to transform them once more into a cadre of grim-faced CIA agents, because bidding is a deadly serious business and every man is your enemy. Each bidder was armed with a stout walking stick with which he prodded the animals unmercifully. In my youthful ignorance, I thought they were simply sizing up how much was fat and how much was bone, until one day a nervous cow shot forth from its rear end a jetstream of brown tobacco juice, and I quickly discovered that the sticks were to steer it towards someone else's brand-new Burberry and away from your own.

In summer, the stench from the tobacco juice would sometimes seep under Grandfather Yeo's back door, but he never seemed to mind. Market day was only once a week, and the job left him lots of time to prepare himself for his true destiny which was a career as a writer. He had already contributed the occasional column to the *Swindon Advertiser,* and had begun to adopt a mode of dress more in keeping with a future Boswell: velvet smoking jacket, brocade waistcoat and a matching pillbox hat with a tassel of silvered threads. A neatly trimmed pepper-and-salt beard and moustache completed the ensemble, and the resultant picture was that of a poor man's King George V. I think he must have become aware of this because it was about then that he developed an urge to acquire a pedigree.

Digging up the Yeo family dirt started as grandfather's hobby but quickly grew into an obsession. There was a spate of unusual comings and goings at the house by the cattle market – the librarian, the postmistress, the town registrar, the vicar, students of history and just plain mongers of gossip. There were frequent day trips by grandfather to London, nosing around the British Museum and the archives at Somerset House. There were interviews with the editor of the local newspaper. And there was finally a pledge to let grandfather share the excitement of his discoveries week by week with the readers of the *Swindon Advertiser.*

After a while, the little snippets picked up on the roadway back through history began to thin out in grandfather's column and it became more and more difficult to hide his disappointment that not the tiniest tincture of blue had turned up in the bloodline. Then suddenly came the day he hit paydirt and set the town agog. He had traced our lineage all the way back to the reign of William II, third son of William the Conqueror and "surnamed Rufus for his red face." History records that William Rufus was killed in a hunting accident in the New Forest and that his body, with the arrow still piercing his eye, was borne back to Winchester on a farm cart. What the historians missed, but grandfather didn't, was that the cart was provided by a Farmer Yeo whose name was plainly painted on the side of it.

The Yeo stock soared and was just about at its zenith when another ancestor surfaced who had been hanged for rape and the articles in the *Swindon Advertiser* abruptly ceased. And, to my knowledge, the roots of the family tree have remained undisturbed ever since.

Grandfather Yeo raised four daughters and three sons, and it came as no surprise to any of them to learn that they were not of noble birth. Most of them had married and had happily accepted their position in society as commoners, albeit middle-class ones. My father, the youngest of the three boys, did nothing to change the pattern and became a tradesman. He went even further than they did in the cause of the common man and married a barmaid.

It was 1911 when a brand-new fascia went up at number three Bath Road, a prime corner location in the Old Town's small but select shopping area. In large gold leaf letters on a black background, it read:

FRED J. YEO
Hatter and Hosier

Life really began for my father the day that sign went up. It ended nineteen years later with a declaration of bankruptcy, and he never got over the shame of it. But that couldn't take away the memories of those nineteen years. Almost at the start of them he met and married my mother. He saw her first while she was dispensing drinks behind the bar in The Goddard Arms just a few doors down the road from "the shop". He wasn't really a drinker and she wasn't really a barmaid. He would only order ginger beer, not for any righteous reasons but because alcohol was taboo for a man with a weak heart. She was only a barmaid because that was one of the ropes to be learned in the business of hotel management which was the family calling. She was twenty-two and exceedingly beautiful. He was thirty-two and wasn't so bad himself. So at the shop, the till had barely been broken in before it was asked to feed two mouths instead of one. Six years on, four hungry sons were also lapping at the family trough. I was the one who came along at the second time of asking.

I wouldn't say my schooldays were on a par with Tom Brown's, but I did achieve a certain notoriety and a small amount of profit by launching my own school magazine. I wrote the text in a special ink and printed it on a gelatin hectograph pudding. It sold like hot cakes in the school playground until I was called in by the headmaster and told that I was seriously eroding the circulation of the official school journal. I could be modest and say I was an average student, but I think I was a mite better than that because I always ended up top in English and second in French. This was mistakenly construed as a flair for languages and landed me in a special Latin class where I never did better than seventh and there were only seven of us on the course.

Less than two blocks from the school was the Swindon Empire where I made my very first appearance on any stage as a bunny rabbit in a local production of *The Arcadians*. Though I was only about ten at the time, I immediately fell madly in love with the leading lady, who was all of twenty-five and quite irresistible with her dainty pillbox hat perched atop her jet black Eton crop. When the cast picture came out, I put an X just above the pillbox and slept with it under my pillow for weeks.

In my particular scene, a group of distinguished local ladies, much too old and far too large, were frolicking about in a meadow singing:

> *Flying nymph and sporting faun*
> *Sport amid the roses,*
> *Flora fresh with dewy dawn*
> *Binds her fairest posies.*
> *Beauty in the shining pool*
> *Mirrors all her graces,*
> *Where the lilies white and cool*
> *Lift their gleaming faces.*
>
> CHORUS
> *Land of love and land of mirth*
> *Land where peace and joy had birth*
> *There the birds have ever sung*
> *Arcady, Arcady, is always young.*

On cue, and looking quite gorgeous swathed from head to toe in rabbit fur, I hopped into the middle of this idyllic scene, paused twice to look and listen, wiggled my whiskers, and hopped off again. Forty-eight years later, a rabbit was to share the spotlight with me on another landmark occasion when I played the lovable alcoholic Elwood P. Dowd and renewed my acquaintanceship with Mary Chase's enchanting creation *Harvey,* arguably (though not in my book), the best performance I ever gave in all those thousand and one first nights.

It was November 1973 and I was at the Vancouver Playhouse

sharing the lead in *Leaving Home* with Kate Reid. We also shared the billing, the accommodation and the number one dressing room which was basically a couple of cells served by a common entrance door. The accommodation was palatial: a townhouse in Kitsilano for the entire run presented to the two of us with extraordinary generosity by Pat Hall, the then chairman of the Playhouse board who said she'd be quite happy to move to her house in Hawaii for six weeks and "leave us to it." In fifty years of touring, I cannot ever recall more luxurious digs. The bedspread, queen-size, was made entirely of wild fox furs. Kate and I were totally incapable of keeping such opulence to ourselves and threw a magnificent party for the cast and crew. I'm sure the genteel neighbours still remember it, for it couldn't even begin until after the performance by which time most of them had gone to bed. Christopher Newton, who was running the Playhouse at the time, allowed as how it was the best theatrical party he'd ever been to.

During the festivities, I overheard him say that he was going to switch the final play of the season and put on *Harvey*. I felt that somebody had stuck a dagger into me. I spun him round quite fiercely and told him that he couldn't possibly do *Harvey* without me. It was my favourite part.

"You'd better come and play it then," said Christopher.

"I can't, I'm booked solid. Can't you keep it for me for next season? About this same time?"

He pulled a Player's cigarette packet from his pocket and emptied the contents on to the table. On the inside tray he wrote LESLIE YEO PROMISES TO PLAY HARVEY AT THE PLAYHOUSE NEXT OCTOBER. "Sign this," he said, and I signed it. About seven months later there was a phone call from Vancouver.

"I have a cigarette pack here that says you belong to me in October. We open on Thanksgiving."

The eminent critic of the *Vancouver Sun,* Christopher Dafoe, started off his review in a grumpy mood. He was irritated at having to miss his Thanksgiving dinner to cover an old hack like *Harvey*. But suddenly he saw how the philosophical outlook of Elwood P. Dowd related very much to the present day and he went on to give us a fabulous review, ending thus:

> Leslie Yeo's Elwood P. Dowd is a sublime creation, so softly fashioned, so beautifully realized in every detail. It is a performance that amuses and touches simultaneously, memorable

in its vividness, enormously appealing in its humanity and warmth. The role of Elwood P. Dowd is a rich prize and Yeo has embraced it and made it his own; a remarkable tour de force.

I don't think I made the review in the *Swindon Advertiser*. And at the site of my debut they now sell groceries. Swindonians still have a theatre but they don't call it the Empire any more. Like so many of its counterparts in provincial Britain, it has had to relinquish its identity to a new master with nobler aims than profit and a close acquaintanceship with the keeper of the public purse from whom all blessings now mostly flow. In the new Wyvern there's carpet in the lobby and no brass to clean. But there's no theatre smell.

two

I was fourteen when my fathers's business failed. I still remember hiding behind a tree across the road from number 36 The Mall, watching all our possessions come one by one through the front door on their way to someone else's home, courtesy of the auctioneer of my father's estate in bankruptcy. We were left with nothing but four bare walls and a roof. My father had a nervous breakdown and the family scattered, settling wherever there was a friend with a warm heart and a spare bed.

As I was the only one of the Yeo boys to make it to secondary school, everybody thought it imperative that I finish my education. I was temporarily adopted by the Dashwood family and lived in upper class comfort until, one day, Dashwood Senior found me reading a book with a plain cover and wrote to my parents suggesting that, in view of the fact that he had a daughter approaching puberty, I should perhaps move on. Another family friend generously picked up the slack. Because he was a bachelor and had no housekeeper, he put me into digs. The name of my first landlady escapes me, but I shall be forever grateful to her for introducing me to the glory of HP Sauce.

The summer holidays came but there was to be no reunion with my family. I was shipped off to Somerset to stay with distant cousins at Hamswell Farm near Bath. Next door to the farm at the bottom of the orchard was Hamswell House, one of England's minor stately homes. The resident squire was a brother of Somerset Maugham, and I found a playmate there in Maugham's nephew Robin who was also home for the holidays and also destined to become a writer.

By English standards, Hamswell was a large farm, and Farmer Sparrow saw to it that there was a large family to run it. His wife's fertility buds blossomed thirteen times before he left her a widow. All thirteen children survived and all lived and worked on the farm. Although the eldest was over forty, he lined up every Friday with the rest of them for his pocket money, which his mother doled out from a large brassbound cashbox. On race days at Bath, there was always a special pay parade with most of the payout ending up in some bookmaker's satchel in the ring.

But it was mealtimes I remember most at the farm. Breakfast was taken on the run, lunch was brought to where the action was in the fields, be it haymaking, harvesting or muckspreading, but dinner was a ritual. The kitchen was mission control with the preparation, the cooking, the eating and the clearing up all taking place within the same four walls. Mum, armed with a carving knife, presided at the head of a large refectory table that at a single sitting accommodated her entire family plus the odd boy friend or girl friend or guest like me. The helpings were generous and the appetites huge. Vegetables were passed round in large white enamel washbowls, and it took three whole loaves of freshly-baked bread to help mop up the gravy.

After dinner, pipes were lit, the girls did the washing up and Mum listened to progress reports and made plans for the morrow. Almost as if by a signal, the girls withdrew to the sewing room, and the door had barely closed behind the last one before someone fired the first fart. Close on its heels came an echo from the other end of the table, then another, and another and soon it was open season. Each effort was greeted with howls of laughter punctuated with cheers for a really virtuoso effort, and the odd jeer for one that turned out to be a little low in decibels. This went on night after night and they never tired of it because the orchestrations were always different. One of the boys, when he was in real form, could render the first six notes of God Save the King in passable tempo though not always perfect pitch.

I'm not quite sure how the rest of the family came to end up in London, but that's where I was bidden for the Christmas holidays. It would be the first time in nine months that we'd all been together. I boarded the train eagerly, laden with textbooks as I was due to sit for my matric in the spring.

The 36 bus from Paddington station winds a fascinating way through the West End until it reaches Westminster Bridge, then spoils it all by picking the most sordid possible route into South London by way of the Elephant and Castle, the Old Kent Road, Walworth, Camberwell and Peckham. It was more than a bit of a shock, therefore, when somewhere in the middle of this stretch, brother John dug me in the ribs and said: "This is where we get off." Had the family fortunes sunk this low?

I found them all crammed into a small flat above a sub-postoffice in Camberwell Green. I wasn't expecting 36 The Mall, but this was barrow-boy country. There was very little in the way of furniture and no tub or shower – just a toilet and a sink with a geyser that had to be fed with a penny to induce it to vomit small quantities of tepid water. This meant visits to the municipal baths which were sordid, stank of chlorine, and were staffed by apes who thumped on the door before you'd even got your clothes off and told you to hurry up because somebody else was waiting.

Brother Fred, the eldest among us, was following the family calling as a salesman in a men's wear store geared to the spiv trade at the Elephant and Castle. He was sixteen. Brother John, who on November 11th reached the legal school-leaving age of fourteen, got himself a job on November 12th as a carpenter at sixpence an hour in a sweatshop making cheap furniture in the East End. My mother was serving as a barmaid at *The Adam and Eve,* Peckham, probably the most notorious pub in the whole of London. Father hadn't found work. Peter was still at school. All earnings were pooled, with deductions only for tram or bus fares and very token pocket money.

John always took the early shift and had a regular routine he followed on his way home. Next day I arranged to meet him off the bus at Camberwell Green so that he could show me the ropes. First he took me to the baker's shop where we waited until five o'clock when what was left of the day's batch went on sale at half price. A few doors closer to home was the fishmongers where he'd pick up a couple of cracked eggs for a penny each. The girl's face dropped as we walked in.

"Sorry John, no cracked eggs today."

He looked so devastated that she darted a quick look over her shoulder, and, with a whispered "Oh well, we'll soon fix that," she cracked a couple for him. It was then that I knew my schooldays were over.

In January, when the Class of '31 straggled up the front steps for their last spasm of high school life, I was not among them. I was sixty miles away climbing a different set of stairs and with infinitely more enthusiasm. I'd struck oil with the very first ad I'd answered in the *Daily Telegraph*, out-charmed them all at the audition and now here I was in the heart of the city of London, one flight up and three to go en route to fame and fortune in the advertising department of Spratt's Patent Limited, dog food manufacturers.

Inside the front door, it was pure Dickens. There was a smell of old masonry kept young with carbolic soap. The stairway was narrow and the steps were of stone, all worn to a groove in the middle and sloping steeply upwards like the lips of so many giant ladles piled up in a soup factory. There was no landing for a breather between flights. You either continued climbing or you took the corridor and your choice of frosted glass doors, each identifying in black letters the body that was buried behind it. There were no windows to light your way because these had been reserved exclusively for the offices, as if the architect had been afraid there wouldn't be enough daylight to go round.

But I saw no sign of gloom on my upward climb that Monday morning. This was the stairway to the stars: a job and twenty-five shillings a week which, after deductions for tram-fare and one coffee and fruit bun a day at the ABC, should add at least twenty percent to the family exchequer. To the Yeo household, Spratt's brought manna from Heaven. To Spratt's Patent Limited, I brought the eagerness of youth, a pronounced West Country burr, and an overwhelming desire to please.

In those early days, the demands upon my energy, time and intelligence were far from life-threatening – and this was just as well because I would need plenty of all three to complete my education which from now on would have to be entirely self-administered. I didn't have to look far for learning aids: I was surrounded by them. The advertising department was one big reference library. This was the creative corner of the company, a cultural clearing in a forest of pen-pushers. Here there was an answer to everything you could ever want to know, just so long as you knew where to look.

It fell to me to keep track of every book as it left its shelf and see that it got safely back there at the end of the day. As most of the traffic took place in the early morning and late afternoon, I had plenty of reading time in between. So, wedged into the undersized well of my paste-and-ink-stained desk, I sat enthroned in this court of literary kings and mapped out for myself a mammoth reading plan to make up for the university I would never attend. Handy to my desk were also a couple of creative shoulders I could peer over and pilfer the knacks of the copywriter and the layout man. And, to add to the momentum, on my sixteenth birthday the advertising manager gave me my very own copy of *Roget's Thesaurus*, coupled with an offer to pay for some night classes on advertising for me at the nearby City Literary Institute. As the cost of an additional course was negligible, I enrolled for drama as well. I little knew at the time that the City Lit would one day become an important farm club for young actors and that I would end up as one of its farmhands. But I had a career as a publicist to complete before that, and I'd yet to write my first ad.

My big chance came when the manager threw a church magazine on my desk and said: "We've taken a quarter page. See what you can do with it."

As the cost of this kind of space was largely looked upon as a charitable donation, the creative department rarely extended itself beyond a bald HAPPY EASTER or BEST WISHES FOR ADVENT from THE MAKERS OF SPRATT'S DOG FOODS. Well, the creative staff had just increased by one and this was his debut. And it might also serve as his entrance exam to a world of bigger things.

By the time I had finished creating, the cost of the original artwork alone for my quarter-page would have paid for Happy Advents in at least a dozen different parishes, a fact which would not have escaped the ad manager but which he generously chose to overlook when he initialled my brainchild and handed it back with a smile. It was my diploma. It was also all the encouragement I needed to put my next plan into effect -- to give Spratt's a house magazine.

The Biscuit was born without any midwifery on the part of the company. The work was done in my own time after office hours, with all the stationery and supplies paid for out of my own money. I wrote the material, typed it, printed it, assembled it and kept the sixpences everybody paid for a copy.

The Biscuit was, of course, a big step forward from my schoolboy effort as one would only expect from a professional copywriter and layout man. The cover was printed commercially on stiff yellow paper with my own India ink drawing of a huge dog biscuit and a hand-lettered title above it. But every inside page was laboriously typed column by column on stencils. Column rules and page borders were hand-drawn with a stylus and thumbnail sketches likewise. There was always plenty of humour, my proudest personal contribution being MY DIRY, purportedly written by an office charlady named Ruby who always knew all the dirt and had a great knack of expressing quite clearly exactly what was going on and with whom, without actually mentioning names. Before press day, I would stay at the office well into the night and run off sixty copies of every page on a hand-operated Roneo duplicator. Then I'd sort them and staple them into the covers. I believe the first edition ran to twenty pages.

By the end of six years, I had crossed out all the adjectives in *Roget's* that could possibly apply to dog biscuits. I was also in a

13

financial rut that was on a steady course about one degree north of the poverty line and running parallel with it. I'd yet to know what it felt like to put my arms and legs into a brand new suit, even one off the peg from the Thirty-Shilling Tailors. Mine still came from the second-hand clothes shop in Camberwell Green.

It was true that my salary had tripled in six years, but that still only made it three pounds ten shillings a week. Ads in the trade papers were offering twice that for a Copywriter and Layout Man. And if you were *just* a copywriter or *just* a layout man, you were really talking money. Which was I? I could hold my own as a lettering artist and often moonlighted as a showcard writer when the sales were on, but my illustrations wouldn't have got me a card in the pavement artists' union. It would have to be copywriting. Besides, copywriters were fetching more than layout men.

When I told Spratt's that I was leaving to join an ad agency as a junior copywriter, you'd have thought that the Chairman was on his deathbed and they were relying upon me to take over. Didn't I know I was one of their bright hopes for the future? That I was on a short list of five young people who were to be groomed for stardom in the company? Did I realize what I was giving up? (I knew one thing I'd kiss goodbye if I stayed -- an extra four pounds a week.) They even whistled me in to see the Chairman of the Board. The closest I'd ever got to him before was on the receiving line at the annual staff ball. He was bright: he locked on immediately to the importance of four pounds a week. If that was all I wanted, that could easily be arranged. I told him that if it had been that easy when I'd asked for it two months earlier, I'd probably never have looked for another job and now that I had one I was afraid I couldn't change my mind. And that little interview set a pattern that I was to follow for the rest of my life. It's not that I'm stubborn, just quick at making up my mind. And once it's made up, I never change it. I'm a door-closer.

I hadn't wasted my years at Spratt's. I'd learned a trade and crossed several key thresholds in my private life. I had begun to sound more like a Londoner than a refugee from a farm in the West Country. I had all but cured myself from blushing for no reason at all and at the most embarrassing moments, like sitting in the barber's chair surrounded by mirrors which flashed my discomfort to every corner of the salon.

I had also been out with the boys and got drunk for the first time. And I'd lost my virginity.

I was just seventeen when I saw her first standing in a doorway, out of the rain, in Soho. She looked as if she'd walked straight off the cover of a movie magazine. I remember her more vividly than anyone else I ever met in my life. If I were an artist I could draw her now. Her hair was dark, slightly wavy and tapered up at the back. She wore a black beret pulled down on the left side and a white macintosh with a wide collar half turned up and a belt tied like the cord of a dressing gown. She was slim and she was young and her name was Jean and to my utter astonishment she spoke with a cultured accent. She cost me all of a week's wages.

She said, "It's a bit small, isn't it."

It was only fourpence on the bus from Fenchurch Street to my next career stop at the Lord and Thomas Advertising Agency, but it was a ticket to another world. After six years in the City on a narrow street condemned to a life in the shadows, Thames House, Millbank was etched against the skyline like a back-lit Hollywood set. It was a skyscraper, all of ten stories high and built with room to breathe and let in the sun on the wide open spaces of the Thames embankment. If you were lucky enough to have a southern outlook, you could press your right cheek against the window, close one eye and just see the Houses of Parliament one bridge up river. And for spiritual guidance you could look clear across the water to Lambeth Palace, London home of the Archbishop of Canterbury.

The agency suite on the eighth floor was a symphony in glass, with see-through walls that gave budding clients a powerful image of a staff of hustlers ever on the move, always at the double and not one them a day over thirty-five. My arrival on the scene at the tender age of twenty-one did nothing to dilute this vision of youth on the march and I knew I could match the others in energy erg for erg. Nonetheless I was more than a little apprehensive when I was ushered into an office all to myself and confronted with my own typewriter, which I felt sure would be expected to spew out the slogan of the month before the end of my first day.

Lord and Thomas was a small agency with big billings. Clients were few but were all major players in the marketplace. This translated into a healthy *status quo*, but a high risk when accounts were on the move and the loss of a single one of them could take seven figures off your bottom line. Trying to hang on to them put an unrelenting strain on the creative department, and undreamed-of opportunities in the way of the new Copywriter and Ideas Man with the junior portfolio.

15

Beyond question, early Lord and Thomas was the period in my life that taught me most how to work under pressure and thrive on it. Stress time at the agency came in batches. It began when the call first went out for a concept for a new national advertising campaign, and never let up until the first ad appeared in print. The account executive always fired the starting gun. He had just returned hotfoot from the client, armed with a budget, an impossible deadline and some blunt words from the man who paid the bills on just what he'd be expecting back from us for our fifteen percent. At creative sessions, you learned to think fast, speak up and get used to being shot down. When the meeting broke up, there would be a mad scramble for a pad, a pencil and an idea. It had only a few hours to germinate before there'd be a recall for a review and a mad scramble back again for a better idea. This cycle would be repeated and the time-frame tightened until one of us came up with the hook on which we could hang the campaign. From then on, all creative thought was channeled into a single fallopian tube from which the agency's brainchild would finally emerge all dressed up and ready for the final presentation to the client. The deadline would be met, the account retained, the agency saved and the client's market share preserved intact.

The only thing that bothered me was that I never seemed to be the one who came up with the hook. But just as I was beginning to worry about the effect of this in high places, I got an unsolicited approval rating from the President himself. We'd all been through the usual wringer to produce a new national campaign for Jaguar cars and had assembled for the final review. The President, an American named Mike Masius, was especially well pleased and singled out the copy department for having done a particularly fine job. The head copywriter without even looking up from his doodling pad gave a dramatic sweep of the arm in my direction handing me all the credit, which was very decent of him seeing that he'd come up with the original idea and I had merely written five or six variations on his theme. But it didn't dilute my feeling of pride one bit when I saw the front page of *The Daily Mail* one morning with nothing else on it but a beautiful picture of the latest Jaguar and six lines of my prose, knowing just what it had cost per word to put them there.

Under the stewardship of Mike Masius at Lord and Thomas, I rapidly matured as a copywriter and also as a man of the world, though my development in the latter area was in no way due to him. That was taken care of by a much lesser light in the agency named Steve Risdon – sophisticate, ex-public schoolboy, socialite and a seasoned member

16

of the Good-Time-Charley Club. I was a social tenderfoot when he took me in tow. On the credit side I suppose I was fairly presentable and a distinct asset when on the prowl for girls in an era when they tended to go around in pairs for safety and hadn't yet learned the danger of prowlers who went round in pairs, too.

Risdon wasn't part of the creative team at Lord and Thomas. His talent lay in providing the agency's top clients with a first-class round of golf and occasionally letting them win, which was the hard part: he had once played for England as a Junior and had a plus two handicap. From the very beginning, Risdon ignored my given name and insisted on calling me Joe because a copy typist from some Latin country couldn't pronounce the letter *y* and always addressed me as Mr. Jo. He even introduced me to everybody as Joe Yeo and, as he was a highly accomplished party-crasher, the introduction got a lot of exposure. I dubbed him Pete, for no better reason than that wasn't his given name either. So Pete and Joe we became and were soon a familiar after-dark duo at some of the lesser known sin spots in Soho and the occasional Mayfair drawing room.

On Saturdays when the agency was closed, we almost always ended up in Fleet Street where we had a mutual chum who was a make-up man on the *Sunday Referee,* not one of the top five but a national newspaper just the same. And they did have as a regular weekly contributor, Edgar Wallace, the leading thriller writer of the day. On Saturdays, he was a familiar figure with his foot-long cigarette holder, scurrying in just under the deadline with the last few pages of his latest short story.

Our day at the *Referee* began with a liquid lunch at the Hole in the Wall, after which we'd weave our way back to the chum's office where he'd arm the two of us with some giant shears and we'd begin trimming the galleys streaming in from the composing room. Fortified by a few more visits to the *Hole in the Wall* during the afternoon, we'd then insist on dipping into the paste-pot and helping him "make up" the late-breaking news pages of the paper. I don't think we could be blamed for the ultimate demise of the *Sunday Referee*, but there were definitely Sunday mornings when I went out to buy my *Sunday Express* and wondered how in the hell a copy of the *Referee* managed to be sitting there beside it.

While it would be true to say that Pete Risdon led me astray in my early twenties, it would be less than honest not to add that I was a willing follower. The agency days were long and the pressure-cooker lid was rarely loosened before seven in the evening. I needed to let off steam, too, and the West End – that renowned reliever of tensions – was only a five minute cab ride away.

There were few human frailties that didn't get an airing during the Risdon Experience. One late bloomer was playing the horses, an omission that I, for once, was the one to rectify. I had been brought up in racing country where local trainers, owners and jockeys had been *habitués* of my father's shop and kept him primed with inside goings-on at the stables. Unfortunately, Pete and I weren't privy to the same kind of information as my father and we didn't do as well as he did. Also, unlike our other diversions, playing the horses was a daytime activity and harder to hide from our more righteous colleagues. It wasn't easy to make the *Sporting Life* look like the *Advertiser's Weekly* through a clear glass door. It also took time to study the form and call the bookmaker, and even the slackest days at the agency were high on the hectic scale. All our accounts were household names with huge appetites for the output of copywriter and ideas men, and there were only two of us to keep up the public demand for the likes of Palmolive soap (NOW SHE'S SCHOOLGIRL COMPLEXION ALL OVER), Pepsodent toothpaste (YOU'LL WONDER WHERE THE YELLOW WENT), Kleenex, Jaguar, Quaker Oats (with all its puffed offspring), and Kotex (NOW WITH LOOPS AT NEW LOW PRICES). And as if that weren't enough, we were all called in one afternoon, told to drop everything and come up with a campaign to launch in England a brand new confection called a Mars Bar.

It is hard to say which put the greater strain upon our staying power: the demands of the day which were mainly mental or the activities of the night which were mostly physical, but our reserves seemed inexhaustible. The only thing we ran short of from time to time was money, and we had a fail-safe way of dealing with that. We'd go to see Harold Lane.

Lane's London Club was a West End landmark, a monument to Edwardian times and a more gracious clientele looking for an evening away from the wife to drink, gamble and watch prizefighting all under the same roof. It was still strictly "Members Only" but Risdon played golf with the proprietor which gave us the entree, not only to the club but to his private office as well. This was up a short flight of stairs beyond a balcony rail overlooking the ring which was the centrepiece of the room. Harold would welcome us warmly and wave to his well-stocked private bar. After two hefty *Black Labels* apiece, Pete would drift over to Harold and ask him to cash a small cheque.

This done, Harold would say, "Let's go and have a look at the bouts." As we leaned over the rail, he would tell us under cover of the ringside clamour that the fighter in the purple trunks would be disqualified in the ninth round. Then he'd take us through the card and tell us how most of the other bouts were likely to end as well. After much back-slapping, Pete and I would wander off, place our bets, and make enough money to cover the cheque he'd cashed plus our cost of high-living for another couple of weeks. This, of course, couldn't go on. Creative juices find it hard to flow when there's a five o'clock deadline to meet and you're worrying about which horse won the four-thirty. And I began to wonder how much longer I would be able to keep from my employers what I could no longer hide from myself: that I was horribly close to becoming an addicted gambler. So one morning I gathered what self-respect and strength of will I still had left and gave it all up, cold turkey, the same way I stopped myself chain-smoking twenty years later. I closed my account with the bookmaker and tore his number out of my private telephone book.

To cover the withdrawal symptoms, I needed a new hobby in a hurry and I found an old one that had never really gone away. Though I had long since graduated from my advertising course at the City Lit, I still showed up for drama once a week. They welcomed the news that my work load would now permit a more active participation in student productions and I quickly found myself cast in plum roles that would leave me little time for a running part as a playboy. One of these was King Henry VIII in *The Rose without a Thorn* by Clifford Bax. I remember I made myself up with a print of the Holbein portrait stuck in my make-up mirror, and I went on to give a passable impersonation of Charles Laughton in *The Private Life Of Henry VIII* – not because I believed that, in the film, he had been at all like the real Henry, but because the public did, and this was now the pattern by which all future Henrys would be judged.

Though amateur companies overflowed with stage-struck women, male roles were invariably filled by reluctant husbands or anxious-to-please boyfriends. Being neither, I was a gift straight from Thespis. I quickly found myself rehearsing leads with three different companies at the same time, as well as being invited to "walk on" with the real actors in the local repertory company at the Penge Empire. You got no pay for this, just your bus fare, and you weren't allowed to open your mouth onstage except in crowd scenes when you went on and did your best to attract as much attention as possible. Per-formances were twice nightly, twelve shows a week; so my leisure hours were now at a premium.

It soon became clear that the Good-Time-Charley Club was about to lose a member and the days of the Risdon Experience were over. It had lasted nearly three years and proved the most expensive part of my education as well as by far the most valuable. I'd had all the behavioural virus shots: early exposure to weaknesses that, if encountered for the first time in later years, might well have become way-of-life threatening. I haven't placed an off-course bet on a horse in almost sixty years or even been tempted to. But I rarely turn down the offer of an afternoon at the races where you can only bet with ready cash and you discover, as they come round the bend and head for the home stretch, that the old tingle you thought was gone for ever has only been hibernating after all.

By far my best stage work as an amateur was achieved at The City Lit where we worked under a professional director. By this time, the Institute had also begun to attract attention as a serious source of drama students. One noted alumna is Pat Galloway, a long-time star of Canada's Stratford Festival. I only discovered this recently, even though she has been one of my closest friends since the early sixties. She looked at me rather quizzically when I asked if we had shared any of the same instructors, and I realized just in time that I must have preceded her at the City Lit by at least twenty years. Why, when we're getting on, do we watch everyone else growing older and imagine we're standing still?

All the City Lit productions were critiqued by a Mrs Roxborough who ran a small theatrical agency. She had been persistently positive about me and had even once said, "If it ever crosses your mind that you might want to become an actor, which God forbid, don't do anything foolish until you've talked to me."

I hadn't thought about it until then, but I began to. A compliment from Mike Masius did a lot for the ego but it couldn't hold a candle to the applause of an audience as you exit after *your* scene. Also, there was serious talk of compulsory military service with God knows how long an interruption to established careers. Better to have one to come back to that you like, rather than find yourself too old to start a new one from scratch. If I wanted to make a change, the time was now. I went to see if Mrs Roxborough was as good as her word.

I was so staggered by my reception that I almost walked out and ended my theatrical career before it began. She was furious with me. I hadn't been fired? Then what the hell was I doing in her office? The theatre wasn't for me. It was for people who either had a private income or hadn't the talent to do any thing else. I had a lucrative job and a future. All I'd get out of the theatre was a bed in an actors' home and a past.

She blasted me for an hour and I sat there and took it. I must have passed the endurance test, because suddenly she switched tactics and promised to help me all she could. She scribbled out a note, sealed it and said, "Go and see this man. He runs a rep company and he's very hard up. If you're prepared to work for very little, he may try you out."

Arthur Lane was an Australian, handsome, blonde, oozing with charm, a good actor, and a wife to match him in all categories. Between them they played all the leads in their weekly repertory company at the Woolwich Empire in South London. Armed with my note from Mrs Roxborough, I introduced myself and told Arthur Lane that I thought I could act. To prove it, I said I would rehearse and play one production for nothing if he gave me a good enough part. After the last performance, he could either say, "Thanks a lot, goodbye" or keep me on and start paying me. He grinned a lovely grin.

"I like your cheek. All right, then. Next Tuesday we start rehearsing *When Irish Eyes Are Smiling,* and you can play the juvenile lead. His name is Gerald and at one point in the play he has to come on in riding clothes carrying his six-week-old illegitimate baby that he's bringing home to mother. If you can play that scene for a whole week without getting a laugh, I'll put you in the permanent company. You've got riding clobber, of course?"

"Of course," I lied and went straight round to the second-hand clothes shop in Camberwell Green.

On the opening night, just before the curtain went up, I stood in the wings and watched with amazement as every other actor desperately took one last look at his lines. I hadn't picked up my script for a week. How those days would change.

I got through the whole week without getting so much as a giggle on my entrance, and Arthur Lane kept me on. My theatrical career had begun. Unfortunately, two weeks later, so had World War II and the Home Secretary closed all the theatres.

three

The bombers didn't show and the Home Office lifted the ban, but the Arthur Lane Players never returned to the Woolwich Empire and I'm still owed the first week's salary I ever earned as an actor. But, paid or unpaid, it was a professional credit and I had a printed programme to prove it. That was all I needed to get me a listing at Miriam Warner's Talent Agency on Charing Cross Road. Miriam didn't have any stars on her books or even feature players. This must have been a terrible wound to her pride since she had given so many of them their very first job, only to see them defect to more fashionable agents at the first whiff of success.

She began by sending me off on "special weeks" to two of the lesser-known repertory companies in Britain at Gravesend and Weston-super-Mare, both of them hiding out on the end of the pier. A "special week" was a misnomer since it took two weeks' work to earn one week's salary. It was pay as you play and nothing for rehearsals in 1939. If you got lucky and were booked for two plays in a row, rehearsals and performances would partly overlap and bring you two weeks' pay for three weeks' work, which put you on a slightly quicker route to prosperity.

After several such assignments, I sensed a distinct danger of becoming looked upon as a professional special-weeker. It was time to discover what the film world had to offer. I accordingly registered with Central Casting where I quickly learned that to make a living as a film extra the last thing you must do is get anywhere near a camera. On my first shoot, I spent a physically exhausting day rioting outside a factory in the East End, while four of my fellow extras hid behind a wall and played poker. They emerged at "wrap" time to line up with the rest of us for our twenty-one shillings in cash and were promptly rewarded for their perfidy with the offer of a second day's work because they hadn't been close enough to the camera to be identifiable in a totally different mob scene to be shot the following day. The conscientious among us like me, who'd been acting our socks off hoping to do a David Niven and get picked out of the crowd, were never given a second chance. We were "over-exposed" and paid off.

Being an extra may have meant a day trip to wonderland for a disenchanted housewife or cigarette money to a pensioned-off civil servant, but to the serious actor it was a demeaning, demoralizing dragdown to the lowest common denominator among the dregs of the job market. The degradation began with the "cattle call" at Central Casting which made you feel like a carcass on a meathook. After a cursory inspection, you were either yanked off your hook to join the rejects or rolled along on your pulley to other indignities further down the line. The cattle theme was continued next day at the studio as you were herded along corridors past heavily laden snack tables all clearly marked NOT FOR EXTRAS and finally quarantined from the rest of the unit in a cheerless room with not enough chairs. You were eventually escorted to make-up by the umpteenth Assistant Director where the girl took one look and decided you hadn't a sufficiently important part to warrant a pat with a powder puff. You were then escorted back again to make sure you didn't contaminate any of the real actors on the way.

I was mercifully rescued from my six week never-to-be-repeated stint as a film extra by an offer to become a member of a brand-new repertory company, opening at the Empire in the naval town of Chatham. It was normally a Variety theatre and suffered a shortage of acts to fill the bill. Its owner Sir Oswald Stoll, head of one of the most prestigious managements in London, didn't want to see his theatre idle and decided to put in a repertory company. The standard was of a very high order and I did wonder how I'd managed to make it as the juvenile leading man with my limited experience until I found out that the director, a Belgian named Yves Renaud, had taken a fancy to me. By the time I'd made this disturbing discovery, the contract had already been signed so I didn't have to buckle on my armour right away. But I decided I'd keep it handy when he began to cast me in all the best parts, strongly suggesting he was in hopes of cashing in later. My problem was suddenly resolved when he got fired for fiddling of quite a different nature. Actors in those days were paid cash. Yves had given Head Office a phoney salary list and since the beginning of the season had been drawing two pounds a week more for each of us than he'd actually been paying out.

I can't say he personally diddled me out of anything. The big diddlee was Sir Oswald Stoll. Yves had signed my contract and faithfully paid me what was on the face of it. He even gave me a bonus by casting me in roles I ought never have been allowed near in a company of that calibre. Not that anybody complained, least of all the naval ratings who packed the place to see me tear off Aubrey in the farce *It Pays to Advertise.* They seemed to be convinced I would turn out to be another Ralph Lynn who'd made his name in the same part long before he got together with Tom Walls and Robertson Hare in *Rookery Nook* at the Aldwych. Few audiences, and occasionally even reviewers, are able to tell the difference between a part and a performance. So all you really needed was one good role to prove you could do it. A pox on all those tiresome stars who loved to pontificate that there were no small parts, only small actors. They spoke from the heights. They had already climbed Everest and not one of them got there by being brilliant in a ten-liner.

There is a big snag in playing to the same audience week after week: once you've proved yourself as a *farceur*, they start looking for laughs in serious scenes where there aren't supposed to be any. This tendency was somewhat exacerbated at Chatham by the presence in the company of an old character actor named Frederick Ross. He had once been a great matinee idol for Oswald Stoll, and he was still a commanding stage presence with a speaking voice that could go two full tones lower than Paul Robeson. A slight unsteadiness due to drink had toppled him from his pedestal but Stoll felt he owed him one last chance. He agreed to pay Ross a handsome salary on condition that eighty percent of it be withheld in London until the end of the season in order to keep him out of the wine and spirit merchants in Chatham. Unfortunately it didn't keep him out of the local chemist's shop where he could buy methylated spirits at sixpence a bottle. On one particular night, in a heavy drama called *Double Door*, Ross made a magnificent entrance and then just stood there making noises like someone having an epileptic fit. These are the occasions when inexperience comes galloping to the rescue. No one has more confidence than an actor at the outset of his career (or less than at the end of it, when you relive every crisis in your theatrical lifetime just before you make your first entrance). So I was able to face Freddie without the slightest semblance of fear. First of all, I had to shut him up, so I raised my right hand like a policeman on point duty and said, "I know exactly what you are going to say," and proceeded to say it for him. I then answered myself and repeated this routine until I had managed to convert the entire scene into a monologue with Freddie contributing little more than an occasional grunt. The navy, of course, loved it and started coming to the theatre regularly each week just to see "that funny old guy who never manages to get a word in." It was a sad end to what had been a brilliant career but also a lesson, in more ways than one, to another that was just beginning.

I had my own priority in the other lessons to be learned by a young actor. They were mostly about love: loving what you were doing and being loved while you were doing it. And not only by your audience, but also by your fellow actors. Particularly your fellow actors. I've nurtured this belief all my professional life and nothing has contributed more to my trail of happy memories or paid handsomer dividends. The first big payout came before the end of my maiden season.

The envy of the entire Chatham company was the leading lady, Helen Sessions: she had another job to go to when the season came to an end. The morning after closing night, she would pack her bags for London, cross the city to Paddington Station and take the Cornish Riviera Express to Bath to begin rehearsals the very next day for a ten-week season at the historic Theatre Royal. Two weeks before departure day, I received a letter with a Bath postmark. In it was an offer from Reg Maddox to join the same company, sight unseen, as leading juvenile man. That could have meant only one thing, so I went in search of Helen. When I found her, I silently held up the envelope, pointed to the postmark and raised my eyebrows. She smiled, I gave her a huge hug and that was all that needed to be said. There was nothing sexual about our relationship, just an immense feeling of mutual pleasure in being on the same stage at the same time, sharing a good script and an appreciative audience. It was a scene that would be replayed often during my career. In fifty-eight years in the theatre, I've landed more parts purely on the recommendation of fellow-performers than for any other reason.

Bath was a stout rung up the prestige ladder from Chatham. The repertory season was an event firmly established on the theatrical calendar, not just a "one-off" to keep a Variety theatre warm. And the Theatre Royal had been built for actors, not unicyclists and kick-lines. You didn't need follow-spots or microphones on a stage where the flick of a feather duster could be clearly seen and heard in the back row of the upper circle. The theatre had played host to all the great comedians and tragedians from Edwardian days, and still attracted actors and actresses of stature in 1940. It was a distinguished ensemble

25

I faced at the first rehearsal. Almost all of them subsequently made it to the West End, although my own arrival had to be delayed by my five years on active service. The one in the company with the biggest future in store was Mona Washbourne, a lovely lady who would find herself in great demand as a leading character actress on the West End stage and in films for the next forty years. Nobody in the Bath audience would have dreamed that she was still in her early thirties, for they rarely saw her without a wig or a character makeup. She was young in heart, too, and always ready to spring to the defence of the younger members of the company like the juvenile man who was first in line when the director wanted a whipping boy. We had such a director and his name was Rex.

In the middle of the season, playwright Philip King arrived to sit in on rehearsals for his new play that we were to try out. He'd yet to write his two great money-spinners, *See How They Run* and *On Monday Next*, but had made an auspicious start with his rustic comedy *Without the Prince*. In his new play, the main character was a boy scout named Ulrick and I was elected to play him. With a minor adjustment to the set of my upper jaw, I found that I could give him slightly protruding teeth, and Philip was ecstatic with the result. Every night, after each scene I was in, I would find him waiting for me in my dressing-room, beside himself with excitement. He promised me faithfully that if the piece ever got to London, nobody would play Ulrick but me. Of course, it never did.

In weekly rep, if you were playing the lead, it was customary for you to be the one to walk forward at each night's curtain call and give a plug for the next week's production. This also gave the audience the chance to let you know by their applause whether you were quite as good in the part as you thought you'd been. Rex had already by-passed me for this honour once before when I was playing the lead. He did it again when I played Ulrick and chose Mona. She was quite distressed and nailed him in his office.

"Rex, this is going to be Leslie's evening. Please let him make the speech."

But Rex said no. He wanted her to do it.

At the first night curtain, Mona started forward, hesitated, stepped back, grabbed me from the line-up and pushed me forward for a solo "call." She played it beautifully, a generous, spontaneous gesture that was twice as telling because it had been totally unrehearsed. The audience loved it. Rex was furious. But Mona was a lady with high principles and she stuck to them all week.

When the summer season came to an end, I saw nothing in my crystal ball except a return to London and a first date with the blitz. The Cornish Riviera Express was already full before it got to Bath, so I parked my one enormous suitcase in the corridor and sat on it. Since it contained my entire wardrobe for a ten-week season, it was big enough for two, and I made room for a musician standing beside his instrument case which was even bigger than mine but too fragile to be sat upon. He'd been standing since Bristol where he'd been playing for a week at the Hippodrome with Henry Hall, the leading big band of the day. When we discovered we both lived about a mile apart in South London, we speedily agreed to split a cab when we got to town.

The train was running late and it was dark before we even made Reading. The German firework display had already started over London and we had a grandstand seat. Although the compartments behind us were blacked out, we could read through the corridor windows the miserable little nameplates that now identified the stations we were passing through. Believe it or not, the big signs that used to stand three feet high at the open end of the platform had all been removed for fear they might be read by German pilots.

At Paddington the taxi queue was four deep and ran the full length of the platform. It would take the entire London fleet to get to us. We humped our suitcases over to the Underground. The body odour that wafted up the escalator smelled like drains at the end of a long, hot summer. The scene on the platform itself was indescribable. There were sleeping bags, cots, mattresses and sacks stuffed with newspapers two bedspaces deep. That left about five feet for people trying to board a train or get off. It didn't really make much difference since there hadn't been one for over half an hour. We fought our way back against the tide of new arrivals and decided that the only way home that night was on two feet. We lugged our suitcases up the slope from the station and out into no-man's-land.

I'll never forget that walk as long as I live. The name of every street we took has etched itself into my memory: Edgware Road, Marble Arch, Park Lane, Hyde Park Corner, along the Mall past Buckingham Palace, Trafalgar Square, Whitehall and over Westminster Bridge and we weren't even halfway. There was still the full length of Lambeth, Kennington and Camberwell to cover before we'd get anywhere near Herne Hill and home.

The blackout didn't mean a thing. Once we got to the West End, there were enough fires to light our way better than any street lamps. Though totally devoid of buses and private cars, the streets were buzzing with ambulances, fire-engines, and police cars. And then we discovered where all the taxis had gone. They'd been pressed into service as emergency fire-engines with auxiliary water-pumps clamped to the back of them.

The only people to be seen were those wearing some kind of uniform or armband, so we stood out. We were constantly screamed at by Air Raid Wardens to take cover but we knew that the legal choice was ours not theirs and we plodded on. Torches frequently flashed on us and our suitcases. Were we plain halfwits or were we looters carrying booty home from a bombed-out building? Each time my musician friend held up his instrument case and murmured the magic words "Henry Hall" and we were happily waved on.

The noise level was horrendous. There were whistles blowing, bells clanging, bombs exploding and anti-aircraft batteries blazing away from every patch of green grass big enough to hold a gun. In a momentary lull, we could hear the one sound that never went away in an air raid – the pulsing drone of the bombers. We began to become impervious to all noises but one – the piercing whistle of a descending bomb that meant it was probably going to land somewhere near you. Only then would we dive flat on our faces and cover the back of our heads with our hands. I don't remember how many dives we took that night. I don't really know why we bothered at all because everyone said that you never heard the whistle of the one that got you.

We crossed Westminster Bridge and now faced the full length of Kennington Road. It was a mile long, straight as an arrow and we could see it all. An ominous glow in the sky ahead lit up the tram tracks like steel ribbons. They pointed right at the glow, due southeast, the same way we were heading. Where home was. We didn't say it, but I knew we were both worrying about the same thing.

My suitcase was now pulling my arms out of my sockets, so I tried riding it on my shoulder. I got as far as Kennington Park and I knew I couldn't lug it any further. I slammed it down and sat on it. Just then I heard voices coming from an Anderson bomb shelter in somebody's front garden across the street. I walked up the path and stuck my head through the small curtained opening.

"Excuse me. I've just carried an enormous suitcase all the way from Paddington and I'll never get it as far as Herne Hill. Could I possibly leave it with you and pick it up in the morning?"

They were a bit grudging but told me to dump it up on the porch. It was too dark to see a number, so I mentally marked my bearings and rejoined my musician friend with a brand new set of springs in my shoes. When I finally got home, the ominous glow, thank God, was still further southeast. I got out a map and measured our route. It had been nearly five hours since we'd left Paddington. We had walked eight miles and I had lugged that bloody suitcase along four of them. Next morning I set out to retrieve it.

The bus got to Camberwell all right, but the entrance to Kennington Road was blocked off. The road I'd walked over only a few hours before was now pockmarked with craters, and pieces of tram track were jutting up like tank traps. The front wall had been shaved off several houses. I remembered that the one I wanted had black wrought-iron railings, a porch and a bomb shelter in the front garden. I stood across the road with my back to Kennington Park and tried to pick it out. Then I discovered that Kennington Road was one long string of row houses and they all had black iron railings and a porch and most of them had an Anderson shelter in the front garden. I tried three houses before I spotted my suitcase on the porch exactly where I had left it. I rang the bell, put on my best "thank you" smile and was greeted by the most violent blast of invective I've ever heard from a woman.

It seems that after I'd gone away the night before, a strange uneasiness had spread through the shelter. What kind of bloke would dump a bloody great suitcase in the middle of the night and go away without leaving his name or at least asking theirs? In no time at all, the shelterers had decided I was a fifth columnist and my suitcase was a ticking time-bomb. Nobody had the guts to stick his head out to look and have it blown off, so they just sat there and waited and didn't get a wink of sleep all night. When it was still there in one piece in the morning, they decided it must be booby-trapped, so they crept past it to the back door and called the police. When the landlady realized the man on her doorstep wasn't one of the boys in blue, she gave it to me with both barrels. So I took my fucking suitcase but I didn't put it where she told me to.

four

The call-up was a rapidly decimating the ranks of juvenile leading men and there was a decided run on hairpieces at Gustave's the wigmaker as talent agencies struggled to fill the gaps. As I was still a few hairs short of toupee time, I was hustled off at a minute's notice to Dundee to play out the end of their repertory season. Already there, and well established in the company, was Max Helpmann who, thirty-five years later, would share a dressing room with me at the Festival Theatre in Stratford, Ontario. Another company member to pop up in Canada was Richard Todd who would be a fellow guest artist in an episode of the TV series *Matt and Jenny*. A film star by this time, Richard had been nominated for an Oscar in 1949 for his Lachie in *The Hasty Heart*.

I hadn't been in Dundee two weeks when a letter arrived marked OHMS with orders to report to the local recruiting officer for a medical and assignment to one of the three services. As a conscript you weren't given a choice: you went where they put you. Max and Richard got identical letters by the same mail but our interviews were set for different days, all consecutive.

Dickie Todd went first, on a Tuesday. He was given to the army and would end up in all the trouble spots, including a drop behind enemy lines with the 6th Airborne in Normandy just hours before the dawn of D-Day. I have thought many times since, that there, but for the grace of God and the luck of the Dundee draw, could have gone I. On Wednesday Max, like everybody else that day, was inducted into the Royal Navy. By Thursday it was clear it was the RAF's turn and, sure enough, I was earmarked for a suit of Air Force blue. I immediately volunteered for pilot training and was put on a waiting list for an interview at the Air Ministry.

Back in London, managements were scrambling to send shows out on tour beyond the reach of the Heinkel bombers, and actors were falling over themselves to join them. I got myself into a strange brew

30

of Variety and straight theatre which was meant to attract both kinds of audiences to houses that normally catered only to playgoers. It was unimaginatively entitled *The Best of Everything*. The producer had assembled a star-studded Variety cast headed by Al Bowlly, Britain's "Golden Voice of Radio," whose reading on the British adulation thermometer in 1940 was bucking Bing Crosby's. His partner was Jimmy Mesene who was another Greek with a golden voice and a similar weakness for all things feminine. The magnet for the straight theatre-goers was to be the personal appearance of Phyllis Neilson-Terry as Kate in J.M. Barrie's one-act play, *The Twelve Pound Look*, a part that had previously attracted many famous actresses including Ethel Barrymore.

The Variety names on the bill would have held their own at the London Palladium in 1940, but the fame of few of them has survived the passing of the years and the Empires and Hippodromes that once headlined them. Even in 1940, nobody wanted to see them in a straight theatre and *The Best Of Everything* was a costly failure. But it was an experience for me that would never be equalled: ten unforgettable weeks to work and play with crooners and comics, jugglers and acrobats, balladeers and belters – those dedicated, down-to-earth, talented, fun-chasing, giving, lovable men and women in Variety. The surroundings were wrong, the show was a hybrid but the people in it were real and I was made to feel that I genuinely belonged. Sure they took the mickey out of me for a while and talked posh whenever I was near because I was "legit" but they loved it when I answered them back in their own lingo with an accent twice as thick as theirs. In no time at all they made me feel like one of them and, as things turned out, by the end of the tour I practically was.

As the company settled down for a pep talk from the producer, the twelve dancers in their rehearsal leotards and little else stood at the back and formed a line from force of habit. Al, Jimmy and I stationed ourselves a few feet behind them admiring the view. Al, who had already done his homework on their front elevations, ambled forward and stopped behind the third girl from the left. He licked his index finger, marked an imaginary X in the air behind her back and rejoined us. Jimmy then solemnly made his choice the same way. They weren't joking either. The pay of chorus girls was appalling in 1940 and the only way they could make a bean on tour was to sleep four to a room. Pairing off with an Al or a Jimmy meant they could live in comparative comfort rent-free, and come back to London with at least some of their pay packet intact. Al remained faithful to his choice all through the tour except for one small lapse. We were in Newcastle and I was in the dressing-room he shared with Jimmy when the stage doorkeeper knocked and said there was a very pretty young lady who wanted to get Al's autograph in person. Jimmy took my arm and steered me gently outside. After a short while, he gave me a big wink and we headed back to the dressing room. As we opened the door, all we could see was Al's bare bottom upside down on the sofa. The girl hadn't been in the room five minutes.

For the first time, I learned the luxury of two and a half weeks of rehearsal instead of five days. The tour was to debut in Coventry and we were to be the very first show in the new 3,000 seat Hippodrome. There we had the full use of the stage and crew for three days before our opening. We needed every minute of the time to iron out the kinks in the big production number which was a re-enactment of the Miracle of Dunkirk, loaded with pyrotechnics, special lighting and sound effects. It was also my big moment.

The scene opened with a life-sized mock-up of a tramp steamer centre stage, seemingly heading straight for the audience. Black smoke belched from the stack, the ship rolled wildly from side to side on hidden rockers and Al Bowlly and Jimmy Mesene, in reefer jackets and seafaring caps, clung to the wheel on the bridge singing:

> *Just a dirty old tramp*
> *Sailing in the blue*
> *Bringing home the bacon*
> *For me and for you*

By the fourth verse, when the hidden crew had rocked Al and Jimmy off into the wings, the backdrop went up to reveal five groundrows of rough seas with spaces between each for ships of all shapes and sizes, pitching and tossing their way across the stage to England and safety. Planes were swooping overhead on wires, bombs were bursting everywhere, the horizon blazed with gun flashes and criss-crossing searchlights and a pall of smoke drifted over the entire scene. As the applause tapered off and the background noise subsided to talkover levels, a spot came up on me downstage left in a fisherman's jersey and cap and smoking a corn-cob pipe. With my foot resting on a log, in the most dramatic voice I could muster, I told the story of Dunkirk in verse, about sixteen of them. I can only remember the first one:

The little ships of England
That sailed the seven seas
From Devonport to Dover
From the Thames up to the Tees

As the lights faded out on me and the little ships, Al and Jimmy rocked back across the stage for a last reprise of *A Dirty Old Tramp*. If the whole thing sounds ghastly today, in 1940 it was spectacular for a road show, and so hot on the heels of the real thing that audiences would be overcome with patriotic fervour.

Every Monday morning in each new town, there was a band call where our Musical Director would teach the local musicians the show. The singers would run their numbers, test the mikes, check the tempos and probably ask for more from the strings or less from the brass. The acrobats would show the drummer where they needed a sting, a sustained drumroll for suspense, a whistle for a flying leap or a cymbal for the climax of a daring feat. The comics would simply cut to cue if they had a vocal.

Three weeks out from London, I arrived for the band call to be told by the stage manager that the army had grabbed our romantic singer and I would have to go on that night and sing *Where or When* at the start of the second half. I was petrified. I had never sung a note in public in my life. I worked with the MD all afternoon and was so scared of blowing the lyrics that I chalked the words on the stage floor where my microphone would be.

The dreaded second half curtain went up and twelve beautifully gowned ballerinas were already into their routine when I walked into my spotlight in white tie and tails and waited for my music cue. When the MD raised his stick and gave me the downbeat, I felt it pointing at me like the muzzle of an assassin's rifle. And that's how I came to make my debut as a singer with twelve ballerinas behind me and Britain's number one crooner below me, sitting in his dressing room listening to me over the PA system and pissing himself with laughter.

One week later, the call-up claimed its next victim and I found myself working with Eddie Leslie and Jean Adrienne as part of their comedy routine. But this time I was in my element and they were quick to see it and make full use of it. We had wonderful sessions in their dressing-room talking about the mechanics of making people laugh.

The precision and the discipline of the comics in Variety always astounded me because they were so undisciplined offstage. They would go into the pub in full make-up and entertain guests in their dressing room during a performance – strict no-nos in legit. But once on stage, they were court jesters in the kingdom of comedy working under their own martial law: once you'd found a new laugh, you never again lost it, or, there's only one sure way of getting a laugh but twenty-four sure ways of killing it.

Archie Glen was a prime example. He was an old north country comic who had been touring the same act round the halls for twenty years, yet he still held an inquisition with his straight man after every performance. "What did you do that you hadn't done before on my line about the cat? We didn't get as big a laugh as we usually do. You were fuzzy on this feed, too early on that one and too late on the other. And what happened just at the moment I put my hand on my heart? You took the attention right off me and I didn't get a sausage." It wasn't so much a criticism as a matter of pride. Many of today's straight actors don't like to be told how to get a laugh. Perhaps we should try a new tack and show them all the things that kill one.

Just as audiences shrank during the blitz, so did the Variety actor's pay. Stars who wanted to tour had to share the financial risk. They had to forego their enormous minimum guarantees and work for a straight percentage of the box-office take. As a performer with no box-office value, I was paid a flat salary come what may. And that's how it transpired that one week I earned more than the great Al Bowlly. The Germans had picked Birmingham as target-of-the-week and plastered it every night. In twelve performances at the huge Prince of Wales Theatre, our biggest house was all of ten people and we grossed £28 on the week. I was paid in full but not one other principal drew a penny.

My most vivid memory of that week was the pub that was closest to the stage door. I'm sure the landlord's name was Bird because I can still see, pinned to the wall of the bar, the cartoon of four bird bodies wearing the caricatured heads of the landlord, his wife and two daughters. Mr Bird should have received a special plaque from the Variety Artiste's Guild. Knowing the score at the Prince of Wales, he announced that anyone in the cast could run a slate for his drinks for the entire week and send him the money later. As he'd built a bomb-proof bar in the basement and we stayed there every night until the small hours, some of the tabs must have been enormous. I'd stake my faith in the Variety profession he was repaid every penny.

The Sadler's Wells Ballet company was also in town and shared our basement bar. They were on guaranteed salaries and insisted on buying us all drinks. Jimmy Mesene fell for one of the dancers and on our last night, we held a mock marriage ceremony with a tablecloth for a veil, a napkin holder for a ring and smouldering ashtrays as censers. After the ceremony we saw them off on their honeymoon to Jimmy's hotel. He had paid his bill in advance that afternoon, ready for an early Sunday train call, and he hadn't a bean left. In the morning, the maid knocked on the door and brought in the breakfast tray. To Jimmy's astonishment it was laid for two. He woke his "wife" and sat there rubbing his hands at the remarkable service when he spotted an envelope propped against the teapot. In it was a bill for two pounds for "one extra occupant in room and one breakfast." I had to go round and bail him out. It was either that or they climbed down a drainpipe.

I had one more call-up victim to replace before the tour ended. This time I was given a week's prior notice, which was just as well because I would have to go on and feed Archie Glen – his straight man for twenty years had gone into the army. We rehearsed every afternoon and by Monday I was ready to go. I was now getting more stage time than any other principal in the show, and I was having the best time of my professional life until the company was hit with an appalling tragedy. It occurred when one of our dates was cancelled and we all returned to London for a week out. On the Wednesday night in the middle of an air raid, a stick of bombs straddled Leicester Square. One came through the roof of the Cafe de Paris killing Snakehips Johnson, the orchestra leader, and half his orchestra. Another fell four blocks away on a flat in Jermyn Street and killed Al Bowlly. On the very same night, several miles away in a home in North London, Archie Glen's only son was standing by the French windows when a bomb went off in the garden and blew the glass right through him.

When the sad company reassembled for the last two weeks of the tour, Jimmy Mesene went on alone in the penultimate spot and sang Al Bowlly's favourite songs. Archie Glen went on every night and made people laugh and came offstage with tears streaming down his face. I even moved into the same digs with Archie because he couldn't bear to be left alone.

When we got back to London, for good this time, no management would look at me with the RAF waiting to pounce at any minute. But Rex Maddox phoned from the Theatre Royal, Bath suggesting I fill in as front-of-house manager for his son Frank who was reporting next day for military service. I was on the next train. The pantomime company was in residence performing *Cinderella*. Frank had only hours to teach me how to be a theatre manager. I earned my keep the first week. One night, upstairs in "the gods" (the upper circle), I counted twenty more people than we'd sold tickets for. They had dodged past the box-office at the foot of the stairs and paid the usher in the balcony half-price for admission. He'd probably been earning a nice private income for years.

Cinderella played out its run and still I had no word from Whitehall. *High Temperature,* starring Henry Kendall, moved in and, as befits a manager, I made a big fuss of him. He was, after all, a big name in the West End and had made a host of films. When he found out I was an actor, he asked me if I would like to take over the part of Freddy for the rest of the tour as he didn't much care for the young man who was now playing it. A farce, with Henry Kendall! I'd love to, particularly as I would spend the opening five minutes of the play every night lying on a bed with the lovely Winifred Shotter. But I explained the hopelessness of the situation as I had already been accepted into the RAF. Harry said that as there were only six weeks left on the tour, he was sure I would make it. (Henry was Harry to his friends.)

So I rehearsed in Bath, played the Saturday night performance as a sort of dress rehearsal, and took off for Scotland on the Sunday. Harry, of course, made a pass at me the first week; but when I gently explained that it wasn't really my thing, he was perfectly charming about it and remained one of my staunchest friends for many years.

I had also undertaken to be Harry's understudy. Once I had the part down, the stage manager called a full run-through for me with all the other members of the cast except, of course, Harry. Farce is very inventive and all *farceurs* tend to introduce a few touches of their own. That night, Harry introduced a few touches of mine.

"You bugger!" I said when he came off, "you were there this morning!"

"Yes, and I liked what you did so I copied it!" he said without any shame whatever. Then he added, somewhat conceitedly when I think about it now, "You'll be a very good comedian because you've got the same gift of comedy that I have: you can speak very quickly and still have every syllable clearly understood."

Harry was one of London's hardest working actors. He owed so much back income-tax that he had to keep the money coming in. By the end of the tour he was very run-down and developed a carbuncle as big as a half-crown on the right cheek of his behind. As he spent most of the play rolling into, out of or underneath a bed, it must have

36

been sheer torture for him to go on. The company went to him in a body and said they'd be perfectly happy to do the play with me to give him a chance to recuperate. He preferred to struggle on, but when he insisted on cancelling a special performance for the troops in Southport rather than let me take his place, he put his selflessness a little in doubt.

At the end of each week, I told my current landlady that, as I wouldn't know my address in the next town until I got there, any mail for me should be marked "return to sender". It wasn't that I deliberately wanted to dodge the column, but I was anxious to complete one last entry on my résumé before signing off for the duration. When we got back to London, I was a bit apprehensive so I went round to the Air Ministry and, giving my very best performance, told them I simply couldn't understand why I hadn't had my calling-up papers. The sergeant went to a pigeon-hole, came back with an armful of envelopes all addressed to me, and threw them on the counter.

"Take your pick sir," he said. "We've been chasing you for weeks. If we'd found you, we'd have yanked you off the stage in the middle of a performance."

Within the week I was in Blackpool lining up for my first crew cut and the suit of blue I would wear for the next five years. On the wall was a recruiting poster of an airman with a tailor-made uniform that didn't look a bit like mine. And underneath, there was the famous motto:

PER ARDUA AD ASTRA
Through Adversity to the Stars

Before the day was out, I would learn the version current among my fellow Aircraftsmen, Second Class:

PER ARDUA ASBESTOS
Fuck you Jack, I'm fireproof

five

I'd like to think of just one thing I did in five years with the RAF that helped us win the war, but I can't. Perhaps things would have been different if I hadn't been quite so colour-blind. I wasn't just your run-of-the-mill reds and greens, I was browns as well. I saw blue roses. I never won at snooker because I had a habit of cueing up on the pink and there's a six-point penalty for that. And menswear salesmen had a field day whenever I came in to buy a new tie.

When this information filtered through to the Air Ministry, my acceptance for pilot training was very hastily scrubbed. They were quite nice about it and explained that runways had traffic lights just like streets did, and you simply had to know when it was time to stop and when it was time to go on. So I missed being one of the Few in the Battle of Britain, and I had to sit ignobly on the ground in East Anglia and watch the gladiators returning from the first thousand-bomber raid.

My new designation was Wireless Operator/Ground. I made up my mind to be a model trainee. Life had already taught me that perfectionism was the only antidote to boredom, as well as the only way of getting any kind of satisfaction out of performing the most menial tasks such as trying to bash holes in concrete with hob-nailed boots on the promenade at Blackpool. We'd do that for three hours at a stretch without making a dent, then come back next day and have another go.

In the afternoons, the powers-that-be would wedge us a thousand at a time into a converted bingo parlour, clap us in headsets and try to teach us how to make a morse key talk. Our sergeant-instructor ignorami had their own special teaching aids. For the hard-to-learn letters, they'd coined phrases that matched the morse rhythm. L, for example, instead of dit-*dah*-dit-dit became "To 'ell wiv it." The letter F, which somehow always seemed to be singled out for special attention, went from dit-dit-*dah*-dit to "Did it hurt you?"

At the end of six weeks, you were either sending and receiving morse at twelve words a minute or you'd gone bonkers and been whisked away to spend the rest of the war as a cook. The final test before the actual whisking began was taken in a specially equipped room above Burton the Tailor in Blackpool. If you failed the test, you didn't rejoin your signals unit and were said to have "gone for a Burton." I'm sorry to have to disagree with the eminent E. Cobham Brewer in *Brewer's Phrase and Fable* but I assure you Cobbie, old boy, that this is the pukka gen.

For those of us who didn't go for a Burton, our basic training was still incomplete until we could master semaphore. I never understood why we had to waste time mucking about with flags because I never saw one again for the rest of the war except up a pole or at the blunt end of a motor boat. As it happens, it did come in handy some thirty years later in Canada when I was directing a big industrial musical for a very partisan audience of Chrysler car dealers. In one particular scene on a dockside, I had the dancers dressed in sexy sailor suits and carrying semaphore flags. To the last eight bars of *Anchors Aweigh* I choreographed them to signal F-U-C-K F-O-R-D. Nobody at Chrysler ever found out, though I was a little apprehensive when we took the show to Halifax which is, after all, a naval town.

As a timely reminder that there was life beyond the Royal Air Force, one day the marquee at the Palace Theatre in Blackpool announced that Ivor Novello was coming with *The Dancing Years.* I had met Ivor several times with Harry Kendall and he had made me promise I'd look him up when he came to Blackpool, so I did. He gave me a stunning dinner, an hour-and-a-half of his enchanting company and the best seat in the house for the opening performance. I sat there and wept, not because I was feeling sorry for myself, not because the show was so sentimental, but simply because it was so good.

For physical beauty, charm and sheer talent, I never met anyone to equal Ivor Novello. He would write the book, compose the music, create the lyrics, play the lead and fill the Palace Theatre at Cambridge Circus for two years at a stretch. He did this at least four times. For some unaccountable reason, his talents never crossed the Atlantic despite Broadway's insatiable appetite for musicals. But in England, Ivor continued to be idolized by the public and adored by his fellow actors. His lovely house "Redroofs" near Maidenhead in Berkshire was always filled with those who needed a helping hand for a couple of weeks, and it finally became a permanent monument to him as an Actors' Convalescent Home. On the day he died at only fifty-eight, they played his music over the PA system at all the railway termini in London and many people went to work in tears.

I was never in love with a man, but if my genes had suddenly gone out of whack and steered me in that direction, it would have been with someone very like Ivor Novello.

Having successfully avoided going for a Burton at Blackpool, I embarked upon the second leg of my RAF journey. This took me to the Wiltshire village of Compton Bassett, not twenty miles from where I was born. Here the day began at 6 am with the door of the Nissen hut banged open by a drill sergeant bellowing "Wakey! Wakey! Hands off your joysticks!" Then Vera Lynn at full blast while you washed, shaved, dressed, made your bed, shone your shoes and cleaned your buttons.

The idea was now less square-bashing and more key-bashing. Bump their morse speed up to twenty-five words a minute and bung some technical know-how into 'em. I made the fatal mistake of becoming too intrigued with the know-how part and found myself yanked off the assembly line and switched to a technical instructor's course. This seemed quite ridiculous seeing that I couldn't tell the difference between a resistor and a condenser.

Nevertheless, it was a challenge I found hard to turn away from. I was still very conscious of my lost learning years and there were plenty of empty slots in the upper storey sitting up and begging for input. What they got now was a crash course in radio theory and the ability to fix the average radio set when it got sick – a tremendous comfort to the local villagers whose repairman had been called up.

Unfortunately, instructor status got you no special treatment whatever despite a pair of acting-corporal's stripes. When the train had called at Compton Bassett, you'd got off at Bullshit Junction and there you stayed, even after you stopped being a trainee. You kept on doing exactly what the trainees did just to set them an example. So you were still awakened at sparrow-fart by the same drill sergeant and the only variation you got on a theme was that sometimes instead of "Hands off your joysticks" you'd get "Bail out of those cockpits," for the mind of a drill sergeant rarely ventured above the navel.

The thing I hated most at Compton Bassett was pay parade. Over a thousand of us would stand at ease on the parade ground, roughly in alphabetical order, and wait until our name was called. If it began with an A, it didn't take long. I was a Y and it never took less than three hours. By the time I'd got to the paymaster's table and barked out "1383055, sir!" and picked up my ten shillings, Abbott was already helping Abernethy home from the pub and I hadn't even had my first pint. I swore that the minute there was a sniff of World War III I'd change my name to Aablonsky.

When Christmas came around, I was still at Compton Bassett along with several hundred others who lived too far away to hitch-hike home and back on a two-day pass. I'd been dying to try myself out as a stand-up comic, so I got together with a piano player and organized a stag party for Boxing Day. I'd been collecting dirty stories for this precise purpose, almost from the moment Chamberlain had got off the plane from Munich waving that silly piece of paper and by this time I had a bookful. I'd even sequenced them into five different twenty-minute routines. I didn't bother to learn the running orders. All I needed was a single key word to remind me of the next story, and someone sitting on the floor to feed it to me during the previous laugh. Compton Bassett got the debut of all five routines, spelled by sing-alongs with the piano player in between. Our unquestionable success was duly noted on our RAF records which always followed you wherever you were posted. From then on, a stag party was demanded of me every Boxing Day for the rest of the war, no matter where I happened to be.

The smell of an audience for the first time for months, started old juices fermenting again. I found a fellow-instructor who was a West End director in peace-time and we put on the Ben Travers farce *Rookery Nook*. We ran for a week without an empty seat (they were free) and immediately got to work on *Thark* as a follow-up. I'm quite sure we'd have gone through the entire Ben Travers canon if something hadn't happened to get me away from Compton Bassett. Some bright brain at the Air Ministry had decided that every instructor on training command should spend two weeks as an observer on an operational station so that we could see how the real war was being fought and come back and tell our trainees exactly what they were in for. Which is how I came to be standing beside the runway of a big bomber station in East Anglia watching a full squadron of Lancasters take off for Cologne on the world's first thousand-bomber raid.

A thousand "bombers" was fantasizing a bit. A thousand planes went up all right but the only way you could turn some of them into bombers would be to lean out of the cockpit window and drop a bomb by hand. But the announcement was great for public morale and a real downer for Jerry, who'd been promised that no British bomb would ever drop on German soil.

The Lancs were due back at 2:24 am and they didn't mean approx. The planning was awesome. At 2:19 we heard the first engines, throbbing with that same strange beat frequency you always got from the four-engine jobs. Almost on the button they began to land with the same clockwork precision with which they'd taken off. We counted them down as we'd counted them up, but this time we came up short. There was an agonizing gap. Then there was a faint hum in the distance and a new surge of hope as the stragglers started to come in, some with an engine smoking or a prop shot away or with a gaping hole in the fuselage. Finally came the worst sound of all, utter silence. Three of them hadn't come back. I asked my guide from Admin if you ever got used to that sort of thing and he said, "No." He took me up to signals and we watched the wireless ops tap out call signs over and over again, then stop and search the dial for responses. They all knew why I was there and one of the operators handed me a spare headset. I heard the faint distress signal at the same moment he did. He interrupted in a flash, got the aircraft's I.D. and told the operator to keep his hand flat down on the morse key until the direction finders had got a fix on his position and could alert the Air Sea Rescue boys. Then he tried to discover how bad things were. In the middle of this exchange, the morse key at the other end suddenly went dead. It was a long time before our wireless op gave up and slowly took off his headset. I thought, "What the hell am I doing in Compton Bassett while all this is going on?"

When I got back, I applied for a transfer. They laughed at me.

"This is Training Command, corporal. No staff ever gets away from here."

"You mean never, sir?"

"I mean not ever." He shrugged. "Unless, of course, you want to volunteer for overseas." The shrug plainly said, "and who'd be stupid enough to walk away from a cushy posting like this for the rest of the war."

"Then please consider me volunteered, sir." My mother would have killed me.

They got rid of me in two weeks. I was posted to a small camp in Dorset to join one of the assault crews being specially trained to spearhead an invasion force and set up advance communications posts. The training unit had taken over Durnford, a famous old prep school in the village of Langton Matravers on the Channel coast eighty miles due north of the beaches of Normandy. Sir Anthony Eden had once been a pupil there. And if that weren't enough fame for one building, Watson-Watt and his boffins had invented radar behind its walls. We even found some old tuned circuits and other remains of their early experiments in the attic.

RAF Durnford had a small headcount and only rated a Squadron Leader for a Commanding Officer. He interviewed every new arrival personally. The minute he opened my file, he pounced. "Ah! An instructor! Just what we need!" And I was grounded for the second time in my RAF career.

At least Durnford wasn't a Compton Bassett clone. Here they practised discipline but eased up on the bull. They weren't dealing with raw recruits, but seasoned W/OPS to be trained for dangerous missions. The C/O made my acting-corporal's stripes permanent and I became "staff" with a lifestyle all of a sudden less rugged than a trainee's. I even had time on my hands. As the unit was starved for entertainment, I asked the C/O if I could build a stage in the mess hall. He had no budget for lumber so we cut through the joists and jacked up an entire chunk of the ancient floor on blocks. The local Women's Volunteer Association made us a primitive front curtain and we were in business. To make the best use of a highly transient talent pool, I ran a kind of Victorian Music Hall with myself as Chairman. On the side of the stage, I sat at a table with a candle in a bottle, a gavel, a tankard of beer and a non-stop line of patter, mostly taking the mickey out of the RAF and any of its local hierarchy who happened to be in the room.

All this still left me time for a social life, and that was taken care of by Joan. Joan was blue-eyed, blonde and shapely. She was upper crust and the English teacher at the Old Malthouse, another prep school right next door and just over the wall from Durnford. It was she who first showed me "Dancing Ledge," a natural shelf in the side of the cliff totally shielded from prying eyes, except perhaps through a telescope from the crow's-nest of a passing ship in the English Channel. On days off, we would rent a couple of hacks from a local farmer, or borrow some bicycles, or simply bask as God made us in the sun and make love on Dancing Ledge.

We had one bike ride I'll never forget. Joan discovered lanes that even the ordnance survey people had missed and one afternoon we found ourselves cycling along a disused road with weeds growing up through the concrete. The silence was uncanny and I should have known something was wrong when we saw a fox break cover. Then a cock pheasant. This was altogether too stagey and I thought, "This has to be a film setup. Any minute now, we'll hear the wind machines and a ball of tumbleweed will come rolling up the hill followed by John Wayne firing his six-guns." There was a shot all right but it wasn't from a Colt 45. It was a 75mm shell and it whined over our heads and exploded in a field to our left. My next shock was the fearsome sight of a squadron of tanks coming over the brow of the hill on my right, firing as they went. I grabbed Joan, threw her into a ditch and jumped in after her. The shells were soon joined by machine-gun fire and we could hear the bullets ripping through the hedge right above our heads. But the most terrifying sound of all with tanks is the clank of the tracks getting closer and closer and not knowing whether they were going to stop. They finally did, three times at the last minute, swivelled, sprayed us with dirt and retreated up the hill only to start the same charge all over again. Joan was marvellous. She got the giggles. For me it wasn't so easy. My brother Peter, in the army, had told me about some mad Aussies on manoeuvres in Norfolk who'd deliberately run their tanks over the "defenders" in a ditch and killed them. They were all Aussies too.

I waited for a full ten bullet-free minutes before I risked a peep through the bushes. There wasn't a tank in sight. Joan and I jumped on our bikes and pedalled like hell. At the bottom of the hill was a guardhouse and outside it, in the middle of the road, stood a bug-eyed sergeant with a face the colour of a pastrycook at the end of a hard day.

"Have you just come through that?"

"We've been in the ditch for an hour."

"Christ!" He reached for the phone, hesitated and pulled back. "Didn't you see the red flag and the sign on the gate?"

"We didn't see a gate. We came through a hole in the hedge."

"Christ!" He put his hand out to the phone and brought it back at least three times. "'Ere, you'd better piss off quick before we all get into trouble."

And that was the closest I would get to an angry gun for the rest of the war.

The Old Malthouse was beautifully run by a surprisingly young headmaster whose name was Stephen Haggard, a nephew of the famous novelist Rider Haggard. In his study he had a signed copy of every first edition of his uncle's works. He showed them to me one Sunday after dinner. Over coffee and brandy, I found out why he had invited me: his science master had just been called up and he was hoping I'd be his replacement.

"It would only be for a couple of hours a week and, of course, I would insist on paying you."

I was flattered no end but protested that my entire scientific knowledge was sandwiched between the first and last pages of the chapter in the Service Manual on electricity and magnetism. Even more to the point, I was already under contract to His Majesty's Royal Air Force and moonlighting would almost certainly upset my C/O. I could also have added that I was a high school dropout but that would have really spoilt the evening. Besides, I had really been more of a force-out, the force being one of circumstances.

Stephen thought Electricity and Magnetism would be just splendid for the boys, especially if I did a few experiments with iron filings. And he was sure he would be able to come to terms with my Commanding Officer. What transpired next was obviously a little gentle blackmail, for the C/O suddenly announced that at long last the Old Malthouse had agreed to allow us the use of its gymnasium for the odd Saturday night Services dance. At the same time, he called me in and told me that although he couldn't possibly condone my double life, he would unofficially instruct the Service Police to look the other way if they saw me climbing back and forth over the garden wall.

So Stephen Haggard added a brand new line to my résumé: Science Master, Old Malthouse Prep School 1942-1944. And he also added to my bank balance with a cheque at the end of every term for almost double what the RAF paid me for the same period. But most of all, he gave me the memory of Sunday evenings in the huge Haggard sitting-room, far away from the war, reading a bedtime story to fifty-odd scrubbed and pajamaed young schoolboys sitting on the carpet in a semicircle round a roaring log fire. It is a picture that has never left me. I can see them all today as clearly as I could fifty-five years ago.

I tended to measure my RAF service by stag parties rather than by years and, including Compton Bassett, I had notched three before I finally left Durnford. The third was a standout, mainly because it was the first time I ever had a female in the audience. I had arranged with the landlord of the Kings Arms nearby to set up a bar in the mess hall, and he arrived with a couple of kegs and his teenage daughter as a helper. I said she couldn't possibly stay because the material would be far too raw for her tender young ears, but he told me that she wouldn't even listen and just to forget she was there. So I did. But the guys in the audience didn't and watching her reactions just made their evening.

I revisited the Kings Arms on a nostalgia trip in 1986 and found a gray-haired sixty-year old lady behind the bar. I reminisced about my

RAF days at Durnford and she told me she'd only ever been once inside the building and that was to help her father run a bar at a troop concert.

"There was a corporal there who stood up and told filthy stories for five hours on end and you know something? He never told the same one twice!"

Durnford had never gone back to being a prep school but most of the old buildings were still there. Up the hill was a new Esso station and I talked to the proprietor.

"Wasn't this where the RAF main gate used to be?" When he said it was, I added, "then that must have been the old mess hall."

"Quite right," he said. "It's now my service bay and a fat lot of help it is. I can only use half the space. You know what those silly buggers did? Sawed through the joists and wrecked the whole bloody floor!"

Soon after stag party three, the war began to catch up with Langton Matravers. British troops were massing in the area and there was heightened talk of a second front. I didn't let the upsurge in military activity cut into my entertainment plans, and I staged my most ambitious show to date – a full length revue. I wrote material and I stole it, some from shows still running in London. We did our own Air Force version of *ITMA* (It's That Man Again), BBC Radio's longest-running and funniest show. It was failure-proof since there wasn't a living soul in our audience who didn't know every character intimately by name, by voice and by catch-phrase. We had plenty of good skits, a dozen first-class one-liners and an aircraftsman who did a hilarious impersonation of Hitler. We had a drill sketch which no longer resembled the one I had seen at the London Palladium, and we had a finale. This was our only serious item and no revue should ever be without one. Ours was inspired by the Dunkirk number in *The Best of Everything* where I had delivered the epic poem on "The Little Ships of England," only this time I wrote one to cover all the major war events to date. Elaborate staging was an impossibility so we rigged up a big white sheet, backlit it and illustrated the verses with a series of dramatic vignettes in silhouette. For the London blitz, for example, we had a cutout of the bomb-damaged side of a house and an old lady in a shawl, picking up some small treasured possessions from a pile of smoking rubble. Simple, dramatic and no scenery to paint.

Of all the claims made upon the human spirit in wartime, patriotism is the one that always evokes the greatest response, and our finale was unashamedly patriotic. During the final verses, a spotlight framed a US Marine in full battle gear backed by a distant military band playing *From the Halls of Montezuma*. Lights and sound then cross-faded to a Russian soldier and *The Song of the Steppes*. Next there was a British Tommy and *Land of Hope and Glory*. In a final tableau, all three soldiers stood shoulder to shoulder, rifles at the ready, bayonet tips touching, as they confronted the common enemy with *Land of Hope and Glory* swelling to a crescendo. It was never too difficult to make a Service audience laugh. It wasn't too hard to make them cry either.

With enormous troop concentrations now within an easy drive, we were swamped with invitations to take the show to other RAF camps. These had to be strictly scheduled in off-duty hours but the resulting tiredness was worth it. I had one other reason to remember that revue. It saved my brother's life.

Peter was the youngest in the family and, as a weekend soldier in the Territorials, he was called up and made a sergeant with an anti-aircraft battery a week before the war began. He was now stationed twenty miles up the road on a hill near Corfe Castle. Peter's unit had never once received a visit from an entertainer of any kind and he was determined that our show should set a precedent. Unfortunately for him, the Germans stepped up their sneak air raids along the coast to such a degree that the day Peter had arranged to come to see our show, the order went out that all Ack-Ack battery personnel should be confined to camp. He *had* to see for himself whether they could possibly supply even the most basic facilities at Corfe, so he took a tremendous chance, borrowed a motor-cycle from the motor pool, rode it to Durnford and took in the show. The first thing he saw as he rode back into camp was one of his trucks up a tree. Stretcher-bearers were running to and fro and there was smoke everywhere. He can't remember which he saw first, his CO or the crater where his own bedspace used to be. He braced himself for a blast that never came. The CO burst into tears when he found Peter was unexpectedly still alive and the almost inevitable court-martial never materialized.

We eventually played the revue for Peter's unit. They had no facilities whatever except a generator which could provide the power we needed. They came to Durnford in the morning, loaded up all the lights and props, hung them and hooked them up according to the lighting plan I gave them, and we did the show in the open air on table tops lashed together. It was one of the most rewarding performances we ever gave. It was the only time we played to a sea of khaki rather than Air Force blue. At the RAF stations, after the show, we were always given a party in the sergeant's mess. At Peter's unit, we were welcomed into the *officer's* mess. And to further illustrate how unimportant rank was on special occasions, I subsequently spent a very happy weekend at Weymouth with a blonde ATS officer.

As spring came to Langton Matravers, so did the GIs, by the thousand. In the Kings Arms you couldn't push your way past them to the bar, and on the beach at Swanage, you couldn't put a pin between them and the local girls. We were given a squad of them to train at Durnford. I was in the CO's office when they wheeled smartly through the front gate and halted on the small parade ground. The minute they were stood at ease, half of them opened their cupped hands and put the stubs of already lighted cigars into their mouths. I thought the CO was going to create a miracle and give birth on the spot. Two weeks later, General Montgomery arrived. Within twenty-four hours, the beach was declared out of bounds to anyone in uniform. At Durnford, we began to be awakened at 6 am by the sound of marching feet, column after column of them. They headed for the hills and they didn't march back again until dark, ten minutes after the pubs closed.

Meantime, my Commanding Officer had called me in and shown me a brand new Air Ministry Order which said that they were now so short of Signals Officers that they were prepared to accept applicants who were colour-blind. There was a proviso that, if accepted, the words COLOUR VISION UNSAFE should be clearly marked in red ink diagonally across the applicant's papers. The CO said he wanted me to be one of the first to apply under the new guidelines. I filled in the forms and he showed me his recommendation: "This is the most commissionable type we've ever recommended from this station."

I was duly summoned to the Air Ministry. I must have safely got through phase one, which seemed to be mainly concerned with one's ability to pick up the right knife and fork at table, because I was passed on to phase two. This was highly technical and might have been a bit tricky for a working wireless operator but was very basic for someone who had been teaching others for three years. At my medical, the ophthalmic boys had a great time. They'd never seen anyone as bad as I was. They brought in the whole department to see the special freak show. I didn't give a damn so long as they remembered to write COLOUR VISION UNSAFE across my papers, diagonally and in red ink and I made sure that they did.

Six weeks after I got back to Durnford, the CO couldn't understand why I hadn't heard anything from the Air Ministry so he phoned them. They told him I had failed because I was colour vision unsafe. It was even written right across my papers in red ink.

"For Christ's sake, don't you even read your own Air Ministry orders?" he screamed at them. "Right," he said to me as he hung up, "we're going to put you up all over again." But the selectors at the Air Ministry weren't big enough to admit that they had made a mistake. I became an embarassment to them when they received my second application and needed to be got out of the way. Within seven days I was on a troopship bound for the Far East. But not before I watched from a grandstand seat the launching of the most awesome military operation mankind had ever seen.

The blast from the bombardment eighty miles away across the channel rattled the windows of Durnford and had us all springing out of bed and diving for the floor in the middle of the night. It was still dark when I got to Dancing Ledge. As I watched the dawn break, a picture slowly come into focus that made anything I saw afterwards in a newspaper or magazine look like a small diversionary attack. I was exactly opposite the landing beaches and everything appeared to be emanating from me. Directly overhead passed dark, menacing shadows of all shapes, sizes and speeds, layer upon layer of them, the bottom ones frighteningly close, all heading due south. There were planes towing gliders, lumbering troop transports, fighters buzzing about like bees each protecting its own queen, and high above them all, the heavy bombers. The first of these were already over the target and a thousand others were queuing behind them for a hundred miles or more. It was like a film loop that kept re-running. Down below, on the water, ships were taking shape in the growing light. The previous day, there was not even a smokestack to be seen in the whole range of vision from Dancing Ledge. Today there were thousands of them, all converging like strands in a spider's web with the centre point dead ahead just beyond the horizon. Some of my trainees and fellow-performers were out there. I wondered how many of them would be in the first wave.

six

More than anything else, I remember the smell of India. I have caught pale whiffs of it since in Barcelona, Jamaica, Mexico City, Lisbon, The Bahamas and Samarkand in Uzbekistan. But not one of them has come close to that acrid assault on the nostrils that came seeping through the stately Gateway to India, down the hill to the docks and up over the rail of the troopship as she tied up in Bombay. It was the perfume of fading petals of hibiscus flowers and ripe figs fallen from a banyan tree, or it was the fetid stench of human feces kept on the bubble by the burning sun, according to how much of a romantic you were. Put me firmly in the former category, for I fell in love with India from the beginning.

We knew that we were bound for the Far East the moment we boarded the old P & O banana boat *Otranto* at Greenock on the Clyde and lined up for an issue of pith helmets that looked for all the world as if they'd come straight from the quartermaster's store of the Bengal Lancers. We waited a long time for the opportunity to ditch them, and we were well clear of the Suez Canal before the first one sailed overboard. Despite the vigilance of the Service Police trying to catch one of us in the act, the wake of the *Otranto* was pockmarked with leather-lined cockleshells all the way to Bombay. Once ashore, three thousand new customers besieged the bazaars for bush hats, Australian style, the headgear of choice among those who had already got their knees brown.

As we descended the gangplank to face the seething mass on the dockside, one of my chums spotted a sergeant frantically waving a sign that said: ANY ENTERTAINERS? REPORT HERE.

"Hey Les," he said, "that's you!"

"What's your trade, Corporal?"

" Wireless Operator."

"Sorry chum, you're one of the untouchables. We can't take

signals or medics."

So the poor old troops would continue to be entertained by the local Ladies Guild because we couldn't win the war without me and my morse key. And instead of a trip to Delhi, I joined my shipmates on the assault course in Bombay at six o'clock the following morning. We just about made the finish line on all fours when our chorus of groans was drowned out by the drill sergeant at full decibels: "All right, you lot! Round the course again! On the double!"

At the end of round two, we dragged our weary bodies to the tail of a long lineup for our first meal call in the open air. I picked up my loaded plate and looked for a place to sit. A kitehawk swooped down over my shoulder and in one pass scooped it clean. I hadn't the heart to queue up all over again so I went without.

For our second day of acclimatization, we drew field rations and set out with rifles and full packs on an eight-hour enforced route march with the mercury climbing faster than we did. A young Flight Lieutenant, immaculate in starched shorts and bush jacket, led the column. He'd carefully walked over the entire route the previous afternoon and made sure it would be no pleasure hike. Not a hazard had been left out. We started out well enough until we came to a *wadi*. Our leader plunged fearlessly forward shouting "Follow me, men!" The next thing we saw was his forage cap floating on top of the water. There had been a thunderstorm during the night and the river had risen several feet. He eventually emerged minus his cap and his dignity and clawed his way up the bank on the other side, screaming out orders for us to follow him.

"Nah. Not bloody likely. Can't swim sir," was the gist of the chorus from the opposite bank. He was so furious he ordered us to march forward waist-deep into the water, left wheel, and wade along the line of the river bank for four hours with our rifles held over our heads. We finally emerged covered in leeches and had to burn them off one by one with lighted cigarettes.

While we were being toughened up in Bombay, the Japanese Eighteenth Army had driven north through Burma and was now knocking on the door of India. My stay in Bombay was abruptly curtailed. I was drafted to a newly-formed mobile signals unit temporarily attached to the headquarters of RAF 224 Group which had been elected to support the army's attempt to stem the advance. As a mobile unit, we were very manoeuvrable. We drove our own vehicles and were completely self-supporting. It mattered not that my total driving experience to date had been a two-day crash course on the country lanes of Dorset.

We set out for the forward areas in convoy. I piloted a water bowser and drove it from one side of India to the other over dirt roads, goat paths and occasional stretches of tarmac. It took over a week. It ended with a spine-tingling navigation of the hairpin bends up and down each side of the Eastern Ghats. You put your vehicle in bottom gear and left it there all the way up and all the way down and still ended up with your brake shoes on fire by the time you had dropped three thousand feet to sea level. We pitched our tents on the edge of the Bay of Bengal and waited for the troop train that would take another seven days to get us and our vehicles to Calcutta and thence to the forward areas.

The Japanese were heading for the crucial port of Chittagong at the same time the Allies were. Luckily for us, General Stillwell cut across from China and stopped them dead on the Indian border. Even luckier, the monsoon came to Chittagong and shelved all thoughts of an immediate operation push-back. But that didn't keep 224 Group grounded. They had a feisty reputation and lost no time in bringing themselves up to full strength and fighting trim. I got my third stripe and became sergeant of the watch on one of the three eight-hour shifts. The airwaves were buzzing, for our Air Commodore, Paddy the Earl of Bandon, was on the short list for every top-secret operational order that emanated in code from Mountbatten's HQ at South East Asia Command. And 224 Group squadrons were never idle. They were out, day after day, on bombing missions, sorties, reconnaissance flights and supply drops to troops that had been surrounded or had infiltrated behind enemy lines.

Our part of Chittagong wasn't exactly bristling with attractions for off-duty aircraftsmen. Group Headquarters had been dumped in the middle of the town's poorest residential district: an island of galvanized iron in a sea of straw *bashas* hemmed in by a network of dirt roads and open drainage ditches. Chittagong proper was a long rickshaw ride away. If you had no spirit of adventure, you were content to stay on site even when it was time to play, for on every station there was always at least one keen type ready to organize your free time into oblivion. But not mine. Nothing was going to keep me confined to base when over the wall beyond the rows of straw *bashas* lay the exciting sounds and sights and smells of a world I'd never seen.

The surest way into this world lay through the front door of a typical Indian home so I struck up a friendship with a Hindu family. This not only marked me "a bit strange" in the eyes of some of my colleagues, but placed my new-found friends under a certain amount of strain with the neighbours, since the clamour to kick the British out of India was growing more shrill by the day. But fraternization wasn't a crime, and soon I was dropping in for dinner at least once a week with the menu augmented by the occasional treat I could scrounge from the kitchen staff at the base.

My host was a *pleader*, a Hindu defence lawyer, but his lifestyle was humble by comparison with his legal counterparts in the west. He was in his fifties but looked seventy and, like so many East Indians struggling to keep up appearances in the lower middle class, he was undernourished. His wife, Susila, was twenty years younger than he and showed no signs of malnutrition, suggesting that her husband sometimes went without to make sure she didn't. Hindus invariably adored their wives, even though almost all marriages at the time were "arranged" and took place when the bride was six and the husband in his twenties or beyond. The child bride would continue to live with her parents until her twelfth birthday, when the husband would receive a message that his wife was now mature and ready to be collected.

My lawyer friend and I had many stimulating after-dinner discussions. When we first broached the subject of independence, he apologized profusely that he was forced to support the cause in public, but secretly he and many of his fellow Hindus dreaded the day when the British would leave. The one thing they could rely on under the British Raj was justice in the courts. God help a Hindu after independence if a Muslim judge sat on the bench, and vice versa. He didn't know then that his home town would end up in Muslim Pakistan, and there would be bloody days ahead along the border.

I never discussed these "at-homes" with my comrades-at-arms. They would never have believed me had I told them that a conversation with an educated Indian was on a far higher intellectual plane than anything I'd ever heard in the sergeant's mess. It would also have been difficult to hide the fact that my sympathies lay entirely with the natives, for I was already appalled at the behaviour of some of the new emissaries to India in khaki and air force blue.

One evening after dinner, while Susila was in the kitchen, my host startled me by asking if his wife appealed to me.

"How do you mean?"

"Sexually."

I couldn't honestly say that the thought had not crossed my mind, but I didn't think it circumspect to let him know that. So I took what I thought was a respectable time to answer.

"Well, yes she does, as a matter of fact."

"Then I wonder if you'd mind? I'm a bit past it and she likes you. And all I want is for her to be happy."

So our after-dinner discussions grew noticeably shorter and, at the first lull, my host would look at his watch and say, "Off you go." Susila and I would then repair to the *charpoy* in the bedroom. He would settle back happily with his paper and the more the ropes creaked on the *charpoy,* the happier he seemed to be.

One evening after we had made exquisite love, Susila announced that she wanted to have a child by me. I told her it wasn't my fault that she wasn't already in that happy state. And what on earth was her husband likely to think about the idea?

"Ask him," she said.

So I did. He just smiled and said, "If that's what she wants."

Pregnancy didn't dull Susila's sexual appetite one whit and it is probably just as well that I finally got posted from Chittagong. The Far East war was about to move south into Burma and I with it. In fact, I was likely to be slightly ahead of it, since the task assigned to my mobile unit was to land with some army units halfway down the coast and help set up advance headquarters for 224 Group.

There was a special kit list for the "forward areas" which was based on the assumption that you might be cut off from all but the most essential supplies for an indefinite length of time. Stocking up at the quartermaster's stores, I was surprised to find myself handed an official issue of two french letters (condoms to a North American) after all the fuss made by Lady Astor. This redoubtable lady had managed to get her hands on a copy of this very kit list and had read it aloud in the British House of Commons. She was outraged that a clean-living young serviceman who had no intention of dipping his wick in the Far East should be forced to carry french letters in his official baggage. The Secretary of State for Air had given Lady Astor his firm assurance that the matter would be immediately rectified. I had another look at the list and he'd been as good as his word. The entry now read:

TWO FRENCH LETTERS *(for carrying watches and other valuables when fording rivers)*

As we embarked at Chittagong docks to prepare for our landing halfway down the coast of Burma, I thought of the assault crews I had spent all those months training in Langton Matravers. The mother ship sailed out into the Bay of Bengal and anchored opposite the island of Akyab. The landing craft were dropped into the water and we were dropped into the landing craft. As a chronic vertigo sufferer, I was in double jeopardy. Climbing into a landing craft down a flimsy rope ladder from the side of a ship that curved away from you at the bottom was every bit as terrifying as the thought of jumping out of one on to a hostile beach.

I'm not likely to forget my one and only amphibious operation. The gnawing at your gut as the front of the landing craft grounds and the flap goes down; the pounding of your heart as well as your feet as you charge up the beach and try to bury your face in the sand ahead of the bullet with your name on it. Only there was no gunfire. Just voices. I finally plucked up enough courage to lift my head. All I saw was a line of excitable Burmese selling fruit.

"Bananas Sahib?"

"Get out of the way!"

"Mangoes Sahib?"

"Out of the fucking way!"

The Japanese had known we were coming. They had left Akyab the day before and moved one island down the coast to Ramree.

We parked our signals truck on the high ground closest to the airfield and set up our antennas. We established contact with rear HQ the day we landed and maintained it non-stop thereafter. It was unfortunate that the high ground was a good ten-minute walk from our tents through snake-infested brush. I hated snakes. Moreover, when going on or off night duty, you made the trip in the dark and you could hear them slithering away from you as you approached. It was no use the RAF trying to assure us that snakes don't usually bite unless you tread on them and then tell us that the beastly things were deaf and couldn't hear us coming. However, the manuals said that snakes were sensitive to ground vibrations. So the quarter-master gave us ankle boots as a first line of defence and told us to tread heavily whenever we were in the jungle. I tramped back and forth to the signals cabin, day or night, like a rogue elephant.

For the next four months, I learned to live without two of life's greatest joys: a hot bath and female company. The Japanese had taken every woman on the island with them and the best I could do for a bath was to stand under a can full of holes while a chum shinned up the tree and poured a bucket of tepid river water into it. I swore when I got back to civvy street I'd never stand under another shower or go a single day without a hot tub. Except for the odd day on my back in an intensive care ward, I've kept my promise to myself faithfully for over fifty years.

One day in Burma stands out among all the others. There was devastating news from Chittagong: my last letter to Susila had been refused. Sgt Charlie Spurway, my opposite number at Rear HQ and my unofficial courier who had been smuggling our letters back and forth with the official despatches, had gone to the house as usual to deliver it in person but no-one answered his knock, even though he could hear that someone was definitely in. He finally decided to push the letter under the door. It was pushed straight back. He went back next day and still there was no answer to his knock. This time he left the letter on the mat. He was able to find out later that Susila had given birth to a baby girl.

I never heard from Susila again. Not a word, not a snapshot of the baby, not even a thank-you letter. Perhaps she was afraid I'd be like Lieutenant Pinkerton and come back to claim the child.

I think about my daughter sometimes and wonder if she has survived the riots, the typhoons, the tidal waves and the famines that have stricken Chittagong over the years. She would be in her fifties now. I don't even know her name.

They gave me the Burma Star when I left Akyab. Not for bravery, just for being there. After four months in the brush, they'd brought us back across the Bay of Bengal to Madras for delousing. We came with scabies, dhobi itch, tinea and prickly heat in every known permutation. A few antiseptic scrubs in a hot tub and a head-to-toe issue of brand-new clothing made a good start on the first three on the list. A daily coating of gentian violet did the rest. It also left us with bright purple balls.

Getting rid of prickly heat wasn't quite so easy and took about as long as the purple dye lasted. The only real cure for prickly heat was to take it to a hill station high above the heat and humidity of the plains. That would have to wait because Madras wasn't finished with us yet. After purification they had us in line for a course of rehabilitation and regeneration.

Madras was the home of the world-famous Madame Matthieu. She had run a brothel there exclusively for British servicemen in World War I and, after some major recasting, was now doing the same for their sons in World War II. She would take care of the regeneration while a team of senior officers and NCOs went to work on the rehabilitation. It was a tough programme of lectures and drills designed to restore some of the bullshit that had worn off as it inevitably will when your only parade ground is a small clearing in the jungle. The Chief Medical Officer kicked off the rehab course with a long dissertation on the perils of venereal disease, graphically illustrated by gruesome film footage of some of its most advanced victims. He set us all a splendid example by being first in line at Mme Matthieu's that same evening.

As soon as the clean-up squad had pronounced us fit to be seen again in public, they sent us to Bangalore, nearest of the hill stations. Bangalore was pukka-sahib territory, staked out years before by the British as a town-size club for the commissioned officer in the regular peacetime army. He was still in evidence in some strength, a reluctant host to the visiting hordes in jungle green bent only on getting rid of prickly heat and having a good time. Just occasionally the hordes went too far. At a dance organized by the ladies of the town, a detachment of Aussies took exception to the presence of several Italian prisoners of war, all immaculately turned out in tailored and starched khaki drill and seemingly in possession of the keys to the city. When the Italians began to "cut-in" on the dance floor, tap an Aussie on the shoulder and expect him to relinquish his partner, there was real trouble. The Aussies began dishing out taps of a less gentle kind and Italians went flying through doors, and I regret to say even windows, until there wasn't a POW left in the hall.

After that, there were no more dances for a while, not even to celebrate V-E Day. They even had a job to rustle up a decent victory parade. After all, where was the victory? Our war was still on. I don't know how the army fared, but an Air Ministry Order was posted announcing that May 8th would be a day of celebration and all non-commissioned ranks were to be issued with two free bottles of beer. The AMO added a note of caution that it might be wise to issue one bottle in the morning and one in the afternoon. This suggestion so upset the non-commissioned ranks that they saved their morning bottle until the afternoon issue. Then they moved in a body to the compound of the senior RAF officer in the garrison and threw both bottles unopened at the front wall of his bungalow. This might have made history as the second Indian Mutiny except that no word of the occurrence ever appeared on any daily report. At that late stage of the war, no senior officer was going to spoil his record by admitting that he had lost control of his troops.

Bangalore holds another, more personal memory for me. My life has seen more than its share of odds-defying coincidences, but by far the most bizarre of them all happened while I was there letting the mountain air get at my prickly-heat pimples. My Signals Officer and I were riding along a country road in a jeep when I sensed something naggingly familiar about a fair-haired memsahib riding a bicycle just ahead of us. Then it dawned and I grabbed my SO fiercely by the arm.

"Hold it, sir! There's not another bum like that in the whole of the British Empire. That's Joan!"

And Joan it was. Blonde, blue-eyed Joan of The Old Malthouse School in Langton Matravers. The last time I had seen her was nine months earlier when we had played our farewell love scene five thousand miles away on a ledge overlooking the English Channel, the night before my departure for foreign parts unknown.

"What on earth are you doing in Bangalore?"

"Looking for you," she said.

"Now don't be silly."

"I'm not. I found out you'd gone to India so I thought I'd come too. I've been here for months." Then she added, "I must say I do miss Dancing Ledge."

I had begun to suspect back in Langton Matravers that I was getting in a little over my head, but this was right down at the deep end without any water wings. She immediately sensed my discomfort and let me flounder in it for several moments before she smiled and said, "Don't look so worried. I've found myself a nice army captain." Then she kissed me on the cheek, shook hands with my Signals Officer and rode off into my past.

I never ran into her again which was surprising because Bangalore wasn't that big a town. It also made the immensity of the odds against our chance encounter all the more staggering. There were over a million square miles of India with RAF detachments scattered over the length and breadth of it, and I could have been stationed in any one of them. There were also nearly fifteen hundred minutes in a day and five of them either way, earlier or later, along that particular road on that particular day and we'd never have met. And she would have gone through life without ever knowing that she had been within a couple of bicycle lengths of hitting the bull's-eye on the target at the end of her ridiculous five-thousand-mile odyssey.

I was really glad about the captain. Joan was a super gal, a classic English beauty, witty, intelligent and fun. But she was not for me. She'd had plans to turn me into a gentleman farmer after the war, with Mummy and Daddy putting up the money. But I didn't want to come back and be a farmer. I wanted to go on being an actor. As I waved goodbye, I found myself hoping they wouldn't send the captain anywhere dangerous.

It was unlikely, as it turned out, because suddenly, unexpectedly, horribly, the war in the east was over. Demobilization, they told us, was to operate on a points system and, as I'd been slow to respond to the call of duty in 1941, I'd have to wait a while. Meantime, I'd be welcome to join an entertainment unit for a six-month tour of all the SEAC bases in the Far East. I told RAF HQ in Delhi, quite bluntly, that the next tour I had in mind for myself was on the Howard and Wyndham circuit in Britain. They'd refused to take me two years earlier when I'd offered myself as I got off the boat at Bombay: I was on signals and couldn't be spared. I was irked at their priorities. They thought that it was easier to stand up in front of a thousand airmen and make them laugh than superintend a watch in a remote signals cabin in Burma.

I outsmarted myself, of course. Instead of taking the opportunity to see still more of the Continent that had captivated me, I found myself bumbling about in Bombay for several weeks. Another Christmas came and I gave my fifth and final stag party. Then early in January, I gathered up my souvenirs and climbed the gangplank of the *Capetown Castle*. I leaned on the rail for one last look at sights I would never see again. I took a deep breath and held it, savouring that unforgettable smell that had first excited me two years before. As the ship cast off from the pier, a Bombay police band on the wharf began to play "Will Ye No Come Back Again?" I wept.

seven

Almost five years to the day that I gave up my name in exchange for a number, the gates of RAF Hednesford closed on my military career and I started the long trek back to Civvy Street and Miriam Warner's Talent Agency. The production team at the release centre had done its best to prepare me for the part: demob suit by Burton the Tailor, deportment by the drill sergeant, hair by the RAF barber and makeup by the tropical sun of India. I was also armed with my first post-war review. My Commanding Officer had written on my discharge papers, "He has taken part successfully in his own time in a great number of service entertainments both as producer and performer and there is no doubt as to his talents in that direction." I walked down the street looking for the first officer I wouldn't have to salute.

Just inside the Agency's glass door, dear old Smithy still sat with his little withered arm held aloft like a spaniel that had just been run over, guarding the inner sanctum where Miriam Warner held court. The outer office was crowded as always with eager young hopefuls, all of them looking ominously younger than before. But when I was ushered into the presence ahead of them, I felt the superiority of the old sweat.

Miriam gave me a big wet kiss and sent me out that same afternoon to read for the part of a RAF wireless operator in an American film called *Twelve O'Clock High* to be shot in England and star Gregory Peck. I gave them a smashing demo on a morse key at twenty-five words a minute, but I didn't get the part because they said I didn't look like a wireless operator. I must have done a hell of a job fooling the Air Ministry for five years.

Two days later, Miriam called me in to meet Basil Thomas who was anxious to cast his next repertory season as largely as possible from returning ex-service men and women actors. Before I left her office, I had signed a contract to appear for a six-week trial at the

Grand Theatre, Wolverhampton, with an option on the management's side to keep me on for the rest of the season. Although she didn't know it then, that little introduction to Basil was to bring Miriam a commission cheque from me every week for the next two years.

All the way back on the troopship *Capetown Castle*, I had been mentally rehearsing my return to the business and I had made up my mind that the first acceptable offer that came along should decide the way I'd go. Would it be the fun route with those earthy, oozing-with-talent, generally working-class but infinitely richer folk in Variety? Or would it be along the carriageway with the ladies and gentlemen in legit? For once, I would have a choice and the opportunity would never come again, for these two worlds were separated by a line of demarcation that was never to be crossed, even though so many Variety performers yearned for the "respectability" of legit and so many legit performers longed for the riches of Variety. Although most of my prewar experience had been in the straight theatre, I'd got my feet wet in the RAF as a stand-up comic, so you might say I was kitted out for either eventuality. But in the end it was hello Basil Thomas and goodbye Variety and probably just as well. A few years down the road those lovely lads and lassies of the Music Halls were to commit mass suicide by taking the entire audience they played to on a two-year circuit of the halls and performing to them all in a single night on television.

Wolverhampton was ranked among the best weekly reps in the country and was one of a chain superbly run by Derek and Reginald Salberg with cousin Basil Thomas. Their flagship was the Alexandra Theatre, Birmingham, and their fleet was strategically spread over the Midlands and poised to infiltrate the environs of London, which it eventually did. The Salbergs ended up with eight first-class companies and no one actor ever managed to play them all. I came closest with seven: Wolverhampton, Birmingham, Hereford, Kettering, Croydon, Penge and Leicester. Somehow Preston never made my résumé.

The birth and blossoming of the repertory system is one of the great romantic chapters in the history of British theatre. Provincial playhouses were enjoying three and four-week runs of West End tours when the movie screen first learned to talk. And when it also started to expand to Cinemascope proportions, playgoers began to defect. The capper came when the mighty Wurlitzer first emerged spinning up out of the floor like something from Jules Verne, flashing, sparkling, twirling, mesmerizing and spitting out decibels that went through walls and across the street into the lobby of the playhouse, luring still more playgoers into the chrome and marble palace opposite.

Years before, when we had to split a pair of headphones and take one drum each to listen to the radio, the loud-speaker arrived to cast a spell over the sitting-room and make people forget all about the living theatre. Some playhouse managers had bowed to that challenge with a temporary shutdown until saner times. Many of them never reopened. This time management knew it would have to find the cheapest possible way to keep the doors open without letting in too much of a draught.

Star salaries would have to go, travel costs reduced and seat prices brought down to *Odeon* levels. Loyal audiences, now thinly scattered over a three-week run, would need to be corralled and packed into a one-week stand. In short, the managers set the parameters of weekly repertory. A resident company would create its own stars and all but cut travel costs completely.

Weekly rep started as a stopgap and ended up as a bonanza. It enticed people into theatres who'd never been anywhere but the movies. It took elitism off the menu and whetted the appetite of the working class. It became the finest school of acting the industry had ever known. It discovered stars and exposed those who didn't really belong. It became a giant farm school for the West End and the number one tour. It gave work and three square meals a day to over five thousand actors.

With the last "all clear" barely wailing into oblivion, new repertory companies began to sprout in every town that could muster fifty thousand survivors. Budding entrepreneurs converted town halls, parish halls, community halls, church halls and, yes, church basements. Even the odd movie house capitulated, though these were mostly "fleapits," as the poorest of them were called. By the time I left England in 1951 there were over four hundred and fifty temples of drama all cranking out a play a week. The standard varied from astonishingly good to unbelievably awful.

Not more than twenty-five companies made the top echelon. This doesn't mean to imply that there weren't any good actors in the other four hundred and twenty-five: many of them were trapped there by a rigid caste system that judged you by the standard of the last company you were in. And yet here was I, bouncing up from nowhere and landing on top of the heap with a gaping five-year hole in my résumé and a row of empty hangers in my wardrobe.

The young actor of today, who wouldn't dream of stepping on stage in his own socks, would probably be quite startled to hear that in 1946, even in a number one company, a repertory actor was expected to provide every single article of modern clothing, seen and unseen, to be worn during an entire season. It was a formidable prospect with something like forty different roles for you to dress. When you were being interviewed for a job, nobody asked what parts you'd played; they only wanted to know how many sports jackets you had.

Five years in the RAF had got my body in great shape, but unfortunately not the same one that used to fill my suits in 1941. I had a problem. However, at the demob centre I'd spotted an application form for a special grant for "tools of trade." As I figured the tools of my trade were clothes, I promptly applied and they sent me £50. Before they had time to think they might have made a mistake, I took myself off to Hector Powe where £50 was good for two made-to-measure suits and a sports jacket. HP wasn't exactly Savile Row but he was several streets closer than Burton's. Up to now I'd always bought "off the peg," so when the tailor stood there with his measuring tape and asked me if I was right or left dress, I hadn't the faintest idea what he was talking about. When we got that straightened out, I agreed to be a fashion pioneer and ordered zip-fastener flies.

Strangely enough, it was dressing the character roles that taxed the actor's resources the most. It was easier for the gals who were always nifty with a needle and thread, but for the men it was a often a question of tracking down the real thing: a pair of pants that had mucked their way through several summers in a farmyard; old hats, caps, boots, ties, scarves, waistcoats and overalls scrounged from bricklayers, garage mechanics, house painters and old clothes shops. It became a status symbol of the successful repertory actor to travel with a hamper full of such trophies.

None of us ever missed a rummage sale. Some of our acquisitions wouldn't have passed muster through a pair of well-focused opera glasses, but with a little chalk on the stains, a touch of flattery from the stage lighting and a lot of flair on the part of the wearer, a bit of Petticoat Lane could invariably hold its own in a Mayfair drawing room.

The only time your wardrobe got a bit of a breather was when the company did a costume play. You could always count on a new release or two from the West End, and *Jane Eyre* and *Wuthering Heights* popped up with unfailing regularity. There was no such thing as a costume shop or even a costume designer in a weekly repertory company. London abounded with first-class theatrical costumiers who'd rent you a complete West End production, or one of the many clones they would make for the actors of all shapes and sizes who would be playing the parts in rep. You might even find yourself in a pair of pants bearing a handstitched label with L. OLIVIER printed in marking ink.

In the tip-top companies, the first rehearsal of each play was always on a Tuesday and the week's routine never varied. Let us suppose that the season opener is to be a farce called *Up in Mabel's Room* and the second play will be Bernard Shaw's *Pygmalion*. Rehearsals for the farce will be a breeze because evenings will still be performance free, so let's pick it up at the start of week two.

It is Tuesday morning and the stage curtain is down to mask the noise of the cleaning staff. You are standing on stage trying to forget the terrors of last night's opening performance of *Up in Mabel's Room*. This isn't easy because you are still *in* Mabel's room, except that her furniture has now been removed and replaced with the pieces belonging to Professor Higgins. The door to the professor's study is not in the same place as the one to Mabel's bedroom, but a couple of telephone books on the floor will serve to remind you of that.

It is ten o'clock and you start to block *Pygmalion*. There is no read-through. You've already done that in your own time over the weekend. By 1:30 the entire play is blocked. You've meticulously logged every move and you are free to go back to your digs and "study" because by tomorrow morning you must know the whole of Act One by heart. At seven o'clock that evening you are back in the theatre making yourself up for the second performance of *Mabel*.

It is now Wednesday morning and you start to rehearse Act One of *Pygmalion* without the book. If you haven't learned the moves as well as the lines, the morning will be difficult for you – and even more so for everyone else. Rehearsals are tight, concentrated. Scenes are worked and polished a segment at a time. Direction is crisp, economical, spot on. If your characterization is missing the mark, you are quickly steered in the right direction. There's no time to argue. By the end of the morning, you run through the entire act non-stop and are surprised to find how far you've come. One more thing before you go: you must rattle through Act Two (with book) to help you with tonight's study. You can't study this afternoon because you have a matinée of *Mabel*.

Thursday morning 10 am. Act Two without the book. You burned the midnight oil learning this one after twice through *Mabel* yesterday. You polish Act Two, recap the moves for Act Three and then go home and learn it. It is probably 1:15.

Friday is the only long rehearsal day. You not only lick Act Three into shape, you have to be sure you haven't forgotten all about Acts One and Two. So you run through them both non-stop as a little refresher. You're home by three o'clock.

Saturday morning: the first thing you notice is that your security blanket has gone. The solid, comforting figure of the director is missing from his perch on the edge of the stage, the curtain is up and there is nothing between you and a yawning chasm of eight hundred empty seats. He's out there somewhere. You can't see him but you'll hear him if he fails to hear you.

You run through the play non-stop just like a performance and you begin to get the feel of the house. At the end of the morning you feel quite exhilarated. You've had a couple of fluffs and a little help from your friends but you've got right through *Pygmalion* without a prompt. Then you get the director's notes and come down to earth a little.

For the first time, you don't have to rush home and study. Everybody heads for the pub, even if it's only for a ginger ale. The team spirit always begins in the pub.

On Saturday evening you have two performances - usually 6 and 8:30. On the notice board just inside the stage door, the cast is up for play number three and a script is on your dressing table. You pray for a small part like the butler.

Sunday – a free day. Well, sort of. You don't go near the theatre but you don't stray far from your script either. This is polishing up day – nails, shoes, lines, performance, costume. As *Pygmalion* is a period piece, for once you don't spend Sunday sorting out your wardrobe for tomorrow, ironing shirts, pressing pants, sewing on buttons, spot removing and trimming frayed cuffs with nail scissors. You remember to read through play number three for Tuesday.

Monday, 1 pm: in costume and makeup and ready to go. The set is up, dressed, lit and the stage crew already drilled. You take a quick walk around. Instead of the telephone books there's now a real door, which takes a bit of getting used to. There are also real stairs to climb instead of just walking on the spot.

There's no such thing as a technical rehearsal in weekly rep. At one o'clock you do it. If there's anything technically wrong, that's where you find out. Only there won't be. At three-thirty you have notes and at seven-thirty you open. Since that first rehearsal on Tuesday, including time for study, you've probably worked a sixty-hour week. Outside the stage door, an autograph seeker asks what you do with yourself in the daytime.

Working in weekly rep was a bit like being a monk: you always walked around with a book in your hand muttering lines to yourself and you kept your mind strictly steered away from all thoughts of sex. I can't speak for the monks: for the actors, the inclination did pop up occasionally but you simply didn't have the time and you certainly didn't have the energy. No doubt that situation would change as you grew a little hungrier and learned to make better use of your time. But the season was young and the rehabilitation of an ex-service man far from complete, so 1946 was seriously shaping up as no-nooky year.

I survived the cut at the end of six weeks but my five fellow demobsters didn't make it. We'd all been away from an audience far too long but I, at least, had managed to keep in touch, if only from tabletops in RAF mess halls.

I'd made up my mind six years earlier at the outset that I'd have something to show for my years away at the wars, even if I came back without the tiniest battle scar. So from the very first day of square-bashing, I kept one ear on the drill sergeant and the other on my drillmates, who were custodians, as it turned out, of a veritable treasure trove of accents and dialects and speech impediments. I listened for the key vowel sounds, the abandoned consonants and the massacred tenses and I mentally recorded them all.

Next I began a collection of character studies, a catalogue of traits and mannerisms that were the trademarks of the members of the most extraordinary cross-section of humanity I would ever encounter again in my lifetime. There was the wimp and there was the bullyboy, the gent and the nose-picker, the sucker and the con man, the intellectual and the dumb cluck: I served with them all and I opened a card on each one of them and stored it away in the filing cabinet under my forage cap. I referred to that file often in my Wolverhampton days.

Instant characterization was the key demand that was made of the repertory actor, and the few who were able to deliver were the ones who got to the top of the tree and stayed there. You arrived each week at the first rehearsal with a firm line on your character and the route you intended to take to translate it into performance language. It had to be there on the Tuesday. Wednesday would be too late to change gears. The rest of the cast would already be in top and running and you'd be a lap behind all week.

The art of quick characterization was not in itself sufficient to keep you out of the labour exchange. You needed other qualities such as stamina, team-spirit, discipline, punctuality, clothes sense, horse sense, drinks sense, a high pain threshold and a low opinion of pills and pick-me-ups. You had a responsibility to keep yourself at the peak of physical fitness and if you faltered, you failed. You went on if you were dying, for there was no such thing as an understudy. I once played a lead with an ulcerated mouth when it was absolute torture just to move my tongue. But once you confront an audience, the concentration demanded is so intense that it blots out everything that doesn't belong to the character you are playing, including pain. Each time I came off and closed the set door behind me I couldn't speak a word. The same thing happened when I had a boil on the sole of my foot. I limped up to the entrance, strode on to the stage, played a long scene with lots of movement, strode off again and limped all the way back to my dressing room.

Keeping the mind fit was just as important as the body. There was that little matter of being able to learn the entire text of a play in just three nights. God or my mother's genes had given me a photographic memory, which saved me strings of sleepless nights endured with such painful regularity by so many of my compatriots. I could mentally photograph the script page by page and, as the rehearsal progressed, I could "see" them turning over. If I wanted a prompt, I'd tell the stage manager, "It's the second line down on the right-hand side" or "third line up from the bottom on the left-hand side, just below that paragraph in italics."

Don't get shocked, young actors. I assure you that the "photographed" script was jettisoned by the end of rehearsal week and the normal memory process took over for performances. Even so, if anyone needed a prompt during playing week, which was rare, I could usually still open my photograph album and help them out.

By mid-season the company was making beautiful music. Everybody was totally in tune with everybody else and nobody was trying to go solo. The prima donnas had long since departed. Even an embryo Laurence Olivier II had been sacrificed in favour of a team player. We now had a company in which everybody was capable of playing the lead and sooner or later would. Between-times, you were a supporting player and you supported. If you didn't, you'd be on your own when it was your turn to lead. And if you still didn't get the message you would join the prima donnas long departed. Thus was the team-spirit instilled, refined and nurtured in the top companies. And thus was the standard maintained. The only thing that mattered in the end was the play.

The true beneficiaries, of course, were the local theatre-going public. They had the chance to see what the playwright really intended them to see: a production undominated by stars in which actors of equal calibre were able and allowed to give the correct dramatic weight to every part in the play and not just one or two of them. So we stopped being embarrassed each time a member of the public told us, "I enjoyed the play much more than I did when I saw it in London," because the chances were they probably did, though they didn't know why. It could have been that, at the Grand Wolverhampton, they had really seen the *play*.

After a run of particularly good parts, I experienced for the first time that magical sound – a round of applause on my entrance. This was to tell me that I was no longer the new kid on the block, that they liked what I did last week and that I'd get an even bigger round next time if they liked what I did this week. This development probably came in the nick of time because, as the juvenile leading man, you were expected to get all the teenage girls a-twitter in very short order. They packed the gallery night after night, for the rock groups had not yet appeared on the scene to drill holes in their fidelity, their eardrums and their pocketbooks. I was also following in the footsteps of Kenneth More, a great idol who had defected to become a film star (*Doctor In The House, Genevieve*) and the heart murmurs precipitated by his departure had yet to quieten down. But I went on to prove just how fickle fans can be.

Basking in this aura of adulation, we would walk in and out of the theatre as if we were passing through the gates of Warner Brothers' studios in Hollywood. Heads would turn and autographs would be sought. If you stopped off at the grocer's you'd often find, when you got home, an extra egg or an illegal pat of butter with your rations which were still restricted to 1/4 lb of butter, 1/4 lb of bacon and one egg per month. Sometimes it worked the other way. One week when I was playing Piers in *Whiteoaks*, the girl refused to give me any rations at all because I'd been "so horrid to that poor little boy, Finch."

Once you became established, you really were a star in a repertory town and they gave you the full star treatment. This, of course, ended dead at the city limits. If you walked down the main street of the very next town, you might just as well have been Roger the Lodger for all the notice anyone took of you. But back in your own small corner of the heavens, you twinkled. You became the guest of honour at society functions and working men's clubs; you opened garden fetes, closed conferences, addressed the Rotarians, read the lesson in church and never got accustomed to the total absence of applause, especially when you knew you'd read it particularly well. On one memorable occasion I was asked to judge a beauty contest for the Ever-Ready battery company and had the extreme pleasure of hanging a medallion round a pretty girl's neck and solemnly saying, "I now pronounce you Miss Ever Ready."

It wasn't absolutely all work and no play in a Salberg company because there was always Cricket Week. Both Derek and Reggie Salberg were potty about the game, although neither of them was particularly good at it. Once a year, leaving cousin Basil Thomas in charge, they would choose an eleven from all the actors in their employ, leave them out of a couple of plays, keep them on full salary and take them on a cricket tour. We would play teams of gentlemen farmers on charming village greens in places such as Datchet, Windsor, Gerrards Cross, and Kettering. We would host the Stage Cricket Club and mingle with some of the mighty for a day both on and off the field. And we would end up at Oxford playing a match against a Drinking Club at one of the University colleges. Beer was served all day in the pavilion, where you waited until it was your turn to go in. Then you walked to the wicket with the bat in one hand and a glass tankard in the other, which you solemnly placed for protection behind the stumps and slurped from between strokes. This was usually a chance for the poor bats to shine because the bowler was even more pissed than they were.

Kettering was a little off the beaten track on our cricket tour, but it was currently Reggie Salberg's "home town" because he was running the company there at the Savoy Theatre. One of his actors, Tim Hudson, was pressed into service for the game as an umpire. I was fielding and we were chatting away at square leg when I suddenly spotted one of the most beautiful women I'd ever seen, walking a golden spaniel along the boundary line. I began to make noises which I thought most closely approximated ecstasy without being positively indecent, and Tim asked me what the matter was.

"There! On the boundary! With the dog!" I positively drooled.

"Yes, my wife," he said.

End of drool. End of conversation. And thankfully the end of an over. I crossed to the sanctuary of the area round the other wicket and the other umpire.

But I'd had my very first glimpse of Hilary Vernon. And what an important event that turned out to be.

69

eight

As word of the success of Cricket Week rippled through the ranks of the acting unemployed, the résumés arriving at the Salberg offices underwent a marked change. Strategically placed among the backup theatrical reviews were clippings from the sports page. And in the saloon bar of the Salisbury, London's theatrical pub of the time, where actors never missed an opportunity to bend a Salberg ear if one happened to be handy, the talk would be craftily channelled into tales of triumphs between the stumps rather than on the boards. With the competition hotting up, I could see that in order to put a lock on my place in the Salberg XI, I'd have to come up with something fairly startling behind the footlights for there was little chance of my doing so in front of the wicket. I was almost back to my pre-war acting form, which wasn't bad considering my creative juices had been growing penicillin for five years. But that might not be good enough to hold my place in the company against a merely passable actor with a devastating batting average. I headed back to Wolverhampton highly motivated to do even greater things with the twenty roles still left for me to play before Christmas.

At this stage of my career, a weekly rep theatre was a learning institution and my fellow actors the faculty. All I had to do was watch, listen and record. And decide when to erase, for even good actors give bad performances on occasions. The Wolverhampton years were by far the most bountiful for me, largely due to the presence in the company of an extraordinary actor called Gerald Cuff. You wouldn't have found his name in *Who's Who in the Theatre* and if you lived outside Wolverhampton you might never have heard of him. Unless you were another actor, that is. To them, from one end of the country to the other, he was king. He didn't have to search for forty different characterizations a season like we did. Every Monday when he walked on stage in costume and full makeup, he *was* another character. And he was also blessed with warmth, that elusive quality without which even the greatest talent never delivers real magic. His range was so phenomenal that it wouldn't be believed if listed on a résumé, so he never bothered to have one. He knew and could reproduce the speech patterns, the mannerisms, the gait, the very aura of someone in any class of society, in any part of the country at any time in history and never be anything less than totally believable.

At the time of my debut with the company in the spring of 1946, he had already completed an incredible ten seasons at Wolverhampton. He'd taken his fans on a world tour through the works of its most famous playwrights. He had romped with equal ease through *commedia dell'arte,* Gogol, Shaw, Shakespeare, Sheridan, Wilde and Coward. He had gut-wrenched them with O'Neill, Strindberg, Ibsen and Chekhov. He'd scared the hell out of them with *grand guignol.* He should have been a great star and many a West End manager had tried to make him one. But unfortunately for them all, his kind of talent attracted offers of job security rare in the theatrical profession and he ended up trapped in the provinces as a prisoner of the repertory system.

From the moment he walked onstage, the audience was totally under his spell. Although they didn't know it, he told them exactly when to laugh, when to cry and when to stop doing either. He could turn moods on and off like switching television channels. He would move a house to tears, walk offstage misty-eyed, give me a huge wink and say, "Silly lot of buggers." But never in one of those moments would he allow himself the indulgence of a genuine teardrop. He would make his audience lose control but never himself.

Perhaps once a season, we'd be given the opportunity to try out a brand-new play never before staged. It was quite an honour if written by an established playwright, less so if it was the work of an unknown. In either case, it gave us all valuable exposure to West End managements who were always on the prowl for a new property. They came to see the play, but when they saw Gerald Cuff, they invariably also wanted him. They would buy the play if Gerry went with it. But Gerry never would go with it because Gerry knew that actors rehearsed a West End production three weeks for free in 1947, and the show sometimes closed after the first week's run. He couldn't gamble away the security of a regular paypacket for what might be a brief flirtation with glory, not with five kids to feed and never knowing when it might be six, for his wife Margery always said, "All Gerry has to do is throw his pants across the bottom of the bed and I conceive."

Gerry's complete indifference to being "discovered" was not shared by the rest of the company. To them, Wolverhampton was a showcase, a stepping stone to films and the West End and we were all waiting for a talent-shopping scout to come by and pick us out of the window. No-one knew in advance when they'd come or even if they'd been until after the event which kept us permanently on our toes. Our biggest heartbreak was to find out that the top talent agent in London had been "in front" the previous night watching your four lines after you had just slogged unseen through three enormous leads in a row and had been brilliant in at least one of them. But thus are careers shaped in the theatre and few actors at the end of a successful one could produce a life's report card that didn't show a high mark for luck.

I was in no hurry for the bright lights of London. I was enjoying life far too much at Wolverhampton. I was also saving money. I had the best digs in town with dear old Mrs Thomas, who fed me like a champion and charged me thirty shillings a week — just about 15 percent of my salary. There was never any time to spend the rest. Unlike most of my fellow actors, I wasn't keeping a second home going in London. But I did send money to my mother every week, as I had done all through the war and would continue to do for the next thirty-five years. That still left quite a lot for Barclays Bank.

By the end of November, I could only assume that the Salberg brothers had selected me as one of the year's Most Valuable Players, for they contracted me for a second season, March to December. They also cushioned the off-season break with an offer of a fill-in at Hereford in the new year. And a carrot that one of my parts there would be Oswald in Ibsen's *Ghosts.*

Gerry Cuff was always paid a retainer between seasons but was already worried about the impending temporary reduction in his salary. He had been working solidly for eleven years but like so many men and women of extraordinary talent in the theatre, he was a hopeless manager of his own affairs. On the last night of the season, he told me he didn't know how he was going to be able to buy Christmas presents for the kids. I dropped my unopened pay packet into the palm of his hand and closed his fingers over it.

"Tuition fee," I said, and I meant it. "See you in March."

This time he really did cry.

Like me, Gerry Cuff could probably look back upon a thousand and one first nights, too, the big difference being that his were all in the *same theatre*. He never did leave Wolverhampton. I heard years later that some far-sighted brewer had installed him as landlord of a local pub. I'd like to think my name crops up sometimes when he's pulling the beer handle and reminiscing about the old days.

It must have been eight years since I'd spent a Christmas at home and Reggie Salberg was threatening to make it nine. He was running a repertory company at the little Savoy Theatre in Kettering in Northants, a short train ride north-east from London. I wasn't due at Hereford until after the holiday and he wanted me at Kettering for the Christmas production, a real Cinderella oldie called *Tilly of Bloomsbury*. I was to be cast as Perce and the part of Tilly was to be played by Hilary Vernon, she of the golden spaniel on the cricket field and the umpire husband Tim. He, alas, would also be in the company.

Reggie was a lovely man but he was a mumbler. He only opened his mouth to eat, to breathe and to make room for a cigar, never to speak. He did that with his mouth closed and merely wobbled his lips. He had a biting wit which never left any teeth marks because half the time you didn't hear it. Kettering was his first crack at running his own theatre independent of the rest of the family, and he'd made up his mind he was going to try a different style of management altogether. He was a bit left-wing and was also having an affair with one of his actresses who openly admitted she'd "fucked her way into the Communist Party" when she was seventeen. This meeting of left-leaning minds led the Kettering company to operate as a kind of high-class commune. Reggie rented, fully furnished, the largest house in the neighbourhood and the entire company moved in. Reggie became the local squire and Noreen, who was a genuine blue-blood with a titled mum, was perfect casting as the Lady of the Manor. They eventually ended up as Mr & Mrs and lived happily ever after, but that was post-Kettering.

My negotiations with Reggie went something like this:

REGGIE (*mumbling*): I can't pay you the fancy salary you get at Wolverhampton.
ME: How much?
REGGIE: Bit more than half. But I'll put you up free at The Grange.
ME: Full board?
REGGIE: Full board.
ME: Brandy after dinner?
REGGIE (*gloomily*): All right, brandy.
ME: Cigar?

REGGIE (*gloomier*): Cigar.
ME: The juvenile girl to sleep with?
REGGIE: That will depend on how good a salesman you are.
ME: Will you put all that in writing?

I wish I still had a copy of that contract, because he did. Brandy, cigars, everything. All but the last item. So I wrote it in as a rider, initialled it and sent it back.

I can still see that huge drawing room at Kettering, all of us in nightdresses, pajamas and dressing gowns, sprawled in front of a massive log fire, scattering cigarette ash on the priceless broadloom and cramming lines from *Tilly of Bloomsbury*. I took every chance I could to sneak a look at Hilary, who was really very beautiful. A couple of times she caught me. In case any of the others had too, I thought I'd better throw up a smokescreen. I grabbed the juvenile girl by the hand and said it was time to go to bed.

"What do you mean?"

"You and I are sharing a room. Didn't you know? It's in my contract."

She allowed me to lead her out of the room thinking it was all a great joke. When I continued on upstairs, she began to become a bit apprehensive. But I was a very good boy. I tucked her into her own bed, kissed her goodnight, and curled up on the floor. Everybody would spend the next two weeks wondering.

About two days before I was due to leave Kettering, I cornered Reggie in his office. As he has been dining out on this story for years, I'd better let him tell it:

"I am sitting in my office when there's this knock on the door and in walks Yeo. 'Reggie,' he says in a very aggrieved tone, 'you haven't paid me my fare.' I was absolutely flabbergasted. I had given him this wonderful part, paid him my top salary, wined him and dined him for two solid weeks with luxury accommodation, gourmet food, brandy, cigars and the juvenile girl for dessert, and he has the nerve to come and ask me for a miserable three and sixpence for his fare back to London!"

It didn't take me long to get back into the Wolverhampton routine because I'd never really left it. All my fill-in dates had been within the Salberg empire. True, living at the manor in Kettering had spoiled me a bit, but a Scots landlady at Hereford had quickly balanced that out. By the time I got to Mrs Thomas's, I was quite ready to be back home.

During the whole of the previous season I had been faithful to my script and nothing else. Now I was ready to stray a little and squeeze some play time into my schedule. On Mondays there'd be a small poker game after the show and once in a virile while I'd ask one of the girls in the cast back to the digs to "go over each other's lines" as the saying went. I would alert Mrs Thomas ahead of time and she would leave out an extra sandwich and cup and saucer. About half an hour after we'd got in, there'd be a knock on the door and her face would appear framed in a halo of innocence and say, "I'm going to bed now. Enjoy yourselves."

I also bought my first car. My bank book said I could and there were contracted paydays stretching far into the future. Petrol rationing had eased up a bit but new tires were still an endangered species. Spare parts only came from wrecking yards. I ended up with a 1939 BSA Scout, very sporty, silver blue and simply demanding to be christened the Silver Bullet. I'm not sure who got the biggest kick out of it, myself or my fellow actors. As my room at Mrs Thomas's was at street level, I found myself being awakened in the middle of the night by taps on the window from actors who couldn't sleep. When I parted the curtains, I'd see someone standing there grinning and making steering gestures. Like a fool, I'd dress and go roaring round the Staffordshire country lanes with the hood down at three o'clock in the morning.

But the Silver Bullet turned out to be the big clincher when they came to pick the next Salberg XI: I had room for two real cricketers and three cricket bags.

The drive south to the duelling grounds would be the Silver Bullet's debut on the open road, only there wasn't much open about it in 1947. For long stretches it was impossible – nay forbidden – to overtake, and every sign of an approaching village might just as well have added BOTTLENECK AHEAD. In those days, to average thirty miles an hour on a long drive would practically qualify you for the Monte Carlo Rally.

Although I had driven a water bowser round the most horrendous hairpin bends on the Eastern Ghats in India, that experience was a quiet Sunday drive compared to the Silver Bullet's coming out party. We had our first flat tire only half an hour out of Wolverhampton. We put on the battered spare, drove very gingerly to the next service station, and waited while they patched the inner tube and plugged the outer one. All five outers were already beginning to look as if they were suffering from a plague of boils. We repeated this routine an unbelievable *four more times* before reaching the end of our journey. The sun was already low in the sky and my spirits even lower as we drove into the stately town of Windsor and stopped at a red light.

The light had scarcely turned green before there was an impatient toot from the car behind me. I slowly put the BSA into neutral, pulled on the hand brake, stood up, turned round and shouted to a tweedy gentleman in an open Bentley, "Fuck off!" in a voice that reverberated down the genteel High Street, bounced over the wall of the playing fields of Eton, and possibly even ricocheted into the grounds of Windsor Castle. Then I sat down very grandly and waited for the light to go red again. By this time a small curious crowd had gathered. When the green came back, I slowly pulled away, giving a royal wave as I did so.

Cricket Week came and went and my batting average stayed right where it was, rock steady at zero. The white flannels and cable-stitch sweater were folded away until the following year, or the next Noël Coward play, and I headed eagerly back to the Midlands. I wasn't so eager when I saw my next part, another sickly juvenile in a wheelchair, smiling in the face of all adversity. I'd really served my time in that department. Besides, this wasn't wartime when you were lucky to find a juvenile who still had his own teeth. The war was over and I was thirty-two with a full set and just what the dentist ordered for a young leading man.

It was a phase we all went through in our repertory years: the juvenile was dying to become leading man, the leading man was itching for character parts because they were more fun to play, and the character actor yearned to go back to being leading man and repeat past triumphs for which he was now too old.

So although life was bliss, you weren't always absolutely potty about every single part you played. But at least you were only stuck with it for a week. In one of my seasons at the Stratford Festival forty years later, I found myself contributing an unsatisfying Capulet in a production of *Romeo and Juliet*, and I was stuck with him for eight solid months. Every time I walked into the dressing room, I felt I was entering the condemned cell. I hung a special calendar on the wall with the *R & J* days heavily outlined in black, and I crossed them off one by one as they passed into history. Towards the end of the season, I even began to cross off half a day in the intermission and the other half as I took off my makeup, I hated my Capulet that much. Fortunately it wasn't my only memory of Stratford. There was also that unforgettable night in June 1975, when the magic of Robin Phillips first reached out and enchanted players and public alike with his stunning production of *Measure for Measure* in which I was lucky enough to play The Provost. Of all the thousand and one, this must be the first night that I will remember the most. Stratford 1975 holds one other, more tender, memory: I met Grete, my second wife-to-be and stole her from her friends in Copenhagen. A graphic artist thirty-three years my junior, she reversed the usual process by inviting me to see *her* etchings. She has kept me young for twenty years and proved that you can love and be loved with intensity twice in one lifetime.

It was a big switch from a wheelchair to the bowels of a coal-mine but that was weekly rep and that was where I found myself after wheelchair week at Wolverhampton. A local miner had written a play about a pit disaster in which men are entombed for several days. A lesser company than Wolverhampton would have balked at the staging demands which called for an underground explosion and collapse of the coal-face in full view of the audience. Meantime, one rehearsal morning we were all taken underground to watch real miners at work. Before we left we arranged to borrow their sweaty, blackened coveralls exactly as they were when they took them off at the end of a shift, and we wore them that way for a whole week.

The scenic people excelled themselves. In saying "scenic people" I do them a great disservice: there were just two of them, a designer/scenepainter and one assistant. Real coal was everywhere, tons of it, including a wall of it for us to hack at with pickaxes. A section of rail had been laid across the stage, and we had a real pit-pony pulling a wagonload of coal. But the big moment was the explosion and the collapse of the pit wall. A chute hidden behind a wall of stacked coal sloped upwards into the wings to an unseen trapdoor holding back huge chunks of black-painted rock, lifted there before each run-through by a sixty-foot electric hoist specially installed for the week. The explosion was deafening. Big sound effects weren't recorded in those days because there were no systems or speakers that could handle the decibels. Instead, several maroons were loaded into a garbage can and detonated electrically all at the same time. It sounded exactly as if a V2 had just landed next door. At the same moment, the trap offstage was sprung and the rocks thundered down the chute and on to the stage floor with a force that shook the whole building and everybody in it. The audience reaction was sensational.

The cost of this effect was an extraordinary outlay for a commercial management with only a one-week run. There was nothing chintzy about the Salbergs.

The pit props eventually disappeared but the coal-dust lingered on and our feet had no right to crunch the following week as we crossed the floor of the courtroom in *The Night of January 16th*. This was a novel trial play in which the actors playing witnesses were planted unseen in the audience. Fans would talk for weeks about their favourite actor sitting right beside them and they didn't even know it until the character was called to the witness stand on stage. I sat there the longest and gave them the biggest shock. I had to jump to my feet screaming, "She's lying! She's lying!," scramble across several knees to get to the end of the row and run on to the stage shouting, "Stop the trial!"

The jury box was onstage, and twelve patrons each night were side-tracked in the lobby and cajoled to sit there instead of in their accustomed seats. They had to deliver their own verdict at the end of the play, for which playwright Ayn Rand had written two different endings. As the defendant was the leading lady and a very popular member of the company, the verdict was always "not guilty." On the very last performance, the management "got at" the jury to bring in a verdict of "guilty" and see if the company was on its toes. The result was pandemonium. The judge, a small part that usually went to a local retired actor, automatically began to discharge the prisoner. The clerk of the court developed a violent coughing fit. The leading lady burst into tears. The usher opened the door of the dock to let the prisoner free, and the stage manager forgot to ring down the curtain. In the end, the electrician mercifully faded out the lights on the frantic picture of the judge searching his desk for the piece of paper with the second ending.

Bringing in a big-name guest star was a dangerous precedent to set in a town like Wolverhampton which had built up its entire following by creating stars of its own. Our management only did it once while I was there and it gave me an undreamed-of opportunity – the chance to play opposite Lupino Lane. In the late nineteen-thirties, he had starred for two years at the Victoria Palace as the first little cockney who inherited a Viscountcy in *Me and My Girl*. Nobody will ever know why the show took nearly fifty years to get to Broadway, especially because when it did, it was as big a hit there as it had originally been in London.

"Nipper" Lane was an acrobatic comic, a powerhouse of energy with a very small dynamo. He was lean and dapper with a pencil-thin moustache, and a well-sharpened pencil at that. A cousin of Stanley Lupino, uncle of film actress Ida Lupino, he was a descendant of a theatrical dynasty that went all the way back to the seventeenth century. He came to Wolverhampton to play in the horse-racing farce *Twenty to One* and I was cast as his feed, the part that had most of the lines and none of the laughs. That didn't faze me at all. I knew from experience that the most successful comics in the Music Halls were the ones with the best straight men, and I intended to show him that such rare animals existed even in a legit theatre miles from a Moss Empire. He cottoned on immediately to my slight Music-Hall flavour and tried out a couple of ad-libs. To his obvious delight, the ball not only bounced right back but landed in the right court. By the end of the two weeks, he had asked me to continue on with him for all his other dates but I explained that I, alas, had several weeks to run on my current contract.

He was fascinating to watch. I was standing right beside him offstage every night when he made his first entrance. The routine never varied. He'd put one hand on the doorknob, cross himself, lick his fingers, touch wood twice and go on. At the end of a big scene, he knew that it only needed a single handclap to start an exit round of applause so he provided the handclap himself.

Exit. Smack. "Come on you buggers!" And the roof would fall in.

He had played *Twenty to One* at the Coliseum in London for a year and ended up buying the rights from the author, Arthur Rose, so nobody else could produce the play without him. He told me one night how he came to be cast in the part at all since it had been announced it would star his cousin Stanley Lupino. Stanley had rung him up in a state of extreme agitation during the first week's rehearsal.

"Nip," he said, "you've got to help me. You've got to take over this part. Arthur Rose hates me. He's been there at every rehearsal. He sits in the stalls and every time I come on I look at him and he starts shaking his head from side to side as if to say, 'This guy's no bloody good at all!' I can't stand it I tell you!"

Nipper took over the part because he knew what Stanley didn't: Arthur Rose had St Vitus Dance and shook his head from side to side all the time. Nip never did tell his cousin.

For several days after he left, I was beset with a great longing for the Music Hall and those lovely people in it. But the warmth of the Wolverhampton audience slowly won me back. They were unbelievably loyal and for years afterwards, in places as far away as Bermuda and St. Lucia and all across Canada, someone from this little town in Staffordshire would tap me on the shoulder and say, "I remember you." In 1986 when I was recovering from a quintuple bypass in Toronto Western Hospital, a lady visiting my room-mate walked across and sat on the end of my bed. She said, "You're Leslie Yeo, I know you are. When I was fifteen I fell madly in love with you at Wolverhampton Rep. What I'd have given then to be able to say I'd sat on Leslie Yeo's bed!"

She was a handsome woman, too.

nine

At the root of the glorious uncertainty that is an actor's life sits its richest source of nourishment, the telephone. The sound of its ring can be the jingle of the jackpot or the clang of the disaster bell at Lloyd's, depending upon whether or not you got the part. Each time you put a finger on the dial, you take a spin on the wheel of fortune. The telephone can bring you five years in a soap opera or five lines in a radio drama. It can tell you that Hollywood just beckoned or that the Straw Hat Players just passed you by. It is a pipeline to that little pool of hope that never quite runs dry, for just when all seems lost, someone will call and prime the pump with an offer that can send you off on an emotional roller coaster ride. There will be peaks and valleys along the way and fame or oblivion at the end of the rainbow. But even if it turns out to be the latter, there will be other calls, other highs and other lows, for an actor's journey never lingers long on level ground. And that beats working in a bank any day.

The phone call that did the most to change my life came in the Fall of 1947 when John Gabriel rang from Birmingham to ask if I would like to join his company going to Newfoundland. I didn't like to tell him I hadn't the faintest idea where Newfoundland was so I said "Yes, of course," and I hared round to the local reference library for an atlas.

John Gabriel was resident director at the Birmingham Alexandra Theatre, flagship of the Salberg group of companies. I was flattered to be asked because the scuttlebutt in the Salisbury was that he was choosing the pick of the Salberg stable. The contract was to be for fourteen weeks, a perfect fill-in for actors laid off between repertory seasons to make way for the annual Christmas Pantomime, where Demon Kings and Fairy Queens took over the repertory stages and held court in the lands of Ali Baba and Sinbad the Sailor. The enterprise wouldn't be a bad thing for management either, for we'd all be back on the market just in time for the end of panto and the start of the new repertory season. All except me, that is. Without the faintest whiff of a rival offer, I had boldly declined a third year at Wolverhampton, following a small difference of opinion about my financial worth to the company at that particular stage of my career. When you were a nobody, you simply had to be tough about things like that. When you were a somebody, your agent was making enough out of it to be tough for you. News of my defection had already filtered through to the teeny-boppers who besieged the stage door at the end of every repertory season with their anguished cries of "are you coming back?" I'm proud to report that the alleyway was stained with tears.

The Newfoundland venture was to be called the Alexandra Company but that was its only link to the Salberg management. The company's "angel" would be John Gabriel's new father-in-law, Sir Eric Bowring, first and wealthiest among the merchants of Newfoundland's capital city, St. John's. Ever since his lovely daughter Pix had graduated from London's Royal Academy of Dramatic Art, Sir Eric had been anxious for an opportunity to show her off in her own home town. Then she married John and Dad had a producer son-in-law to show off, too. What could be more natural than to sponsor a visit by a repertory company and kill two birds with the same ten thousand dollar bill, so to speak, for that's about what it finally cost him.

Newfoundland had been settled for almost four hundred years. It was Britain's oldest colony and her first toe-hold in the New World, so St. John's was by no means virgin territory even to theatrical marauders. At least one touring company had played there in the early eighteen hundreds. The last to call with any regularity was Florence Glossop-Harris whose English company always stopped off on its way to the West Indies, Bermuda and the Bahamas in the late nineteen-twenties. Flossop, as she was affectionately called, was never one to miss an opportunity. She would whisk the company ashore for a couple of quick performances while they were busy restocking the ship's bar. There was always a star name in the cast, and in St. John's they still talk about Roger Livesey (*Colonel Blimp* in the movie, for those of you who stay up to watch the late, late, late show) who made the trip several times and became a great local favourite. So when the Alexandra Company arrived in 1947, they didn't exactly find themselves dumped in the middle of a cultural tundra.

John Gabriel may not have been a true pioneer but he was a theatrical first just the same. He brought a company of actors from England for the sole purpose of presenting a season of plays in St.

John's and nowhere else. Englishmen have been knighted for less.

There wasn't an actor in Britain who wouldn't have traded his toupee for a break from eight years of restricted travel, currency control and going without. But John Gabriel needed performers who could deliver West End polish with only six days' elbow-grease. He began with the pick of his Birmingham company: Eileen Draycott, Roy Hannah, Pauline Williams (next stop Australia as the first star of the new National Theatre), Stephen Ward, Raymond Frances (soon to become a big hit as Inspector Maigret on BBC Television) and Raymond's wife, Margaret Towner, along with set designer Barbara Addenbrooke, carpenter William Longstaffe and stage manager Ronald Lane. From outside his Birmingham company, but having guested for John on occasion, there were the lovely Hilary Vernon from the Kettering company, myself from Wolverhampton and Alec McCowen, an ex-Salbergian who in terms of fame and fortune would ultimately outpace the lot of us. He has put Broadway and London in a tizzy on several occasions, notably on-stage with his one-man show *The Gospel According to St Mark*, and onscreen in *Travels with My Aunt* where he stole the film clean from under Maggie Smith's well-established nose.

These were the new Good Companions who converged on London Airport that December morning, and I like to think J. B. Priestley would have been proud of them. Flying the Atlantic was still something of an adventure in 1947. Most of us had never been off the ground and everybody was trying very hard not to look nervous. Hilary wouldn't let go my hand, even as we boarded the plane, so it was just as well we were sitting together. The moment the engines began to roar, I could feel her fingernails digging in, and long before we were airborne she had gouged her own runway down my palm.

We were aboard a Super-Constellation flown by AOA, the old overseas leg of American Airlines. There was only one class, plenty of leg room and no such thing as three seats abreast. Flying was a long way from becoming a mass transit system, and the sardine packers wouldn't take over the check-in counters for some years yet. Best of all, there was a bar in the belly of the aircraft, with high stools, space for the counter-leaners and even room to walk about.

The whole trip took about eighteen hours. It seemed as if we never stopped landing and taking off so the palm of my right hand got a real workout. We refuelled at Shannon, Reykjavik, Goose Bay and Gander. Goose was the worst. The terminal building was just a converted hangar, only nobody had done much converting except to add a few stacking chairs and a Johnny-on-the-spot. The only refreshment to be had was foul coffee made with evaporated milk because there apparently wasn't a promising-looking udder within a thousand miles. But it was Gander we dreaded the most. There had been a couple of bad crashes on the airfield and it was said that pilots didn't like to land there. They didn't, but not for that reason. They were afraid of a sudden fog that would prevent them from getting away again.

Sir Eric Bowring had designated the Great War Veterans Association (GWVA) to be our hosts, and hopefully beneficiaries of our box-office. They despatched an ambassador to Gander to shepherd us through Customs and Immigration, bed us down for the night and see us safely on the morning flight to St. John's. His name was Cam Eaton. Once we were all legally standing on Newfoundland soil, he took us for a small celebration into the largest bar I'd ever seen. Aptly called the Big Dipper, it had a fireplace that must have been fully twelve feet long with a roaring log fire the full length of it. The only dipper in the bar when we arrived was a BOAC pilot with a big wooffler moustache sagging under the weight of a prolonged soaking in pink gin.

"Where have you all sprung from?" wooffled the hole under the moustache.

"London," we chorused.

He squinted in the direction of the window. "In *that?* Jesus, you're lucky you got here. They tie theirs up with bits of string."

Hilary started edging towards me and I hastily buried my wounded hand in my trousers pocket.

After a few drinks, we all opted for an early breakfast and made total pigs of ourselves by putting away a two-month ration of eggs and bacon at a single sitting. Then we went to bed. The Airport Hotel was a one-level network of adjoining prefabs, with walls so thin that you could hear someone unzip his fly three doors down.

I awoke early. My stomach was still on English time and it was chiming the breakfast hour. I thought I might sneak back to the dining room for seconds. When I got there I found the others ahead of me, all twelve of them, tucking into double double eggs and bacon. This was shaping up to be quite a team.

When we finally lifted off for the comparatively short hop to St. John's, we could still see a few chunks of mangled metal from the planes that hadn't made it. My right hand thanked the Lord that the dark had hidden the evidence from us as we'd come in to land the night before.

After a photo session at Torbay Airport, we motorcaded into the city, eager for our first look at built-up North America with its dinky white picket fences, broadloomed lawns and sunporches with cushioned hammocks where the paperboy tosses the morning edition from his bike as he rides whistling by.

Your first shock is that there isn't a single picket poking through the snow and not enough porch to stop stray dogs from peeing on the morning paper. Every front door you pass is a single step up, right off the sidewalk. The houses are in rows, but they're not row houses as we understand them because no two of them are exactly alike. Built entirely of wood, they stand tightly shoulder to shoulder like an Elizabethan man-o'-war broadside on to the worst that the Atlantic gales can throw at them. They are strangely all about the same height, as if everybody had run out of money at the same time, with the result that the line of rooftops ripples into the distance in perfect synch with the contour of the road which is undulating. Then you think about it and find you aren't shocked at all because what you are looking at is really rather beautiful. And you get a queer feeling that there's an unseen presence just behind you looking over your shoulder, seeing exactly what you are seeing, only about two hundred years before you did. And that's the picture the city intends to preserve. St. John's has Heritage Police and they are vigilant and have teeth. In the morning sunlight, the street is a symphony in colour and the watchdogs don't intend to let anybody change a note in the score.

I was glad to find that we were billeted smack in the middle of this area of St. John's, for the preservation of the past did not extend to the suburbs. The War Vets had arranged to put us up on full board at the old Balsam Hotel, which was probably the closest thing to theatrical digs to be found anywhere on the island. It was also not far from the theatre and this turned out to be a big plus when the blizzards began to blow. The only minus might be that we were not used to being The Good Companions twenty-four hours a day. Back in Birmingham, Wolverhampton and Kettering, "Last call please!" in the local was usually the signal for the portcullises to come down on our private lives until rehearsal call at ten the next morning. At the hotel, we all had separate rooms, of course, but some of them were divided by mere sliding doors. Would fourteen weeks at the Balsam reveal all?

Our first priority, we were told, was to sign the book at Government House. Then, in due course, we'd receive the King's invitation to some soiree or other, for Newfoundland was still a full colony and rated a Governor-General. His Majesty's current representative was an appointee of the newly elected Labour Government in Britain, and it was common gossip that he'd been sent across the Atlantic with the express purpose of unloading Newfound-land as a British responsibility and getting it to confederate with Canada. In a stroke of diplomatic idiocy the Foreign Office chose to send, as its final representative to what was probably the hardest drinking corner of the British Empire, a former coal-miner named Gordon MacDonald who was a teetotaller.

From that time on, the only liquid served at Government House, apart from tea or coffee, was a non-alcoholic punch. Her Excellency the Governor's wife could never understand why, at all the levees, so many guests were pissed by the end of the evening. She had mixed the punch herself and knew exactly what was in it. What she hadn't seen was the guests arriving and car doors opening long before they reached her main entrance, and bottles being stashed right and left in the shrubbery that lined the driveway.

Our "theatre" was Pitt's Memorial Hall, the assembly room in a Catholic girls' school opposite the Basilica and just down the road from *The Nickel*, a movie house that showed nothing but Westerns. The current joke going the rounds was for somebody to stop you and say with a really worried look, "Did you hear they're closing the Nickel?"

"No! Why?"

"They've got to shovel the horseshit out of the aisles."

John put us to work immediately on the opening play, Terence Rattigan's *Flare Path*, one of the newest releases from London's West End. It was about a fighter pilot who loses his nerve, and it put me back into an RAF uniform and a whole host of memories. Thanks to Mr Rattigan, I had received some extraordinarily rapid promotion: there was now gold braid where before there had been only common sergeant's stripes on the uniform I'd taken off for the last time back in – was it really less than two years ago? My God, I'd done eighty-eight plays since then. By the time we left Newfoundland, I'd have knocked up a century and still be carrying my bat. And that was just since the war. I'd racked up at least another sixty-odd before I was even called up.

John didn't rush the rehearsals for *Flare Path*. For one thing, he wanted time to bring the stage up to scratch technically. He'd left a very sophisticated plant behind him at the Alex, Birmingham; and judging from the theatrical supplies pouring in from New York, he intended to turn the little Pitt's Memorial Hall into a carbon copy.

Once *Flare Path* was on, we'd be back to the deadly play-a-week grind; so we all took the opportunity to get in a little heavy socializing. It wasn't difficult to find. In fact it came looking for us. Newfoundland is practically a synonym for hospitality. We were never just watered and fed; we were feasted. It was Christmastime and you could almost hear the tables groaning. The first full-company invitation came from the house of Gordon Warren, the local sheriff. He spotted Ray Frances and me positively drooling at the sight of an entire round of Stilton cheese, a hundred-percent export item from Britain for at least the last nine years. The top had been gently disturbed and was peacefully marinating in fine port when our observant host calmly sat the two of us at the buffet table. He gave us each a large plate, an oversize napkin, a dessert spoon and said, "dig in." You couldn't insult a classy cheese like Stilton by showing it a common cracker, so we ate it straight by the spoonful. I regret to say that for the first time in our lives we both found out what it really meant to eat yourself sick. We just made it to the back door.

So overwhelming was the hospitality in St. John's that we never did find out what Sunday dinner was like at The Balsam. It was the company day off and nobody ever lacked an invitation out, usually preceded by a Sunday drive before dinner. The furthest you could go on a paved road out of St. John's was thirteen miles, but you could see practically as many late model cars on that stretch as you would at the New York Motor Show. Hilary and I were in an enormous Buick coupe one Sunday when our host pulled in to the side of the road.

"Drink Bridge," he announced, then opened the trunk and produced a bottle of rum and four glasses.

A bit further on, we came to another bridge. It seemed that was Drink Bridge, too. So was the one after that. When we all met up at the Balsam at the end of the evening, the sitting room reeked of rum.

"Drink Bridge?" I asked them.

"S'right," they said.

I'd hate to be taken for a Sunday drive today. There's a paved road right across the island all the way to Port aux Basques.

In every house we visited, and there were many, there was a rare elegance hiding behind those clapboard exteriors that seemed to belong more to the other side of ivy-covered Cotswold stone. The richness of the furnishings and the decor decidedly spoke of an Old Country heritage and a distinctly luxurious lifestyle. It was said that there were more millionaires per square mile in St. John's than in

Houston, Texas. Confederation hadn't yet hit the Newfoundland history books and income tax was only five cents on the dollar. There was no industry to speak of and the city was really one vast trading post. Every famous brand-name had an agent, like Jim MacNab who got some part of a cent for every tin of Campbell's soup sold anywhere on the island. I wondered what the agent for Johnnie Walker was worth. The country's main source of tax revenue was customs and excise, which must have made shopping fun for the rich, nerve-wracking for the middle class and a rare outing for the poor.

But there was no shortage of people shopping for theatre tickets. Bowrings had wisely priced them for all pockets and the word was out that some performances were already sold out. This was tremendously exciting news and, for me, a load off my mind that had no right to be there in the first place. All that expensive equipment flying in from New York had got me worrying about the War Vets and what they were going to get out of our visit.

This was something new. I'd never given management so much as a passing thought before. They were there when you wanted them – payday, raise-time, and an emergency first-aid post for financial crises. At the moment, of course, management wasn't "there." It was still sitting in its office back in Birmingham. Perhaps that was it. John Gabriel was a RADA man, not Dale Carnegie. He could manoeuvre his troops on stage with the best of them, but did he really know that the bottom line was where you made your last stand?

As a final assault on my fast-growing sense of responsibility, a hefty consignment of auto-transformer dimmers weighing about two hundred pounds apiece arrived from New York *by air!* I suddenly became so jittery I had to go and hide. It didn't come to me until weeks afterwards that this must have been the moment that I contracted the actor-manager virus, with this particular attack of hypertension being the first major symptom.

I remember thinking *Flare Path* an odd choice for a season opener, but after a thirty-year theatre drought, who was to know what local tastes were? For anybody under the age of fifty, we'd probably be the ones creating a taste for them. They were in good hands. John's production was up to anything I'd seen outside London and in theatres far better equipped than Pitt's Memorial Hall. Yet *Flare Path* didn't fill it. When they added up at the end of the week, we'd played to just over seventy-five per cent of capacity.

Now, seventy-five percent was surely not to be sneezed at. No entrepreneur in his right mind would budget higher than that. St.

John's was a small town; Pitt's was a five-hundred-seat theatre. With seven performances, seventy-five percent would add up to 2,600 bodies a week, nearly nine percent of every man, woman and child in the city, an astounding achievement.

Meantime, while the fighters were landing and taking off in *Flare Path* by night, we were rehearsing premeditated murder by day with the good old pot-boiler *Night Must Fall* by Emlyn Williams. This was to be John Gabriel's big showpiece as Danny with Eileen Draycott as the murderee in the wheelchair.

Hilary and I had scenes together and arranged to go over them back at the Balsam after the *Flare Path* performance. She had a room with four solid walls on ground level. I was one floor up and was only a sliding door away from Alec McCowen. I went down to her room. We rehearsed away until I said that it was a bit chilly and why didn't I pop into bed. She said, "All right," and as I climbed in, she said, "Don't you dare do anything."

"Certainly not," I said, but of course I did. In fact I overdid – to such a degree that after two very happy weeks I had to ring up the company doctor, a war vet named Jim Roberts. He had volunteered his services to the group and very generously offered to come to the Balsam when I told him over the phone of the intimate nature of my problem. I met him in my old room upstairs. After a few pointed questions he suggested that I might have been going at it a bit too hard. He suggested I take it easy for a while and my problem would go away on its own. Which I did. And which it did.

A year and a half later, Alec McCowen came down to play a guest role at the Penge Empire in South London where I was performing for the season. It was the first time I'd seen him since St. John's.

"How's your whatsit?" he asked innocently.

"My what?"

"Your whatsit." And he pointed to my crotch. "Everything all right now?"

It took me a moment or two.

"You bastard! You were behind those bloody sliding doors! You heard every word!"

And he shrieked with laughter.

Night Must Fall gave the customers an extra thrill on the Wednesday night. Danny had just left Mrs. Bramson dead in her wheelchair when it slowly started to roll down towards the edge of the stage. What was poor old Eileen Draycott to do? She was dead. She couldn't come back to life and put on the brake. A fast-thinking patron in the front row saved the day, the play and possibly Eileen Draycott. He crept forward, lifted his hand above his head and grasped the front wheel until the curtain came down. She was a gutsy old lady and she ran it dangerously close. One night, in a terrible blizzard, some of the patrons even had to climb out of bedroom windows to get to the theatre. We never thought Eileen would make it from the Balsam. After several tries through howling winds and waist-deep snow, we finally plonked her on a kid's sleigh and pulled her there.

Attraction number three was John Patrick's lovely play *The Hasty Heart*. When you can look back upon years in weekly rep and a tally of five or six hundred plays, you realize how few roles you would want to play a second time, even if you could still do so physically. My list would probably stop at ten, but one of them would unquestionably be the Yank in *The Hasty Heart*. I'd already played him twice, once at Wolverhampton and once at Birmingham and I loved him. In fact, he was probably the reason why I was in St. John's right then. He is an absolute charmer and he stutters. He has one magnificent moment in the play when he recites non-stop the names of every book in the Old Testament, all thirty-nine of them. This was the one long speech in which I decided that he would *not* stutter, just because everybody would be expecting him to. I kept them waiting until the very last book. "M - M - M -" I stammered. "M - M - M -" I turned my back on the audience. "M - M - M-" I moved as if to go off the stage. I went off the stage. Then immediately, I returned. "M- M- Malachi!" And I went off. Of course it stopped the show.

There are directors I know today who would have called me "very naughty" for doing that. But then, there are directors today who think getting a laugh of any kind is being naughty. Some of the drama schools are even more hysterical about that sort of thing. I think it's high time we dumped a cylinder of laughing gas in every Actors' Studio, with an automatic timer that gives it a squirt every hour on the hour. That way we might end up with a generation of new actors who know how to play comedy and give some incentive to playwrights to go back to writing them.

The Hasty Heart ambled along in the same seventy-five percent attendance groove. And like *Night Must Fall*, it had its own special moment of unrehearsed drama. In this wartime play, we were all ward-mates in a field hospital in the jungle with the set just a straw *basha* with six rope beds. One of us was supposed to be a black GI nicknamed Blossom. After what practically amounted to a house to house search, we found the only black man in St. John's. He was a night-watchman named Clifford Earle, who agreed to moonlight and hold down two jobs at once. Blossom has the most tender moment in the play. There is a dour Scot named Lachie who has spurned the hand of friendship from us all. Blossom, our last hope, is to present Lachie with his most treasured possession, a string of native beads. On the night in question, we all looked expectantly towards Blossom's bed. But Blossom the actor didn't move. Blossom the night-watchman was sound asleep.

I edged towards his bed and gave it a sharp nudge. Then a sharper one. Suddenly there were two big brown eyes staring vacantly up at me. I frowned and jerked my head towards Lachie. Not a flicker. I mouthed the word "Beads." Not a glimmer. I hissed the word at him. The eyes got bigger. Finally, in a stage whisper that could have been heard across the road at the Basilica I said, "Give him the fucking beads!"

His hand hit his forehead with a loud smack. "Oh my Gaad!" he wailed and grabbed the beads.

On the Monday of week four, a minor miracle happened; we had to turn people away at the door. We did it again on Tuesday. By Wednesday morning there was a waiting list for the rest of the performances that week. The play was *Arsenic and Old Lace*, more affectionately known to actors as Lace Knicks and Old Arse. Why the sudden stampede? Was it conscience? Was it because Lace Knicks was a big recent hit? So were several others on our list. It couldn't have been word of mouth because the rush began before the first performance. Whatever it was, it was short-lived. The following Monday we were back to our loyal group of seventy-five percenters. And that's where the meter stuck.

I began to suspect that our beneficiaries, the GWVA, were going to come up empty-handed. Suspicion almost became a certainty when I asked John Gabriel one day if he would ever come back to St. John's and he smiled wryly and said "No." This surprised me, because at least he now knew how much a week it cost us to be there. I did a few sums of my own and the figures fairly danced off the page. All we had to do was make the productions fit the stage rather than make the stage fit the productions.

A couple of other company members who had heard John's "No" were also thinking along the same lines I was. So we all got together and even went as far as looking for an alternative hall for a return visit. That was until John convened a special company meeting and proceeded to blast the hell out of us.

"There are two or three among you who are apparently making plans to return here under your own steam some time in the future." He went on from there. Deceitful, unprofessional and dirty were the words I remember because they hurt the most. Someone had to disturb the air of innocence which had suddenly descended upon the room, so I spoke up.

"But John, I asked you if you would ever come back here and you said 'No'."

"Yes, but that was just a casual remark made over a cup of coffee. It never occurred to me it was a serious question."

"It never occurred to me it wasn't," I answered. But even as I said it, I knew I couldn't have added "Scout's Honour."

There wasn't a peep out of the other two. So that was the last peep they ever got out of me on the subject. From then on I went it alone. I made no attempt at secrecy – what was the point? I established a firm line of communication with Gordon Stirling, barrister and head of the old boys' association of Bishop Feild College (Feild with the funny spelling was the name of the bishop, not the college sports ground). The College hall had a hundred more seats than Pitt's Memorial. I negotiated a rental, found out the rates at the Balsam Hotel and recorded the cost of space in the local papers. I talked to printers, carpenters, electricians, handymen, the trucking company, the phone company, the shipping company, in fact, anyone who supplied any goods or services we might have to purchase locally. But there was one question nobody was able to answer. Why did Lace Knicks beat the pants off everything else at the box-office? If we could work that one out, St. John's was ours.

I wrestled for days with the Alexandra playbill. Somewhere on that list was the key. What was it that *Arsenic and Old Lace* had that the others lacked? What was the uncommon denominator? It finally hit me. Apart from *The Hasty Heart*, every other play on the list was English.

Newfoundlanders would rightly pride themselves on being more British than the passenger list of the *Mayflower*. But the winds of temptation from the southwest were nibbling away at the corners of the Union Jack. Their way of life was slowly tilting towards Yankee-dom. Their currency was the dollar. Their radio dramas were rudely interrupted by someone trying to cure bad breath, they drove their cars on the wrong side of the road and they even blew their noses into bits of tissue paper instead of a good solid linen handkerchief.

The Alexandra Company ended up ten thousand dollars in the red, which worked out to a loss of almost a thousand dollars a week. On top of that, I heard that Sir Eric Bowring had made a donation of a thousand or two to the War Vets. Although the Alexandra Company's actual running costs remained a closely guarded secret, Gordon Stirling had no trouble in getting me a copy of the certified box-office returns. That was a hell of a lot more to go on than John Gabriel ever had. All I needed to do was work backwards.

I told Gordon he'd have to be very patient. There was no hope of a new company the following winter, because there was far too much homework to be done. There was also the little matter of finding a partner. No, I didn't want a sponsor. I was a child of the commercial theatre. I wanted an investor, a person of the theatre who believed in the viability of the project as vehemently as I did and was prepared to put his money where his vehemence was.

John had arranged for the company to go back to England by sea. We were booked first-class on the *RMS Nova Scotia,* and the comings and goings on the wharf on departure day must have been the social event of the season. Enough bottles were left on board to put the ship's bar out of business for the entire voyage. There was a message from Mr Caterpillar Tractor, Ches Pippy, to say that there was a whole smoked salmon for me in the ship's freezer. George Crosbie had already put a 24 lb case of margarine for each of us in the ship's cold storage and arranged with Lever Brothers in Liverpool to see us through customs. As we cast off and headed through the Narrows, I wondered how long it would be before I saw that rugged shoreline again.

ten

I had played farewell scenes before on the platform at Euston Station at the end of a tour, but the one with Hilary was different. This time I really minded. This is not to imply that I had been less than honest with the other ladies. I hadn't. I'd been absolutely up-front with all of them. I'd made it quite clear from the outset that there was no signpost that said ALTAR on the road we were about to travel. Both my wives could have testified to this from personal experiences, and once we were married, both did, frequently and with great glee to all my friends.

I was rapidly closing in on thirty-three and it was time to hang up my playboy boots. I'd never even had a place of my own. Five years in provincial theatre digs and five in RAF Nissen huts had combined to make a gypsy of me ever since 1939. And before that, as my brothers had all fled the coop, I'd been left to provide a home for my mother and a put-u-up bed for me between jobs. It was to Mum's place I now headed with my case of margarine and my ten-pound smoked salmon. Since she had no fridge, the first thing I did before it completely defrosted was to flog it for thirty shillings to a restaurant round the corner.

My mother was a gutsy lady who had kept my brother Fred's West End menswear shop open all through the air raids while he took refuge in the country. She liked to live close to the shop and had been bombed out twice. She resettled for the final time in Bayswater in a small flat in which she had curtained-off a corner for me. She was still out all day running the shop, so at least I'd have some time to sort out my papers on the floor, a system I had perfected over the years on many floors in many places.

I was eager to get at the Newfoundland pile while I was still on an emotional high and my memory was fresh enough to fill in the gaps. There were floor plans and wiring diagrams and specifications and catalogues for every conceivable supply or service. There were notebooks crammed with names, addresses, telephone numbers, distinguishing marks, idiosyncrasies, advice solicited and advice unsolicited. And there were figures. Sheet after sheet of columned foolscap with possibilities, probabilities, best and worst and even worse-case scenarios, calculations scribbled on scraps of paper, on backs of envelopes, napkins, cigarette packets, menus, even toilet tissue. For one passing moment, I felt a small seed of doubt crawling about in my lower intestine looking for a spot to germinate. What in the hell did I think I was up to? I had no money, I didn't know anybody who had money, and I hadn't the faintest idea where to *look* for somebody who had money.

But my stubborn streak won as it usually did. I had something to sell and I knew it. It wasn't ready for market but I knew what had to be done to make it ready. Time enough then to start thinking about a buyer. First, I needed a working title. Something to inspire confidence in a prospective partner and a feeling of expectancy in an audience. I settled on London Theatre Company.

To launch a theatrical enterprise, you need two distinct budgets: the Production Budget which has to cover the cost of everything it takes to get the show on the road and back home again, and the Operating Budget which tells you the cost of keeping the curtain going up and coming down without going broke in between. The latter is called the "Weekly Getout." or more simply "The Nut." This has to include its weekly share of the Production Budget, which is amortized over the length of the season. Preparing these two budgets was now my number one priority.

All I had to go on from the Alexandra Company experience was their certified box-office returns. I could only guess at their expenses, though it would be an educated one because I knew they had lost $10,000 in twelve weeks. I added this deficit, at the rate of $800 a week, to their average revenue of $2700 per play. This clearly meant they'd *spent* $3500 a week just to stay alive. So to bring a humble repertory company from England to a tiny school hall in St. John's, Newfoundland in 1947 had cost, in 1998 dollars, the equivalent of $25,000 a week. This was a sobering thought and a shocking revelation to a penniless embryo actor-manager planning to launch a second expedition. To give it any hope at all, the London Theatre Company would have to slash the Alexandra costs in half. Any conjecture on how I was going to perform this miracle was cut short by the arrival of my mother with a fourteen-week accumulation of telephone messages including one marked URGENT to call Reggie

Salberg at an unfamiliar London number.

Reggie, it transpired, had taken over the lease on the Penge Empire in South London, an ex-Variety house that had been trying to make repertory pay for years without success. I had played there as an amateur way back in 1938 when it was run by Harry Hanson, a flamboyant impresario who was never seen without his toupee. In actual fact, he had three; one short, one medium and one long-haired. Every three weeks he would tell his secretary he was going out to get a haircut and come back an hour later having switched from the long-haired version to the short one. Every Sunday at home he'd switch again, and it never seemed to bother anybody that his hair only grew at weekends.

Penge Empire was really too large for something as intimate as repertory, but Reggie had it all worked out. He wouldn't carry fourteen permanent actors like they did in Wolverhampton, paying eight of them for doing nothing when a play only had a cast of six. Penge was three stops down the commuter line from the richest talent pool in the entertainment world. He would rely on just six "regulars" to build up a fan following, and job in the other actors a play at a time. Would I be one of the six starting immediately?

He was offering me the actor's dream: a regular showcase bang on the doorstep of every talent agent and management in London. The chance to live at home, make all the film auditions, see all the new plays and hear all the latest gossip in the Salisbury. There was just this one snag. I had a new baby to bring up, only christened that afternoon. I didn't want to stunt its early growth by sheer neglect and Reggie was talking about a contract right through to December. I'd put nothing in the London Theatre budget for preparatory work; so until we opened our box-office, the new baby was going to need child support. I might as well get that from Reggie as anyone else. He offered to do that handsomely to the tune of twelve pounds a week. Other managements in the London suburbs were getting away with ten. But I suspected he meant to get a lot for his money. You don't build up a following playing small parts. I was sure he'd have me in every play unless he did *The Women,* and even then I just might find myself going on in drag.

It was now imperative for me to find a quiet place of my own where I could learn a monstrous quota of lines and use the floor as a filing cabinet if I wanted to. I found one in Smith Terrace, an exquisite cul-de-sac in Chelsea, home of the rich and famous in the art and entertainment world. I thought they wouldn't mind if I only took a small single room. My next door neighbour was Percy Marmont, a famous silent film star with two beautiful daughters. At the corner of the street, I shared the same local with Robert Newton, then at the peak of his fame both as an actor and a drinker.

The Silver Bullet could get me to Penge in half an hour, and there was an extra petrol ration for business travel. For eleven weeks I didn't escape a single hour of rehearsal time, but I still managed to squeeze in my first session wrestling with the London Theatre Company budget. We were rehearsing the Aldwych farce *It Pays to Advertise,* and although I was playing the lead, I'd done the part recently at Wolverhampton and still remembered the lines and all my funny biz. That left my afternoons free.

My target for expenses, set in indelible ink, was to come in at $1750 a week lower than the Alexandra Company. If only I'd been able to find out *how* they'd spent their $3500, my task might have been a lot simpler. Without doubt the killer had been transportation. There was only one class by air and it was roughly the same as first class by sea – $480 round trip per person, $6700 for a company of fourteen. (For an idea of costs in today's dollars, multiply all figures by seven)

There was absolutely nothing I could do to reduce transportation costs, unless I sent them steerage, which would be unthinkable across the North Atlantic on a seven thousand five hundred ton cork like the *RMS Nova Scotia.* But what I *could* do was amortize the same total over a longer period of time. John Gabriel, with only twelve playing weeks, had no choice but to write off his travel costs at $560 a week. With a twenty-six week season, for instance, I could amortize exactly the same amount at only $260 a week, a saving of $300 on the "Weekly Getout" and a full twenty percent knocked off my target. The London Theatre Company made its first major decision: the season would be twenty-six weeks long.

I began to have an impact on the Penge audience early. A gentleman in the balcony had a heart attack and was carried out moaning all through one of my scenes in *The Shop at Sly Corner*. And during the run of a rarely done Priestley play, *How Are They at Home?*, an usherette brought me a note torn off the corner of a programme on which a patron had scribbled, "Will the gentleman in the Squadron Leader's uniform kindly button up his fly?"

But that was small stuff compared to what happened in Somerset Maugham's *The Sacred Flame.* I was sitting once again in my most unfavourite spot, a wheelchair. A flying accident had seriously damaged my marriage equipment, pathetically soon after taking unto myself a beautiful young bride played by Elizabeth London. We had a very tender love scene at the end of the first act and it did go on a bit. Much too long for one member of the audience because he got up to leave in the middle of it. The clatter of the seats springing back as people stood up to let him pass was like a slow handclap and just about as encouraging. I gripped Liz's hand, smiled my wheelchair smile and hissed through my teeth "don't worry!" To my horror, our interrupter, instead of making for the doors, headed down toward the stage. He grasped the orchestra rail, leaned in and shouted up at us, "Ducky darling nonsense! Lot of bloody trash!" and stumped out. Those were the exact words. They were burned on my brain as if with a branding iron and the scar remains after forty-eight years. As soon as the interrupter had gone, we carried on with the scene and of course got a round of applause for our courage.

As my character died at the end of Act One, I was excused from taking the final curtain call. I got out of costume and makeup as fast as I could and attacked the poor front-of-house manager in the lobby.

"What the hell was all that about?" I asked.

"Now don't get upset. The poor fellow explained to me that he had been jilted that morning by his girl friend and your long love scene was just too much for him."

"Oh great! And are you going to explain that to the audience?" I asked, rather reasonably I thought.

Our spurned lover wasn't the only hazard when it came to playing that particular scene. There was another. It happened not just once but every night of the run. The stage lighting system at Penge was closer to state-of-the-ark than state-of-the-art. It was one of the last few remaining theatres in England that still had salt-and-water dimmers. For the uninitiated, a dimmer is something that fades the stage lights up or down. With the primitive salt-and-water system, there are two or three rows of antiquated earthenware drainpipes standing on end, and in the bottom of each is a layer of concrete and an electrode connected to one end of a circuit. The other end of the circuit is joined to an iron rod dangling immediately above each drainpipe which is filled with salt water, a conductor of electricity. As the rod is lowered into the salt water, the circuit is completed and the light comes on. The lower the rod goes and the closer to the electrode, the brighter the light becomes and vice versa.

In my last scene in *The Sacred Flame*, my life was supposed to ebb beautifully away in an orange beam of fading light from the setting sun. Long, slow "fade-outs" today are achieved by simply pressing a key on a computer. At Penge, the electrician painstakingly took twenty minutes to turn his master wheel a notch at a time to lift twenty-four iron rods slowly up through twenty-four drainpipes. The trouble was that if the rods stayed too long near the top, the water started to bubble with the heat and I ended up my tender scene with a premature death rattle that sounded like twenty-four saucepans all boiling potatoes.

During my whole tenure at Penge, I would have to confess that a part of me was always two thousand miles away in St. John's. Except while I was actually on the stage. With a play a week, anything less than total concentration would be disastrous. I've tried it and I know. With six months on tour in the same part, you could practically work out your football pools and tear off a dramatic strip at the same time. But not in weekly rep. So the minute I made an exit, I left my current character onstage and became an actor-manager offstage. And that's how it came to me one day as I sat in my dressing room at Penge that all those guest artistes constantly streaming in from uptown were, in effect, giving the London Theatre Company an unsolicited audition if I only took the trouble to evaluate them. So I started keeping a record book. It only had two categories: OFFERERS and NON-OFFERERS. To be an Offerer, you not only had to be a good actor by London Theatre Company standards but you also had to perform well offstage too. I couldn't take trouble-makers two thousand miles and be stuck with them for six months. As I had a dread of dear friends picking up the book and finding themselves listed as Non-offerers, I always kept it well out of sight.

The twin demands of Penge Rep and the London Theatre Company left little time for any kind of personal life, which was just as well since Hilary and I were finding it increasingly difficult to meet. She was currently touring Ireland with the somewhat passé but still vibrant musical comedy star Jessie Matthews. I did pick up my old friendship with Henry Kendall, who was now in his fourth year at the Ambassadors Theatre in *Sweetest and Lowest*, the third of the incredibly successful *Sweet and Low* revues. Harry had moved into a luxury apartment at 22D Ebury Street, not far from Buckingham Palace and just a floor and a ceiling away from the flat where Ian Fleming would shortly create the character of Agent 007, James Bond. Harry would sometimes call me backstage on a Saturday night, often in tears because his latest lover had taken off complete with his silver cigarette case or some such treasure. After a morning rehearsal and two performances, I would drive up to Ebury Street, hold his hand, dry his eyes, get him gently sloshed and put him to bed. Then I'd have a couple of stiff ones on my own and flop out exhausted in the spare room.

Sometimes, when I knew in advance that I'd get away from rehearsal early, Harry would take me to lunch at the Ivy and introduce me to all the famous names who always stopped at his table. "Of course, you know what they'll all be thinking, don't you?" he said archly one day, and I told him I really didn't give a damn.

But my afternoons in the West End weren't always social. It was here I would find the answers to many of the blanks in the London Theatre Company budget. I had already talked to Strand Electric, the stage-lighting people, and I subsequently spent a fascinating couple of hours in their demonstration theatre in Covent Garden. Their engineers had taken my floor plan of the Bishop Feild Hall stage and gone to immense trouble to completely re-rig their own showroom stage, which wasn't that much smaller, with the most versatile lighting set-up they could think of for a repertory season using the minimum amount of equipment. They had even put up some token scenery and proceeded to "light" a couple of scenes. We put the system through its paces with myself posing imaginary artistic problems and they coming up with genuine lighting solutions. By the time they'd finished I was quite excited, particularly as they didn't seem to mind when I broke the news that purchase was out of the question. They happily promised to work out a rental figure which would decrease every week we kept the equipment, complete with compartmentalized crates for road and sea travel, colour filters, spare bulbs, pre-formed cables and anything else they thought we might need for a six-month season and wouldn't be able to get at short notice. Or even long notice for that matter.

After Strand, I felt encouraged enough to tackle Gustave the wigmaker and Michael Ellis who ran the stage costume department of Moss Bros. Gustaves were quite adamant that a twenty-six week rental meant twenty-six times the weekly rate, whether the wigs were used in England or in Timbuktu. In a six-month season, I'd be buying the damned things nearly three times over. Wigs would clearly have to be a capital item and I didn't want too many of those. Michael Ellis showed symptoms of being much more malleable.

Life was full to the brim in 1948, and not a moment went to waste or lacked pleasure. There was work, there was money, there were wonderful parts to play, superb fellow-actors to play with, the most supportive management in Britain and all the ingredients of a big adventure simmering on the back burner. And we all had such tremendous belief in ourselves! This was how my Pen Portrait started off in a Penge programme way back in 1948:

> ONE-TIME JOURNALIST who forsook Fleet Street for Drury Lane but went by way of Woolwich, Gravesend, Chatham, Bath, Dundee, Wolverhampton, Hereford, Newfoundland and Penge.
> FOR FURTHER HISTORY, look up *Who's Who* in 1968.

The same programme contained another interesting comment on the times. The management announced that the recent reduction in the entertainment tax would be passed on to the patrons and the new prices would be (with dollar equivalents in parentheses): Stalls 3/- (60c) Back Stalls 1/10 (40c) Balcony 11d (20c) At these prices, Reggie would have to sell eighty of his best seats just to pay me my salary. Using the same arithmetic at Canada's Stratford Festival prices today, I would be earning nearly $5000 a week!

My father always told me that he dreaded the day when he wouldn't have enough to do. I could never understand that at the time but I do now. In fact, I almost dread the day when I won't have too much on my plate: the higher the pressure the better I work. So I decided to give myself some more and began putting the finishing touches to a play I had begun writing between dodging king cobras and promotion in the Burmese jungle. Then came the wonderful news that Hilary was coming down to Penge to play the lead in *Lottie Dundass,* which put all thoughts of being a playwright or a playboy or an actor-manager right out of my head. They all came surging back, though, the moment she left, for it had become agonizingly clear that she'd never have the courage to leave her husband Tim while we were still in England. A return visit to St. John's now became more vital than ever. I got down on my hands and knees and started poring over the files looking for a new glimmer of hope.

eleven

Just as I was getting a firm grip on the London Theatre Company budget, the British Chancellor of the Exchequer lost control of his and down went sterling. The same pound note that twenty-four hours earlier was good for four dollars' worth of supplies and services in St. John's would now buy only two dollars and eighty cents' worth. I would have to begin all over again.

Devaluation hadn't even made my possible disaster list and that really bothered me. We could have been halfway across the Atlantic with fourteen actors under watertight contracts and irrevocable financial commitments in two different capitals. What a script for a horror movie that would have made.

My big worry now was dates. An early October start was essential for a twenty-six week season that wouldn't run into the summer doldrums, and we'd never make it now in 1949. Nineteen forty-eight was already history. I'd wasted a whole season at Penge riding a merry-go-round trying to catch the horse in front.

I didn't want St. John's to cool off. I wrote Gordon Stirling to put everything on hold but be sure to keep the candle burning in the window. I signed with Reggie for a second season at Penge beginning in March, and I couldn't resist the offer to fill-in a couple of the dead months at the new Salberg company in Leicester. That left me just two weeks to revise my budget. I was halfway through it when Newfoundland became the tenth province of Canada, making mincemeat of the old customs-and-excise regulations and a whole segment of my calculations as well. For the budget, it was back to the massage parlour once more.

I returned to Penge to find that Reggie had made a few trades in the off-season. Oliver Gordon was appointed the Director of Productions and there was a new scenic designer named George

102

Paddon-Foster. Although none of us knew it at the time, they were both to play key roles in the story of the London Theatre Company.

Oliver's new title marked a historic change in theatrical nomenclature. Hitherto, the man who manoeuvred the actors between the sofas, the chairs and the standard lamps on stage had always been known as the Producer. Only on a film set was the Director the actors' traffic cop. Henceforth, the Producer in the theatre would be the one to supply the money, like Reggie.

I also moved house at the start of Penge Two. I'd been wasting too much time driving back and forth to Chelsea four times a day. I teamed up with one of the new regulars, Anthony Sagar, and we found a luxurious, unfurnished and highly expensive upper floor flat on what appeared to be Millionaire's Row in nearby Sydenham, about five minutes from the stage door by Silver Bullet. The rooms were enormous and we had practically nothing to put in them. I'm sure the neighbours wondered for weeks when the big furniture van was going to arrive.

Early in the new Penge season, the following note appeared in the theatre programme. It was placed immediately after the announcement that the next week's play would be *Hay Fever* by Noël Coward.

> ACTOR PLAYWRIGHT
> On May 30th, we are presenting a new play by a somewhat less famous playwright. It's a comedy-thriller and it's called "And the Whistle Blew." The name of the author – Leslie Yeo. It has an outstandingly good part for an actor whose work he admires very much. The name of the actor – Leslie Yeo. But there are other good parts as well, and the whole play should prove excellent entertainment.

In true keeping with dramatists of the male persuasion, *The Whistle* had a cast of ten men and only one woman. Hilary, who had that very week joined the regular company, made a splendid start by refusing to play it because she said it was such an awful part.

In my entire theatrical career, nothing has ever matched the horror of that first night of *And the Whistle Blew*. Not only did I have to face hearing lines that had never before been bounced off a public ear-drum, but also I'd been stupid enough to cast myself as the chief bouncer. I'd gone to great lengths to structure the funny lines, feed them meticulously and space them strategically. I braced myself for the first of these, delivered it loud and clear and heard it plop onto the

103

stage floor like a bag of wet feathers. Half a page further on, I gave them a fill-in line that didn't matter a damn and it brought the house down. So much for constructive playwriting.

Although the birth of *And The Whistle Blew* was duly recorded in *The Stage,* nobody ever offered to become godfather to a second production. A few of the Penge patrons wrote. The letter I liked best came from a lady who said she didn't really like the play because it was too funny.

Despite *And the Whistle Blew* and plays by more famous playwrights, the Salbergs found, like others before them, that there just weren't enough patrons to satisfy the voracious financial appetite of a theatre as big as the Penge Empire. They decided to call it a day. They sold the building to their one and only bidder, Essoldo Cinemas. But they went out in style. For the very last performance, Reggie invited every guest artiste who had appeared during the previous two years, and at the end of the play, over a hundred of them poured on to the stage to take the final curtain call. And final it would be as far as live theatre was concerned: within days, a movie screen would sadly hang right there where they were standing.

After the last member of the audience had gone, the curtain went up again and Reggie made a rather moving speech to the cast, the staff, the crew and the invited guests. He told them of his long struggle and that his own salary had been £5 less than he'd paid his top actor. As one voice, everyone shrieked "Too much!" which at once brought the proceedings down to a less emotional level. Reggie then announced that, as drinks could not legally be served in a movie house, the bars would reopen and all drinks would be free. Moreover, the bars wouldn't close until there wasn't a drop of anything left. And so began the best, the biggest, the longest and the loudest binge in my entire sixty-odd years of concentrated socializing. I left at 4 am and everybody was flying. On my way up to town at eleven next morning, the stage door was still open and I looked in. A hoarse group was singing barrack-room songs round the grand piano. Two people were sound asleep on top of it. The cleaning ladies lay flaked out in the aisles like ninepins in a bowling alley after a strike. Bodies sprawled everywhere, draped over the footlights, hanging out of boxes and wedged under seats. In the bars, a few actors were still on their feet and mixing their own cocktails from bottles that were normally not on speaking terms. Reggie told me later that the party went on most of that day. It was Sunday, October 16, 1949.

For the first time in four years I was out of a job. But not for long.

Henry Kendall was having a big success at the Comedy Theatre in *On Monday Next* by Philip King and had been asked to direct a company to take it on tour. He offered me the second lead. I had to negotiate terms with the producer, Peter Dearing. The next time I'd come across Peter would be twenty years later at the Grand Theatre, London, Ontario when I went to adjudicate his production of *Marat/Sade* for the Dominion Drama Festival.

I hadn't been on tour since before the war and a break from learning lines would be like a couple of weeks on the Riviera. Cast in the lead role was an Irish actor, Terence de Marney, whose sole claim to fame was playing the *Count of Monte Cristo* for twenty-four episodes on BBC radio. But it made him a star. He had a magnificent voice but not much else and knew as much about playing comedy as a laughing hyena. But he was willing to learn, and every night on the road I would pick out three sure-fire laughs in the script, drill him on exactly how to get them and stand in the wings to make sure he did. Unfortunately the tour didn't last long enough to turn him into a real comedian.

Provincial audiences weren't mad about *On Monday Next*. Cardiff hated it. So did Glasgow. Manchester absolutely loathed it. They didn't really like it much in London either. But it packed them in at the Comedy Theatre for a year just the same. They didn't know they'd hate it until they got to the theatre because they'd been conned by the reviewers who had loved it. It was an *in* show, a slice of life backstage. Suburbia had never been backstage, didn't want to and didn't know what the hell was going on. The play was about an awful repertory company putting on a dreadful piece called *The Morals of Melisande*. It began with actors still floundering through an early rehearsal with scripts in their hands. Harry Kendall had papered all four walls and the ceiling of his dressing room at the Comedy Theatre with abusive letters from theatre-goers. My favourite was one that "thought we'd never see the day when West End actors would walk onstage still reading their lines." It was signed "Disgusted bus load from Windsor."

The tour of *On Monday Next* wasn't a total write-off because, as so often happened in my life, it led to other things. Terence de Marney had the rights to a play called *Madam Tic-Tac* as well as the backing to put it on in the West End. He had signed the famous French actress Françoise Rosay for the lead and, wonder upon wonder, there would be parts in it for both Hilary and myself. Terry had been able to hook Madame Rosay only by casting her son in a leading role. While she was quite brilliant, he was a non-offerer and we closed in three weeks.

The morning after opening night, my telephone rang and a voice said, "This is Emlyn Williams."

I said, "Oh yes, I'm sure."

The voice chuckled and said, "I am Emlyn Williams and I saw your show last night. I had to go because Françoise is a great friend and once played a part for me. I thought it was a dreadful play but I liked you in it, so you see it doesn't matter if you're in something bad as long as you are good yourself."

He went on to tell me that he had just written a new play called *Accolade* and I would be perfect for the part of the cockney butler. He explained that he'd always been writer, director and star of his own shows, but for the first time, he had decided to relinquish one of these roles. The play would be directed by Glen Byam Shaw. Would I meet them both at the H.M. Tennent office next morning?

I phoned Harry Kendall and gave him a full report. He told me that of course I'd got the part. Famous authors and star actors didn't phone you personally just to tell you that you were being considered.

It was the one and only time I was ever in the tiny lift that took you up to the office of the most illustrious theatre management in the land. Emlyn greeted me himself and said that I already had two-thirds of the management on my side, the writer and the star; all we had to do was to convince the other third. And he introduced me to Byam Shaw. Despite Emlyn's assurance that I was dead right for the part, Mr Shaw wanted to audition me, and we all trooped downstairs to the stage of the Globe Theatre where he proceeded to find fault with almost everything I did. I found out later that he had already promised the part to an actor chum of his currently playing in the famous try-out theatre, The Embassy, Swiss Cottage and hadn't said a word to Emlyn. I had a chum in that company, too, and he told me that the actor in question had come to him two weeks earlier for some coaching on the way to speak cockney because he didn't know how and he'd just landed a cockney part in the West End.

If this was the devious route to stardom, they could have my seat in the spaceship. I'd take Newfoundland. And I went back to the file with a vengeance.

I'd got the budget down to saleable proportions, not right on target but a full $1500 a week below what it had cost the Alexandra Company. It was June 1950 and time to begin a serious search for a partner. It would be December before I found him. Luckily I was offered a lucrative fill in at Richmond Theatre, just down the Thames from the West End, where Oliver Gordon had gone straight from Penge and taken George Paddon-Foster with him.

To go back to the weekly grind after a nine-month breather on the road made you realize just how an escaped convict must feel after he's been recaptured. Particularly if your first chore back in the repertory pen was to learn Valentine in *You Never Can Tell* in three nights. I've always found Shaw the most difficult of all playwrights to memorize but also the hardest to forget. Good lines settle in and mature in the memory like fine wine. Rubbish rots there. We did one of the latter variety at Richmond and halfway through the playing week, I suddenly said to a fellow actor, "I've played this damned part before." And so I had. It had taken a week of rehearsals and three performances for my memory to recognize a single phrase of it.

Funny things, lines. Actors have a multitude of weird and wonderful ways of committing them to memory, but once they're in storage I believe we share a fairly common system of recall. We fluff the same phrases, miss the same cues, go blank at the same moments and stumble over the same *non sequiturs*. I always mark these trouble spots with an asterisk in my rehearsal script and never go onstage without taking a quick look at them. Sometimes I've found myself rehearsing the same part years afterwards and marking a brand-new script. When I've later compared it with the earlier one, the asterisks were in almost exactly the same spots. I've even compared notes with another actor who had played the same part. He didn't use asterisks, but the lines he'd marked were basically the same ones.

Back in 1983, Eric House and I had both accepted bookings to appear the same week in different productions of *The Gin Game*. Eric was one of the actors I most admired in Canada and was always first on the list of people I would think of whenever I was casting. *The Gin Game* was a two-hander. He would play it in Hamilton and I thirteen hundred miles north in Thunder Bay. During the course of the play, Weller and Fonsia play fourteen complete games of gin rummy, all different and all properly scored on a pegboard. Eric and I both opened on the same night and at approximately the same hour. I called him the next morning to ask him how everything went.

He said, "Great! I cut two complete gin games in the first act."

"You didn't!"

"I did. Games number six and seven."

"You want to know something?"

"What?"

"I cut the same two."

twelve

Summer began a slow dissolve into fall, the leaves stippled the backdrop of Richmond Common with bright new colours, the London Theatre Company file grew steadily fatter, and the needle on my lifetime theatrical-production meter edged closer to three hundred. It had been a hugely enjoyable season. That is, until Black Saturday. That was the day I walked through the stage door, looked at the notice-board for the cast list of *Harvey* and was stunned to find that I wouldn't be playing Elwood P. Dowd.

I had yet to play Elwood so I had no proprietary rights, but I couldn't believe that Oliver would bypass the regular company for such a plum. Nothing caused more anguish in a repertory company than bringing in an outsider – unless, of course, the outsider was a "name." Ours wasn't, and I made a mental note that *Harvey* would be on our first list of plays for St. John's where outsiders would be well out of reach.

We had other guests who were much more welcome that Richmond season. They were old special-weekers from the Wolverhampton and Penge days. One such was Russell Thorndike, brother of the famous Dame Sybil. Russell was renowned in his own right as the literary creator of *Doctor Syn,* that rum-running parson of another age, always astride a fast horse, cassock billowing in the wind, leading the revenue men in a merry chase across Romney Marsh. After the first morning's rehearsal, I took him into our stage door local, The Cobwebs, for a welcoming drink. After a few minutes, Russell asked the landlord what date it was.

"October the tenth."

Russell paused for a moment, beamed and then said very loudly, "It's my birthday!" and of course the landlord bought him a drink. So did everyone else in the bar who wasn't stone deaf.

When we got outside, several free rounds later, I turned to him and said, "Russell, you had a birthday when you came down to Penge last year and that was in May."

"I know, dear boy, but they do love the chance to talk to us theatricals, don't they?" He told me that when he was on tour, he automatically had a birthday every Monday in each new town.

He was a terrible giggler on stage, and this particular week we had another guest in the company who was even worse, an actor named Frederick Piper. The three of us were playing the inseparable trio of Tappercoom, the Mayor and the Chaplain in *The Lady's Not for Burning*. Russell and I were sitting on a bench downstage, and Freddie was standing behind us trying to describe somebody he had just seen walk through the archway, only he couldn't think of the word "archway." He stammered, he started making shapes with his hands, which became more and more suggestive. He finally settled for "orifice," whereupon Russell and I swivelled our bottoms sharply downstage, hunched our shoulders and shook. Freddie had the worst job. He was facing the audience.

Soon after the run of *The Lady,* the backstage corridors began to pile up with steamer trunks, skips, kitbags, carrier bags, battered suitcases and brown paper parcels. This sent a clear message that the final payday of the season was close at hand to be followed inevitably by the dreaded chore of evacuating a dressing-room that for the best part of six months had been home, laundry, kitchen, card-room, bar and seduction chamber. Although I had been "asked back" (as they say) for the following season, the annual Christmas pantomime was panting to get in and every inch of dressing room space was earmarked for Cinderella, Prince Charming, the Ugly Sisters, the Twelve Tiny Tappers, the Fairy Queen, the Demon King, the jugglers, the knockabouts, the magicians and all the impedimenta that went with them.

Managements considered straight actors too genteel to be cast in pantomime, but occasionally a member of the repertory company was let loose on the part of the Demon King because it was non-singing, non-dancing and all he had to do was ham it up just a bit more than he'd been doing all year. For the rest of us it was mackerel three times a day until the new season started in mid-February. At least, that's how it always used to be before the Beveridge Plan came into being and made actors eligible to draw the dole.

Unfortunately for the rest of the unemployed in the area, most London-based actors elected to register for unemployment pay at the Marylebone Labour Exchange, close to Madame Tussaud's. During the pantomime hiatus, reps disgorged actors from all over England and payday at the Marylebone Labour Exchange became one gigantic class reunion. With one accord they came, from their pads in Paddington, their closets in Chelsea and their bedsits in Bayswater, converging upon Marylebone Road. They arrived on foot, by bike, by bus, in beat-up Bentleys, but mostly by taxi which was a terribly expensive way to pick up the pittance they were about to receive and be truly thankful for. But how else should an actor travel? You really couldn't be expected to mix with the *hoi-polloi* on the Underground.

They came arrayed in their most outrageous party frocks, often highlighted by some period piece that had mysteriously failed to find its way back to Moss Bros after one of the season's costume dramas. They screamed endearments at each other across the road, tied up the traffic and generally behaved as if they were playing a crowd scene in *La Dolce Vita.*

Although I liked to show up for the fun, I'd always been spared the actual indignity of having to line up for my daily bread by a last-minute offer to fill in between seasons somewhere else. This time it was the lucky people of Eastbourne who were to be given the opportunity to see me in ten of the West End's latest releases, beginning with Dr Sloper in *The Heiress.* Five full years since demob and here I was still batting a thousand: four and a half complete repertory seasons, five fill-ins, one tour and one fleeting glimpse of the West End.

When I told a group of rapt Russian actors in Leningrad many years later that I had once played two hundred different stage roles in the space of five years, there was a good old-fashioned gasp. And when the diaphragms of twenty-four Stanislavsky disciples suddenly snapped into action all at once, that was a gasp. They told me that no play in Russia ever got near an audience until it had been rehearsed for at least six months and the most credits an actor could therefore hope to claim in a five-year stretch of his career would be ten.

I was a member of a "cultural delegation" on that fascinating trip in 1988. *Glasnost* was a brand new baby barely six weeks old. For the first time since any of them could remember, a Russian could experience the joy of talking to a foreigner without feeling the hot breath of a KGB agent on the back of his neck and hearing the skin-tingling scratch of a pencil on a notebook. At a film studio in Tashkent, we asked a group of directors what kind of films they planned to make under their new-found freedom and got a somewhat surprising answer.

"We've already made them. They've been hidden in the basement for years. Now we can dust them off and bring them up!"

Eastbourne turned out to be no ordinary fill-in. It was how I came to meet Harry Reynolds. He was a Producer, or so the programme said. I confess I inwardly questioned the production savvy of someone who would select a seaside resort town like Eastbourne in the middle of the off-season. Any actor who'd ever played on the end of a pier could tell you that the locals never went near the theatre, because in the summer they were too busy making money and in the winter they were too busy spending it somewhere the sun was sure to shine. Then I read his bio and discovered that what Harry really produced was films, a vocation, according to him, that largely entailed bringing together a scriptwriter, a director and a group of men with money who wanted to rub shoulders (or other things) with a film star and weren't averse to opening a generous expense account to bring it about. This chemistry didn't always result in something being recorded on celluloid, but in such cases, Harry explained, it was still necessary to spend a bit even to find out that the project was not viable.

He did make some films. And he certainly appeared to have made some money. He lived in great style in a huge apartment in Baker Street, and when he could see how impressed I was with his pad, he told me with a grin that it was the registered office of two of his current film production companies.

I never did solve the mystery of why Harry would want to exchange the opulence of the film world for the poverty of the provincial theatre, and it didn't take long for Eastbourne to prove that it wasn't a very wise move. Nearing the end of the season, I stuck my head into his office just as he was going over the latest bad news from the box-office and was greeted with, "Why does everything I touch in the theatre turn to ratshit?"

Without thinking I said, "I know a town where it wouldn't."

"Where?"

"St. John's, Newfoundland."

"Where the hell's that?"

I told him. About the Alexandra Company, about the theatrical history of St. John's that made Eastbourne look like the boondocks, about the box-office potential with seat prices four times what they were in England, about the budget I'd gone over so many times I practically knew it by heart. I'd waited three years to tell somebody. I'd written the script, learned it, directed myself in it and gave it my all.

After I'd finished, he gave me a long look, taking stock of me but giving no indication whatever what his thought machinery might be up to. He was probably thinking, "The son-of-a-bitch gave me a hell of a hard time when I negotiated his salary. That could be a plus." I did a bit of stock-taking of my own and said to myself, "He's really not bad-looking. Lips a bit too much Victor Mature, perhaps, but I can see the kind of charm that might talk some grown men out of their money and some grown ladies out of their virtue."

Suddenly he shot a series of questions at me that proved he wasn't a complete dilettante in the theatre. What's the percentage gate needed to break even? Forty-seven. What's the weekly nut? Two thousand dollars. What's that in pounds? Seven hundred and fourteen. How long a season? Twenty-six weeks. Why so long? Why not try it out first for a shorter time, say thirteen weeks? Because shipping fourteen actors back and forth across the Atlantic is our biggest cost item and I need every one of twenty-six weeks to earn a share of it back. Trying to do it in less is what killed the Alexandra Company. How do you know they'll stand us for twenty-six weeks? I didn't even blink at the "us." And how much capital will it take? Two thousand pounds.

He scribbled behind his left hand and without looking up said, "Let me have a look at your budget tomorrow. If I like what I see, I could probably come in at a thousand and twenty."

I should think he could, the cheeky bugger! Did he think I couldn't count? Fifty-one percent, a controlling interest? I said I didn't know about that. I'd bring him the budget but I'd have to go and think it over, too.

I certainly would! That still left nine hundred and eighty pounds to find and I had forty in the bank. But the ball had started rolling and even though it was veering up an alley which wasn't quite the one I might have chosen, I just knew I had to keep it on the move. So I went to see Oliver in London.

Oliver Gordon was the role model for all teddy-bears. He was also one of the most highly regarded directors in the repertory system. He knew the routine, had refined it, polished it and practised it longer than almost anybody in the business. He had tremendous rapport with his actors because he always did his homework and never wasted their time. When he was called upon to make an artistic decision, he wasn't always right, but he comforted himself with the thought that you simply could not do an Ingmar Bergman every time when you were churning out one production a week.

There wasn't much he and I didn't know about each other professionally and even less that we didn't agree about. We had gloried in the same triumphs and cringed at the same clinkers. Even the lids on our private lives had begun to loosen and soon there were few of my innermost secrets he hadn't winkled out of me, but not, I hasten to interject, a morsel more than I'd managed to winkle out of him. So when I told him about my talk with Harry Reynolds, all he said was, "When do we go?"

I told him to hang on a minute because Harry wanted control with fifty-one percent. That still left forty-nine percent for the two of us – twenty-four-and-a-half each – and I didn't even have the money for the four-and-a-half.

"I couldn't borrow it from you could I?"

"Of course you could, cock." And that was how the London Theatre Company was born and Oliver Gordon came to sign the birth certificate.

He was christened Oliver Gordon Battcock on a date that the winkle pin never did manage to pry out of him. He was raised in a country vicarage where his father had scrimped and saved out of his wretched parson's stipend to send him to Harrow. This was a terrible mistake according to Oliver, because for years afterwards he had been obliged to cross to the other side of the street whenever he saw an old school chum approaching, since he himself didn't own a bowler hat and wasn't carrying a rolled umbrella. But there was one bounty he picked up in his years at Harrow. They taught him how to play cricket.

Battcock! What a wonderful name for a wielder of the willow! But in the end, it wasn't the bat but the ball that brought him glory. He bowled his way into the record books. He even googlied himself into the captaincy of Bucks, a minor county to be sure but a major honour in cricket land.

For years, the battle for Oliver's devotion wavered between cricket and the theatre, and neither of them ever really won. Perhaps their biggest tussle took place when Oliver was a struggling young actor, out of a job, broke, depressed and down to his last mackerel when the phone rang. Not once but twice. The first offer was to join an undistinguished little company in an uninteresting little town at an unattractive little salary. But it was work and it was spending power and it was for ten solid weeks. The other offer was from the selectors to play cricket for England in a side about to leave for a tour of Canada. As a non-professional he would, of course, be one of "The Gentlemen" and not one of "The Players." In plain language, this meant that he would live and travel free but wouldn't get paid. How he must have agonized over that inevitable decision to swap valour for a pay packet, for he knew that in doing so he was throwing away the right to wear an England cap and blazer on any cricket field anywhere for the rest of his life. It was the saddest story I ever heard him tell, and his eyes clouded as he told it.

Although his concentration on the cricket field was so fierce as to make him almost demoniacal and his focus in the director's chair was never less than razor sharp, at almost all other times he appeared to float through life in the middle of a dense vague cloud. He couldn't see out and, as far as he was concerned, nobody could see in. Like the time we were at Piccadilly tube station and he let out a tremendous belch in the middle of the down escalator and practically blew a brand-new parting in the Brylcreemed hair of the young man with his arm round a girl one step below us. Brylcreem turned in a rage and was all ready for a punch-up until I grabbed his arm and hissed in his ear that my friend was "a little bit gone in the top story." As I hustled Oliver away from the danger zone he said: "What's up cock? Is it anything I did?"

He'd had three wives, all of them sexy young actresses of impeccable breeding. Each time, he was carried away with the novelty of it all for the first week or so, then quietly ambled back into his cloud and forgot about them, and they all ended up cricket widows and left him.

What I didn't know about him at the time was that he had invested in theatrical enterprises before. In fact, every penny he had ever made in the theatre, he had always put back. And he had never once recovered his capital outlay.

I intended to see that the pattern of his life was about to change.

thirteen

Oliver and I were primed and ready to go but, the pin was still missing from the starting pistol: Harry hadn't signed on. After my meeting with Oliver in London, I pushed the Silver Bullet hard all the way back to Eastbourne. I had to catch Harry before the dress rehearsal. It was the last play of the season and in six days he'd be gone. He had to make up his mind and he had to make it up now. I had an opening performance in a few hours and uncertainty and first nights didn't mix.

I nailed him in his office and everything was going swimmingly until I mentioned London Theatre Company.

"What's the matter with Mid-Century Entertainments?" (They're the ones who'd signed my Eastbourne contract.) "We're incorporated, we've got stationery printed, report forms, a head office in Baker Street —"

"That's your company, Harry. This is going to be our company. Oliver's, yours and mine. 'Leslie Yeo, Oliver Gordon and Harry Reynolds Present...'" He didn't even blink at the pecking order.

I wished he hadn't mentioned Baker Street. I remembered the film companies both paying the rent and it made me nervous. Mental note to self: see to it that nobody could draw a cheque on the London Theatre Company account without two signatures.

Harry was still dickering when I left him to make up for the dress. I fluffed several times during the run-through which wasn't like me at all. When it was over, he came into my dressing room, held out his hand and said, "Okay, it's a deal." I went on that evening and out-Laurenced Olivier. It was almost three years to the day since I'd watched the gap in the rocks at the entrance to St. John's harbour get smaller and smaller as my dream and I sailed back to England. Before I left Eastbourne for the last time, I drew a box on the wall of my dressing-room and hand-lettered inside it in my best sans-serif: THE LONDON THEATRE COMPANY WAS BORN HERE – FEBRUARY 19th

1951. Back in London, I phoned Oliver. We'd just nine days before rehearsing again at Richmond and I needed every minute of his time until then. Harry wanted some of it too.

It was an unlikely brew that gathered at Baker Street as the Board of the London Theatre Company. Oliver was a pussycat, Harry was a tycoon and I was stubborn as hell – all the ingredients for a fiery future. Our only hope was to spell out terms of reference so clear that even legalese couldn't muddy them. I told Harry with my best company-director smile that the significance of the fifty-one/forty-nine percent split had not been lost upon Oliver and myself but that this, of course, would only apply to financial input and out-take. In all other matters we would be a council of three. As soon as he could have partnership agreements drawn up, we would all meet again, sign them and put our cheques into the kitty. Harry demurred at the urgency of having to fork out so soon. I told him that three reputations were at stake, mine most of all as I would be making the commitments. I wasn't going to pledge any part of it until the money was safely in the bank; I wouldn't even write and tell St. John's we were coming. We held the signing ceremony fourteen days later.

We'd no need to waste time on planning sessions. I'd had an ACTION SHEET on standby for eighteen months. It was well mottled with coffee stains and scotch-glass rings, meticulously detailed and fully prioritized. Heading the list as it always had was the budget, and I wanted to have one last crack at it. The only option left for a major saving that I could see was to ditch one body and save a pay packet, a room and board, and a berth on the ship both ways. I asked Oliver if he could manage with twelve performers instead of thirteen and he said, "Of course, cock." That squeezed the WEEKLY GETOUT down to $1,850 and there the wringer stuck. It wasn't a bad spot to stick at. We'd slashed the Alexandra Company's running costs by forty-seven percent.

With an acting company of twelve, we settled on a split of seven actors and five actresses (as female performers were still called in 1951). The ratio of seven to five might change to fit the final choice of plays, but nothing except an act of God would tamper with the total of twelve. This would include the director (Oliver), the manager (me), the stage manager and two assistant stage managers, all of whom would be experienced performers who could double-up onstage. The final member of the expedition would be the scenic designer who only ever performed with a paintbrush. The first London Theatre Company would be thirteen strong. We couldn't afford to be superstitious.

I phoned the Furness-Withy Line to find the first ship due to dock in St. John's in October. The *Nova Scotia* would arrive "about the fifth or the sixth." They couldn't be more precise because they never knew how far they'd have to detour round an icefield or a force-seven gale. Looking on the worst side, the company would arrive, albeit a little wobbly, on October the sixth which was a Wednesday. It would be tight but possible to open the following Monday. Actors booked for a full repertory season still rehearsed one week without pay and got nothing for travel time. I had allowed for two week's rehearsal of the opening play. We'd use the free week in London and pay the cast to rehearse on the six-day voyage. Right on budget. I booked eleven first-class berths on the *Nova Scotia*, "passenger names as yet unknown," and wrote to Gordon Stirling that we would open on Monday, October 11th. The scenic designer and I would fly to St. John's three weeks ahead of the company. It was now the end of February, D-Day minus 196. Only we didn't have a General Staff to work out the logistics. We had me.

Oliver and I took the phone off the hook and spent the first day picking plays. It wasn't hard to think of titles. The difficulty was whittling the list down to twenty-six. I'd already played in nearly three hundred and Oliver had directed even more. Audience appeal was paramount but we had to be sparing with the potboilers. We might need some for another day. We also had to be wary of large-cast plays. Anything over twelve would call for local casting and there was no professional talent pool in St. John's in 1951. Once we'd chosen the twenty-six, we juggled them into a running order with one eye on audience build and the other on spacing the workload. We didn't want any nervous breakdowns.

We looked at our first cut and thought how we'd love the chance to present that identical playbill at a theatre in England in a town that had never seen any of the plays before. We were a little heavy on farce perhaps but drama, mystery, light comedy, broad comedy, romance and a tinge of the sensational were all represented, topped off by a Shakespeare and a musical revue to finish the season. Nine of the twenty-six were full costume productions. Nobody could accuse us of trying to do things on the cheap. On the contrary, the budget alarm-bells started to go off. I thought we'd better have a quick talk with Michael Ellis at Moss Bros Stage Costumes before we got too locked in.

We came away with a superb deal. Shipping costumes back and forth for each production, said Michael, was for the birds. Sailings were infrequent, cargo holds were often full and consignments got bumped. Railway clerks, shipping brokers, and customs inspectors were morons and shipping companies were thieves. A single basket would invoke the minimum freight charge: for the same price you could probably ship a full production of *Cavalcade.* "Give me a cast list and enough time for fittings," said Michael, "and I'll have the costumes for the entire season at Liverpool ready to travel with the company as personal baggage and avoid the freight charges altogether." Six months later we could bring them all back the same way. For this privilege, he would charge us four weeks rental per costume instead of one. This sounded sweet music to a cost-conscious ear. When we did a rough costume count based on the plays we had just selected, Michael's figure made it look as if he'd been snooping in my briefcase.

We now faced an awesome task. Moss Bros would need full cast-lists and everybody's vital statistics by the middle of July if they were to fit, alter and pack every costume in time for the *Nova Scotia.* This meant we'd have to cast all twenty-six plays before we left England. Not just the period pieces, the moderns as well. Nurses needed costumes. So did butlers and army officers and London Bobbies (show me an English mystery play without one). It was now March and we had yet to hire our first actor. We would have to cast by category – LM for leading man, JG for juvenile girl – and add the real names later.

One bit of casting was never in doubt. Our scenic designer simply had to be George Paddon-Foster. He not only painted scenery better than anybody else but also he knew how to build it. And he'd be the one to train a local stage carpenter, since we'd already decided that to bring one from England with return fare and room and board constituted cruelty to budgets.

George was all agog. Even though he'd be on the Richmond payroll and not ours until we actually left London Airport in September, he was always there whenever we wanted him, perched aloft on his paintframe at the back of the Richmond stage, like a sitting duck waiting for his brains to be picked by a couple of vultures. Only he didn't wait. He *offered* to take all nine period plays, read them and draw up a costume plot for each of them. A costume plot is a blueprint for the supplier, listing in detail every costume and quick-change for every member of the cast. This left Oliver clear to concentrate on casting. While he was doing that by category, I'd be learning how to run a box-office.

For two afternoons a week, sandwiched between the morning rehearsal and the evening performance, I'd join the girls in the front-of-house at Richmond Theatre to learn the tricks of the ticket-selling trade. This turned out to be nothing so simple as just taking the money and handing over a ticket. The box-office was highly systemized. Correct recording and reporting was crucial. An error in the count of a single ticket per performance at our scheduled top price would amount to a staggering $10,000 in a twenty-six week season. This error would be further compounded by over or underpayments to authors and tax collectors who worked on percentages of the gross take.

In the days before *Ticketmaster*, each performance had its own copy of the seating plan on which locations were crossed off as they were sold. Season tickets were marked "S" because they were worth less than the printed value on the ticket: it was from the seating plan after each performance that you worked out exactly how much the attendance had been worth.

I also learned how to "dress" a house. With only four seats left in a particular row, you'd never sell to a party of three and leave an empty single. And on thin nights you wouldn't cram everybody into the front rows. Instead you'd scatter them in groups well spaced all the way to the back so that everybody who was there would think the house much better than it really was.

I ended my crash course at Richmond with a graduation ceremony in the Manager's office. I left well loaded with champagne, good wishes and copies of all the report forms I'd need: Daily Sales Report, Daily Box-office Return, Weekly Getout, Weekly Box-office Return, Stage Manager's Daily Report and umpteen others designed to give a printer enough to retire on. My head was buzzing as was amply demonstrated on stage that evening. We were in the middle of the run of *The Late Christopher Bean*, a piece about art forgeries in which I was playing the detective. I took off my costume and makeup at the end of Act Two and was halfway through the stage-door on my way to The Cobwebs for my nightly pint when the stage manager grabbed me and shrieked the dreaded words, "You're off!" I'd missed a stage entrance.

"No, no, old boy, my part finishes in Act Two. I – Oh my God!" I dashed on stage. Act Three began where Act Two left off. At the end of Act Two I'd been wearing a trench coat, a trilby hat and a thin pencil moustache. I now walked on minus coat, minus hat and minus moustache and the audience must have ended up minus its marbles.

On another occasion, I was so tired after the show that I borrowed a couple of benzedrine tablets from Reg Biggs, the landlord of The Cobwebs. I had a big lead to play the following week and a stack of lines to learn that night. I simply had to stay awake. I went home, swallowed the benzedrine, sat down, opened the script and immediately started to nod off. I jumped up, shook my head, walked briskly round the room a couple of times and tried again. My chin immediately hit my chestbone. From then on I was afraid to sit down at all and spent the next three hours on my feet plodding non-stop round the room, script in hand, trying to stuff lines into brain cells that were distinctly inhospitable. Next day Reg Biggs was beside himself with remorse. He'd given me sleeping pills by mistake.

If I'd had a grain of sense, I'd have ditched Richmond and put myself on the London Theatre Company payroll. God knows, there was enough to do to fill every day to the brim from now until departure date. I was an administrative staff of one and already committed to a sixty-hour week. But there was nothing in the budget for a full-time manager. Besides, the first sign of a paycheque with my name on it would almost certainly spark a slew of bills from Baker Street for services rendered, although there wasn't much rendering going on there at the moment. Harry was far too busy forming another company for a summer season at Ventnor on the Isle of Wight.

So I coped, as I'd learned to do under pressure since the day I'd first walked into an advertising agency. And fifty years and a quintuple bypass later I'm still here to prove that you can. I've even found that the best antidote for overtiredness is for someone to step up the action and stiffen the challenge. I was seeing plenty of both at the moment. The costume contract had been signed, Strand Electric Stage Lighting had agreed on a magnificent reducing rental, payable four-weekly in arrears, and a sound system had been leased at a rental payable four-weekly in advance. Applications had gone out to play agents for the performing rights for the twenty-six plays and I had started rounding up sets of scripts. It was time to begin looking at actors.

Oliver and I each wrote down the names of the twenty-five best performers we'd ever worked with, never mind age or gender. Then we checked for duplications, possible alcoholics and potential shit-disturbers. They were a dangerous species to have in a company living and working in the kind of close quarters ours would be. We boiled the remainder down to a joint list of first and second choices in each category and set aside the remainder as they say in the cook-books. Then we talked tactics. Within hours of calling the first actor on our list, the tom-toms would begin and Oliver's phone would become a hotline for chums and he was very bad at saying no. I told him he had an easy out: he had two partners and casting would be a three-way decision.

Before putting finger to phone, we'd have to be ready with an offer. It would be useless talking dollars and cents to actors who had been weaned on pounds, shillings and pence, so we'd keep it very simple. We would provide them with free room and full board, and for spending money we'd give them their English salary converted into dollars at the generous rate of three to the pound against the official rate of 2.80. If they felt so inclined, they could save their entire salary (one of them did!). If they wanted to spend it, they'd find prices in St. John's would be higher than those in London. So our top actor, who was earning fifteen pounds a week in England, drew forty-five Canadian dollars in St. John's. At approximately the same point in time, the Canadian Repertory Theatre in Ottawa was paying the professional members of its company forty dollars a week and they had to house and feed themselves.

Most of the names on our first-choice list were working in the top reps scattered across the country, and tracking them down turned into a waiting game for returned collect calls. But the responses when they came were excitingly positive. It was some time before we met our first refusal. This very disappointed invitee had a prior commitment. Ever on the lookout for ways of conserving precious dollars, I even persuaded two actors who were family men to take half their salaries in sterling each week by direct payment into their bank accounts from ours in London.

With the gossip already in full flood in the Salisbury, Fleet Street couldn't possibly be far behind. Sure enough I soon received a phone call from a reporter with the *News-Chronicle*. He seemed particularly intrigued with our financial plans to pay for everything possible in sterling before we left, thus conserving our dollar income for items that could only be paid for on the spot, like salaries for instance. I was stunned to read the following headline in the next morning's paper:

ACTORS MUST LIVE ON ADVANCE TAKINGS

All my romantic ideas about Fleet Street evaporated at that moment, and they've never really come back, particularly in view of the aftermath of that somewhat dishonest piece of reporting. First on the blower was an angry voice from British Actors' Equity Association. It wasn't too hard to calm them down. I was a highly respected member of the Association, having served on several committees, and we would be a full Equity company. Harry, who would be signing the contracts, already had a substantial bond deposited with the

Association which would more than cover the mandatory two weeks' pay for everyone in the event of failure.

The second part of the aftermath was a little more ominous. In the mail, an envelope arrived with the words ON HIS MAJESTY'S SERVICE where the stamp ought to be. Inside was a letter informing me that I was required to present myself to the undersigned at his office at the British Treasury in Whitehall the following Tuesday at 10:30 am. Required, not requested. That sounded ominous.

At the appointed hour, a secretary showed me into the office of Mr Undersigned (I don't remember his name). Without the head looking up, a finger pointed to a spot in front of his desk. It was a long walk and the broadloom pile was so deep I felt I should have been wearing showshoes. Even though nobody asked me to sit down, after a respectable pause I did anyway. The pen continued to scratch away and I lit a cigarette. At this the head lifted slowly, gave me a long cold stare that reminded me of a dead cod on a fishmonger's slab. He turned back to the pen-scratching. Finally, His Majesty's surely most uncivil civil servant leaned back, methodically screwed the cap onto his fountain pen, painstakingly set it in precisely the spot it had probably occupied for the past twenty years, turned to me and proceeded to blast my head off, rather like a sergeant-major who'd been to Eton.

How dare I arrange to take a company of actors out of the country without consulting them? Didn't I know there were strict currency controls? I confessed I genuinely thought they'd be pleased. Wasn't England short of dollars? Indeed they were, he told me, and he didn't intend that I should help them to become any shorter. If we ran into any trouble in Canada, I needn't think for a moment that the British Treasury would relent and let us transfer capital from England because they wouldn't. And what's more, every cent we took in over there had to come back immediately to England. It was illegal for us to have dollars in our possession. And we'd better not try to open a bank account in St. John's. That was illegal too. If we did, they'd know immediately.

The longer the tirade went on, the more my niceness ebbed away. As I hadn't been able to get much of a word in for some time, I stood up. This shut him up long enough for me to say, "I'd like to tell you how I plan to deal with this problem, may I? The minute I get off the plane I shall apply for Landed Immigrant status and anything I do from that point on will be none of your bloody business. And since Britain doesn't require any help from me with its dollar shortage, what supplies I need from outside Canada I will steer to the United States. Good morning."

I'd like to be able to say that my brush with bureaucracy ended there but it didn't. I had a somewhat similar session with a gentleman at the Department of Health and Social Security. He wasn't as arrogant as Mr Undersigned but he was snide. Maddeningly, smilingly unhelpful. I simply wanted to know whether actors working outside the country should continue to contribute to the health plan since they wouldn't be in a position to make use of any of its services.

"Oh yes. Still have to pay, you know. Don't dodge it by leaving England. Oh no."

"How much will I have to deduct? Your tables are all in pounds. We pay in dollars and the exchange rate varies."

"That'll be a nice little sum for you to work out, won't it?"

"I see. What happens if they need medical attention while they are there?"

"That's one of the little problems you'll have to face, isn't it?" I suddenly felt awfully glad to be leaving England.

Meanwhile, just over a hundred miles and a ferry ride away on the Isle Of Wight, Harry Reynolds was sitting in the theatre manager's office on the pier in Ventnor busily casting his own London Theatre Company. Totally unknown to us, he was luring performers to his summer ensemble with the promise that at the end of the season he would take them all to Canada. All, believe it or not, included the director! Fortunately for my blood pressure, I didn't hear a whisper about any of this until forty years later. Even more fortunately for our enterprise, Ventnor joined Eastbourne on Harry's "ratshit" list and folded long before the scheduled end of the season. So nobody got to go to Canada except John Holmes, the stage manager. He alone in the Ventnor company had had the sense to make Harry add a Canada rider to his contract. It was John Holmes who told me this horrendous story in 1991. Even after forty years, my blood almost curdled at the thought of Harry, the only one of the three of us authorized to sign contracts because of the Equity bond, presenting us with his list as a *fait accompli*. I don't know how we'd have got out of it, but I'm quite sure we'd never have set sail.

Harry mentioned not a word of this when Oliver and I arrived with our casting complete and contracts ready to be signed. He merely said that he had already contracted a stage manager at a salary to be negotiated. So we negotiated with John Holmes, who turned out to be very experienced and an invaluable cameo actor.

The rest of the company, for posterity, were Hilary Vernon, Geoffrey Lumsden, Sheila Huntington, Rosemary Rogers, Dorothea Rundle, Michael Atkinson, John Woodnutt, Paul Williamson and Gladys Richards. Gladys was a native-born Newfoundlander, who had been working in the theatre in England, and we thought that fact might help the box-office. But if anything it worked the other way. There is no mystique in showcasing your own, and Canada doesn't go in for home-made heroes. They'd rather somebody else did the making and then cash in later by bringing them back.

The casting was now complete and the time for George and myself to leave was alarmingly close. But the action sheet was full of ticks and the blanks were rapidly filling in: buy the train tickets to Liverpool, check that all the suppliers will make the deadline for the *Nova Scotia*, confirm that all the actors have passports, send out the scripts for the first play, book a London rehearsal room and so forth.

On my last night at Richmond, as I carefully packed my makeup box for a long journey, I wondered if I'd just rung the curtain down on the last part I'd ever play in England. It wasn't as a matter of fact. But it was the last but one.

fourteen

If you were looking for time in 1951 to reflect undisturbed upon past misdeeds or future follies, you could have done worse than board a TCA North Star bound for Newfoundland where you could count on at least fourteen hours of it. More if you overshot Gander and got taken on to Montreal which you too often were. Stray talk wouldn't have distracted you, for none of it could top the chatter of four Rolls-Royce engines at full throttle chewing their way into a prevailing wind.

Were I to make that identical trip today I would without question have made use of every moment of my time. My briefcase would have been open and my calculator finger a-quiver before we'd even got off the ground. But this was 1951 and I was thirty-six and totally without fear of flying or failure. I saw no necessity whatever to sit and stew for fourteen hours over what I might have overlooked. I'd been doing that in England, waking and sleeping, for the past fourteen months. This was the time to relax with a book and a scotch which would taste all the better because they were serving it at duty-free prices.

A stewardess friend had told me, "If you get overcarried, make a hell of a fuss and they'll get rid of you first. They won't want you stirring up the quiet passengers." I put the theory to work in Montreal. Within an hour of clearing immigration, George and I were on a plane heading back the way we'd come.

We found a hole in the mist, which wasn't always there when you needed it, and touched down in Torbay. There was no mistaking the tang of the sea air that came at you through The Narrows, picking up the flavour of the fish flakes on the way. I was back. I felt like MacArthur.

It was September 14th, a Friday. In my pocket I had thirty dollars and not a penny in a local bank. No nice letter of credit, no comforting little wallet of travellers cheques. Ten pounds was the limit leaving England and they didn't take any chances. You went through customs coming into the country and you went through customs going out. In view of my brush with the bureaucrats in Whitehall, I'd fully expected that word would have gone ahead and George and I would be strip-searched at the airport, so I was even afraid to stuff a few extra fivers inside my socks.

I didn't tell George, but we were now about to face the three most crucial days of the entire undertaking. I'd had to take just one little gamble. We were well financed but our money wasn't the right colour: we had no dollars. The only way we could get some was to open the box-office. And the only way to open the box-office was to place some ads in the local papers. Would they give us credit, or would they, like so many newspapers when they smelled "theatre," demand cash on the line? This was the one pot-hole on the entire critical path of the London Theatre Company that I'd been unable to fill in before leaving England.

The dollar crunch had always been at the top of my worry list. I knew I could only go so far in paying sterling for everything; sooner or later it would end up in a Canadian customs shed and somebody would have to come and bail it out. Meantime I couldn't open a box-office without tickets, and George couldn't start building sets without canvas, paint or lumber. I'd been chipping away at our problems for over a year, and our salvation now lay in the laps of a couple of newspaper proprietors. I'd managed to get this far with the help of a little luck, a lot of optimism, an occasional abuse of the Yeo charm, and Fred Ayre.

Fred Ayre was top management at Bowrings, the big store on Water Street. I'd written to Sir Eric Bowring, angel of the Alexandra Company, to ask if we could set up a ticket booth in the store as our predecessors had done. I got a letter back from Fred saying that he'd been instructed by Sir Eric to "look after us." Although I intended to interpret Sir Eric's orders rather liberally, I played my hand with Fred very carefully. For at least three postal exchanges, we wrote of nothing but the setting up of the box-office. I gave him my ideas, he sent me his. I sent a rough layout, he sent me a scale drawing. I amended it, he sent a colour rendering. Each time, he assured me that the entire cost would come out of Bowrings' display budget and I was not to worry. (He really did poke his finger through the bars, didn't he?)

At the fourth time of asking, I thought I'd try a gentle P.S.: "There are a few small items I'll need to ship ahead of the company. Could I consign them to Bowrings and have your shipping department clear them through customs ready for my arrival? My timing would be crucial. I will, of course, square up with you as soon as I get there."

The usual time went by and there was no reply. I began to get a little agitato, not because I might have to go back to the top of my worry list, but because I might have offended Fred. Finally, there it was on the mat, an envelope with the Bowrings logo. Fred's answer was: "Okay, but..." He would open an account at Bowrings in the name of the London Theatre Company but there would have to be a credit limit of one thousand dollars, terms strictly thirty days net. I couldn't have breathed any easier if I'd won the Irish Sweepstakes.

I didn't need my shipping list to know what our priorities were: the top worry had always been the tickets. There was no way I could pay a Canadian printer in dollars for a full season's supply, so I'd have to import them. English theatre tickets weren't printed individually on pasteboard like they were in Canada, but on paper, three stubs to a ticket and bound in books according to seat prices. So the same firm that supplied all the houses in the West End of London added a strange new theatre to its list, Bishop Feild Hall, with seat prices to be printed in an unfamiliar currency. The order was for the entire twenty-six week season – 182 performances, 738 books, 98,644 tickets all priced, dated and seat-numbered and paid for in sterling. I did a quick calculation of the duty and federal sales tax on that little lot and was relieved to find there would still be some of our credit left to bring in paint and canvas, neither of which was available in St. John's, at least not the kind that George wanted. Scenery canvas was a very special animal and you bought it by the bolt. As for paint, George always mixed his own from powders. We consequently ended up in a warehouse in London's East End where George spent a blissful morning drooling over the latest hues while I watched the sacks pile up. Every time a new sack joined them, the adding machine in my mind gave another nervous click. But when George had finished his shopping spree and I had checked and rechecked the tax and duty, I knew we'd make it. All I had to do now was find a freighter that would dock in St. John's at the right time and not start the meter running too early on our thirty days net. That done, our dollar crunch would be all but over.

The moment we'd checked into the Balsam, George went off in search of his imported canvas and paint, and I headed for the office of the local Lord Beaverbrook, Jim Herder of the *Telegram*. Just in case things should go wrong, I'd sent Fred Ayre another little gentle P.S.: "Can you slip a little slug in the middle of your back-page ad in both papers on

Friday September 17th announcing that the London Theatre Company ticket booth will open Monday morning on your main floor?"

I was renewing a social acquaintanceship when I called on Jim Herder. He'd been at all the Alexandra Theatre Company parties. So instead of shunting me down to the office of his advertising manager, the aforementioned was shunted up to see me. This put me in a strong position, for it was unlikely that an underling would be brash enough to bring up anything so sordid as credit references to a friend of the boss. And so it was.

I'd already had a short recall session with myself about the old days in advertising and quite a lot of the jargon had come back. You didn't talk about advertising, you called it space. And you didn't measure it in column inches like they did in England; here everything was calculated in lines. I talked like a man who'd been through it all before and knew exactly what he wanted.

"We'll need a display ad 48 lines across two columns every day six days a week for twenty-seven weeks – twenty-six weeks of the playing season and the week before opening. We'll also need a few specials starting with tomorrow. It would seem to me that we should be looking at a space contract, say, 10,000 lines? (an enormous saving on the ordinary single insertion rate)."

I was smilingly bargained down to 5000 lines and reminded that if I used less I'd be backbilled at the full rate. I was also too late to make Saturday's paper. This was a blow because the *Telegram* didn't come out until midday Monday. Could they stick in a short news item tomorrow? They could. I had a release ready. I signed the space contract, gave them the release and the copy for Monday's ad, beamed and left. Nobody mentioned a word about money. As I walked out through the main office, the receptionist's face was buried behind a spread-eagled copy of the evening's edition just off the press. There we were on the back page in a box surrounded by lots of white space. Good old Fred.

George, meanwhile, had been checking out the space that we'd booked for a possible carpentry/paint shop at the back of the now defunct Baird's department store on Water Street. David Baird had kept in touch since the Alexandra days and had offered us first refusal at a rent that sounded like a charitable donation. It was warehouse quality with a high ceiling, a huge hot air blower hanging from it, hot and cold running water, a work bench, and easy access to the loading dock so that moving scenery in and out would be a breeze. George loved it. Time to go and see Fred Ayre.

The ticket booth grabbed your attention as if somebody had banged a gong beside it the minute you got inside the front door of Bowrings. And to see LONDON THEATRE COMPANY for the first time in big, bold letters was a moment of some emotion.

Fred had laid on a box-office assistant for us within the salary range we had discussed and she was to start the next morning. I arranged to meet her there first thing when we would rack the ticket books and go over the routine. There was one other new staff member we had to find – a stage carpenter for George. The Lord must have been looking over us that day because that was when Ira Butler came into our lives.

Gordon Stirling, president of our hosts, the Feildian Athletic Grounds Association (FAGA), had found Ira for us. He didn't have to look far. Ira was the groundsman for the school playing fields and a great deal handier than you'd any right to expect a handyman to be. As his was mainly a summer job, if we hired him in the winter it would help the FAGA. If he was any good it would certainly help us. George and I interviewed him that night and took him on. We hadn't yet been in St. John's twenty-four hours. It was three more days to D-Day, where D stood for Deliverance. We were still cash-strapped but we wouldn't starve because we were on full board at the Balsam Hotel and could eat on credit.

On Saturday morning I received an astonishing phone call: "This is Hugh Baird of Baird Motors. If you're going to be here for six months you'll be wanting some wheels. Come and pick what you fancy on the used-car lot and let me have it back when you've done with it." I'd never even met him.

Like a good Englishman, I chose an Austin A40.

While Ira took George on a tour of the lumber yards, I briefed our new assistant on the tricks of the box-office trade: marking off seating plans, "dressing a house" and the mechanics of a three-stub ticket system – two to the customer and one in the cashbox, which must balance with the take at the end of the day.

It would be season tickets only for the first week, cash down for twenty-four shows and two shows free. And you got to sit in the same seat on the same night every week, so the sooner you booked the better the choice. I wasn't going to impede the cash flow by making people wait while we pulled the tickets from twenty-six different books; so I had a set of master seating plans from which you chose your seat and we took your money and marked your name and you picked up the tickets later. You also had the advantage of seeing who would be sitting next to you and changing your location if you didn't like the scenery.

There was danger in this system. As long as the tickets were still in the book there was a risk you might give them to the wrong person or even book the same seat twice. I impressed upon our gal how vital it was to record first names as well as surnames. Like the Newfoundland song said, there were lots of Ryans and lots of Pittmans and that went for the Bairds, the Munns, the Parsons and the Crosbies as well. People got very possessive about permanent seats and I didn't want to start any family feuds. Finally we were ready and I shut up shop. We'd have to wait until Monday to know if St. John's was ready for us. I drove down to the wharf.

I was surprised to find the dock door open on a Saturday afternoon and even more startled to see a pile of wood sticking out. There was also the unmistakable buzz of a saw. Inside, the finished framework of the first scenery flat lay on the floor with George close by like an enraptured father gazing upon his firstborn. This was no handyman's work. Ira was a carpenter. He also had the keys to the manual training room at the college and the entree to a whole range of power tools. He handed me a delivery slip from Horwood Lumber made out to The London Theatre Company. It was rubber-stamped CHARGE. "They know me down there," he said to my raised eyebrows. I started to get the feeling that everybody was desperately anxious to see us succeed. Of course, we might have been basking a bit in the aura of the Alexandra Company which unquestionably had departed with a pristine slate.

George was genius material. I seriously doubt if we would ever have ventured beyond Richmond Common if he'd said no to us. He not only designed sets and painted them, his working drawings were like an engineer's, detailed and to scale. He knew where all the stresses were and where the reinforcements would have to go. He knew what needed to be turned on a lathe and what could be done with a spokeshave. Like the actors, he would have to turn out one play a week, only his work would double if there was a set change.

Scenery in 1951 meant canvas flats of varying shapes and sizes lashed together with cleat-lines and held upright with stage braces. At the end of the week, all the flats went back into stock to be repainted for some future set. After six different layers of paint, they became too heavy to handle for quick scene changes and were recanvassed. But the frames lived on, unlike so many of today's sets, built like battleships to withstand a year's run, which usually turns out to be three and a half weeks, and then trashed because storage space is too expensive.

Our opening production was no ordinary challenge for George because our scenery cupboard was bare. Every flat had to be built from scratch, "sized" and painted, to say nothing of French doors, room doors, cupboard doors, reveals, windows, stairs, a landing and some bannisters. What the heck, he had three weeks. It would be like working in the West End. I succumbed to North Star fatigue and went to bed.

On Monday morning there was a small lineup at the box-office. I'd set our prices at $2, $1.50, $1 and 50c. That meant a pair of the best seats would cost $96 for the season (about $700 in 1998 money), payable in advance. By the end of the day, fifty-two lovely people had plonked down their cash and chosen their spot. Next morning I opened an account at the Royal Bank, paid off Bowrings, and dropped in at Citizenship to apply for Landed Immigrant status and activate my threat to the gent at the British Treasury. We'd seen our last dollar crisis. Dilemmas there would be, but not that particular one.

It's a matter of some pride to me, living today in an era when representatives of Arts organizations hop on and off planes like Dodgem cars and flit halfway round the world at the drop of a Canada Council grant, that no one from the London Theatre Company set foot on Newfoundland soil in the entire preparatory period, from the end of the Alexandra Company in 1947 to the opening of our season in 1951. For one thing there was no budget for a reconnoitering trip. And for another, I'd done the homework before I'd left. I'd met all the right people, approved the theatre, measured out the stage, spaced out the seating, drawn up a seating plan and found accommodation for the actors. Homework and correspondence coped with the rest.

Even the long distance telephone was rarely called into play, for the British had still not learned to conquer their fear of the pips which chipped in relentlessly every three minutes to remind you how fast your money was being spent. As recently as 1979, the year I ran the Shaw Festival, I had occasion to call Sir John Gielgud at his home in Aylesbury, Bucks to ask him if he'd like to come and direct *You Never Can Tell*. His valet answered the call. There was a distinct scurrying of feet and Sir John came to the phone quite out of breath.

"C-Canada? Good Heavens!" I explained the reason for my call. "Yes – well – yes. We mustn't spend time talking on the phone, must we? I'll have another look at the play tonight and you can call me again tomorrow."

He beat the pips by at least a minute.

fifteen

I'm a list addict and always have been. The one for "things to do around the house" is thirty-five years old and still on active service. Things get crossed off, things get added and things just sit there. Some have been sitting there for thirty-five years. The first item on my list for St. John's was "set up the office."

Above the stage at Bishop Feild Hall were the dressing rooms, three of them, plus a toilet on each side. You reached them by a flight of very narrow stairs running parallel with the back wall. You often had to take these full tilt during a performance, and if you were unfortunate enough to be wearing a crinoline, the language sometimes got a bit colourful and just occasionally seeped through the scenery to the people in the front row.

I picked the middle room on stage right for mission control. The men in the company would dress in the two rooms on either side of the office which would double as a dressing room for me. On stage left, the stage management would get the room nearest the stairs and the ladies the other two. There were no stars in weekly rep and no star dressing rooms, though there was a certain status in sitting nearest the door. Occasionally a performer would invent a weak bladder and try to beat the system.

I plonked my old Underwood portable in the middle of the table of the middle room and, as it was the only piece of office equipment we had, I crossed off the first item on my list.

I next found an accountant and asked him to help me open the books. I should say "book" because that's all we had at the beginning – a Receipts and Disbursements Journal. He made a few sample entries in pencil that could be erased later, rapidly showed me how to total them across and down and make them balance, and that ended my lesson in book-keeping. Skimpy though it was, it started a love affair with figures which has lasted to the present day when, in my eighties,

I still produce a personal budget for the year on the first of January. What's more I stick to it, which would have astonished my teachers who for years had peppered my report cards with "he must do better at maths."

The printers were next. We were going to need display cards for hotels, corner stores, drugstores, libraries and anywhere there was a notice board, and I'd elected myself to distribute them. I'd bought the design in England at a bargain price from a commercial artist who was undergoing hunger spasms. I now had a cut made for the cards and two smaller ones for our newspaper ads. It was a basic white on black design of a proscenium arch with LONDON THEATRE COMPANY in lights, framed by a pair of stage curtains tied back to reveal the name of the current play.

Bowrings had undertaken to print and supply our programmes free in exchange for the sole advertising rights and Fred Ayre began clamouring for the editorial content. I put on my PR hat. Several others were already hanging on the rack – Box-office Manager, Book-keeper, Advertising Manager, Front-of-House Manager, delivery boy, and mealtime relief box-office assistant – not forgetting I'd also be playing the lead in the first three plays. I wasn't setting myself up as a candidate for martyrdom, but I was going to save every salary I could until I could see a definite pattern emerging from the box-office. It wasn't as if we were moving into an established theatre with an experienced staff and a regular following. We were taking over a school hall that was going to have to learn to become a theatre and do it with a box-office assistant, stage electrician, stage carpenter, ushers and programme sellers all in their rookie year as professionals.

That evening, Gordon Stirling paraded his front-of-house troops for inspection. He had done an outstanding job. He'd recruited teams of ushers, cloakroom attendants and canteen helpers, each with a team captain. He'd scheduled them, complete with backups, for every performance right through to Christmas. All were senior students, Old Feildians, their wives or girl friends, and every one of them was a *volunteer!* With backups there must have been nearly a hundred of them. The Association's reward was to be the income from the cloakroom and the profits from the canteen. Edgar House, headmaster of the College, subsequently wrote in his book *Edward Feild – The Man and His Legacy*: "The annual profits to the FAGA from the London Players were never very great (upwards of $2000) but the FAGA directors felt that it was a very worthwhile venture which helped to pay off the debt on the bowling alleys." The helpers had one other perk. They got to see the play for free. Judging by the way they scrambled for empty seats the minute the doors were closed, they must have thought it quite a perk.

Gordon asked me if I would give them a short briefing. I sat them down, walked out on to the stage and faced our very first audience. This was a slight challenge to the emotions. I took my time finding a spot where I could sit on the floor and dangle my legs over the footlights, Danny Kaye style. I looked out at the eager faces, all leaning forward rigid with expectancy, mouths slightly ajar, eyes glistening as if they sensed we were on the brink of a great adventure and they were going to be part of it.

I told them just that. I said how grateful we were and also how professional we all were, which I was sure they would all want to be too. I told them how heavily I would be depending upon them because there would be times when I was playing a part onstage and wouldn't be able to see the house in.

I passed round some specimen tickets and explained the routine. I told them we planned to flout North American tradition and charge for programmes like the English did – ten cents a programme. I would provide them with a change float each night. The boys would have pockets, but what about the ladies? They assured me they would each make their own attractive little pouches to hang around their waists.

For fun, I asked them if the seats they were sitting in were comfortable and went white when they all shrieked "No!" When they saw the look on my face, they roared with laughter and assured me that the audiences would come well prepared mentally and many of them even physically because they'd bring their own cushions. The seating really was horrible – batches of slatted stacking chairs battened together. They couldn't be anchored to the floor because it was *terrazzo,* and I wondered how much somebody must have paid the Fire Marshal. I explained that although we would have the exclusive use of the auditorium, this being a church school, the boys would still assemble for prayers every morning. As this would almost certainly play havoc with the seat alignment, the first job for the ushers on arrival each night would be to straighten the rows and line up the end seats exactly on their marks. No, there weren't any marks there now but there would be tomorrow because I intended to put them there myself with a paintbrush after I'd been busy with a tape measure.

I went down on to the auditorium floor and we tried a dummy run with some of them acting as ushers and some as ticket-holders. It didn't take us long to discover that the seat numbers were almost totally indecipherable. Better now than on opening night. Gordon Stirling undertook to find 550 new seat numbers by the following evening and his troops would all come back and stick them in place. Whatever other troubles might be in store, I didn't think running the front-of-house would be one of them.

According to the master plan, the company would now have assembled in London, spent a week rehearsing the opening play with an Assistant Stage Manager reading in for me and entrained for Liverpool. The opener was to be the tried-and-true farce *Rookery Nook* by Ben Travers. The idea was to continue rehearsals on the voyage, but it turned out that Father Neptune wanted to play whenever the company wanted to work and the best they could manage most days was a line rehearsal.

The box-office had now switched to ticket sales for single performances and the cash flow took on a new spurt. George and Ira had finished the set and would have it up and ready for the company's arrival on the Wednesday. I had tracked down one of the Alexandra Company electricians and our staff was complete. He was Art Noseworthy, a good old Newfoundland name and a good old Newfoundland nature. Forty years later, he would end up in tears when I dropped in to see him quite out of the blue. He was a working electrician by day, with a burning ambition by night to go into business for himself. We were fortunate that we found each other when both our needs were greatest.

I put him to work immediately hanging the lighting pipes. All the equipment rented from Strand Electric in London was in the hold of the *Nova Scotia*. To clear customs, hang and focus was going to take us right down to the wire. I got Ira to make some racks in the room on stage right to accommodate fourteen hampersfull of costumes, some of which wouldn't be worn for at least four months. Then I went to check out the Balsam Hotel.

Actors were nothing new to Mary Facey: she'd housed the Alexandra Company four years before. Not a facial muscle gave the tiniest twitch when I told her that Hilary and I would be sharing the same room. I had booked single rooms for all the others.

I always felt "Hotel" was a bit fancy for the Balsam. It raised your level of expectancy above what you were to find. Balsam House might have been better. "Hotel" suggests transients and almost all the inmates were permanent residents, mostly retired gentlewomen. Mary and I both agreed at the outset that the old ladies should not be exposed to the goings-on of actors at play; so we took over the entire annexe with our own sitting-room and a silver-birch log fire always available at the scratch of a match. We were even segregated at mealtimes, for our hours were not those of normal men and women. This gave Mary the chance to slip us all a chop when everybody else was having moose.

Actors lived so much of their lives in theatrical "digs" that they wouldn't be too shattered with the Balsam. After six days on the *Nova Scotia* it would probably seem paradise, even though we travelled them first-class and the dining room was like Maxims afloat. The only trouble was that their stomachs would be taking a bit more of a beating than they'd have done on the Rue Royale. Hilary and I had gone back on the *Nova Scotia* in 1947. It was only a 7500 tonner and the Atlantic rollers batted it about like a pingpong ball. It pitched, it tossed, it rolled, it yawed, it did everything but turn upside down and once it almost did that. We were in the middle of dinner, those of us with cast-iron stomachs, when the plates actually sailed over the raised rim of the table and crashed in a heap on the floor. But she looked steady as she goes when she came through The Narrows that Wednesday morning.

I was waiting on the quayside with a couple of photographers as she tied up at Harvey's Wharf. Most of the cast were at the rail, waving and shouting. I caught Geoffrey Lumsden's voice above all the rest, "We're broke. Send us money!" A couple of others took up the cry and soon everybody was chanting, "Money! Money! Money! Money! Money!" with hands outstretched like a bunch of beggars. They weren't joking either. Before they were allowed off the boat, I had to square their bar bills with the purser. Surely Oliver would have remembered to advance them all a week's pay in Liverpool? But where was Oliver? The group at the rail opened up and there he was, famous all-round athlete, jogger, demon spin-bowler of Bucks county, sagging at the knees and propped up by two hefty crew members. His face was chalk white. He'd been desperately ill for the entire voyage. For the rest of his life he would never again set foot on a boat, not even a punt in Hyde Park. He grasped the rail, pointed at me and screamed in a voice that bounced off the bollards, "You bastard!" The London Theatre Company had arrived. At least twelve British passports recorded the date for posterity – October 3, 1951.

We lost no time in putting everybody to work. We were all wedded to the Salberg plan which meant Wednesday would be the first rehearsal of Act I without book. We were right on schedule. In fact, we were ahead because the set was up. Ira was already busy building set number two which George would have to start painting the following Tuesday. The *Rookery Nook* set wasn't yet dressed. George had picked up a few knick-knacks but none of the major pieces. This had now become a priority.

I introduced Oliver to Edgar House, the school headmaster, and in true Newfoundland fashion he immediately asked Oliver to dinner. As Edgar himself now tells it: "We were sitting in the front room having an after-dinner coffee when Oliver suddenly said, 'I say, that's a smashing sofa. It would look great on the *Rookery Nook* set. Could we borrow it?' A couple of armchairs next took his eye and before I knew where I was I had to spend a whole week with a house only half-full of furniture. For pure protection, I took him round town the next day and introduced him to all the used furniture dealers."

Even so, down the road, many a patron would gladly part with a prized piece for a whole week to share the spotlight with the cast and get feature billing in the programme. On one occasion when we simply had to have a sofa that was spanking new, we twisted Fred Ayre's arm and borrowed it from Bowrings' furniture department. The week following the play, a customer came into the store and wanted to buy the sofa he'd seen on the London Theatre Company stage. The one they showed him was identical.

"I don't want that," he said. "I want the one they actually sat on." From then on, Bowrings was a pushover.

We held back our welcome party until everybody's lines were down and locked in. Then, true to the Salberg tradition, Friday was declared "office" night – an after-show drink with the management. No outsiders, just the actors, so they could let their hair down without putting our public image at risk. It also turned out to be an excellent opportunity, after sufficient fortification, for anyone to bend my ear if something was really bothering them.

There wasn't much bothering anybody that particular evening. They were in a ripe party mood and, judging by the rate the spirit level was dropping in the bottles on the table, any damage done to the digestive system aboard the *Nova Scotia* had been strictly temporary. George and Ira and Art were inducted into the family and from then on were never very far from its bosom.

I told them all that the advance was good and the excitement was high. The first night wasn't sold out but would be close enough and it was all solid gold, no paper. Not that I was anti-paper: sometimes when you were touring a sleeper, it would slumber all week unless you got a houseful in somehow to go out and talk it up. But on this occasion I felt we already had enough paying customers to spread the gospel according to Ben Travers.

We had chosen *Rookery Nook* as an opener because a farce had topped the box-office during the Alexandra Theatre season and this was the grand-daddy of them all. It was the first of the Aldwych farces to bring together the famous team of Ralph Lynn, Tom Walls and Robertson Hare. It was full of good parts which would hopefully establish several of the new faces at one go. It also had particularly good roles for Hilary and myself. If any box-office appeal had lingered since 1947, it might just give us a jump-start. We needed St. John's to get the repertory habit early. We didn't have the time or the money to build.

If any of the cast woke up with hangovers, they left them at the Balsam, for the Saturday run-through fairly sizzled. No *farceurs* could touch the English at the top of their form. They tossed lines back and forth like a well-played volley at Wimbledon with no return ever appearing quite what you expected. The result was a spontaneity that made every performance look like a first night. Timing would change and characterizations would grow but the discipline would remain, for we all knew that a lack of it was death to farce. I tried to explain that once to a class of third year drama students at Dalhousie University in Halifax and you'd have thought I'd just told them the earth was flat.

Finally one of them ventured, "Bit premeditated isn't it?"

"Yes," said I, "acting is premeditated. You learn the lines, don't you? You've learned the moves. You don't make them up as you go along? The secret is that you don't let the audience know it's premeditated. That's where the acting part comes in."

Although the cast was now free until the dress rehearsal on Monday, they'd spend much of Sunday sponging and pressing the pick of their personal wardrobes to wear at the country house named "Rookery Nook". The stage management were far from free because they were the real workhorses in a company like ours. I wondered why anybody ever took on the job. Gathering props alone for a different play each week was a horrendous job, even in a town where you knew people and the company had a well stocked prop room. John Holmes and his helpers struck out on both counts, and as they'd arrived with only three business days to go before opening, I hired them a local assistant for ten dollars a week. Her name was Sylvia Wigh and she only lasted five weeks. But she was to turn up again on a later page in our history.

Art Noseworthy had wrought miracles installing the electrics. In forty-eight hours he'd hooked up the dimmer board and hung, lamped, cabled and tested every lighting instrument. He must have worked right through the previous night, and that was after I told him we couldn't possibly afford his hourly rate and he'd have to work for a flat weekly fee. He loved the job and he loved us. He once told me that if he were ever granted one single wish, it would be to sit out front just once and see what happened when he pulled the levers. It was the only complaint I ever heard him make. His "lighting booth" behind piled-up packing cases on stage left totally obscured his view from all but the stage manager who called the lighting cues.

Oliver lit like he did everything else, rapidly, well-homeworked and with tremendous effect. The emergence of the lighting designer as a member of the creative team was still at the tentative stage in British theatre and was greeted largely with hostility by the old school of directors. I held out as long as anybody and still instisted on lighting my own shows even though I was colour-blind. I finally capitulated in 1967 when, to the chagrin of a top auto-executive, a green cyclorama showed up in a big scene in one of my Chrysler spectaculars at the O'Keefe Centre in Toronto.

Oliver had no problems with colour. He would lay three flat washes over the entire stage, one red, one yellow and one blue and, with clever mixing of the intensities on the dimmer board, could end up with any colour in the spectrum including white or close to it. Then the sculpturing would begin. Beams from hard-edge spots and soft-edge fresnels would marry and give birth to highlights and shadows, shafts and patterns, warmth or chill, as well as shadings that would transform a flat column into a round one, helped considerably by the masterly brushwork of George Paddon-Foster. At the end of it all, George would stand there as if in a trance and say, "What a beautiful picture! Pity the actors have to come on and fuck it up." Because that's what he always said.

Not this lot, George, I told him. For once we had a bunch that were capable of upstaging him instead of the other way round. They were good, they liked the stage, they liked the set, they liked him, they liked each other. Six months down the road might be quite another story, but right now all they wanted was to get up there and do it, and on Monday night they were going to peak. I was all set to peak along with them until Harry Reynolds arrived unannounced, uninvited and unwelcome from England.

sixteen

I've degenerated into a chronic worrier. There's a Bunsen burning at the bottom of my esophagus. It wasn't there in 1951 or the London Theatre Company would never have happened. But it's forty years on and it's life after Harry Reynolds, to say nothing of Harry Reynolds II, yet to be encountered. Young, budding entrepreneurs, never, in your desperation to get launched, peddle fifty-one percent of your vision, your baby, unless you have the guts and the stamina to guard your minority stake even to the point of utter ruthlessness.

When I suggested a rather urgent meeting, Oliver suddenly had something important to do. He smelt confrontation and he ran. Perhaps it was just as well because he usually ended up feeling sorry for the other guy. I'm a sucker too but I'm also a Gemini and can put on a pretty good show of being just the opposite when necessity nudges. I led Harry up the stairs into the office and sat him on the lone spare bentwood chair while I took up the commanding position behind the Underwood.

"Not exactly Baker Street, is it?" I began. I chucked a copy of our budget across to him. "And that's not exactly a Harry Reynolds production in Cinerama is it? Why in the hell did you come, Harry? There's nothing in there for you."

"I go where my money goes."

If he'd told me that before, his money would never have left England. Was he mad? This was the theatre, not the fantasy world of film. Oliver and I weren't a couple of sugar-daddies looking to pat a film star's fanny. The positions were reversed. Harry was the fanny-patter now and we were the ones making the picture. We were all keyed up to work our arses off to see that we got our investment back with interest and that would go for his share as well. All he had to do was sit back and not spend a cent we hadn't budgeted for. He wasn't exactly doing that, was he, lolling about at – I suddenly went icy cold.

Where *was* he staying? *What? Not the Hotel Newfoundland?* I couldn't believe it! I was nearly in tears. For the cost of a single room there, I could house *and feed* seven members of the company at The Balsam.

The tragedy was that Harry didn't really see what all the fuss was about. This was the way he lived. He'd never had working partners before, just sleepers. Sleep wasn't something his current partners were getting much of. He'd be able to rack up plenty, for there was nothing for him to do in St. John's that I couldn't and wasn't doing already. It was time to tell him the facts of London Theatre Company life. Oliver and I were taking thirty dollars a week, a salary equal to the lowest one on the payroll. He would get the same. The Balsam part of the package was worth $22.50 a week. Where did he plan to find the shortfall? Did he have a secret cache of dollars?

"Take it out of my share of the profit," he said airily and breezed out.

Profit? He'd just upped the cost of making one by a full ten percent. For over a year the budget had been inviolate. It was the Bible, the prospectus that had attracted the capital, the promissory note against my personal integrity. In my language, when circumstances changed, you didn't change the budget, you changed the circumstances. It was our bottom bottom line. Harry had breached it and put the whole project in jeopardy. It was heartbreaking.

There isn't a more exciting sound backstage than the buzz of an expectant first-night audience on the other side of the front curtain. I tingled as I sat with the office door ajar, making myself up as Gerald Popkiss in *Rookery Nook.* Oliver and Harry were doing their stuff out in the lobby. Since our one box-office assistant finished at five at Bowrings, Oliver manned the lobby phone from six o'clock on and tonight it was ringing off the hook. I'd impressed upon them both the need to be totally ruthless in selling unclaimed seats fifteen minutes before curtain time. We were going to lick the "no-show" syndrome early.

Fred Ayre had inveigled us into letting Bowrings put on a short fashion show as a curtain raiser to *Rookery Nook.* It was not your average David Merrick programming but what could we do? We really owed him. As the last of the latest in camiknickers sashayed off into the wings, the furniture was put back on its marks and John Holmes called "Stand by please." This is the signal for most actors to have a quick feel, the gents in the area of their flies and the ladies in the vicinity of their bosoms. After that it varies. Some actors cross themselves, some touch wood, almost all of them moisten their lips. I usually snuck a last quick look at the script before lodging it behind a cleat-line.

"House lights – out."

We couldn't see but we could hear them fade because as they went down, so did the buzz. When it was almost silent, there was an ominous *crack*. Then another. And another and another, as if a dozen people were suddenly snapping firewood over their knee at the same time. Backstage, we all played "what the blazes is that?" in dumbshow. What on earth was it? There wasn't a titter from anyone out there so it had to be something they were used to. My God, the chairs! They creaked! The bloody chairs *creaked!*

What in the hell was this going to do to us? People would be afraid to move. They were sitting on a flat floor. Every time the person in front leaned one way, they'd have to lean the other and there would be a chain reaction of creaks going all the way back to the last row. It didn't matter so much with *Rookery Nook* because you could always shift your weight from one cheek to the other in the middle of a laugh, but what about the quiet plays? Before I had a chance to worry, the curtain was up and the romp was on. *Rookery Nook* was not the most intellectual beginning to a slice of Canadian Theatre history but it was a successful one, and history isn't too interested in failures. In today's corporate buzzwords we'd probably have had a Mission Statement and it would have read: "Give us your bums, we'll deal with your minds later." When I look over the playbill now, I think that's exactly what we did. We gave them an intellectual shot about once every six weeks.

Reviewers are never mad about farce, which is a pity because it is by far the most difficult thing to play. When I've directed a farce, I've sat behind them on first nights and watched them. They take on a kind of hurt look whenever the audience seems to be having a particularly good time. I felt sure Alison O'Reilly, critic for the St. John's *Evening Telegram*, was a member of the same club. She was, after all, a professor of English at the university by day. But you'd never have guessed either of these things from her opening review which we all thought ecstatic. It wasn't until the real raves came later in the season that we recognized she'd been a mite generous over *Rookery Nook*. And if we'd needed any further proof that farce simply wasn't her cup of screech, she subsequently described William Douglas Home's *Chiltern Hundreds* as "a delightful comedy – not farce which blatantly contrives at mirth and relies so desperately on the physical and the sensational for its laughs." I hoped she still had some generosity left because she would be called upon to sit and squeak through three more farces before the season was over.

About midweek, the Lieutenant-Governor and his entourage paid us the first of many visits. An aide interrupted the rehearsal in the morning to brief us on the protocol. As His Honour first came into view at the auditorium entrance, there would be a sustained drum-roll until he and his party had reached their seats. At that moment, the drum would give way to the first six bars of "God Save The King."

Tape decks hadn't yet found their way into prompt corners. Most theatres were using twin turntables with a "cuebar" system in which a series of adjustable rods were preset at the appropriate length, one for each cue, so that you could drop the needle on exactly the right groove. There was also a fair bit of rapid record-changing involved and unfortunately for us the drumroll, the King and the opening cue for *Rookery Nook* were all on different discs. So when the great man arrived he was greeted with a splendid drum-roll but instead of "God Save The King" he got "Alexander's Ragtime Band," which was a singularly unfortunate choice because at that particular time, Lord Alexander was Governor-General of Canada. His Newfoundland representative, Sir Leonard Outerbridge, fought heroically to stem a fit of the giggles, but the aide-de-camp had no such sense of humour and gave me absolute shit the next morning.

By late Saturday night, we had the answers to some of the questions that had worried us most during the preparation years. The big one was that the spirit of Florence Glossop-Harris lived on. The appetite for professional theatre she had aroused in the 1920s and John Gabriel had whetted in 1947, was hungry for more in 1951. *Rookery Nook* had come in at sixty-five percent of the gross. In bodies, that meant almost seventy percent because the unsold seats were usually the more expensive ones. More significant still, in dollars we had topped the opening week of the Alexandra Company whose box-office returns had been the magnet that had first drawn the elements of the London Theatre Company together.

According to the Alexandra records, we should have been able to anticipate eleven more weeks of the same but we had a different set of variables. They had put all their eggs into a twelve-week basket; we'd made an omelette of ours and spread them over twenty-six, and who could say how much that would affect the thickness of the spread. They'd also announced that all proceeds would be devoted to a charity, the Great War Veterans Association. The only charity we were devoted to was the Reynolds, Gordon and Yeo Retirement Fund and there was no PR value in that. We would have to wait at least one more week to see just how much these two things were going to matter.

Our biggest Saturday surprise was the size of the kitty from the programme sellers – $180 collected a dime at a time ($1260 today). Harry immediately suggested we divvy it up between the partners as a perk. As this would effectively triple our pitiful salaries without affecting the budget, I agreed. I also quickly calculated that sixty dollars times twenty-six weeks would almost repay the capital I'd borrowed from Oliver. I went to the bank on Monday and established a special sinking fund to that end.

Saturday nights were highly organized. While Harry and I were upstairs in the office trying to make two plus two equal five, Oliver was onstage with a crew of six trying to make them do the work of ten. The minute the final curtain closed (after five calls in the case of *Rookery Nook*) the actors scurried off, usually to a party, and the crew scurried on: John Holmes and his two assistants; George and Ira, who had created the set and knew best how to take it apart; Art Noseworthy, who had wired and now had to unwire it, and Oliver, who in reluctant deference to the North American way of life had bought his first pair of jeans. The audience was played out with very loud recorded music to cover the noise of the set being struck. Within seconds of the main doors closing behind the last *afficionado*, the stage curtains were thrown open. The walls and furnishings of *Rookery Nook* were lifted piece by piece from the stage to the auditorium floor and carted off to the lobby. Nobody came back empty-handed because the *Born Yesterday* set and furniture were just along the corridor where they had been off-loaded earlier in the day. Some time about then, Art's wife Dorothy arrived with coffee and sandwiches for everybody and began what was to become a weekly ritual.

By 2 am, Harry Brock's penthouse was up and basically furnished and that would be it until Monday morning. Nobody went near the theatre on Sundays. I did a rough tally and calculated that my work week had been just over ninety hours, and that didn't include learning the part of the talkative Harry Brock.

Years later, Art confessed that he often broke the Sunday rule to sneak in and wire up the practicals like the telephone bell, the chandelier, the wall brackets, the reading lamps and the hidden floods to create moonlight, sunlight or fog outside the windows. I suspect this also gave him time on Monday morning for a couple of emergency calls that would take him two steps closer to the formation of Art

145

Noseworthy Ltd.

Before the first schoolboy appeared on Monday morning, the last traces of rural England were carted from the lobby to a rented truck and returned to their rightful owners in Rennies Mill Road. Then everybody moved backstage and started to think American. The penthouse was ready to receive the stage management's haul of frilly curtains, cushions, scatter rugs, ornaments, knick-knacks and whatnots – all in Billie Dawn's best worst taste. While the set was being dressed, Oliver lit it and set sound levels. At eleven sharp, he ran the crew through every curtain, light and sound cue and rehearsed the scene changes down to seconds. At 12.30 the cast arrived, made up, got into costume and walked around the set for the first time. They found the light switches, tried the doors, timed their entrances and checked their props. At one o'clock they did it, just like a performance, and that meant you stopped for nothing unless the set fell down. Such was the repertory routine and they were all old hands at it. The audience, unfortunately, wasn't.

The attendance curve for *Born Yesterday* took a nasty down-turn from opening week, and *The Heiress* didn't fare much better despite an absolute rave from Alison in the *Telegram*. The *Daily News* came forth with this little gem: "Leslie Yeo as Dr Sloper was surprisingly good. In the former plays, he gave one the impression that he was trying to imitate Bob Hope whom he faintly resembles." *The Heiress* proved one thing, though: there wasn't a creak to be heard once the curtain went up. At the end of each scene, it sounded like the finale of a military tattoo, but during the scene, all was silence.

When *The Chiltern Hundreds* failed to break the box-office pattern, despite a brilliant performance by Geoffrey Lumsden as the Earl of Lister, it began to look as if we were down to the faithfuls and there just weren't quite enough of them. The immediate financial drain on Oliver and myself was minuscule compared to Harry. Every bite he took in the Newfoundland Hotel dining room would now be eating into his capital investment.

One morning during our fourth week, George Crosbie came quietly into the hall and sat down watching the rehearsal. George was President of Lever Brothers (Newfoundland) and a friend from the Alexandra days. He was also an uncle of John Crosbie, who became a minister in Brian Mulroney's cabinet.

"How are you doing?" he asked.

"George, we're so close. We need just another hundred people a week to break even. That's only fifteen people a night."

"Is that right?" He gave my shoulder a grip of encouragement and without another word went straight down to the box-office and bought a hundred seats. He distributed them in pairs to members of his staff, many of whom had never seen a professional play before. It was our first week without a loss. Some of them must have got hooked because we just edged into the black the following week as well. This gave me the chance to ease up on the pressure in my programme editorials and give the audience a pat on the back for a change:

> You have proved that such is your love of the theatre that you can endure two hours on a hard seat and that they do not squeak because you are obviously too interested in the play to become restless. This hardness will be remedied. Cushions are already on order. In the meantime, by all means bring your own.

When the cushions were finally installed, they didn't do a thing about the creaks. They were only a pathetic half-inch of foam between two sheets of blue plastic, but they saved the most delicate bottoms from being branded with slat marks every theatre night and well into the following day.

From the very first week, there was one performance that we never had difficulty in selling out – our Saturday matinee. The seats ranged in price from twenty-five cents to one dollar and our audience ranged in age from about five to twelve. These were our real fans. Their loyalty was totally unaffected by the choice of play, the reviews, the weather, or the fickleness of human nature. It mattered not to them that something unspeakable was happening at Deadwood Gulch or the Circle Z just up the road at The Nickel movie theatre, or that it cost fifteen cents more to come to us. There, they would join with the rest of them running up and down the aisles shouting *bang! bang!* With us they would sit for two hours glued to a seat that creaked if you dared to move. However biting the wind, however deep the snow, they'd be there in their snowsuits, their mittens and their pretty toques with the pompoms on top. These were the real faithfuls. Some day, maybe another thirty years hence, some band of travelling troubadours will rediscover John Cabot's land and wonder at the trained theatre audience they find there.

seventeen

I had to make room on my rack for one more hat. Bonnet might be more apt, since the designation I overlooked in my job description of an actor-manager was Den Mother. No theatre company away from home base should ever be without one.

Actors seem to run on a special kind of adrenalin that is only activiated by stage lighting. Safely within its ambience, they become masters of another world. Back home in the dim light of a forty-watt bulb, they rejoin the less than ordinary run of mortals. Simple arithmetic is beyond their ken and a problem is something that will go away if you close your eyes. Actors are a self-run business, a corporation of one, and their account book is a cookie jar. Incoming mail often piles up unopened because they can't look a bill in the face, while stale-dated cheques that could have paid them pile up unopened alongside. As a breed, they are generous, spoiled, charming, over-worked, underpaid, irresistible, lovable children, who should always be part of some den mother's brood wherever they are and essentially so when they are two thousand miles from home. Someone has to make sure they've written to the wife this week, sent off their child support or paid their union dues. To eleven of these lovely people, it fell to me to become their confidante, psychoanalyst, moral adviser, financial consultant and sometime shoulder to cry on.

Payday was the popular time for the baring of souls. The "ghost walked" from 11 am on Fridays, and each cast member would choose the right moment to leave the rehearsal and pop into the office above the stage. If they closed the door behind them, I knew they'd come for more than just their pay-packet.

Financial problems cropped up most and could usually be resolved with the offer of a small loan. Domestic worries called for less material but equally demanding resources like gentleness, tact and a sympathetic ear that wasn't pressed for time. On occasions, these sessions would become quite emotional and nothing I could say or do seemed to make any difference. At such times I would pass them the telephone and say, "This one's on me. Don't get carried away and remember there aren't any pips when you call from this end." This was expensive psychiatry but it usually worked and the prescription was rarely abused.

Keeping up company morale was as vital as keeping up the bank balance and I was responsible for both. Their physical well-being was in the hands of Dr Frank O'Dea who had generously donated his services as the company doctor, since Newfoundland had no equivalent of the British Health service. I didn't tell the girls, in case it gave them any ideas, but he was also a highly qualified obstetrician.

The thing they all missed most was the English pub. It was almost traditional to nip in for a pint on your way home to slog away at the night's quota of lines. The closest to a pub atmosphere was to be found at the Crow's Nest, an ex-officers' club perched atop forty-nine rather intimidating wooden steps halfway between Duckworth and Water Streets. One day, to our immense delight, an envelope arrived with an honorary membership card made out to each one of us for the duration of our stay. It wasn't that there was ever any difficulty in getting a drink after the show: there were standing invitations galore to drop in if the porch light was on, and Rennies Mill Road porches were usually lit up like guiding lights to Alcoholics Anonymous. It was just that in somebody's house, you couldn't have your script open on the bar and memorize half a page of tomorrow's lines between throws at the dartboard.

Newfoundland hospitality was legendary and our dance card was always full. Someone had put the word around that actors are always hungry after a performance, so we found ourselves being offered not only any drink that appeared in *The Bartender's Manual* but also a huge spread. As a good actor-manager, I began to become concerned about everybody's waistline. These had sort of settled into dimensions imposed by post-war rationing, and fourteen baskets of pre-fitted stage costumes were dependent upon their staying that way. There was also the question of stamina. I finally had to make a rule not to accept full company invitations on line-learning nights : Tuesdays, Wednesdays and Thursdays.

There was a moment of high excitement when Princess Elizabeth and Prince Philip paid a visit to St. John's, and it was rumoured that Government House was trying to squeeze a night at the theatre into the royal schedule. Unfortunately, jet lag robbed the box-office of a royal boost, but we all took an hour off from rehearsals and joined the crowd on Water Street waving our miniature Red Ensigns. As we made more noise than the others, we were rewarded with our own special royal wave. It was a beautiful Fall day and they were riding in an open limousine. The *Daily News,* which didn't seem to run to a proof-reader, described next day how "the Royal couple were in full public view every foot of the route and couldn't even enjoy a private poke with decorum." The edition sold out very early in the morning. My previous favourite in the *Daily News* had been the report of a society wedding in which it described the bride as wearing a dutch cap trimmed with sequins.

High Temperature, our second farce of the season, topped the *Rookery Nook* box-office by a whisker and *Wuthering Heights* did almost as well the following week. We had wiped out our early losses and a small profit on the season was staring us in the face. We'd read the market correctly: St. John's adored farce and heavy drama, rather like any repertory town in the north of England.

Since I had toured in *High Temperature* in the early days of the war, I directed it. Oliver played the Harry Kendall part and was brilliant. He had a long, sad face which looked even longer and sadder because his forehead now went all the way up, over and down to the bottom of his neck. Every time he appeared, you simply couldn't help feeling sorry for him. This was an enormous plus in a play where he constantly found himself half-undressed in somebody else's bed with never an evil thought in his body.

On this note of personal triumph, Oliver flew off to England at the end of the week to keep a long-standing commitment to direct *Cinderella* for Derek Salberg at the Alexandra Theatre, Birmingham. There he would control an orchestra of twenty and a cast of a hundred and would introduce to the British public for the first time in a starring role, a promising young comedian named Norman Wisdom.

Week after week in the programme notes, I had been steadily flogging the theme that if you want a permanent theatre, you must come every week. The fickle factor was too high to be healthy. Just before Oliver left, I asked him to write something with a real hearts-and-flowers flavour and he came up with this wrencher: "Audiences have been on the small side which may bring our season to an end at Christmas. I shall be anxiously awaiting a cable to know if I am to come back."

Just as Oliver's departure to produce a panto reminded us that Christmas was at hand, so did the box-office receipts which plunged alarmingly. That was enough to bring Harry out of the woodwork. We were in the middle of a rehearsal of *Charley's Aunt*, the choice for Christmas week, when he walked into the hall without a word of greeting and sat down at the back. I smelled trouble. He'd never been near a rehearsal since the day he'd arrived. I had no idea what he did with himself all day, except relieve the box-office girl for her lunch hour at Bowrings. There was no TV in his hotel bedroom or anywhere else in Newfoundland for that matter.

He fidgeted about until the creaks drove us mad. Suddenly he sprang up and stormed onto the stage.

"What the hell do you all think you're doing? You're yawning your bloody heads off! You're walking through the goddamned play! It's disgusting."

I tried to stay calm but if there was anything guaranteed to set me off it was injustice and he was being unjust. Of course they were tired! Their job was to be entertaining onstage and off, and in St. John's, the "off" part was non-stop. But not a speck of tiredness had ever showed up in an actual performance.

After a brief shouting duel, I finally ordered Harry off the stage. As he didn't stop when I did, I shouted "Cast dismissed" in a voice that would have topped six of his in unison and went back to the Balsam. In seconds, I had undressed and was sleeping the sleep of total exhaustion. The rest of the cast made a bee-line for the Crow's Nest.

I've no idea how long I'd been out before a knock on the door woke me. Harry walked in and threw a letter onto the bed.

"That's your notice. I've booked you on a plane for Monday week."

"You can't fire me. It's my company."

"That's not what a judge would say."

"Well in that case, you'd better book a passage for Hilary too."

"Oh no! She's under contract. I took up her option, remember?"

As a hedge against total disaster, everybody had been contracted for six weeks with an option on the management's side for the rest of the season. Harry had signed the original contracts as an existing management that had lodged the required deposit with British Actors' Equity Association. He was also required to sign the options and he'd given them to me to distribute six weeks earlier.

"Harry," I said pityingly, "you don't think I was stupid enough to give it to her, do you?"

The corner of his mouth started to twitch. He went out and slammed the door. I dressed as fast as I could and called Hilary at the

Crow's Nest.

"We've never taken up your option," I hissed at her.

"What? What? What are you talking about?"

"That-letter-from-Harry-I-gave-you-about-six-weeks-ago-taking-up-the-option-on-your-contract?-You-never-received-it-okay?-Can't-stop.-Bye."

I drove to the office which now boasted a cupboard, and took out every script for every play remaining on the schedule – fourteen sets of them – so there was absolutely nothing for the company to start rehearsing the following Tuesday. (To help conserve our capital outlay in England, I had tracked down every script needed for the season and borrowed them all from managements I had worked for, mainly the Salbergs.) I loaded the car and drove round to Audrey (wife of George) Crosbie's house on Rennies Mill Road. I dumped the scripts in her basement and asked her to forget I'd been anywhere near her house that morning. Then I went down to the Crow's Nest. It wasn't long before the phone started to ring.

I signalled to the bartender that I wasn't there even though his shouted "For you Les" made it obvious I was. This little game was repeated every ten minutes until the bartender said, "I think you'd better take it, Les."

"Yes?"

"You have half an hour to return those scripts to the office or I'll have you arrested for theft."

"Well now, Harry, even in the remotest corners of the British Commonwealth of Nations, I don't believe you can be arrested for stealing your own property. Those scripts were loaned to me. Not to Mid-Century Entertainments, not to the London Theatre Company, to me. Personally." And I hung up.

Minutes later, a taxi-driver appeared at the door and said somebody wanted to see me outside. I picked up my coat, waved to the others and ambled as nonchalantly down the forty-nine steps as the danger factor would permit.

"The Hotel please," said Harry.

"No. My place if you don't mind."

Once we were alone in my bedroom at the Balsam, this is what he said: "You've beaten me. Nobody has ever done that before. If you will come and work for me, I'll give you ten percent of everything I earn."

I couldn't believe what I was hearing. Did he really think he could buy me? I totally ignored his offer and gave him *my* terms instead. Number one, he would never again show up at a rehearsal. Number two, the sooner he went back to England the better it would be for his bank balance and for my personal equilibrium. Two days later, his wife and two children came in on the London plane for Christmas and it suddenly became clear what had sparked his furore. He'd invited them when business was picking up and he thought he could afford their fare. Today he knew he couldn't.

With Oliver in Birmingham and Harry in limbo, I made some rapid unilateral decisions. I got the rent reduced on the auditorium from $350 a week to a basic $200 plus a percentage. And our most expensive employee, Art Noseworthy, without the slightest hint from me, insisted we cut his salary by twenty-five percent. Rehearsals quickly got back on track, if not immediately to normal. But there was one aftermath that disturbed me: the person who had secretly agreed with Harry to take my place in the director's chair was Geoffrey Lumsden, a long-time friend and an actor I greatly admired. I had stood up and defended the company. When his turn had come to defend me he had failed. I never really forgave him.

But it was Christmas and *Charley's Aunt* would open on Christmas Eve and I would be playing Fancourt-Babberly. And George had given us not one but three gorgeous sets all, God alone knows how, painted in the space of a single week. The box-office would be one day short, for we wouldn't play on Christmas Day, but we stuck in a couple of extra matinees and did a splendid week. The kids at the Saturday matinee were in hysterics, especially when we extended the chase to take us right through the house to the lobby and back again down the other aisle.

Every member of the company spent Christmas Day with a St. John's family. "Reservations" had started coming in weeks before, and right up to Christmas Eve there were calls to make sure no one had been forgotten. In every house, there was a gift on the tree for the guest. For two lucky actors, their hosts had even booked a transatlantic telephone call to their families at home, quite an event in 1951.

The Christmas lull spilled over into January but Harry still lingered on and I started to get worried about our dollar drain. The only other excitement was generated by Geoffrey Lumsden who was having an extra-marital affair with Rosemary Rogers. One Sunday morning, when the sun was shining on a brand new layer of untrodden snow, the two of them decided to tackle a climb up Signal Hill. It was impossible to tell where the road stopped and the ditch began and Geoffrey ended up buried to his waist and screaming in agony. Rosemary got him out with some difficulty and did what she'd read somewhere was the only way to deal with frostbite: she grabbed a handful of snow, put her hand down inside his pants and massaged his peter, to the utter astonishment of a handful of citizens who were on their way to church.

Oliver returned from Birmingham to find peace that he never even knew had been disturbed. The first St. John's payday of the new year had pepped up the box-office and soon we had three hits in a row: *The Perfect Woman* allowed Sheila Huntington to show off her splendid body; *Jane Eyre* allowed Hilary to show off her extraordinary ability to make people cry; and *Present Laughter* allowed me just to show off as Garry Essendine, the pampered actor. Our old friend *Harvey* came next, and attendance was all set to continue dizzying upwards when King George VI died and the box-office with him. Gloom settled over the loyalist town, and what had promised to be a record-breaking week just dwindled away. The only other thing I remember about that week was hearing on VOCM radio that the King was in Westminster Abbey "lying on his brier."

After the first night of *The Perfect Woman*, an officer from the U.S. Navy came round to see me. He'd been bowled over with the show and he didn't care what it cost, he just had to take it to Argentia, the naval base in Placentia Bay, eighty miles from St. John's over very rugged roads.

"When? We play every night except Sunday."

"It was Sunday I was thinking of."

He had it all worked out. He'd seen us several times before, but this was the play he'd been waiting for. After the last performance on Saturday, they'd take us and the set to the base, give us a hell of a party, put us up for the night, we'd do the show on Sunday afternoon and then they'd drive us back.

Of course, it was impossible. But then, the whole concept of the London Theatre Company had been impossible, and here we were. I told him I would talk to the company and let him know the next day. I also had to check with George and Ira about getting set up for the Monday opening of *Jane Eyre*.

Next morning I informed the U.S. Navy that the company was mad keen. I got them all a good fee. On Saturday night the set and the furniture didn't stop off in the lobby but continued on down the front steps into an enormous military truck, with all the lifting for a change being done by American sailors. The actors, each with costumes, makeup and an overnight bag, piled on to a bus to be greeted with

154

champagne, smoked salmon sandwiches and a U.S. Marine playing a guitar. Under those circumstances, a two-hour drive over a dirt road was like riding the Orient Express.

We were greeted by a huge log fire, a banquet table dressed to match the meal scene from *The Private Life of Henry VIII* and an enormous banner that said WELCOME LONDON PLAYERS. They'd promised us a hell of a party and they delivered. And so did we that afternoon to the best audience I ever remember playing to.

In February, the message finally got through to Harry that the best chance he'd have of getting his money back was to keep it out of the hands of the Newfoundland Hotel, and he booked a flight back to England. Before he left, we all went to a lawyer to incorporate the London Theatre Company under the laws of Newfoundland. I still didn't trust those jokers in Whitehall.

Harry's departure didn't noticeably increase my work load but something else did. Geoff Stirling (no relation to Gordon) phoned from CJON that he'd finally found a sponsor for a weekly radio show I'd suggested. Our sponsor was to be Standard Manufacturing, the leading paint-maker in Newfoundland, and part of the deal provided our scenic designer, George Paddon-Foster, with an unlimited supply of all the colours he wanted. Our two theatre reviewers sang George's praises so often that he constantly upstaged the leading actors. Standard were quick to bask in the glory with the claim that he used their paints exclusively, though I doubt if they foresaw just how voracious an appetite some of his largest brushes had.

Our radio programme was to be a game show that we intended to call "Keep Talking." It was a terrible steal from the BBC, but it would be good PR and give the company some pocket money. We would record it before a live audience after the show on Monday nights, starting immediately. As it would involve three of the girls and three of the boys each week, I planned to rotate them so that everybody got a crack at the kitty. As if I hadn't enough on my plate already, I agreed to be the host of the programme. They would each get thirty dollars, and I would get fifty because I had to do all the homework, like dreaming up the questions and scripting the opening and closing, and also because I was the boss. This meant that the weeks they did the radio show, the actors doubled their stage salary. Paul O'Neill was already making considerable use of the company in schools broadcasts for the CBC, and all this was adding up to a very tempting package to be able to offer contenders for next year's company. Oh yes, Virginia, there was going to be a next year. I had a few small changes in mind, but we'd be back.

Just before rehearsal one morning, John Holmes approached me with a look of awe and whispered that the Archbishop wanted me on the office phone. Archbishop? I'd never spoken to an Archbishop before. It must have been twenty-five years since I'd even said hullo to a curate. I couldn't imagine why he would want to talk to me.

He said, "Is that Mr Yeo?" When I said it was, he told me he'd heard we were planning to put on *A Streetcar Named Desire*.

"Yes we are. As a matter of fact we are rehearsing it right now."

"Then I have to tell you that if this play goes on I will be compelled to ban it from the pulpit on Sunday."

"Oh." Over half our audience would have to choose between us and purgatory. "Have you ever seen the play?"

"No."

"Have you read it?"

"No."

"Oh" again. And a well-timed pause. "I find that quite extraordinary, Your Grace, that you would go into the pulpit and ban a play that you've never seen and you've never read."

"Some of my people, however, have."

"Have they? Or have they just *heard*, do you think?" The film hadn't even hit St. John's yet. "Would you like to see the play, Your Grace? We do a run-through on Saturday mornings, just like a performance except that we will not be in the proper costume or on the right set. Why not come and judge for yourself?"

To my immense surprise, he said he would.

"Not a word about the Archbishop," I hissed to John. At the end of the morning I casually mentioned to the company that there would be a gentleman with a clerical collar watching the Saturday run and would they please refrain from saying "Fuck!" if they blew their lines.

I was playing Stanley Kowalski and therefore couldn't sit with His Grace during the run, but he waited for me. "It's a very, very fine play," he said. "I think it will be misunderstood, but I wouldn't dream of telling anyone they mustn't see it."

Streetcar set a box-office record that would stand unchallenged for nearly four years. That should have been enough to make it my happiest memory of the season but it didn't end up that way. Hilary played Blanche Dubois, and in all the years we were together, it was the only time I ever saw a part take her over. For three weeks she *was* Blanche. She was torture to live with during rehearsal week, hell during playing week and impossible the week after. She was brilliant in the part, better than Vivien Leigh who was always such a wonderful technician but never really moved you. Hilary made you cry.

Tennessee Williams was one of the first playwrights to call for a divided set. The genius of George Paddon-Foster reached its zenith with his composite creation of a seedy corner of New Orleans with acting areas on three different levels: a ground floor flat, the one above it and the alley-way that ran alongside, all on a stage with a thirty-foot opening. With 105 light cues, the visual impact was breathtaking. Behind the scenes, Art Noseworthy moved dimmer levers with hands, knees and feet and plugged and replugged circuits like a telephone switchboard operator on election night. But the Archbishop was right. The play was misunderstood. With a packed opening-night house half-filled with novice theatregoers, there were embarrassed laughs in the wrong places. When the curtain came down on the first act, Hilary broke into hacking sobs which quickly turned to hysteria, and I had to administer a good old-fashioned face slap.

We met Tennessee Williams, Hilary and I, for a brief moment in New York many years later. Kate Reid and Zoe Caldwell, both chums, were co-starring on Broadway in *A Slapstick Tragedy* and we went down for the opening. The author came into Kate's dressing-room after the show to thank her for her performance and she introduced us. He shook hands limply, stammered a few unintelligible words and fled. This little mumbling mouse was the man who was able to wield a pen so powerful that it could take over a person's mind and wall it in for three solid weeks?

Fan mail wasn't a feature of repertory life in your home base but *Streetcar* yielded Hilary a small shoal. All the writers without exception hated the play but had fallen so profoundly under Blanche's spell that they felt they had to write and tell her so.

Then there was the Saturday matinée. After each performance it was customary for someone to give a plug for the next week's production. During *White Cargo* week, when we announced *Streetcar*, we thought it advisable to suggest that the play was not suitable for children. By phone, by letter and in person, I was bombarded by irate mums who said their child had never missed a play since the season began and why should they be made to miss this one? I explained that nobody said they couldn't come; we merely suggested they shouldn't.

Came Saturday, they were all there, the same eager little faces, the same pompoms, the same little fur-trimmed mitts clutching a nickel for a programme, specially reduced for matinées. I don't think they understood a word of what was going on, but they were far more controlled than the grown-ups had been on the Monday night. And when they left, I think they went home under a kind of spell too.

eighteen

Of all the calls on an actor-manager's time, the most demanding for me was collecting, vetting and writing the material for a sixteen-page programme week after week. But we had to give them something for their dime. There was BACKSTAGE GOSSIP (not all of it got into print), a cast member's BIOGRAPHY (not all of it true), a plug for NEXT WEEK'S PLAY (one you simply must not miss) and an EDITORIAL (ticking you off in advance if you did). There was also the centre-page spread, stating who was playing what, where and when in time. This was the page still in the Underwood when it hit me that we'd come of age.

21st PRODUCTION
Week commencing February 24th 1952
"CLAUDIA"
by Rose Franken

For twenty-one weeks we'd kept up this murderous pace and no one was even winded. We'd got the key of the door and practically the keys to the city. We were the talk of the town, the antidote to short days and long nights. We were the chat of the cocktail circuit and the topic on the back seat of the bus. We had become part of the winter way of life.

The management wasn't making a mint but you could say that it had acquired fiscal respectability. And my personal bank balance was more than merely respectable, it was positively middle-class. For one thing, I never had time to go shopping. Once a week to the liquor store and once a day to the smoke shop and that was it. The rest headed straight for the vaults at the Royal Bank of Canada. With the windfall from the radio show and the share-out from the house programmes, I'd been able to pay off my loan to Oliver a full six weeks ahead of schedule. Now I *really* had a stake in the company. It was mine, paid for, and it was there to speak for me when we started to talk about season number two.

Hilary and I also had a twenty-first to celebrate: twenty-one weeks free of longing, devoid of lies and cover-ups and assignations in unromantic places. It was the longest time we'd ever been together, and we didn't want it to stop, even though we rarely saw each other in the waking hours except at weekends and onstage when we were both in the same play.

We had eased into the habit of spending Sundays in upper class splendour with David and Mary Baird on Rennies Mill Road. Mary was a Topping and her cousin Dan had once owned the New York Yankees. David was the son of a Water Street merchant who had owned Baird's now-defunct department store. After the show on Saturday nights, Hilary and I would arrive with our toothbrushes, soothe away the week's worries with a few gentle nightcaps by the fire, flop out on the canopied bed in the guest room and turn off our built-in alarm clocks. In the morning, we would go for a barefoot stroll round the bedroom up to our ankles in broadloom and end up in the *en suite* bathroom with the gold-plated taps. From then on it was dressing-gowns until lunchtime and the first martini.

Some time in the afternoon, David would ask Hilary the question that had been on every Sunday agenda since almost the first week: had she written *the* letter? Both Hilary and I had long since known that we couldn't face a replay of our goodbye scene at Euston Station in London when we had come back from Newfoundland in 1947. I had gone one way and she had gone another, back to her husband Tim. This time she knew she would have to write and tell him that she and I would both be taking the same turning. She had put it off and put it off and now there were only six Sundays left. To make matters worse, she confessed she had been sending him conscience money every week, even though he was earning a regular salary with the Salbergs. So now he would be losing not only a wife but an income as well. The degree of difficulty factor was rising.

We all knew that the time had finally come and I'm ashamed to confess that David and I got her a little pissed, put a pen in her hand and chanted in unison, "Dear Tim." After several aborted beginnings, she wrote the letter, addressed the envelope, sat back and looked at us defiantly. Very slowly, and wisely without ceremony, David crossed to the letter, picked it up, folded it into the envelope and held it out.

"Want to change your mind?"

"No."

"Stick out your tongue then." He very gently glided the gummed flap across it from one end to the other, pinched the letter shut, kissed it and put it safely in his pocket. And that was my personal life taken care of for the next twenty-two years.

Now if only the same could have been said for my business life. I wasn't planning to fly that solo either. Nor was I thinking of a three-seater. The end of the current season was alarmingly close and I needed at least two hours of concentrated Oliver. And that wouldn't be easy, seeing that he was up to the top of his hairless head rehearsing two plays at the same time, one of them our most ambitious production – *The Taming of the Shrew.*

To do Shakespeare in a week is like trying to skip through *War and Peace* on a Sunday afternoon. Just to cast *The Shrew* was a nightmare, with eighteen speaking parts and a total acting strength of twelve. We had to find six local actors who could fill not only the roles but also the costumes we'd brought from England. We never did manage to get George Paddon-Foster in front of an audience, but we press-ganged his stage carpenter Ira Butler into making "a brief but effective appearance as a cringing, tumbling kitchen boy," as the *Daily News* put it.

We preceded the *Shrew* with a play that left out Geoffrey and Rosemary and gave them double the usual time to learn and rehearse Petruchio and Kate. So it was Oliver who became martyr of the week with his mornings spent directing half the company in *A Lady Mislaid,* his afternoons directing the other half in *The Shrew* and his evenings doing his usual stint on the box-office phone in the lobby. On one such evening, his day didn't even end there. I grabbed him and a bottle of scotch and yanked him off to the Balsam for a serious look into our crystal ball.

For a man who was about to come through a theatrical venture with his capital intact for the first time in his life, Oliver showed remarkable aplomb at the news that there would even be a small profit. He took a long look at the scotch he'd just poured, picked up the bottle and calmly added another couple of ounces. He could, of course, take the money and run, but I knew he'd never be able to do that any more than I would. So we started right in on season number two: what we'd learned from number one, what the future promised and what we had to do to hold it to that promise. As I tended to see things through the window of an adding machine, Oliver said little except to pop in the odd "Whatever you think, cock."

My whatever thinking right then was that the St. John's season was too long. Although we had a solid base of steadies, the fickles were getting too many chances to pick and choose. We had to cut down the options and still retain twenty-six working weeks to amortize our pre-opening costs. Maybe a short diversionary trip to "Canada," as its newest citizens still called the mainland, would worry a few of the fickles into joining the ranks of the steadies. Halifax loomed largest on our horizon. Surely a whisper of our prowess had carried that far? For next to nothing, I could re-route my return air ticket and find out.

"Why don't you do that, old boy?"

Next on my worry list was the Christmas doldrums: two horrible weeks when the glitter in the gift-shop windows lured theatre ticket money away from even the most ardent followers. We couldn't afford to close because, unlike a rep season in England, our actors still had to be paid, housed and fed, and every little helped. How did the English reps cope with the problem?

"Pantomime!" we chimed in unison. Spend the dead weeks rehearsing a panto, open on Boxing Day, play twice daily, sell out and in two weeks take in four weeks' revenue. But that was in England. Would St. John's dig panto? Could we even stage one with a thirty-foot proscenium opening? Could we find a piano player to sound like a twenty-piece orchestra? Could we persuade a dance school in St. John's to transform eight of its brightest students into Ziegfeld girls by Christmas?

"We could have a go," said Oliver. And he ought to have known whether we could or not: he'd directed some of the most lavish pantos in Britain for Derek Salberg. Every panto of Derek's packed the Alex, Birmingham for eight solid weeks and even then only just made back its enormous production costs. The profits came over the next five Christmases when the productions were rented out complete with sets, costumes, props, book and music to leaner managements in lesser towns. Derek, Oliver felt sure, would give us a wonderful deal as renter number six.

Pantomime was probably Britain's only best-selling product that had never made an export manifest. It was a spectacular, colourful, broad, fall-on-your-fanny comedy with a man in drag playing the "Dame" and a girl playing her son, the "Principal Boy," usually long-and-shapely-legged in flesh-coloured tights and a top that made a mini-skirt look like a chastity belt. The whole affair rode on the faintest thread of a children's fairy story, liberally laced with local references and current top-of-the-pops tunes with doctored lyrics. Local gags began immediately to germinate in my mind, for nobody was going to play Dame but me.

So three big decisions were made: we'd return next year, we'd try a tour to Halifax, and we'd present a pantomime. Right Oliver?

"Right cock." Then, after a pause, "What about Harry?"

"Fuck Harry," I said, and we went back to the theatre to see the house out.

Up in the office, I started a new list: SEASON II. By nine o'clock next morning I'd crossed off the first item: an urgent letter to Strand Electric in London. To freight all the stage-lighting equipment back to Liverpool, truck it to London, relabel the same crates three months later and send them all the way back again seemed a terrible waste of money to a dedicated cash conservationist. Could we store everything in St. John's and suspend the weekly rental until we reopened in October? Likewise the sound equipment people? Back came letters from both to say that we could. We'd made the first dent in our second year's budget.

William Shakespeare cast his magic spell upon the box-office and all who patronized it as he'd been doing the world over for four hundred years. *The Shrew* brought great kudos to the company and fleeting fame to six local actors: Michael Cashin, Marie Darcy, John Carter, Ira Butler, Doug Brophy and Sarah Fletcher. Alison O'Reilly thoughtfully recorded their names in her *Telegram* review. She even gave mine some prominence for a rendering I'd felt sure would be too broad for her delicate taste-buds:

> As Grumio, Leslie Yeo accomplished the feat of making one of Shakespeare's more tiresome clowns completely diverting. The abandon of his antics was wonderful. He surrendered himself to the "rough-house" of his role and by his clownish laughter, knack of mimicry and half-wittedness was one of the most engaging persons on the stage.

By heck Virginia, we'd have her enjoying farce next! But not this season. We were all out of farces and were fast coming up to Kleenex time with that fail-safe weepie *Smilin' Through*. In St. John's, something with a whiff of the Auld Sod was practically a city ordinance for the week of St Patrick's Day. And for every husband who couldn't bear to sit and watch the damage to his wife's mascara, there'd be two others who'd choose *Smilin' Through* for their annual shot of culture just as they had picked *Peg O' My Heart* in the Alexandra season four years before.

After that came *The Ghost Train*, two paces lower still down the cultural path from Padua, except that it could claim to be a classic of its own in the comedy-thriller genre. The star of the evening is the train itself which is never seen but is decidedly heard, smelt and *felt*, all without the help of a single recorded effect. This fact is made clear in advance to the audience in the programme notes, and if you don't get an ovation as the train comes thundering through the remote Cornish railway station, you know you have failed. Arnold Ridley, the author, tells you how to make sure you won't.

"First, you take ten Boy Scouts ... " and he goes on to describe in meticulous detail the drill and the weaponry required: oxygen cylinders, whistles, hammers, mallets, snares, wire brushes, smoke box, thunder sheet, milk churns and light slots revolving on a gramophone turntable. I still remember John Holmes standing in the wings like a conductor with his own private orchestra bringing each section in on cue.

More recent revivals have turned to modern sound reproduction with massive woofer speakers that will drive a rock beat downwards through three condominiums to reach yours and still shatter your eardrums. But the *floor* won't shake. In Arnold Ridley's *Ghost Train* it does, because the culminating drill calls for two of the train team to run across the back of the stage behind the set, pulling a heavy garden roller over slats nailed to the stage floor so that as you sat in the audience, you *felt* the floor tremble. And that's the effect that brings people to their feet. We didn't have boy scouts but we found ten students just as prepared and they got an ovation every night.

In a span of just three weeks from the time the curtain had first gone up on *The Taming of the Shrew*, the box-office delivered to us a net profit equivalent to a thirty percent return on our entire original investment. And we still hadn't reached the pot of gold at the end of the rainbow. Our twenty-sixth and final week was a sellout.

All season long we had been promising our faithfuls a musical revue as a going-away present. Its title had never been in doubt but its content had been in a state of flux until the very last moment. We called our revue *Screech* after the local brand of pure Jamaica rum that had been the primary cause of Newfoundland hangovers from time immemorial. We began scrounging material even before we left England and as John Woodnutt had been in revue, we appointed him scavenger-in-chief. He took the job very seriously, read the local papers from cover to cover every day and pumped us unmercifully for titbits of gossip picked up at parties. The first rehearsal of *Screech* was barely two weeks off when John finally put the cork in the bottle.

Screech was the start of a dynasty that would dominate the box-office and the local conversaziones for six years. Actors who had never danced or sung a note in public became Fred Astaires and Judy Garlands. All became masters of the send-up. Newfoundland made fun of England, England chuckled at Newfoundland and actors sent up each other. Michael Atkinson impersonated Geoffrey Lumsden as Heathcliff in *Wuthering Heights,* Geoffrey impersonated himself in *Smilin' Through* and we all impersonated somebody who was anybody locally. Two ladies with thinly disguised names of local socialites sat in the window of McMurdo's Restaurant on Water Street and exchanged confidences on all the well-known names that passed by. We called it "Coffee at McBurpos." We parodied the fashion show that had begun our season, only this time using ourselves as male models. Bowrings were still brave enough to supply the outfits which, to their chagrin, were slightly doctored before opening night. Not a sacred cow was left unmilked. With the discovery and blossoming of Andreas Barban as composer, vocal coach and musical accompanist, the fun was fast, furious and totally non-stop as revue must always be. It ended with a rousing rendering of *There's No Business Like Show Business* by the entire company as we all climbed the gangplank to George Paddon-Foster's mock-up of the *RMS Nova Scotia* on its way to snowbound England.

Alison began her review thus: "Last evening Bishop Feild Hall was second only to the famed Gaiety Theatre in London ... "

The extraordinary exhilaration of that final week was marred for me by some unpleasantness from a totally unexpected quarter. But it didn't spoil it for the others because I didn't tell them about it. I had been summoned to the sanctum of the Chairman of Bowrings and as I opened his door I immediately missed the aura of warmth that had always radiated from the desk of the genial Sir Eric. In his chair now sat his nephew Derek, a rather pinched and weaselly fellow not noted for his charm, a deficiency that he immediately proceeded to demonstrate. He didn't ask me to sit down. He left me standing there like an employee who had been caught with his hand in the till. He told me quite bluntly that Bowrings was under new management and that its attitude to the London Theatre Company was about to change. The following year there would be *no* credit, *no* borrowing of props from the store and *no* supply of free programmes from the printer. We could, however, still keep the box-office space on the main floor, which was nice of him seeing that two thousand people a week would be wearing out his carpet on the way in to buy tickets. Of course, they might just buy a few other things on the way out, too. I smiled. I thought that might spoil his lunch.

There is a creed among Newfoundlanders that no one shall leave their hospitable land with the slightest cause to speak ill of it, and this somehow made my meeting with Derek Bowring that much more of a shock. He didn't conform. So I didn't either. I wasn't an actor for nothing. I put on a great show of being immensely pleased about freeing up the programme for all those other merchants who'd been dying for the chance to buy space all season but couldn't because Bowrings had cornered the market. This should provide us with enough new revenue to pay the printer and leave us with a handsome surplus and make things so much *easier* for us next year. As far as the box-office was concerned, I would have to sleep on that one and would let him know in a couple of days. I thought that might give him time to have a nice little nightmare featuring his biggest rival, Lewis Ayre, standing outside Bowrings' main door and directing two thousand theatre ticket buyers to his own emporium next door. Lewis would have taken us, too. But I resisted the temptation because I'd be simply taking my private quarrel public. I would also be needing the box-office for one more week before I left and I wanted to be sure that people still knew the way.

The company didn't all sail home aboard the *Nova Scotia*, but the ones who did got a wild send-off from the townspeople. Oliver flew home. John Holmes stayed on in St. John's to become an announcer with VOCM Radio. Sheila Huntington went to have a look at New York and in no time at all met and married a Latin American diplomat at the United Nations. Hilary and I stayed behind for another reason that only Oliver knew about and happily endorsed. The actors who didn't return with the main company on the boat received the equivalent of their fare back to England in cash and signed a statement that they hadn't been stranded by the London Theatre Company.

Hilary and I gave St. John's a couple of weeks to realize how much they missed the company before announcing a farewell performance for the two of us. I had a hunch that I was going to need a little more capital than I possessed for the launch of season number two. For our benefit production we chose *The Voice of the Turtle,* the three-hander John van Druten comedy that in New York had enjoyed one of the longest runs in American theatrical history. Out of my own pocket, I paid a handsome fee to George to design and paint the set and also to Gladys Richards, staying in St. John's for a while with Mum, to play the third part. I kept completely separate accounts for the production so that not a single expense was borne by the London Theatre Company. St. John's turned out in loyal strength, and by the end of the week I had considerably enhanced my financial position. Oliver was absolutely delighted when he heard. Harry was incensed.

I returned the Austin to Hugh Baird, paid all the bills and picked up a first draft of our financial statements. I had Art disconnect the dimmer board and lighting control panel and store them at Baird's wharf for the summer. The rent on this space would be our only expense while we were away. We decided to leave the lighting instruments hanging right where they were, all positioned and cabled ready for our return in the fall. But we did take the precaution of removing the fiendishly expensive 500-watt bulbs just in case there was some budding Edison in grade twelve who could figure out a way to power them up again.

George hung up his paintbrushes for the summer and took off for a look at the United States, financially fortified by the cash equivalent of two fares, one to England and one back again, ready to rejoin us for season number two. Hilary and I headed for Nova Scotia.

nineteen

Halifax smelled good right from the start. The Queen Elizabeth High School Auditorium sat there like a WELCOME mat in the middle of the most prominent and accessible spot in the city. Compared to Bishop Feild the Queen Elizabeth was palatial with 1250 tip-up seats, a sloping auditorium floor and a sixty-foot-wide stage opening. There was only one snag. The rent was in line with the going rate for palaces, too. No special deal for a full week. Simply multiply the single performance fee by seven, they said. When I suggested we might just as well forget Halifax and take the company to Broadway, a special meeting of the School Board was hastily convened. The members were mostly Scots and weren't about to see a wee windfall for the ratepayers vanishing in a cloud of Sassenach dust. By tradition, they were also masters of the mean bargain. I wasn't too bad at that myself and made them empty their sporrans a little more than they intended. Even so, we ended up paying four times as much rent per week than we did in St. John's. Halifax theatre-goers were going to have to dig a little deeper.

The auditorium superintendent would have to be dealt with, too. He'd settled in to a comfy routine of a couple of bookings a week and was almost in shock at the prospect of having to work the full six nights he was paid for. He also regarded the place as his own personal property. In the first half-hour I'd heard quite enough of *my* auditorium and *my* stage. He had me feeling I should have gone down to my socks before daring to set foot on it. That was the moment I looked down and made the appalling discovery that I was standing on hardwood. No architect who'd done his homework would have specified anything but softwood for a stage floor in 1952. How else would you be able to stop scenery from falling flat on its face? It was held upright by stage braces fastened to the floor with stage screws. A stage screw was hand-forged with a large loop for a head, one that you could wrap your hand round rather like a giant corkscrew and twist into the floor

168

in a hurry when you had a quick set change.

"*Screws!* In *my* stage floor?"

I'm glad he said it then and didn't save it up for the Fall. All we'd need with a quick "get-in" would be a showdown with a house-proud janitor. I went straight out and found a local sailmaker to run up some miniature sandbags like the ones the film people used to anchor their braces to concrete floors in the studios. Next I tracked down a Girl Guide mistress whose troop would usher and sell programmes for a donation of twenty-five dollars a week. I picked up an advertising rate card from the local newspaper, fixed up advance box-office facilities at Phinney's the stationers on Barrington Street and booked the best of the rooms behind the bed-and-breakfast signs that ringed the High School auditorium. I finally dropped in on the Provincial Treasury and confirmed the ugly rumour that theatre tickets were subject to a 12 ½ percent hospitals tax – not something you'd want to find out after a five-week supply had just arrived from the printer. Only then did Hilary and I get on the plane for England.

I waited until we were in the airport cab well on the way towards London before I allowed myself the luxury of feeling tired. I had played in seventeen out of twenty-six productions, mostly leads, directed four others and business-managed the whole shooting match with the solitary help of a lone box-office assistant. It was inevitable that my mind should flash back to this particular moment of reflection twenty-seven years later when I was appointed Artistic Director of the Shaw Festival at Niagara-on-the-Lake and presented with an administrative staff of thirty-seven, all of whose names and fancy titles were emblazoned like an honours list on the back page of the theatre programme. I remember causing something of a stir at my first meeting in the Boardroom when, befitting a true child of the commercial theatre, I suggested that the back page was surely a monument to our inefficiency and not really something we should brag about.

Oliver had a spare room waiting for us in his flat, four stone flights up and no lift, in Redcliffe Square just off the Old Brompton Road in South Kensington. There was also a huge pile of large manila envelopes that couldn't possibly contain anything else but a résumé and an eight-by-ten glossy.

"Over five hundred of them," gloated Oliver, "all dying to get out of England and come with us next season."

"Oliver," I said, brutally *non sequitur,* "we have to get rid of Harry." His happy grin did a quick cross-fade to his spaniel look. "Has to be done, old boy. Sorry. I can't go through a rerun of last Christmas."

I told him he needn't worry. I would do all the talking. I might have to be a bit of a bastard, but no more, I assured him, than Harry had been to me at the Balsam back in December. I knew exactly what I had to do, how I had to do it and when, which would be just as soon as I'd managed to get over prop-lag or whatever it was we called it in the days before jets. I have never been one to shirk confrontations. I don't enjoy them but I have to get them out of the way. A problem that sits on my shelf grows bigger, at least in my mind if not in reality. Oliver and I were at Harry's flat in Baker Street within the week.

I kicked off the meeting. If it sounded off the cuff, I can assure you it was anything but. I'd been quietly rehearsing myself for days.

I began with the financial statements. They were the first ones I'd ever really studied and I was fascinated by them. In later life I would be called upon to present dozens of them as Honorary Treasurer of no less than four large theatrical organizations, one of them for twenty-two years – the ACTRA Fraternal Benefit Society with assets in excess of a hundred and fifty million dollars. But this was my debut. I didn't know then what I know now and I didn't want to muck it up. The auditors had helped by picking out the highlights for me but these still had to be properly fed and timed like the best lines in any good play. And of course I saved up everything for the punchline: we had earned a net return of 130 percent on our original investment.

Before Harry had a chance to start mentally spending his share, I told him I was afraid the auditors hadn't left him with much after deducting the cost of his family's air tickets and the bills from the Newfoundland Hotel. Minus, of course, the $22.50 a week we'd have paid for him had he stayed at the Balsam. Oliver's dividend and mine would be a clear two thousand dollars apiece. So now, all that remained was to realize our assets, consolidate our sterling and dollar bank accounts and wind up the company.

I was dying to sneak in a quick glance at Oliver but I didn't dare. I didn't want to give any suggestion of collusion which there certainly hadn't been. I'd kept him totally in the dark about what I was going to say because I wanted him to look genuinely stunned. He did. So did Harry.

"Wind up? We made a profit for Christ's sake!"

"Yes, but why did we make a profit, Harry? Because I did four people's jobs. That profit is just about what it would cost to take three more bodies to St. John's, pay them, feed them and ship them back again. We'd end up breaking even. It's not worth the worry. Besides, nobody but an idiot would do it all over again: four people's work for one person's salary for twenty-six weeks and then come back here and hand you half the profit? No thanks. Nothing personal." I smiled, a really warm one. I stood up and started shovelling papers into my briefcase. Come on Harry, that's your cue for God's sake! The pause was becoming unbearable so I tossed in the alternate ending: "I suppose if we all owned equal shares and I got *some* help, I might have another crack at it, but – " I left the word hanging there. We'd almost got to the door before he called us back.

"All right, supposing I did agree to a three-way split. Would you go back then?"

"Oh, I don't know. I'm really awfully tired, Harry. How do you feel, Oliver?"

"Whatever you think, cock."

"You're a great help. Well– " I sighed. My pause beat anything we ever got from the great Macready. "All right, Harry. I'll have one more go." And in my best throwaway technique, I tossed in, "You'll work out how many shares you'll transfer to each of us? For cash, of course."

Oliver maintained his poker-face all the way along the corridor, into the elevator, out through the lobby, into the street and round the corner. Then he exploded with glee.

"You bastard!"

"But Oliver, I told you that's what I was going to be." It was only a small dose compared to the one I dished out at our next meeting one week later.

We had given our cheques to Harry for the shares we were buying from him, initialled the minutes recording the transfer, signed each other's share certificates and applied the company's great seal that I'd thoughtfully brought back with me from the lawyers in St. John's. Harry handed out the new certificates like prizes on speech day. When I was quite sure we had the right ones, I grasped Oliver firmly by the hand and said, "Old boy, that's a third of the vote you're holding there. Here's my third. Between us you and I now control the company. Be seeing you Harry." As I turned to wave, I saw the corner of his mouth start to twitch, just like it had in my bedroom doorway at the Balsam.

I whisked Oliver off to lunch and a quick martini before remorse had a chance to set in and start making me feel as big a shit as I knew he felt. We went to Simpsons in the Strand which should always be reserved for the highest celebrations. There, the chef rolls to your table a whole baron of beef in a silver tureen and carves it before your eyes.

At this same Simpsons, far too few years later, this lovely man and

I were to share another lunch that would be our last one together. He was dying of cancer and made it up the grand staircase unaided though in great pain, just to prove to Hilary and me that he was going to be fine and there was nothing for us to worry about.

They held a memorial service for him at the actors' church, St Martin-in-the-Fields, where the flower of the profession and the cricket world met and remembered him in the light-hearted fashion that he would have wanted. Finally someone said, "And now I think Oliver is waiting for us all at the Salisbury." And everybody walked the few yards up St Martin's Lane to the actors' pub and drank one last toast to Oliver Gordon Battcock.

Gearing up for season number two was a cake-walk compared to number one. It was the difference between packing a suitcase for the summer holidays and kitting yourself out for a six-month safari into the unknown. This time we knew what to expect when we got there. We also had an advance routine that had already proved itself and laid bare its weaknesses; we had clear box-office indications of what St. John's liked, what it didn't like and what it might learn to like with a little coaxing. And we no longer had to work double shift in England. We had both saved up enough to carry us comfortably through the summer. From here on it would be all London Theatre Company.

Even Baker Street had gone way down on the worry list, though it was still holding one trump card that bothered me – the Actors' Equity performance bond. There was no way Oliver and I could tie up for six months a deposit with British Actors' Equity to cover two weeks' salary and the cost of a return ticket for every actor on the payroll. This meant the contracts would once again have to be issued in the name of Mid-Century Entertainments who already held a big enough Equity bond. It also meant Harry could refuse to sign them, insist on some nominations of his own or pull the plug on the whole operation if he felt peeved enough. Somehow we had to weasel our way into the Theatrical Managers' Association. Their members operated as a kind of Lloyd's of London who guaranteed each other in the event of default. They were big league and powerful enough to call the shots with Actors' Equity. Their word was their bond and that covered any of their members. I asked Oliver if perchance he knew anybody in the TMA.

"Of course cock, Biff Killick. He's on the Board. And he's also president of my cricket club."

And *that* is how we came to join the greats in the Theatrical Managers' Association. Operation Harry was almost complete. But not quite. The *coup de grâce* was still a month or so away.

Once again Oliver and I set out to choose, cast and costume twenty-six different plays. First we studied the popularity poll for 1951. Aside from the revue, *Screech,* box-office honours had ended up in this order:

> *1. A Streetcar Named Desire*
> *2. The Perfect Woman*
> *3. Jane Eyre*
> *4. High Temperature*
> *5. Wuthering Heights*
> *6. Rookery Nook*
> *7. The Taming of the Shrew.*

What we obviously needed was *Jane Eyre II* and *Wuthering Heights III.* There were plenty of farces left but a scarcity of costume dramas. But now our audience had been broken-in, Oliver and I both felt sure that they'd stick with the pack if, every five weeks or so, we gave them something they ought to see rather than a play we knew they wouldn't be able to stay away from. Once we'd agreed on a playbill, we went to see our old friend Michael Ellis, theatrical costumier-de-luxe at Moss Bros, drenched him in well-deserved flattery, gave him a personal thank-you cheque worth about a month's salary and came away with the same generous rental deal as before.

This time we wouldn't need to cast by category (LM for Leading Man, CJ for Character Juvenile). We already had the actual names of most of them. We hadn't managed to land everyone on our wanted list but we'd made an impressive start. The others would come from lesser lists like second choice, third choice and last resort. Anywhere but from an audition.

There is a growing belief among new actors coming along that it should be mandatory for managements to hold auditions before choosing actors for any part whatever and that the mere possession of an Equity card bestows upon them a God-given right to be an auditionee. This makes about as much sense as telling a grocer he must interview every cocoa salesman before ordering a case of Fry's. I have to say that, after almost sixty years of auditioning and being auditioned, I have acquired serious doubts about the reliability of this

173

method of putting the right actor into the right part when it is to be performed before a live audience. Auditions can be faked. Auditioners can be fooled. Many of us, in our early theatre days in London, knew of an actor who would get the script ahead of time, be vigorously coached in the audition scene, get the part and invariably be fired before the end of the first week's rehearsal. An audition can tell you whether an actor looks right for the part, sounds right for the part, but it can't really tell you whether he or she can *act* the part. And unless you are a dwarf auditioning for Jack the Giant-Killer or a six-footer reading for Tiny Tim, it doesn't really matter a damn whether or not you look the part provided you can act it and you have a big enough make-up box.

Films, of course are different. Under the microscopic eye of the close-up lens you simply must look the part, and they don't seem to mind so much if you can't act it so long as you can think it. But for the live theatre, those catering to the audience of tomorrow will need to take a long hard look at the present system which, with its ever-more-stringent performers' union code, tempts managements to audition local performers for parts already secretly awarded to a foreign actor. This engenders false hopes in the actor at the bottom of the ladder, demeans the actor at the top and provides a feeding trough along the way for the director who is on a power trip. Some auditioners are now but a mere step away from committing actor abuse.

It was always our view in the London Theatre Company that the only audition that really counted was a public one in front of a paying audience. To that end Oliver and I would climb into his battered Volkswagen and drive two hundred miles, if needed, to see someone actually perform. As a commercial company, unsponsored and unsubsidized, we were in no position to invest a trans-Atlantic fare and a watertight six-month contract in somebody who couldn't.

There was a well-tried format to be followed when casting a repertory company like ours. We would need a leading man and a leading lady, a character man and a character woman, a juvenile man and a juvenile girl and two character juves, one of each sex. (It is interesting that tradition should have reserved the genteel term of "lady" exclusively for the leading actress: from then on, respect goes steadily downhill to "woman" for the character actress and mere "girls" for the rest.) These eight players were the basic minimum and could be augmented with utility actors. If the budget would stand it, a utility actor might be replaced with a second leading man or lady.

The London Theatre Company of 1952-53 carried an acting

strength of twelve, with actors outnumbering actresses by seven to five, simply because playwrights wrote more parts for men than for women and still do. The genius of George Paddon-Foster would again be responsible for our visual impact and this time we would bring a business assistant for me – Rae Ellison. She had been doing a similar job at Bromley Theatre on the outskirts of London and had a photograph of herself presenting a bouquet to the Queen Mother which would look good on the front page of the St. John's *Daily News.*

We had lined up an even stronger company than the previous year. We were no longer an unknown quantity and it was easier to get good people. John Woodnutt would be back and would bring his actress wife Roma Haycock as Assistant Stage Manager. We'd have a new stage manager named Richard Eastham who had already toured Canada with the Sadler's Wells Ballet Company. Joining Hilary on the distaff side would be Jacqueline Lacey, who, apart from anything else, could sing and had just the right legs for our first Principal Boy in the pantomime *Cinderella;* ex-Salbergian Ruth Perkins, who had endeared herself to me by playing the role that Hilary had refused in my play *And The Whistle Blew;* and a remarkable young character actress named Avis Lennard, who, at twenty-six almost never played a character under the age of fifty. She was to become a great local favourite and return with us for four successive seasons. The newcomers among the men, all capable of playing leads, were David Morrell, Charles Mardel and a young leading man, straight from the Old Vic, named Anthony Newlands. The 1952/3 company was now complete and committed.

Harry sat biting his nails in Baker Street waiting for our call for a long time. When he obviously couldn't stand it any longer, he rang and asked when he was going to sign the contracts. I told him breezily that Oliver had already signed them in his first official act as a member of the Theatrical Managers' Association. I could almost hear his mouth twitch over the telephone.

We wouldn't be needing his help either in obtaining performing rights for the twenty-six productions. I was going to be very unpatriotic and book them all through New York because, while I was clearing the rights to *Voice of the Turtle* for our personal benefit performance in April, I made the astounding discovery that New York play agents charged only a four percent royalty for all but the very latest releases from Broadway. In Britain, they started off at ten percent and stayed there, even for hoary old potboilers like *The Ghost Train.* Diverting lucrative business away from her shores brought a few screams from British play agents and undoubtedly caused much gnashing of dentures at the British Treasury, but it yielded the London Theatre Company a cash bonus of six percent of the entire week's takings for over half our productions. I suspect a certain gentleman buried in broadloom at the Treasury would have been even angrier had he known that we'd converted sterling capital into dollars without breaking a single currency law. We had paid for last year's supplies and services in sterling, earned it back in dollars and kept them in Canada to capitalize our company under a Canadian charter.

Things were going so smoothly that Oliver and I both agreed I should take up Basil Thomas's offer to make a triumphant return to Wolverhampton after a five-year absence to "star" in the actor-proof part of Garry Essendine in Noël Coward's *Present Laughter*. I'd have an easy two weeks because I'd only just finished playing him in St. John's. On the Monday night, when I made my first entrance at the top of a magnificent Cowardian staircase, the welcome couldn't have been more tumultuous if I'd been The Master himself. It continued the same all week, and the emotional strain as I made my farewell curtain speech on the Saturday night was hard to handle. It would have been quite uncontrollable had I known at the time that I had just given my last performance on an English stage.

It wasn't, however, to be my final *production* in the U.K. I was to do one more twenty years later, as a director. It was late in 1972 when Don Lander phoned from London.

"Les, the Brits have never seen a big industrial show, North American style. How would you like to come and direct the first one?"

Don was President of Chrysler U.K and several years shy of his anointing as head of Canada Post. He and I had worked on many a Chrysler show together in his capacity as Vice-President of Chrysler Canada. An industrial car show was a mega-musical in which the stars of the show were the latest new cars. The twenty top actors, singers and dancers were the supporting cast. They were backed by a twenty-four piece orchestra and lavish stage settings. These shows were high-budget, high-pressure and high-paying. Don's offer was sumptuous: a free service flat in Berkeley Square, my Canadian Industrial director's fee, and an obscenely high per diem at a time when, believe it or not, you could eat out in London for half what it cost in Toronto. He could have got away with far less generous terms if he'd told me right at the outset that I would be directing the show at one of the most famous theatres in the English-speaking world – the Theatre Royal, Drury Lane.

176

I naturally assumed that Chrysler had managed to catch the Lane empty at one of her rare moments between long runs. I was therefore quite startled on the plane over to pick up an English newspaper and see a large ad for a live stage production of *Gone with the Wind* "now taking bookings for the next three months" at our very theatre.

The fact that Industrial shows were usually performed at ten o'clock in the morning and the curtain didn't go up on *Gone with the Wind* until eight in the evening didn't console me at all since the stage settings required for the Chrysler Show were not within a continent of Margaret Mitchell country. The "Burning of Atlanta" was hardly a suitable backdrop for the reveal of the latest Chrysler Cordoba. I had seen and marveled at this particular scene the night I arrived. They even had Rhett and Scarlett crossing the stage in a buggy pulled by a horse that had been trained to shy at the flames, rear up on cue and prance offstage on its hind legs. The production was spectacular, Hollywood gone live with scenery changing by the minute before your eyes. Fast-changing stage sets were "flown" in and out on counterweighted lines and Drury Lane must have had a hundred of them, every one loaded to the full. Unfortunately, I needed forty for the Chrysler Show so we had a problem. I insisted that I must have complete use of the stage for five full days before showtime. The costs would be horrendous but were not my problem. Working out the logistics was.

While I rehearsed the cast for a week in a rehearsal room, I selected the "lines" I would need to hang the Chrysler sets and fly them in to the exact positions where they would be needed. On the evening before our first in-theatre rehearsal, at the end of the performance of *Gone with the Wind,* a brand new crew took over the Drury Lane stage, let down the lines I had selected, removed the GWTW scenery from them and carried it offstage into two enormous pantechnicons which were then parked overnight in an adjacent carpark. The moment the dock doors were clear, two equally large pantechnicons moved in and disgorged our scenery into the waiting arms of our night crew, who then hung it on the now-vacant lines and reweighted them. A complete false stage floor with a built-in turntable was then off-loaded and installed. By 8 am the stage was ready for me, the regular house crew came on duty and we went to work. At 3 pm on the dot, the entire midnight process was reversed with the last piece of GWTW scenery barely in position before the curtain went up on the evening performance. In five days of this horrendous routine, the Drury Lane crew grew steadily wearier, weathier and more and more determined not to let me down. With seven Chrysler shows already behind me, I knew from experience that we were going to make it, until that fateful morning when I arrived at the stage door at 7.30 am to be greeted by a white-faced resident stage manager saying, "Sorry Les, you can't have the stage today."

I have a special vocabulary for occasions such as this. A reasonable translation would have been, "What the hell do you mean, I can't have the stage? We do the show in three days! I've got to have it!"

"Terribly sorry Les, but the poor old horse got over-excited in the "Burning of Atlanta" last night. He just made it offstage and dropped dead of a heart attack, still in the shafts. I've got to spend all day rehearsing the understudy horse."

And that's how Britain's first Chrysler show nearly didn't make it. It did, of course. It always does. And the slight sluggishness here and there was probably noticeable only to me. When I left, I gave every member of the magnificent Drury Lane stage crew a bottle of scotch.

In 1952, twenty years before that Chrysler show and not all that far from Drury Lane, I was riding on the top of a double-decker bus when something caught my eye that gave me a nasty twinge of guilty conscience. Sitting on the sidewalk was a row of theatre seats. Remembering my promise to St. John's to do something about those squeaky chairs, I got off the bus and walked back along Kingsway. I found myself standing outside the famous Stoll Theatre which was in the process of reseating the stalls. The seats that had nobly served their time were no longer young but still quite magnificent. They were elegant examples of old world craftsmanship that no longer existed. They were enormous, almost armchairs, with fully sprung tip-up seats and padded backs upholstered in rich red plush. Here and there, the sun picked out a spot that had worn to a dark pink but that didn't even show inside a theatre which never saw a sunbeam.

I found the manager and discovered that these were seats with a history. At least one member of every Royal Family all over the world had sat on them at one time or another to watch stars as far back as Irving and Terry and Tree. The two most recent celebrities to occupy them had been honeymooners Elizabeth Taylor and Michael Wilding just two weeks before.

The manager was asking ten shillings ($1.40) a seat. I phoned Gordon Stirling in St. John's, got him to pledge the FAGA to share the cost of buying six hundred, and closed the deal. Then began a series of woes that taught me never again to be that impetuous in my

178

business life.

The first shock came when the shipping agents told me it would cost fifteen times what we'd paid for the seats just to crate them. I'd made a terrible error in not discovering they couldn't be dismantled like their modern counterparts and shipped in neat stacks of arms, backs and bases. They had been made in the days when seats were built to last, locked together for life with mortice and tenon and glue in inseparable blocks of eight. We'd end up crating as much air as chair. In desperation, I got Furness Withy to agree to ship them uncrated at our own risk. Since that ruled out Insurance against damage, I took out some out of our own: I bought an extra four hundred seats. Off the thousand went to Liverpool just as they were and onto the *RMS Newfoundland*, sister ship to the *Nova Scotia* which would be bringing the company two weeks later. Then I sat down to contemplate the other fruits of my impetuosity, like the damage to our seating capacity. It was likely to be considerable. Eight of the new seats would take up as much space as ten of the squeaky ones.

I began to draw up a new seating plan. If we were going to reseat we might as well do it properly. On a flat floor it was essential to "stagger" the seats so that you never sat directly behind the person in front but in the gap between two of them. This meant losing yet another seat in every second row. By the time I'd finished we'd lost almost a hundred seats, seven hundred sources of revenue per week, an economic disaster.

The only tourniquet I could think of to stem the bleeding was to get rid of the centre aisle. St. John's was quite rightly a very fire-conscious city, but surely the fire people would see that three aisles were not needed now that we had tip-up seats and three less sitters per row to evacuate in an emergency. I passed the argument on to Gordon Stirling, with backup photos and dimensions of the new seats and the proposed changes to the seating plan. I asked him to put on the pressure because I wouldn't be able to open the box-office until I knew exactly what seats I would have to sell. Which led to problem number three.

The order had already gone in to the ticket printers based on our old seating plan. There might be time to change it but something told me to leave it as it was. Anything could happen between now and opening night. The fire people might say "No." The ship carrying the chairs might be two weeks late or even hit an iceberg. Better to have too many tickets than not enough. We could always tear out the ones for seats that were no longer there. It turned out to be a wise decision.

179

We didn't go right back to the status quo but we were forced to compromise for reasons we hadn't even thought about.

I now had nothing left to do in London but a hell of a lot in St. John's, not the least being the first-time job of selling several pages of advertising space in the house programmes. Oliver left Hilary and myself out of the opening play which meant we could both fly to St. John's about three weeks ahead of the company. At least, that was the idea.

If you are going anywhere by plane or bus or train or even dogcart and I am a fellow passenger, don't get on it. I am the patron Jonah of travellers. I have broken long-distance records all over the world where "long" equals the time it took to get there. My TCA trip with Hilary in the Fall of 1952 still holds the cup.

It was a Sunday evening at Heathrow when we taxied out to the runway, spent longer than usual waiting for clearance from the tower and taxied back again. We deplaned and were advised that there would be a twenty-minute delay due to engine trouble. This slowly grew to one hour, two hours and finally four before we were all herded on to a bus and driven to a hotel in Kensington just round the corner from Oliver's flat that we'd left only a few hours earlier. As we had already been through exit customs, we were "in bond" and were not allowed out of the hotel or to come into personal contact with anybody who might slip us a wad of illegal currency. At 5:30 am we were dragged out of bed, loaded on to the same bus and taken back to the airport. This time the plane took off and deposited us in Shannon for refuelling and a hot meal in the terminal plus a look at the world's first duty-free shop. We reboarded the plane, taxied out to the runway and replayed the exact scene we'd performed the night before at Heathrow except that it was a different engine that had now joined the cast. As there were no understudy engines at Shannon, they would have to fly back empty to London on three props for a replacement. They'd be back for us in twenty-four hours. To appease the uglier passengers (which included me), they took us all on a bus tour of Galway Bay and then bedded us down for the night at the airport hotel. In the morning, we were roused once again like the dawn patrol and reboarded the plane. It was now Tuesday.

We refuelled without incident at Keflavik and Goose Bay and were finally headed for Newfoundland and Montreal, when word came from the captain that we would be overshooting Gander because it was fogged in. I looked through the window. It was a bright, sunny day and you could already see the Island of Newfoundland clear as a bell.

I gripped the arm of the stewardess and fiercely pointed her finger at it. She very smartly whisked me off to the flight deck where the captain sat me down in the co-pilot's seat and slowly brought down my blood pressure. Landing two passengers and their luggage at Gander, he gently explained, meant another hour-and-a-half delay for over a hundred passengers already two days behind schedule. He'd rather offend the two of us than a hundred of them.

By the time we got to Montreal, the last plane had already left for St. John's. It was overnight stay number three. We got to our final destination late on Wednesday afternoon. Alcock and Brown had beaten us by nearly two and a half days back in 1919.

twenty

The miseries of the preceeding days quickly melted away under the warmth of George and Ira's welcome and soon the talk was only of the future. The set for the opening production was already built, sized and thirsting for paint. What should they start on next? I rounded up Art Noseworthy, our comptroller of the volts and amps, and we all went to the Balsam for a briefing and a reunion drink from my duty-free bottle.

We would follow five plays at Bishop Feild Hall with five at the Queen Elizabeth. I hated like hell to tell them that they wouldn't be the same five. I wanted to play safe with Halifax and include two proven money-spinners from our first season in St. John's.

The big problem would be Ira's. George would still have to come up with a set a week and he wouldn't give a designer's damn whether he painted it in Halifax or in St. John's. Ira would have no choice. Every piece of scenery for Halifax would have to be constructed in advance in our scene shop at Baird's Wharf, since there were no facilities for building sets backstage at the Queen Elizabeth. You could paint but you couldn't carpenter. And there'd be a janitor walking around with a magnifying glass just looking for the first speck of sawdust.

Then I dropped the real bombshell: we would close on the Saturday night in St. John's, strip the stage, whisk everything and everybody off to the airport and open in Halifax the following Monday. We were venturing into the unknown and couldn't afford to lose a single night's revenue. Even so, I can't believe how the cautious me of today could have taken such an enormous gamble. November was fog month and Torbay was top of the league for cancelled flights. Two weeks without a single plane in or out was the current record and counting. I can remember a time when the flights were grounded, the *Nova Scotia* couldn't come into port because the sea was frozen over and the train was stuck in a snowdrift on the Gaff Topsails. St. John's was virtually in a state of siege. Luckily we weren't going anywhere at the time except back and forth between Bishop Feild Hall and the Balsam Hotel.

After I'd topped up their glasses and coaxed the colour back into their cheeks, we started to draw up battle plans. George would have to design every Halifax set in advance. Ira would take the floor plans and meticulously tabulate each piece of scenery, window, door, fireplace, shelf, staircase, window seat, pelmet and built-in cupboard: everything that couldn't be borrowed and had to be built. Against each item he would then indicate where it would come from – stock, re-use or build – and then get busy on the build part. He could save himself work and us shipping costs by noting that any piece used in production number one in Halifax would already be on the spot and available for repainting for production number three and so on. He'd also get another break: *She Stoops to Conquer* would be on both playbills. All he'd have to build would be the extra pieces to turn the set into a stretched version for the Queen Elizabeth's sixty-foot stage. All the St. John's scenery would be shipped ahead by rail and ferry with the set for the opening production painted and ready to put up. That gave him seven weeks at the most and he'd still have to keep George happy with the weekly set demands for St. John's.

Art's job would be to list every item of electrical equipment, assign it a packing case number and make sure the cases were big enough to receive it. They hadn't been opened since the day we first arrived in 1951 and our inventory had grown a bit since then. I would be responsible for the logistics of getting everything and everybody there on time.

George and Ira, who'd thought I was being kind, now knew the real reason why I had squeezed the production budget to take them on three weeks early. I'd given them a hell of a challenge. Could they meet it? They'd have died rather than tell me they couldn't. Then I went to see Gordon Stirling.

The fire people and the City had approved the new seating plan with conditions: the seats had to be permanently anchored to wooden strips with a strict minimum space between rows. The *Newfoundland* had already docked and the seats themselves would be off-loaded in the morning. Gordon promised to pick me up at the Balsam and take me down to the wharf.

I saw the flashes of red plush on the dockside long before we got to the bottom of the hill but something was wrong. They weren't shaped like seats. When we got closer, I could see why. Our thousand seats were a tangled pile of matchwood.

For a long time I just stood there. I couldn't move. I couldn't speak. I couldn't look at Gordon. Just at that pathetic heap of theatrical history. I tried to think positive but I couldn't. I'd been rash, I'd let our theatre-goers down, I'd thrown away a stack of money.

Finally I said, "Let's go and get Ira."

Ira took one look, put his arm round my shoulder, gave it a powerful squeeze and said, "Now don't you be worrying, my son."

The salvage work began immediately. Dave Baird, out of the kindness of his heart, gave us a spare warehouse right behind the scene-shop. Gordon mustered his volunteer ticket-taking army, and they went to work in shifts with Ira as foreman, splitting his time between them and George. First they isolated any group of chairs that could still stand up unassisted. Then they sorted the rest into four piles: seats, backs, sides and junk. I armed them with half a hardware store and left them to it. I was badly behind in my schedule as an ad salesman.

It took me a week but I signed up twenty-nine different advertisers. They chose their own spaces from a twelve-page mock-up, anything from one-eighth to a full page. And every one of them signed up for the entire season of twenty-one weeks. I promised them all there would be a half-page editorial on every double page spread. I worked out that after paying the printer, we'd end up with a net new revenue of nearly a hundred and eighty dollars a week, almost ten percent of our total running expenses. God bless you, Derek Bowring.

Each time I dropped into the salvage room, my feeling of utter hopelessness ebbed, but only a little. The finished clusters of threes, fours and bigger were growing, but with a gut-wrenching slowness. Box-office opening day loomed and I had to know exactly what the final tally would be. Ira would only volunteer a tentative two hundred and fifty. Out of a *thousand?* I begged him to do a wreck by wreck recount and squeeze it up to three hundred. That would at least cover the $2 and $1.50 sections on the main floor. I didn't want the fifty-centers at the back to feel slighted, so we would arrange to put their slatted seats on risers and give them a periscopic view. The balcony was stepped and already had the best view of the stage. It could stay as it was.

I went back to the office, drew up a new seating plan and gave a rush order to the printer. The new arrangement had cost us forty-two seats – forty-two paying customers on "house full" nights, nearly three hundred on a capacity week. I put the box-office assistant to work

Right: my mother
with her youngest
son Peter, c.1920.

Below right: the rest
of us – myself, Fred,
John, c.1918.

Below: my dad,
before he was
married, c.1910.

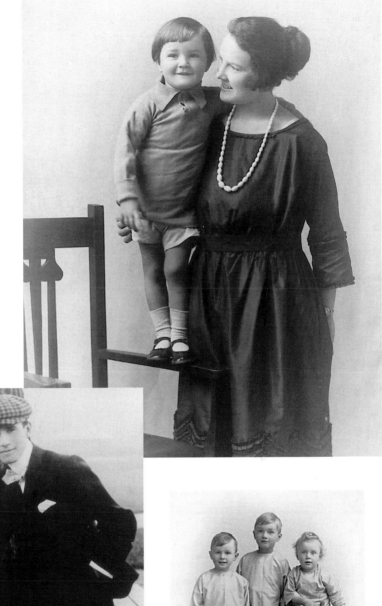

Opposite, top left: I become an actor in 1939 – and this is the glossy I sent round to talent agents to let them know it.

Opposite, top right: a new publicity shot in 1946 to tell the same agents that I'm back from the war.

Opposite, bottom: set design by George Paddon-Foster and (inset this page) house programme for the premiere of my play *And the Whistle Blew* at the Penge Empire, 1949.

Above: playing Dr Sloper in *The Heiress* at Eastbourne in 1950 – too young for the part!

WITH THE ALEXANDRA COMPANY IN ST. JOHN'S, 1947-48

Left: The first English company in thirty years arrives in St. John's, Newfoundland, in December 1947. Left to right: Raymond Frances, Alec McCowen, Roy Hannah, Eileen Draycott, Pauline Williams, Hilary Vernon, Stephen Ward, Pix and John Gabriel (the producer and his wife) with Margaret Towner between them, Barbara Addenbrooke (set designer), Bill Longstaffe and Ronald Lane. I seem to be hidden behind Barbara, just under the TCA roundel.

Opposite, below: Being hidden in the above group, I took no chances and parked myself next to the producer (John Gabriel, beside the Customs officer). In the centre is Hilary Vernon whom I would one day marry.

Below: as the USAAF Lieutenant in *While the Sun Shines*, February 1948. Standing behind me are Alec McCowen, Hilary Vernon, Roy Hannah, Raymond Frances and Pauline Williams.

WITH THE LONDON THEATRE
COMPANY IN ST. JOHN'S, 1951-57

Top left: the play being rehearsed
for the following week is Agatha
Christie's *Murder on the Nile*, but
the set is for the current production
of *Seagulls over Sorrento*. Oliver
Gordon sits in the director's chair,
Freddie Davies is the prompter in
the corner, and the actors are (L-R)
Bill Glover, Joseph Shaw, Ronnie
Fraser and Jack Hine.

Partners in the London Theatre
Company, clockwise from above:
    Leslie Yeo, Actor-Manager
    Hilary Vernon, Leading Lady
    George Paddon-Foster, Designer
    Oliver Gordon, Director

A publicity shot:
hearing Hilary's lines
at a hotel in Halifax.

Above: *Johnny Belinda* broke box-office records in St. John's in 1952, but the next year died 900 miles away in Halifax. Hilary, as the deaf-mute Belinda, is being seduced by Charles Jarrott as Black Macdonald.

Opposite, top: Our sixth and last company being interviewed at our theatre by the American base radio station VOUS. Note the Stoll theatre chairs in the front row. Sitting on them are Oliver Gordon and Nancie Herrod; standing behind are Elizabeth Howe, Bill Glover, Gillie Fenwick, Ronald Fraser, Joseph Shaw, Mary Williams and Freddie Davies.

Opposite, bottom: Gillie Fenwick and Bill Glover give me a hard time as the Petty Officer in *Seagulls over Sorrento*, February 1956.

Marguerite's entrance in the ballroom scene in *Camille*, which played eleven cities from Nova Scotia to Niagara Falls in 1954. From left: Avis Lennard, Bernard Thompson, Honor Shepherd, Kevin Stoney, Sally Day, Hilary Vernon, Robert Dorning and Charles Jarrott.

THE LONDON THEATRE COMPANY ON TOUR, 1954-55

Above: Hilary, Honor Shepherd, Bob Dorning and Patricia Gould seem happy to let Denny Spence worry about whether they left anything on the train.

Opposite, above: Our 1954 company disembarks from the ferry in Sydney NS in the middle of winter and begins a tour that will end in Niagara Falls in midsummer. Me, Joseph Shaw, Avis Lennard, Victor Adams, Patricia Gould, Denny Spence and Anthony Sagar.

Right: Boarding the famous Newfie Bullet in St. John's, 1955

Above: The 1954 company on the sidewalk in front of the old Grand Theatre in London, Ontario – me, Hilary, Bob Dorning, Honor Shepherd, Kevin Stoney, Sally Day, Ken Basquette (theatre manager), Charles Jarrott, Barbara Bryne, Bernard Thompson and (in front) Avis Lennard and Anthony Newlands.

Opposite, above: Sunday was always open house at the Yeos, and this was one of them during our 1954 summer season in Niagara Falls. Note the bearded George Paddon-Foster, second from right, who was rarely coaxed out of his scene shop.

Opposite, below: Bob Dorning and I discover cake-mixes and try one out for the company.

Above: THE ADVENTURE BEGINS...
Eileen Draycott, Hilary, myself and Pauline Williams
land in St. John's with the Alexandra Company in 1947.

...AND THE LAST CALL
The last remaining players of the sixth and
final London Theatre Company leave St.
John's in 1957 for a new life in Toronto –
Stanley Rixon, Nancie Herrod, Bill Glover,
Joseph Shaw, Gillie Fenwick, Moya Fenwick,
with myself seeing them off.

ON STAGE AT THE SHAW FESTIVAL (all photos by Robert C. Ragsdale)

Above: Paxton Whitehead as King Magnus, myself as Boanerges and Patrick Boxill as Proteus in *The Apple Cart*, 1976.

Opposite, above: Michael Bradshaw as Joseph Percival, Tom Kneebone as Bentley Summerhays, Zoe Caldwell as Lina Szczepanowska, myself as Tarleton and Betty Leighton as Mrs Tarleton in *Misalliance*, 1966.

Opposite, far left: James Valentine as Valentine and myself as The Waiter in *You Never Can Tell*, 1979.

Opposite, left: Kate Reid as Lady Catherine Champion-Cheney, myself as Lord Porteous and Hiram Sherman as Clive Champion-Cheney in Somerset Maugham's *The Circle*, 1967.

ON STAGE AT THE STRATFORD FESTIVAL
(all photos by Robert C. Ragsdale)

Above: Frank Maraden as Sir Andrew Aguecheek
and myself as Sir Toby Belch in *Twelfth Night*,
1975.

Opposite, above: playing Duke Senior to Brian
Bedford's Jaques in *As You Like It*, 1977.

Opposite, below: myself as Capulet and Florence
Paterson as The Nurse in *Romeo and Juliet*, 1977.

My all-time favourite role: as Elwood P. Dowd
in *Harvey*, which I first played in Newfoundland
in 1952. This photo, by Glen Erikson, is from the
Vancouver Playhouse production in 1974.

removing all traces of forty-two numbered tickets for every performance for the entire season. I checked every discard before she threw them away.

When we opened the box-office at Bowrings the following Monday, the line-up was twice as long as the year before. This time around, season-ticket subscribers would be allowed to keep the same seats all season and pay for only five shows at a time in advance. More regulars were what we needed now, not ready cash. What a difference a year made.

As soon as Oliver had seen the cast safely onto the boat train for Liverpool, he boarded a plane where nobody got seasick and flew into St. John's. The war cabinet was now complete and discussed strategy. The moment school was out on Friday afternoon, the first consignment of rebuilt chairs would move in. They wouldn't all be ready and would still be arriving in dribs and drabs all through the following week. We had to hire a skilled furniture maker to do the final battening together into rows of fifteen. Ira's first priority was to George and the two of them would erect the set for our opening play the same weekend. Once it was up, Ira would transfer his talents back to Operation Seat Salvage.

Oliver told me Harry was mad as hell he hadn't heard a word from me about our plans or our progress. I'd already given his early niggling letters the big chill. When they turned nastier, I took them and Oliver down to our lawyer, Fabian O'Dea, who would one day become Lieutenant-Governor of the Province.

"How much information on our day-to-day operations do we have to send him, Fabian?"

"You don't have to send him any if you don't want to."

"We don't?"

"Not a thing. All he's entitled to receive are the financial statements once a year."

"Oliver," I said, "We've just had a board meeting and imposed a total news blackout."

The second London Theatre Company arrived with a splash. The *Daily News* devoted the entire front page of the second section to pictures, motivated I was sure by the paper's new drama critic Grace Sparkes, our unpaid PR officer and tireless champion throughout the rest of the life of the London Theatre Company.

Once the cast moved onstage, we reluctantly had to stop the hammers of the chair restorers and restrict their work schedule to afternoons and evenings. Some of the anxiety must have shown up in our faces because once the cast had finished their first rehearsal and had lunch, the entire company came back to the theatre in work clothes and asked what they could do to help. We gave them needles and thread, furniture polish, Brasso, fabric shampoo, rags, brushes and vacuum cleaners. In three afternoons they had every completed chair in antique showroom condition.

We made opening night with a couple of hours to spare. It wasn't the Stoll Theatre but it didn't look much like Bishop Feild Hall either. And it wasn't Terry or Tree they saw, but Roland Pertwee's *Pink String and Sealing Wax,* a murder mystery with 1880s charm. Despite the drop in our seating capacity, we were right up there with our opening figures for the previous year.

But week two was the key. In 1951 it started a four-week nosedive at the box-office. This time I couldn't believe it. We topped week one. We'd found the magic formula and didn't even know what it was. Could it be that Hilary and I were making our season debut in two wonderful parts as Frank and Ethel in Noël Coward's *This Happy Breed?* Was St. John's trying to send us a message that we didn't really need to forsake them for five weeks and go to Halifax? Or was it the seats? When week three beat week two, it had to be the seats. God Bless London Transport and the 68 bus that took me down Kingsway that summer afternoon.

During *This Happy Breed* week, the passenger agent for Trans-Canada Airlines came to see me. I'd booked the company on the early morning plane to Halifax three Sundays hence and I had told him to reserve space for a stack of excess baggage which would include all our lighting equipment. He had come to measure and record the size of every packing case. One thing really worried him: the maneuverability of the dimmer board. It was not only big, it was heavy. The turnaround time at the airport was strictly twenty minutes because fogs were known to come down pretty fast. At TCA's instigation, a crew arrived immediately after the Saturday night performance of *This Happy Breed,* manhandled the dimmer board and its packing case down the front steps into a van, drove it to the airport and waited for the arrival of the identical North Star that would ship us all to Halifax two Sundays down the road. For twenty minutes they rehearsed loading and off-loading the board into the luggage bay and timed it. Then they brought it back to Bishop Feild Hall and Art hooked it up again for the dress rehearsal of *She Stoops to Conquer* on the Monday.

She Stoops was a recurring favourite on repertory schedules and I had played every major man's role but one, old Hardcastle. Wouldn't you know it, that was the one Oliver wanted me to play? I was all of thirty-seven and the oldest man in the company; so I had to put aside the hard-learned lines and fond memories of my Tony Lumpkin and my Young Marlow to tackle Hardcastle. In the middle of the run, Rae Ellison, my new admin assistant, came to tell me Harry Reynolds was on the phone and he was calling from the Newfoundland Hotel.

He couldn't have timed it better. Another couple of days and I'd have already left for Halifax. I said to tell him we'd meet him at the lawyer's office in an hour.

"What the hell are you guys trying to do to me? You've brought my bloody ulcer back!"

"What's the problem Harry?"

"I haven't heard a bloody word! Surely I'm entitled to know what's going on?"

"Well actually, no." And I tossed the ball into poor old Fabian's court.

Harry immediately wanted us to buy him out. I told him we'd be happy to give him back his investment.

"That's all? You're not going to give me anything for my share of future profits?"

"There won't be any profits, Harry," I told him cheerfully, "Oliver and I will divvy them up as a salary bonus."

When his lip began to tremble, I started to feel sorry for him. Even more when he said rather pathetically, "Aren't you even going to pay me my fare?" I looked at Oliver. His spaniel eyes plainly said, "Can't we?" I nodded to Fabian. And Harry took his money and his fare and walked out of our lives. I got on the plane for Halifax at the end of the week with my snowboots weighing like bedroom slippers.

While Oliver staged two more plays in St. John's, I had just two weeks to open the advance box-office and spread the news that the British were coming. The first ads appeared in the *Mail-Star* and announced that tickets at $3.00, $2.00 and $1.00 plus tax were on sale at Phinney's the stationers on the second floor. There would be a ten percent discount on a season ticket for all five productions. As I walked through the front door of Phinney's the first morning, the girl on fountain pens came running across excitedly and said, "You're going to do terribly well. We've never had a queue up there before."

At the first lull, I took two comps to the *Mail-Star* for the drama critic. I was told that the paper not only didn't have one, but also didn't consider that sort of thing a newspaper's responsibility! I got the same message at the *Chronicle-Herald*, which was hardly surprising since both Halifax papers were owned by the same company. As an advertiser entitled to some editorial support, I was grudgingly told that if I found a critic and the material was any good, they'd print it but the writer wouldn't get paid. All I had to do now was find someone who'd do the job for the sheer glory of two free seats to the first professional company to visit Halifax since Sir John Martin-Harvey.

I had found accommodation for Hilary, Oliver and myself on South Park Street at the Sword and Anchor Inn, a rare flavour of old England with large rooms, fourposter beds and fireplaces. it was a Balsam Hotel with four stars. While I wasn't letting one or two good weeks in St. John's go to my head, I felt the three of us had earned a step up from the bed-and-breakfast circuit. I hadn't been there a week before I received a somewhat ominous phone call from a man who identified himself only as a member of the local stage-hands' union.

"I hope you're not thinking of bringing your company here for five weeks and not using our boys in the local?"

I told him I hadn't even thought about it.

"Then I'd think about it if I were you," he said, and hung up.

A professional stage-hands' union, in *Halifax?* They didn't even have a theatre. They'd had one once, the *Capitol,* but that had been showing movies for donkey's years. Was this a union of geriatrics? And how often did they think you should work to be able to call yourself a professional? The *Capitol* went live maybe twice a year, once for a hypnotist and once for an evangelist. Canada's National Ballet hadn't yet been born and the Canadian Opera Company had never been out of Toronto.

I checked with the School Board office. They had no agreement with the local and didn't want one. We were not to worry because there was a city bylaw that made it illegal to picket School Board property. It wasn't quite so easy not to worry when the messages turned uglier, like "Don't go near any dark corners on your way home tonight." And it wasn't always the same voice, which was even more disturbing.

As our Halifax season progressed, the telephone threats became more intermittent but no less intense. Although the Sword and Anchor was walking distance from the auditorium, I insisted on a cab for the three of us whenever it was dark.

The auditorium had its own crew of senior students who knew their stage and were well trained and highly disciplined. I'd found that out before I'd booked it. And budgeted for them. They had already stacked our carload of scenery neatly backstage and segregated the pieces marked PW for *Perfect Woman,* our opening production. George had given me a list of furniture to round up and it was all there waiting for him in the wings. I'd balked at getting the props. The stage-manager and his gang could do the propping in St. John's and bring everything with them.

If I'd thought my horrendous three-day trip out from England had left me with a pronounced fear of "no flying," I was wrong. I didn't even check that the North Star had left Torbay before I confidently went out to the airport to meet it. I gave Rae Ellison hand-drawn maps marking each B-and-B location for the company and told her to go and be a shepherdess. The rest of us saw the electrics safely onto a truck and went straight to the auditorium. On the way, Oliver brought me up to date on St. John's.

Jane Steps Out, a Cinderella story, had held its own. Then *Johnny Belinda,* with Hilary in the name part, had broken every box-office record but one - the first season's *A Streetcar Named Desire.* Fourteen more patrons on the week and it would have beaten even that. This was tremendously exciting news. In five weeks we had averaged 74½ percent, 2635 people a week, more than one in twelve of every man, woman and child in St. John's.

Halifax looked promising, too. The advance was good but mostly for the first play. They were being a bit canny about season tickets. They all wanted to try the jacket on for a week before they bought the suit.

Over five thousand of them thronged the Queen Elizabeth for *The Perfect Woman* and appeared to have had a rip-roaring time. But was it what they'd really expected? Was it the right choice for an opener? Half them said no, for two thousand five hundred of them stayed away from play number two. And this was our blockbuster *Johnny Belinda!* I had made a terrible error in taking for granted that Nova Scotia tastes would be the same as Newfoundland's. I should have known just by listening to them talk. These were the sounds of cultures much farther apart than mere mileage. The Newfoundlander spoke in bright colours, with the rich burr of Devon and Cornwall and counties from across the Irish Sea; the Nova Scotian in muted pastels, with the lilt of the lowlands of Scotland. Of course they were different. While Newfoundland loved farce, Nova Scotia thought it trivial, even improper. One lady was so shocked at *The Perfect Woman,* she asked for her money back for the other four plays. St. John's would flock to see a play with a movie title, even just after it had been screened there. Halifax would take the Scottish view and say, "We've already paid to see that once." I am not trying to pit province against province, but merely want to point out the challenge that faced an actor-manager trying to choose a repertoire that would maintain its appeal across the vast distances and cultural regions of a country like Canada.

After we had struck the *Johnny Belinda* set on the Saturday night, we couldn't follow our usual routine and set up for *Harvey*. The stage had to be clear on the Sunday for a Salvation Army prayer meeting. I wasn't surprised on Monday morning to find that they'd removed all traces of the London Theatre Company in the lobby. But I thought it a bit much that they'd draped all individual photographs of the players in black cloth. We may have had a bad week but we weren't holding the funeral yet!

Harvey brought almost half our defectors back to the fold and still more rejoined them for *She Stoops to Conquer*. But we were stuck with another farce for our closer, *See How They Run,* and we lost them again.

I had approached the School Board and offered to do a special Wednesday matinee of *She Stoops to Conquer* for fifty cents a head, but they decided the students couldn't spare the classroom time for the Goldsmith classic because they "didn't see how it related to the current school curriculum." A few weeks earlier they had spent a studious afternoon on a field trip to the local Coca-Cola bottling plant. But I mustn't be unkind to Halifax. They did us proud. We only had one losing week.

With one more year to go on his pantomime contract with Birmingham, Oliver had to leave us after the last night of *Harvey*. He'd already directed the stretched version of *Stoops*. I would have to take over the director's chair for *See How They Run*. Before he went, I was able to give him a review of our progress and prospects that were now looking decidedly upbeat. I told him it was vital for us to build up formidable reserves in the company in case we should run into a bad harvest. But with no Harry now to provide for, I didn't see why we shouldn't build up our personal reserves at the same time and we could do that by doubling our own miserable salaries. Oliver held up his hand with mock solemnity and said, "Carried."

"Now don't go back to England and tell everybody we've hit a gold-mine. They'll all want to come and they'll ask three times the salary." He promised me he wouldn't but I knew he would. One drink and it would go through the Salisbury like a flash-fire.

We agreed on one other thing before I saw him onto the plane. We had a vacancy to be filled on our Board of Directors. Why not appoint our two most valuable assets, Hilary and George, and give them each a five percent piece of the company? "Carried," said Oliver again.

Once the set was up for the final production, George and Ira saw the rest of the scenery onto the train and flew back to St. John's. They had a mega-production, *Cinderella,* to build and paint in just two and a half weeks. Rae Ellison had already gone ahead to re-open the box-office.

Halifax had been a bold experiment so early in our history but it had been a rewarding one. We had found a new market. We had discovered that people would still come to the theatre in the dead dull weeks before Christmas if they were given no other choice: we'd limited them to five weeks and it was either then or miss us altogether. And we had given the company not only a break from the set menu at the Balsam, but also the novelty of eating out on a per diem. Now they were all anxious to get back to home base and a St. John's Christmas which had already become legendary. As the North Star climbed higher and the vast landscape opened up, I wondered how many other Halifaxes were out there waiting for us beyond that grey horizon.

twentyone

This time we didn't leave it entirely to the hosts and hostesses of St. John's to give the company a Christmas they'd never forget. We played Santa Claus, too. We let them all loose on an English pantomime, not something they'd ever find in their Christmas stockings if they were working in repertory in England. Pantomime was the preserve of the Music Hall artiste, but there weren't any in St. John's to laugh us out of town. So we put away the Repertory rule book, broadened our guidelines to decorum and good taste and gave the company a ten day fling on the Variety stage where egos run free and it doesn't matter a damn what the director told you because once you are out there you're on your own. But you'd better know your way around, for it can be awfully lonely if you don't.

There is a moment of sheer terror when you first step on to a Variety stage: the imaginary "fourth wall" is no longer there and you suddenly find yourself eyeball to eyeball with the local greengrocer, for you are playing *with* the paying customers instead of *for* them. More frightening still is the fact that the greengrocer's face will tell you quite plainly whether he is with you or agin you in what you are trying to do. But if you are good enough and it is the former, you will be able to take him gently by the hand and lead him up all kinds of fascinating alleys, for participation is the lifeblood of pantomime.

Putting on a panto at all, especially in only ten days, calls for a rare blend of daring, dexterity, dedication, endurance and financial bravery. While it was true that we had no evening performances to worry about and could rehearse eight hours a day once we got back to St. John's, it was also true that bones were crying out to climb back into their sockets after hours of unaccustomed choreography, and singing voices were starting to crack the minute they got above middle C. But from the cast quarters not a squawk was heard because everyone was having *fun*. And that's what made *Cinderella* the triumph it unquestionably was.

As a spectacle, St. John's had never seen anything quite like it. The costumes alone would have cost ten times our total box-office take for a month if we'd had to make them. And although we were the sixth set of bodies to wear them, they showed not a wrinkle of age or weariness. The wardrobe warehouse in Birmingham was the Salberg bank, with every costume a deposit that had to earn a yearly dividend. Consequently no torn piece of taffeta went unrepaired or missing spangle unreplaced after each venture into the marketplace. All we had to do was alter them to fit our own peculiar bulges or lack of them, and that kept a local seamstress busy on the side of the stage right through to the very last minute. Fittings were done on the fly between entrances and exits during rehearsals.

George Paddon-Foster outdid himself with stage settings right out of Disneyland, all of them engineered for mobility on a stage totally lacking the necessary machinery or manpower. Three of the sets demanded the full stage: a bustling street scene, Cinderella's kitchen and the Prince's palace. Fast set changes, which deliver their own special magic, were accomplished with that priceless legacy from the Music Halls, the frontcloth, which dropped in to mask the feverish activities of the scene-changers while leaving a mere three feet of space for the comics to work their tried and true pantomime routines. These could always be milked indefinitely until the scuffle of the last pair of stage-hand sneakers could be heard scampering off into the wings.

Hilda Brinton, the local dance teacher, had chosen her six best pupils and had drilled them all summer as chorines to tunes we had already chosen in the spring. She now turned her attention to the principals. Few repertory actors had ever learned to foxtrot, never mind chasse. They'd always been working in the evening hours while their chums were jiving it up at the local palais. But Hilda kept the steps simple, drilled the cast hard and made them all look like honour graduates from Arthur Murray. Andy Barban, our *Screech* pianist was down at auditorium floor level conducting with his left hand and playing with his right.

Unlike most pantomimes, *Cinderella* doesn't have a "dame" but the two Ugly Sisters are always played by men, in this case David Morrell and myself. My only previous encounter with *Cinderella* had been in 1940 while I was managing the Theatre Royal, Bath and waiting for my call to arms. As the six white ponies pulling Cinderella's coach were being fractious, I went on as a flunkey in powdered wig

193

and satin knee breeches and held their heads. They practically mashed my left instep to pulp before the run was over but that isn't what made that production memorable. In the cast were the two most famous Ugly Sisters of the day, Bartlett and Ross, and I watched them every night. Thirteen years later, I remembered all their best gags and a few of the corny ones as well. There is nothing wrong with corn but you can't be apologetic about it. If you attack it head on and deliver it as if shelling out nuggets of great wisdom, it never fails. I also laced my part liberally with local references in true pantomime tradition.

The Dame is a lovable character in most pantos but not in *Cinderella*. The Ugly Sisters are hated because they are so awful to poor little Cinders. As David and I prepared to go off in our finery and Cinderella made one final appeal to be allowed to go to the ball, all she got from me was, "Certainly not! You have the housework to do. You have to scrub the floor, do the washing up, make the beds, empty the chamber pots – " At this point I'd stop and walk right downstage with my warmest smile and say to the kids, "Shall I let her go?" And they'd all scream, "Yes!" whereupon I'd stamp my foot and say, "Well, she can't go!" and stump upstage. Five times I'd lead them up the same garden path with myself getting more and more honey-tongued and the kids getting more and more hysterical. Then I'd deliver the punch line and exit. The *Sunday Herald* was the St. John's answer to Britain's *News of the World* and was loaded with reports of sex-related crimes and misdemeanours. My final exhortation to Cinderella was: "And don't read the *Sunday Herald* in bed!"

By tradition, every pantomime has a "transformation" scene. *Cinderella* has one of the best when the pumpkin and six white mice turn into a coach to take her to the ball. We didn't have six white ponies but George and Ira brought magic to that tiny stage just the same. When the Fairy Godmother appeared in a puff of smoke and sent Cinders off to get the mice and a pumpkin, they were brought on seconds later, not by Cinders, but by a double wearing identical rags and a duplicate blonde wig. The double sat downstage with her back to the audience while Cinderella did her lines offstage through the fireplace, at the same time frantically getting into her ballgown. When the Fairy Godmother finally waved her magic wand, there was thunder and lightning and a mighty flash that dazzled the audience long enough to allow the double to dash offstage and the beautifully begowned Cinderella to dash on in her place. At the same moment, the rear wall of George's kitchen set parted and there was Cinderella's gold coach twinkling with fairy lights and just the rear end of a white horse with a tail that really swished! When the coachman let down the steps and opened the door, our stage was so shallow that Cinderella actually climbed up into an empty void and sat on a golden chair perched on a hidden riser, but there wasn't a child in the audience under or over sixty who didn't believe our heroine was sitting in a coach with four solid gold walls.

For George's final wonder, the curtain rose at the start of the second half to reveal the Palace ballroom complete with grand staircase and almost the entire cast, in crinolines and doublet and hose, dancing a minuet. There was no room for the Berlin Philharmonic, so we hid them offstage in a large audio unit.

Boxing Day fell on a Friday in 1952, leaving us only two performance days for that week. We stuck in two full-price extra matinees and filled the house four times, equivalent in money to two-thirds of a capacity six-performance week. The second week, we were faithful to our Saturday regulars and kept their matinee at half-price. The eleven performances were a virtual sellout. In eight days, in a 459-seat theatre, we played to over thirty-six hundred people.

The big surprise with *Cinderella* was the reaction of the local Americans. Ever since our first arrival in 1951 we had been building up a solid fan following at nearby Fort Pepperell, the U.S. Air Force base, but I felt sure they'd forsake us for pantomime week. "Mime" to an American meant a show without words. But they came anyway and from that year on, they were hooked on British panto. We could always measure the strength of their support by the amount of American currency coming into the box-office. We accepted the U.S. dollar at par even though (read it and weep) the Canadian dollar at that time was worth four cents more than theirs.

I doubt if any GI specifically asked for a posting to Pepperell because of a local amenity called the London Theatre Company, but few who'd ever served there would have denied that once a week we provided a king-size break in the numbing routine of life on an isolated station. And they went to extraordinary lengths to show their appreciation. They plugged us ceaselessly on the base radio and in their daily newspaper; they switched the award for "Airman of the Month" to dinner for two and a pair of free tickets to the London Theatre Company; they pulled strings for any actor wanting a visa to visit the States at the end of the season; and they flooded us with party invitations. At one of these, we met a Walt Disney cartoonist who was making a USO-sponsored tour of the base hospitals to draw caricatures of the patients. He had a go at all of us but I was the only one in the company who failed to end up with a memorable souvenir. "I can't do you," he said, "you keep coming out like Bob Hope." And he tore me up.

It was during the run of the pantomime that I first began to worry about Ira. He and George Paddon-Foster, who had both spent days on end in the sceneshop creating the magic for *Cinderella*, now were onstage every night, speeding up the set changes to make sure that nothing broke the spell. It was impossible to be around Ira and not notice him. He was ruggedly handsome with dark curly hair, a stitched-on grin and the physique of an Olympic athlete. He was a bundle of coiled energy thirsting for action, like someone always on the starting blocks waiting for the gun to go off. In almost two years, I'd never seen him sit down. Or without his grin. Then one night in *Cinderella,* I made a quick exit into the wings and caught him out on both counts.

"Are you all right, Ira?"

He crunched my right shoulder so that it practically joined the one on the left. "Now don't you be worrying, my son. 'Tis a little 'flu I have, is all."

George and Ira were inseparable. Oliver and I nicknamed them the Gershwins. Once panto was over, I began dropping in on them regularly at Baird's Wharf. Ira really worried me. He was going visibly downhill. By the beginning of February I became seriously alarmed. He had begun to turn yellow. I sent him home immediately and called Horace Rosenberg, our new honorary company doctor who had volunteered to take over from Frank O'Dea. Ira had cancer. Within twenty-four hours he was in hospital and in three weeks he was dead. The company was stunned. George, who had made few really enduring friendships in his entire lifetime, was almost inconsolable.

We said goodbye to Ira in the parlour of the little house he had built for the wife he had brought from Britain after serving there with a Newfoundland regiment during the war. Until the service began, we had no idea that he had been a devout Jehovah's Witness. The "minister" entered wearing a light grey suit with a hand-painted tie and proceeded for more than an hour to read quotations from a large Bible copiously spiked with hand-torn newspaper bookmarks. I remember watching each one flutter to the floor as he read passage after passage purporting to provide holy proof that Ira must have been a wicked sinner or he'd never have died. For the bereaved widow, there was not a crumb of comfort. We were absolutely appalled.

Ira was probably the least sinful person I ever met. He was a simple man, lovable and much loved. His passing cast a pall over the company who had adored him, as had the company before them. He was part of our history. He had been with us from day one. He had built our first scenery flat. Testimony to his skill, love and dedication now filled half a warehouse. He was only thirty-nine. If he had been designated a spot alongside the sinners in the next world, there wasn't much hope for the rest of us.

Almost my first act upon returning from Halifax had been to get rid of every printed form reading MID-CENTURY ENTERTAINMENTS LTD. It was time to start flaunting the LONDON THEATRE COMPANY name on box-office returns and in correspondence with suppliers, author's agents and future actors. Our new letterhead still gives me a thrill when I look at what is probably the only surviving copy:

LONDON THEATRE COMPANY LTD.
PRESENTING ENGLISH PLAYS & PLAYERS IN
CANADA

DIRECTORS:

OLIVER GORDON) Joint
LESLIE YEO ʃ managing directors
GEORGE PADDON-FOSTER
HILARY VERNON

HEAD OFFICE:
ST. JOHNS,
NEWFOUNDLAND, CANADA
LONDON OFFICE:
47, REDCLIFFE SQUARE
S.W.10   Ph.: FRE 8896

Cash was now flowing freely into the bank and it even had time to sit there and look smug for a while before flowing out again. The moment had come to start building up some material assets. First we bought a company car and repaid Hugh Baird for his long-standing kindness in providing us with free wheels for almost a year and a half. Hugh was the Austin dealer. Canada was big car country and Austin were small car makers; so we bought the biggest he had, an A90. Next I wrote to Strand Electric in London and told them a huge fib. I said I'd been offered a tempting purchase deal from Century Lighting of New York, whom I knew to be their most hated rivals. If, however, they'd give me a bargain buyout price for the equipment we were now renting, I just might be tempted to stick with Strand. I wrote something similar to the sound equipment people. Strand bit but the sound boys didn't. We bought the lighting outright but still paid rent for sound equipment, which would go back to England, never to return, at the end of the season.

The first play after panto was a Christmassy piece called *The Holly and the Ivy,* and it just scraped through as a plus at the box-office in a week that was traditionally negative. From then on there were dips and there were spurts, but the spurts spurted more than the dips dipped and the curve of our season average kept on climbing. Not a single play showed a minus until we got to Holy Week when we were hopelessly outdrawn by the Basilica. We were both doing the Easter story but ours was a modern version called *The Vigil* while they stuck religiously to the classic script. To be honest about it, they also had bigger stars and flashier costumes than we did.

But *The Vigil* was only a temporary blip on the prosperity graph. We were a success and I was quite unready for it. Worry was what kept me going. Without it my mind had time to dwell on other things, like dishing out all my favourite roles to someone else in the company because of some fiddling management chore. It had never been fiddling before, it wasn't really fiddling now and it simply mustn't be fiddling in the future because it fiddling well had to be done. But some of the spark had gone out of the challenge.

Success was spoiling Oliver's fun too. He loved his nightly stint on the box-office phone in the lobby. Now it was being ruined half the time because there weren't any seats left to sell. He'd just put the phone down when I walked through on one such evening.

"What do you think some silly twit just asked me?" he said. "Do you have your radio on? I said `No, I don't even have a fucking radio!'"

"You didn't really say that, did you Oliver?"

"Yes old boy, why?"

"You were probably on the air."

"What?"

I had to explain to him how deejays sometimes picked telephone numbers at random and the first thing they always did was ask whether you had your radio on. Oliver's voice was getting very well known to theatregoers both as an actor and a telephone operator. I spent an anxious half hour waiting for an angry call. I can only think that someone at the radio station had been very sharp on the bleeper button.

Probably the only people in the entire city of St. John's who weren't overjoyed at our success were the movie moguls. I'd heard rumblings about pressure being brought to bear on City Hall to revoke our special exemption from the local entertainment tax. Sure enough, Mayor Harry Mews called to tell me reluctantly that we would have to begin paying it the following season. I could see that we were a double bind to the movie house boys. They were losing market share to us and feeding our future as well. St. John's playgoers thrived on movie titles. Every time the cinemas did a film based on a play, we'd do it live as soon as possible afterwards and hit them even harder with a record week. Nineteen fifty-three was a vintage year for film titles. We did *This Happy Breed, Random Harvest, The Seventh Veil, Rebecca* and *Johnny Belinda*. Everybody came to see who was best, Hilary or Jane Wyman. If the members of the Academy had all lived in St. John's, Jane Wyman wouldn't have stood a chance.

But our proudest moment of all was the box-office revelation that way up with the money-spinners on our hit parade were our two classics: Goldsmith's *She Stoops to Conquer* and *The Merchant of Venice*. Excluding the panto and the revue, this is how our second season's productions crossed the finish line:

1. *Johnny Belinda*
2. *She Stoops to Conquer*
3. *The Seventh Veil*
4. *The Merchant of Venice*
5. *This Happy Breed*
6. *Rebecca*

Hilary had played the lead in four of the six.

If we'd thought *Cinderella* was tough in ten days, we looked back upon it as a gentle warm-up when it came to *The Merchant*. We had brought Elizabethan costumes first worn by Alec Guinness and his Shakespearean Company for a cast of twenty-nine characters, fifteen of them size and shape unknown. We had nineteen speaking parts to allot and only three of them female. We lowered the ratio a bit by casting Hilary as the Prince of Arragon. If he had never been played camp before, he should always be in the future. We managed to persuade a couple of radio announcers to be seen as well as heard for once. We gave them small parts. That still left us with a long list of non-speaking servants, noblemen and ladies-in-waiting. If we ended up with a local bartender playing a nobleman and a society lady playing a washerwoman, we weren't making a social statement but merely choosing bottoms that best filled the costumes.

By the time we had finished, the local acquisitions outnumbered the regular company. Most of them could only rehearse evenings. Since the stage was busy every night with *To Dorothy a Son*, we scattered them in groups all over the school – in classrooms, stairwells and corridors. We rounded them all up at the weekend and put the jigsaw together on Sunday. It was the only time we ever worked a seven-day week. How the school managed to put up with us during that week and the one that followed, I'll never understand. We practically took it over. We kept the janitor on the go at all hours; we kept lights burning that should never have been on; we commandeered the gymnasium for an overflow dressing room; and we had so many students working for us that there must have been a horrible paucity of homework handed in. Two of the busiest of these students were Bob Cole and William Rompkey whom we'd taken on as extra Assistant Stage Managers for the production. Both had served us in this capacity before and their experience was invaluable. Bill Rompkey is now a Liberal Senator in Ottawa. Bob Cole became a play-by-play commentator on Hockey Night in Canada and was recently inducted into the Hockey Hall of Fame.

All in all, *The Merchant of Venice* was a splendid confection. But it was our company doctor, Horace Rosenberg, who put the icing on the cake. Cocking a large snook at the paranoids who were beginning to murmur anti-Semitism, he personally opened our production with a rich baritone rendering of *Che Fiero Costume* by Giovanni Legrenzi. Horace had also composed and arranged music to Shakespeare's song "Tell me where is fancy bred" and he sang them in the casket scene, in costume of course, with his own quartet. Atmosphere music was specially recorded for us by Wynne Godley, the celebrated oboe player with the Boyd Neel Orchestra. We did an extra matinee for the schools on the Wednesday, and by the end of the week the entire company, the College staff and at least one member of thirty different households were exhausted.

We considered our *Merchant* a class act, but from that time on, Oliver and I decided to let William Shakespeare rest on his laurels at the Old Vic in London.

We took one big gamble in 1953. We repeated a play the Alexandra Company had done only five years earlier. It was the farce *See How They Run* and it did almost as well for us as it had for John Gabriel. This was an enormously comforting discovery for a company eating up plays at the rate of twenty-six a year. Farces were our most bankable commodity. Now it looked as if we could not only cash them in, but also count them as continuing assets. We only did one other farce in 1952-53 and that was *Love's a Luxury*. It earned the rare distinction of making the press a second time in one playing week:

> When Gerald Raymond's truck left the road and cracked off a light pole at Bay Bulls Big Pond Road at 9.15 Saturday night and plunged half the city into darkness, the London

Theatre Company interrupted *Love's a Luxury* and gave an impromptu show in emergency lighting.

Every actor has a party piece and we all trotted them out. I even remembered a few stories from my old RAF stag book and quickly cleaned them up a bit for general consumption. But as the Hydro truck seemed destined for a long stay at Bay Bulls Big Pond Road, we finally ended up finishing the play by candlelight.

Soon the end of the season was upon us and it was revue time again. We christened the 1953 vintage *More Screech,* with John Woodnutt once again elected brewmaster. There were twenty-four items on the bill and not one of them flopped. The biggest hits were the ones with any kind of local reference, which gave us a clear blueprint for the future. The standouts were "The 14th Veil" which burlesqued Hilary's dramatic tear-off with Tony Newlands in "The Seventh Veil," "The Cascara Sisters" (played by men of course), "The Great Phoodini" in which all the conjuring tricks went wrong, and a couple of hilarious skits written or devised by two local celebrities, Bob MacLeod and Don Jamieson. First there was "The Heart's Disease Glee Club": Newfoundland already had a Heart's Content, Heart's Delight and Heart's Desire; so we decided to add a new one to the gazetteer. Bob MacLeod had run the St. John's Glee Club for years. Nobody knew their idiosyncrasies better than he did or was more gleeful in sending them up.

But the big hit of the evening, and our most daring attempt at political satire to date, was a sketch entitled *The Cabinet Meeting.* Political satire? It was pure political slander. But as it was devised by Don Jamieson who owned half a radio station, half the *Sunday Herald* and half the credit for Joey Smallwood's continuing occupation of the Premier's office, nobody said a word. Don would eventually become a senior minister in the Trudeau cabinet and end up as Canada's High Commissioner in London.

In our skit, we made no attempt whatever to disguise the names of the unfortunate ministers we lampooned. We even made ourselves up to look like them and we shamelessly exaggerated their well-known failings. We were altogether very daring, but Don Jamieson's name on the programme was our guarantee of a safe passage through the week and even future seasons. The seeds had been sown: all we had to do was to keep them fertilized with up-to-date political gossip and there'd be even riper harvests ahead.

Every seat for *More Screech* was sold out for the entire week before anyone even knew what was on the menu, a London Theatre Company first.

It was just after the revue that I first met Premier Joey Smallwood, the man who had guided Newfoundland into Confederation. We were all having Sunday brunch at Mrs Godson's in Holyrood and I was introduced to him.

"I know all the things you've been saying about me down at that theatre," he said with a wagging forefinger.

"But you've never been to see us, Mr Smallwood."

"No, but my ministers have. And they all come back and report to me. *Verbatim.*" And he stared at me accusingly. But I saw the twinkle in his eye before I dared to put one in mine.

True to the precedent we had set the year before, in 1953 we gave Canada two more new immigrants. At the end of the season, CBC St. John's snapped up Charles Mardel, and wife-to-be Ruth Perkins stayed behind with him. We also kept up our mating average: Jacqueline Lacey and David Morrell decided they'd liked their trial run in St. John's and announced they'd make it legal as soon as they got home.

Meanwhile, back in Britain, the buttercups were out and so were the mowers, busily cutting twenty-two-yard-long swaths across the village greens. Oliver was already mentally back at Datchet dreaming of maiden overs, but I couldn't let him go until we'd talked about season number three. I had some changes in mind that were big enough to call for a new mandate. This time, "Whatever you think, cock" would not be enough.

The sitting-room in the Balsam Annexe was strangely silent as its four remaining residents sat down to talk about the future. I began by giving Oliver, George and Hilary a short recap of the past. As our accounting system had blossomed from a single disbursements journal into a full set of ledgers, I was able to predict with some confidence that the auditors would value our net worth at the end of season number two at just under $15,000 (over a hundred thousand in 1998 dollars). This may seem small potatoes in today's world of Arts and Culture but my share of it was no mean two-year return on my original capital of £40.

"Now what does everybody want to do? Come back here year after year and get rich? Or strike out across the Gulf of St Lawrence and find out if we're really as good as we think we are?" As long as he could get the next plane to a cricket field, Oliver was quite happy to let me take Hilary, George and the A90 through the Maritimes and across Ontario to scout every town with a population at least as big as Greater

St. John's. As a final item on the agenda, I suggested that the time had come to distribute a little of our wealth but still leave enough to finance a possible tour. We settled on a dividend that virtually repaid us our original capital investment and still left us plenty to work with. Oliver had broken a lifelong chain of unprofitable ventures and I had honoured a secret pledge to myself that he would. George and Hilary got a small windfall for no investment at all, and, in addition, George once again took his fare back to England and out again in cash so that he would be able to coast comfortably through the summer. Oliver would have enough to be able to lead the life of a gentleman and buy himself several new pairs of white flannels.

twentytwo

For most of our 1952 company the great adventure was over, but for four of us it was only just beginning. While the others sailed east on the *RMS Newfoundland,* back to weekly rep English-style without the drop-in privileges of Rennies Mill Road, Hilary, George, the A90 and I went west on her sister ship the *Nova Scotia* in search of pastures new. In no time at all, we were in Halifax and that was enough to trigger my budget machinery which I always kept on standby. Why not sail next year's company from Liverpool right through to Halifax and open the season there? A one-way plane ticket would get us back for our Newfoundland season and save us a round-trip fare to Halifax in the middle of it.

We found the Furness Withy office, tied up the best berths on the first boat due into Halifax in October, and put a tentative lock on the Queen Elizabeth Auditorium for the five weeks after that. Was our friend the janitor still there, enquired George with his most charming smile? He deserved an Oscar for feigning pleasure at the news that the king still sat upon his backstage throne.

When we picked up the A90 at the wharf, we didn't immediately steer south-south-west and take the golden road to Ontario. First we wanted to have a look at Sydney, which meant backtracking 262 miles east through Cape Breton. Sydney conformed to our touring specs: population over 30,000 and squarely on our travel route. We'd go through it anyway if we brought the company overland by Newfie Bullet from St. John's to Port aux Basques and then boarded the ferry to North Sydney. That was all part of the master plan. I hadn't told the others yet about the master plan. I thought I'd let it unfold gently as we went along.

The nub of the plan was that the company would tour everywhere by rail, just like Irving and Terry and Sarah Bernhardt had done decades before us. British touring companies always went by rail because if you bought twelve passenger tickets, you got your own private luggage van free. If your company was too small, you simply bought twelve tickets and threw away the ones you didn't need. Your private luggage-van was coupled to the back of your train, decoupled at your destination and shunted into a siding for immediate off-loading into a truck.

When I first tackled CN in St. John's about this long-standing custom on British railways, they laughed. Then somebody leafed through their own rule book and found it was there too. That little discovery laid the foundation stone of the master plan when I first began to draft it in St. John's halfway through the 1952-53 season. I started off with a map of Eastern Canada and a stack of yellow pins. I stuck one in every mainland town of 30,000 people west of St. John's right through to the Southern Ontario/U.S. border. Then I went to the Memorial University library and steeped myself in statistics. Thirteen yellow pins found a target and would stay there only if the stats failed to turn up the faintest hint of a negative. I went out of my way to look for one. How did local incomes compare with the national average? What was the ratio of blue collar workers to white? How many of the given population would count English as their first language? What was early closing day? Was there a predominant local religious sect that regarded theatre companies as PR agents for the devil? How many city newspapers were there to demand a slice of our advertising pie? What kind of local competition could we expect for the entertainment dollar?

I also had to know how long it would take us to get from one yellow pin to the next and where the snowbelts were that might try to stop us. I wrestled for days with train and ferry schedules and left a wide margin for error after asking CN and CP pointblank whether I should take their printed times as gospel or wishful thinking. I contacted three provincial governments and thirteen city halls and uncovered a few surprises. I found that Confederation with Canada had not bestowed upon Newfoundland corporations (that was us) the right to ply their trade in other provinces without first obtaining a licence from each of them. There would also be an entertainment tax to collect with the rate changing every time we crossed a provincial border. And I learned that public holidays varied not only from province to province but also from city to city. This was vital foreknowledge for the stage manager with a quick get-in on a strange stage and not a hardware store to be found open in an emergency. Like replacing a smashed doorknob or a mangled hinge on the very French

205

windows that the murderer had to open dead on cue.

I'd done the homework, now for the field trip. The thirteen towns that had passed the stats test would almost certainly make the tour list barring plague, pestilence, famine or just plain bad vibes when we came to look them over. This wasn't going to be so much a reconnoitering trip as a series of confirmation classes. I'd circled the thirteen on our road map and the sequence we would play them in and this was the itinerary I intended we should follow. I wanted to be back in England in three and a half weeks; so I'd been absolutely brutal about our schedule: a day and a half to scout each location, half a day for travelling to the next one and no time between them for seeing the sights.

All the way from St. John's, on the boat and on the road, I had been carefully briefing the others on the scouting routine we would follow in each town. Sydney would be our test run. First we'd have to find somewhere to stay the night. In the morning we'd head for the offices of the school board. After we'd toured all the schools that had a stage, we'd select one of them. There I'd off-load George with his tape measure, his notebook, his eight-page questionnaire and a camera. I would head back to the office to dicker with the Super-intendent of Schools. With such a quick turnaround, Hilary would spend most of her time packing and unpacking and keeping us supplied with goodies on the journey. As she was also our navigator, she'd would have plenty of homework to do, too.

On the eve of our test run, I got out my nit-picking comb and had one long last look at the master plan. The following day, it would cease to be a plan and start to become a commitment, and the name and reputation of the London Theatre Company would be on the dotted line. There would still be room to juggle with the future, but the past would be locked in as fast as we left it behind us with no escape hatch for second thoughts. I instinctively picked up our itinerary one more time for a quick reassuring look at life after Sydney.

Moncton and Saint John would be next. For the first time, I realized from the map how much closer they were to Halifax than to Sydney. In fact Halifax, Moncton and Saint John all sat in a neat arc circling our home base in St. John's like the flight path of a carrier pigeon reluctant to leave. And that also meant they were all roughly the same distance away in North Star miles.

"George, I've had a brainwave. Why don't we do a mini-tour of the Maritimes, tack it on to the end of the Halifax season, give ourselves a dry run and find out firsthand just exactly what we might have overlooked before we take the big plunge west? We could just as easily fly the company back to St. John's from Moncton or Saint John as from Halifax."

I knew the moment I said it I was going to cost myself a large dollop of sleep. Taking two towns out of the main loop and tightening up all the others at this late stage was major surgery on the master plan. Travel times had been scrupulously clocked, checked, rechecked and performance dates pencilled in, waiting for the confirming ink. But George thought it was a great idea. I stayed up half the night and revamped the entire schedule.

In the morning, we discovered that there was only one high school with a stage in Sydney; so I drove George there and left him. George was the precursor of the Technical Director. We didn't call him that because the position hadn't been invented yet. But he was the perfect TD by any modern standards, and, by the end of the day, he knew that stage and its limitations better than the people who had built it. He drew up a complete stage floor plan to scale and checked all the sight-lines. He listed, measured and photographed every piece of stage drapery, hanging or available to be hung, movable or fixed. He noted every spare inch of pipe space overhead to which we could clamp a spotlight. He checked that there would be enough power for us to take a feed from the main breaker to our portable lighting board and measured how long the heavy cable would have to be. He phoned the local electrical contractor and tentatively booked him to do the hook-up. He traced an access route to the stage from outside the building with no sharp corners that would stymie a 12 ft by 6 ft piece of scenery in a hurry. He ended with a report on the extent or absence of box-office facilities in the front-of-house, the state of the dressing-room accommodation and the attitude of the janitor. By the time I picked him up at the end of the day, he had the senior student in charge of the stage waiting for me. We talked terms, numbers and dates for a student crew for get-in, get-out and running the show. Then we went off to dinner.

My own day hadn't been exactly an afternoon stroll. Back at the School Board office, I had bargained the rent down for a two-night stand, blocked off the dates, paid a deposit and picked up a numbered seating plan for the ticket printer. My next job had been to find somewhere to put an advance box-office. Fred Ayre, my early saviour at Bowrings in St. John's, had taken my list of circled towns and given me a personal letter of introduction to his opposite number in the leading department store in each one of them. In it, he referred to me as "the sparkplug of the enterprise" and he stressed the immense value to the store of a steady stream of ticket buyers. He enclosed a photo of the booth they had built for us at Bowrings and said it had been worth every cent it cost them. We were never turned down once.

The following morning, George went off to find and fix a trucking firm to ferry the scenery and props from the railhead to the auditorium while Hilary and I cornered the publisher of the local newspaper. We talked about how much advertising space we'd need (which pleased him) and how much editorial coverage we'd expect (which didn't). But we parted friends, picked up George, formed an inspection team of three and went looking for bed-and-breakfast signs for housing the company. By lunchtime we were on our way to Moncton.

In 1953, the Trans-Canada highway was a mere dotted line of hope on Nova Scotia road maps. Its forerunner was a two-laner, winding and hilly with the traffic bunched in convoys behind the slow movers, like stock car racers under a yellow flag. Fortunately, every five miles or so there would be a small stretch of three-lane to create a passing zone and give the speedsters a chance to get back into the race. Both the A90 and its driver, notwithstanding a Canadian apprenticeship served solely on the lone thirteen miles of paved highway beyond the city limits of St. John's, held their own with all but the madmen.

Faithful to the Sydney formula, we clinched Moncton and Saint John in record time, closed the folder on the mini-tour and went back to worrying about the big one. We now faced the only horrendous leg on our scouting journey west to the teeming towns of theatre-starved Ontario. The revised plan for the maxi-tour called for the company to open in Sydney, skip the Maritimes and then head direct for Montreal for what we all hoped would be an extremely lucrative stopover. While the company would make the long hop from Sydney in comparative comfort aboard Canadian National's crack train, the Nova Scotian, our reconnoitering group would have to make it in the Austin and although we had already got as far as Saint John, New Brunswick, we still had six hundred miles to go. This would be the one time we couldn't make the trip in the half-day allotted for travel.

As the beauty of the newly-awakening trees flashed by all too quickly in a disheartening blur, I became growingly aware of the awesome distances that faced theatre companies bent on touring in Canada. What we were now planning in terms of mileage from Sydney to Montreal would be the equivalent of taking an English company from Birmingham to the south coast, ferrying them across the English Channel and training them through the whole of France to play a season on the Spanish Riviera.

We started dreaming of HOUSE FULL signs the moment we saw the crowds thronging downtown Montreal. But when we got to the city centre and saw the magnificent facade of Her Majesty's Theatre, I knew Montreal wasn't for us. We'd be condemned to total anonymity in a school auditorium with one of the finest professional playhouses in Canada sitting empty down the road. Her Majesty's had flourished in the days when Broadway and West End runs were measured in months instead of years and the greats were forced to go on tour to keep the bailiffs at bay. But it was now 1953, and with TV emerging as a lucrative fill-in to keep the stars at home, pickings had become slim for theatre managements in cities like Montreal. Her Majesty's had been reduced to hosting "number two" or "number three" tours of a Broadway hit or remaining dark. And the manager didn't think it was worth turning on the lights for an unknown company from England without a star name. We were very welcome, of course, to *rent* the theatre and pay the crew, the orchestra and the publicity, and they would be very pleased to throw in the ushers and box-office staff with the rent. And we were very pleased to thank them very much and drive on to Kingston. The distance from Sydney to our second date had just grown bigger.

Our list of prospects was now down to ten and we booked them all except one. By journey's end we had logged almost five thousand miles of hard driving over roads that still had a long wait ahead for super-highway 401 to come along and bulldoze the kinks out of them. And it had taken us over three weeks to do it. Since we badly needed some sightseeing relief, I broke the rule a couple of times. The first occasion was after St Catharines, where we were far too close to one of the world's great wonders to deny ourselves the memory of that never-to-be-forgotten first glimpse. As we neared Niagara and the traffic got thicker, we suddenly became aware that American cars overtaking us deliberately slowed down and ran level with us long enough for the entire carload to press its noses against the windows and goggle at us as they went by. When other drivers started queuing up to do the same, I thought we'd better pull off to the side to see if we had a flat tire, a piece of loose chrome flapping in the breeze or a couple of beavers mating on the roof. But there was nothing unusual that I could see; just a dusty old Austin A90 with Newfoundland plates. The plates! That was it, of course. The Americans expected to see us all swathed in sealskins and carrying harpoons.

Our second diversion was on the same day that we clinched a week at the Grand Theatre in London. With Stratford a mere forty-five minutes away, no theatrical worth his Equity card could have failed to feed his curiosity about the rumours that were wildly circulating in that spring of 1953. When we got to Stratford and asked for directions, not a local appeared to have the faintest idea what we were talking about. It was quite by accident that we stumbled on a bunch of burly workmen leaning on their shovels beside a large hole close by the Avon. They didn't know exactly why they were digging it but they thought it was for "some kind of thee-ater". The city was less than three months away from the launch of the Stratford Festival.

After London, we had one more town left to vet. For the weary scouters, Windsor was the end of the line. And for the fourteen-strong touring company, it was clearly way beyond it. We were as far from Halifax as we could possibly go and still be in Southern Ontario. And Halifax was where the company would have to end up to board the boat that would finally take them home to England. I couldn't fly them back from Ontario: their baggage would have weighed more than they did. Repertory actors travelled with their entire wardrobes and, in addition, we had over twenty company baskets of period and panto costumes that we could wangle back to Liverpool free as part of the generous personal baggage allowance for first-class steamship passengers. Halifax it would have to be. Windsor was simply too far for a leg all to itself; so we lopped it off, settled on London as our furthest point west and saved the tour about three hundred miles. And Windsor joined Montreal on the list of towns whose citizens would never know what they had missed.

The scouting trip may have been over but the driving wasn't. I now faced fifteen hundred miles of it if I wanted the car waiting for me in Halifax in October. George wanted to do some sketching on the Toronto Islands. We dropped him off at the Y and went on to Montreal. There, something thankfully happened that told me I no longer had time to be a car jockey. I picked up a message already several days old to call Ken Basquette at the Grand Theatre in London. After talking to him, I hastily put the car into storage and got Hilary and myself on the first plane to London, England. I needed an urgent session with Oliver. He and I had a big decision to make and no time to make it in. Basquette's American summer stock company, after several years at the Grand, had just advised him that this would be their final visit, and he was offering us the same slot in 1954. There was just this one little problem: London wanted us the first week in May; the tour I had just booked would end in Kingston the first week in April. What on earth was I to do with fourteen hungry actors for the four weeks in between?

I've never slept on a plane. I've never been able to. I've managed to go off quite soundly on a groundsheet under a tree in Burma in the middle of a monsoon, on the heaving deck of a troopship in a gale in the Bay of Biscay, in the orchestra stalls during the third act of a very boring play and in somebody else's bed when beside me lay every reason why I should try to stay awake, but never a wink have I snatched on an aircraft. And for once in my life I was glad. I had come aboard with a problem and I needed all the waking time I could get to solve it. Until I had, I wouldn't be able to call Ken Basquette, and Oliver and I wouldn't be able to begin lining up actors for our next season because we wouldn't be able to tell them how long it was going to last.

The answer, if there was one, lay in the tour itinerary that had been spread out for hours on my seat table: Sydney, Hamilton, London, St Catharines, Kitchener, Ottawa, Peterborough, Toronto and Kingston in that order. Somewhere on that tight list, I had to find a window I could pry open and let in four weeks. And it had to be somewhere near the end of the schedule because no power on earth was going to persuade me to backtrack and rebook the entire tour. I had arrived at one of those rare moments in my life when I knew my own limitations and, rarer still, was prepared to admit it. I was exhausted. I needed a holiday and I intended to have one, my first in fifteen years.

If only I'd known about the London offer sooner, it would have been easy. I'd have given an extra four weeks to good old reliable St. John's and delayed the start of the tour, which would have had us landing on Ken Basquette's stage doorstep just at the right moment. I would also have been able to take a great load off my guilt-laden conscience. In my eagerness to carve the London Theatre Company name in larger letters, I had allowed myself to forget that we owed our very existence to the people of St. John's and I had butchered their next season down to a miserable eleven weeks. Now the mini-tour would gobble up another two of those at the front end and leave them with only nine. While everyone agreed that six months was outstaying even a Newfoundland welcome, to cut them down from twenty-six productions to twenty-one to nine in three consecutive seasons was cruelty to fans at the very moment that they were beginning to multiply.

But there was an even bigger load on my mind just then: what to do with a company of actors tuned to concert pitch, costumed and propped and nowhere to play for four weeks in an area where nobody had ever heard of them. It was agonizing just to think of passing up a summer at the Grand: two months of living in the same digs with bags properly unpacked and not just sitting there with their lids open. And working in a real theatre with a fully equipped stage to play on and a trained audience to play to after weeks of striving to create a breath of atmosphere in high school auditoriums. There had to be a solution. And of course there was.

The final tour date was to be Kingston and it was there I had planned we should pack our bags and head for Halifax and the boat home. And that's where I found the window, right between our arrival in Halifax and boarding the boat: we could play a second season at the Queen Elizabeth Auditorium. It would already be twenty weeks since our previous one in October and I was sure they'd stand us for another four. Then, instead of embarking for London, England, the company would entrain for the other London in Ontario, just in time for a May third opening.

All I had to do now was convince Oliver – and even more to the point, myself – that we were strong enough to withstand this double-barrelled assault on our finances: two totally unplanned and unbudgeted seasons and a three-thousand-mile-round trip separating them.

twentythree

Rain stopped play long enough for me to grab Oliver and switch his mind off cricket and on to the London Theatre Company. In a corner of the tin-roofed pavilion at Datchet, I sat him down on a cricket bag and battled the hammering of the raindrops for his attention while I told him the story of our travels. In less than two hours, we set the parameters for season number three, committing the partnership to a highly ambitious programme expanded from twenty-six weeks to thirty-eight. A daring seventeen of them would be in virgin territory where John Gabriel's Alexandra Company had not already blazed a trail and left a legacy of invaluable statistics.

The rain stopped, the sun came out and Oliver happily led his team back onto the field, his mind now free to decide the kind of horror he would hurl down from the bowler's end on to a lovely wet wicket. Another winter had been taken care off. Another summer was to be enjoyed to the full. His faith in me was absolute. I thought how lucky I'd been to pick him for a partner.

Although I hadn't promised that the mainland tour would make us a fortune, I'd been bold enough to pledge that there would be enough cash in the kitty to pay the bills if it didn't. Only a disaster of monstrous proportions would prevent that. Even after paying ourselves back our original investment, we were still left with an accumulated surplus for working capital that was bigger than the one we started out with in 1951.

It never occurred to Oliver or myself to dip into this accumulated nest-egg because we didn't really look upon it as rightfully ours. It was an advance from the paying customers against future deliveries, and if they ever stopped coming, we might end up having to give it all back. Besides, capital appreciation was never the main objective of the London Theatre Company. It was formed to provide us with an income as well as an opportunity to work alongside actors we wanted to work with in plays that we wanted to play for people who wanted to see them. The income had to be substantial enough to keep us going during the off-season months when there was considerable preparatory work to do and nothing coming in to pay for it. During the entire life of the London Theatre Company, none of its partners ever drew a penny off-season, or off-site while the season was on.

By the time our second season ended in the spring of 1953, getting through the summer was easy. We had given ourselves a couple of raises, and the company had paid our full living expenses on top of our salaries, as it did for all our other actors. Hilary and I even considered taking a real holiday, a luxury we'd never before been able to contemplate as working actors in England. Vacation pay was still twenty years away from a place in the Actors' Equity rule book. That meant double jeopardy every time you took a holiday. For two weeks, you earned nothing and you spent twice as much as usual.

For over two years we had been nursing the memory of a conversation with a film cameraman who told us he'd just come back from paradise. He had spent six weeks on location in the Mediterranean shooting *Pandora and the Flying Dutchman*, starring Ava Gardner and James Mason, in the tiny fishing village of Tossa del Mar on the Spanish Costa Brava. There the sun always shone, the skies were ever blue, living was cheap and visitors from another country were practically an undiscovered species. I still had the scrap of paper with the address of the *pension* the cameraman had stayed at. Someone must have told him that Hilary and I weren't married because he had taken particular care to warn us that passports had to be surrendered when you checked in at your accommodation and el Spanish were a bit old-fashioned. So after we wrote off to the *Pension Simeon* and booked a double room, Hilary and I went in search of a Notary Public to change her name. For half-a-crown and as long as it took to raise her right hand and place her left one on the Bible, Mrs Hudson became Mrs Yeo. And nobody in Spain would have a clue what the words "name changed by deed poll" meant at the bottom of her new passport.

Oliver decided to make the ultimate sacrifice and give up three weeks of cricketing to join us in Spain. While we were still in London awaiting confirmation from Señora Simeon that she could accommodate him as well, we all three watched the biggest parade of world leaders in history riding in open carriages to Westminster Abbey for the crowning of Queen Elizabeth II. After the procession had passed, we mingled with the huge crowd in The Mall and ran into more

Newfoundlanders we knew than we ever expected to encounter along Water Street on a normal day in St. John's. Here was a heaven-sent opportunity to repay some of the fabulous hospitality they'd lavished upon our company for two straight seasons. We rounded up Harold (Fish) Lake and his pretty wife Robyn together with Nancy and Dick Winter (he was an aide-de-camp to the current Lieutenant Governor), and we booked a table for seven at the Caprice – *the* place to eat and be seen doing it if you were an actor. You could always get a reservation for dinner even if you weren't top billing because, in the evenings, all the stage luminaries were busy acting their socks off to keep their names in lights, and most of the film stars were at home learning their lines for the next day's shoot. Lunchtime at the Caprice was an entirely different matter. To get a table, you practically needed to enter wearing the Order of the Garter.

Hilary and I had a quick look round for celebrities for the benefit of our friends from St. John's and could only point out the un-mistakable bulk of Al Parker, London's top talent agent, sitting a couple of tables away with a stunningly attractive young woman whom neither of us had ever seen before. Next morning, her picture on the front page of the *Daily Express* identified her as Audrey Hepburn signing her first Hollywood contract to star in a film called *Roman Holiday.* As if trying to make up for the lack of celebrities, Dick Winter practically became one by trying to light a cigarette from the candle in the middle of the table with a spill torn out of the evening paper. This brought waiters rushing to our table from all directions with Ronson lighters already ablaze. For an encore, Dick and Fish refused to let us pick up the check. To make sure we didn't, they stood up and scattered five-pound notes all over the table and left. What was I to do? I had to be sure there was enough. I whispered to Hilary and Oliver to join the others in the lobby and I sat it out. I put on my most nonchalant air that I usually reserved for Noël Coward plays and held up a very genteel finger for the waiter.

"You'd better just count it and let me know if there's enough," I said, as if that sort of thing happened every day.

There was more than enough, so I left a handsome tip of my own which made me feel a lot better. But Newfoundland had once again scored a direct hospitality hit with no answering fire.

Our cinematographer, like his camera, didn't lie. Tossa was paradise. The sky was blue, the water was bluer and sparkling clear as an advertisement for Schweppes. You could drop a flat pebble from the top of the small sea-wall and watch it see-saw all the way down to the ocean floor. Every cottage in Tossa gleamed as if lovingly lathered daily with a fresh coat of whitewash, and the beach was deserted save for the women squatting on the pebbles to repair the fishing nets still wet from their all-night soaking offshore as their husbands hunted sardines by the powerful light of acetylene lamps. Nobody in the village spoke a word of English: if you wanted something, it was phrasebooks or point.

At Señora Simeon's the *pensionnaires* already in residence greeted our arrival with considerable reserve. Obviously they didn't relish the thought of having to share their private Eden with three more people. After the thaw had set in some time later, they confessed that they'd been highly intrigued that Hilary should be travelling with two male companions, both apparently virile and of similar age. When they first heard Oliver's alarm clock go off at six am for his morning jog, they were convinced that it "must be those theatricals changing over."

With only a handful of other visitors, there were enough little sandy bays to go round for each group to have its own private beach. And all for thirty shillings a week ($4.50 Canadian), which covered room, laundry, all meals and as much local wine as you could drink. Ten years down the road, the sky would still be blue but the Mediterranean would be too polluted to reflect it and would end up a murky green; tourists would be ten deep on the beach and the fishermen's wives would be banished to their own backyards to do their mending; the locals would all be talking English with a cockney accent, and the *bodega*, which once sold nothing but sherry from a choice of thirty-five casks, would have turned into a soda-fountain dispensing Coke and Pepsi and would be fronted by a plate glass window on which a finger dipped in whitening had written: A CUP OF TEA AS MUM MAKES IT. We went through two world wars to preserve a way of life for our children. Why did we throw it all away in peacetime?

But it was still paradise in the summer of 1953, when Hilary, Oliver and I lay under a *sombre* on our still private beach and read plays. Two each a day was mandatory with a strict rotating system so that we each read the whole pile. Though some of them we knew and had played before, we had to take a fresh look at them through the eyes of managers rather than performers. We made notes for each other on probable box-office reaction, staging problems, casting limitations and any special costume or prop requirements. In addition, in the two years since we'd all been away from the British scene, a host of new releases had emerged from Broadway and the West End: these had to be read and evaluated, too. Between readings, we sunbathed, swam and drank champagne cocktails at twenty-five cents a crack.

One morning, the fishing-net repair ladies arrived on the beach at daybreak to find their working space considerably reduced by the appearance overnight of a portable theatre. There was a solid wooden stage at one end and at the other, a marquee boldly lettered *Teatro Principe*. The space between them was boxed in with canvas to put a roof over the collection of loose stacking chairs plonked straight onto the pebbles. A playbill announced that a Spanish Concert Party had come to town and would play twice-nightly for four days.

It was inevitable that we should get to know some of the players, for the smell of greasepaint seeps through all cultural and social barriers. It wasn't very long before they discovered that we were *artistas* like themselves. They spoke no English, we spoke pidgin Spanish, and we both massacred phrases in French. But we communicated, for all theatre people speak the same language whatever the tongue: the manager wasn't spending nearly enough on publicity; the leading lady was a bitch and was probably sleeping with him; and all the performers were worth far more than he was paying them. But it was good-natured criticism, for there is no more enjoyable company than actors in their off-duty hours, especially after a couple of drinks which we were very happy to provide at those prices.

The group was no tacky concert party from the end of the pier at Southend-on-Sea. Their show was expensively costumed and highly professional, with talented performers and a three-piece band in the pit. But they had never played Tossa before and were a few years ahead of the holiday hordes from England and Germany, and audiences were thin. We went to the second show every night even though we couldn't understand a word of the comic routines. We just took our cue from the locals and laughed whenever they did. Each day we would meet the cast for an after-lunch liqueur or three and we never let them pick up a tab. On their last day, the lunch session stretched a bit and my management side got worried about their early performance. The stage manager was promptly despatched to the tent to tell the first house audience to go away and come back later for the second show. To this performance, we all floated a couple of hours afterwards, but not before we'd had a private talk with the drummer. We had some last-night gifts we wanted him to hand up to the cast as a surprise at the end of the show. This was a custom not practised in the Spanish theatre and we had to explain the drill.

As the show neared its end, we could see that the drummer was getting a bit over-anxious, shuffling the gift packages around between drumbeats. The final act on the bill was the comic. Before the poor man could get out the punch-line of his last and best gag, there was a resounding drum-roll from the orchestra pit. The comic was left standing with egg on his face while the drummer proceeded to introduce his *amigos* in the front row who were all fellow *artistas de Canada* who had gifts for the whole company as was the custom in their country. The cast came on, the gifts were handed up (cigars for the men and perfume for the ladies), and the curtain came down to tumultuous applause which followed the three of us all the way out of the "theatre."

Tossa del Mar wasn't the only gift that filtered down from the gods that summer of '53. There was also Monica Wilkinson. Ninette de Valois, *grande-dame* of the famous Sadler's Wells Ballet, lost the queen-pin of her support staff when Monica came knocking on our door in search of a more adventurous way of life. Her timing, like most of her other attributes, was impeccable, for 1953 was unquestionably shaping up as the year of adventure for the London Theatre Company.

Gaining Monica doubled the size of our administrative staff. For the first time in three years I would have help during the planning stage and I would never need it more. The reconnoitering tour and the Spanish interlude had eaten away a huge chunk of our preparation time. With all the new touring dates added to our schedule, some aspects of the workload had multiplied by ten. Travel people, school boards, box-office sites, truckers, ticket takers, ushers and bed-and-breakfast brokers scattered over half Ontario were anxiously awaiting written confirmations. There were tickets to be ordered from the printer for ten totally different seating formats and price scales; performing rights to be tracked down, negotiated and deposits paid; costume plots, prop plots, itineraries, advertising schedules and contracts to be drawn up. We shoehorned Monica and a brand-new portable typewriter into a cramped corner of Oliver's flat and went on a hunt for actors.

Finding enough of them itching to go to Canada was easy. Picking the right ones was the hard part and it was getting harder. We'd used up most of the actors we'd worked with before and wanted to again, and we were running out of excuses for not hiring the ones that we didn't. For the first time, we'd have to do our own talent-spotting and not leave it all to the Salbergs. And with actors about to be locked in to nine-month contracts with no escape clause, we needed to be better than good at it.

The pile of résumés was bigger than ever. All it took was one glimpse of Oliver, Hilary or myself having a quick nip in the Salisbury for the bush telegraph to spread the word that we were back and casting again, and an avalanche of mail would descend upon Redcliffe Square.

For our first two seasons, all the pile ever got was a cursory flip-through to see if it contained a familiar face that we hadn't thought about. We had never been interested in rooting out budding talent only to find out two thousand miles from home that it was never likely to flower. But now we had no choice. There would always be an element of the unknown in the actors we chose, whatever it said on résumés that could be heavily booby-trapped for the unwary. Career histories they may have been but they were written not by historians, but by actors who might not be such sticklers for the facts. Some actors were even known to list parts they wished they'd played rather than parts they had. We'd recognize the title of the play and the name of the character, but we'd never heard of the company it was supposed to have been played in. The thickness of the résumé was nothing to go on. Often it boiled down to the thinnest genuine experience. Take away the parts played in high school and local amateur societies, and a single sheet could have done the job.

Most actors in their early days actors flirt a little with the truth without getting found out, but one girl we interviewed was unlucky enough to claim to have played the lead in a production I had been in myself at Richmond. She brazened it out when I challenged her, saying she would go straight home and bring me a copy of the programme to prove it. That was the last we ever saw of her. In the end, you found yourself hooked by the cool confidence of an actor or actress who simply stated: REPERTORY SEASONS IN BRISTOL, MANCHESTER and SHEFFIELD. You would take it for granted that they must have played at least a hundred roles and didn't feel it necessary to name one of them. Then the voice of suspicion whispered that they might all have been walk-ons, so they too, like all the others, had to take the final test and prove that they could really deliver in front of a paying audience.

For four weeks, we didn't miss a night of repertory theatre within a hundred miles of London: six nights a week for Hilary and me and five for Oliver because on Saturdays he was the player with an audience of his own in the bleachers on the cricket ground. We didn't always agree about the merits of the actors we saw, and it only needed the slightest reservation from one of us for the name to come straight off our shopping list. Nobody ever made the team without a solid three-to-nil endorsement. One actor who was dying to come with us in 1953 was Edward Mulhare. Oliver was all for him; I felt we could do better. A few years later, Mulhare took over from Rex Harrison in *My Fair Lady* on Broadway. Oliver never said "I told you so" and I still didn't concede that I was wrong. No doubt he'd have been a whiz as Professor Higgins in *Pygmalion*, but how would he have made out as Heathcliff in *Wuthering Heights* that same season?

We had already passed Michael Ellis's absolute deadline for the costume plot at Moss Bros before we filled the final slot in the acting company and began pencilling a name against every part in every play for the entire season. To calm Michael down, we added to his private cash bonus before sending the first actor along for a costume fitting. Michael, who was always a bit hysterical, had a genuine problem: he was having a run on some of the plays we had chosen. Where he couldn't draw a costume from stock he would have to tailor-make a new one to our own actor's specifications. The biggest beneficiary of this bonanza was Hilary. Michael personally designed every gown she wore as Marguerite in *Camille* and had his top cutters tailor them especially for her. And all at standard rental prices.

We set a huge precedent for a repertory company in 1953 by sending every member of the company to one of London's leading theatrical photographers for a portrait session at our expense. The repertory actor of 1953 was still expected to provide his or her own photographs for display in the theatre lobby. This arrangement didn't always harmonize with the billing, particularly when a well-heeled young pup with a walk-on part would arrive with his own easel supporting a frame showing his unknown face from four different angles, while the leading actor's presence in the company was miserably reflected by a single unframed eight-by-ten glossy twenty years old and curling at the edges. It became quite clear that the latter kind of display would not do in a department store window on High Street, Ontario.

We also splurged on an additional actor for the 1953 company. We would be fifteen strong, and strong was the key word by any repertory standards. Avis Lennard and Anthony Newlands, two standouts from our previous season, unquestionably excited by the prospects of a mainland tour, decided to sign on for another nine months. Kevin Stoney finished the West End revival of *Journey's End* just when we wanted him. Honor Shepherd completed her long West End run playing the name part in *The Perfect Woman* in time to join us with her husband, character actor Robert Dorning. Charles Jarrott, a young leading man, would eventually become a director of feature films as a direct result of coming with us to Canada. Sally Day, our ingenue, would find herself a husband who was a vice-president of CP Hotels. And an all-new stage management team would face our toughest assignment yet – touring. The SM would be Bernard Thompson. His assistants would be Denny Spence and Barbara Bryne. Barbara would lose no time at all in proving that she was a character actress of no ordinary ability, and she would end up as probably the London Theatre Company's single most notable gift to Canadian theatre among all the actresses we brought over and left behind.

Just as Monica and I were packing our bags for Canada, word came from Hilary's husband, Tim, that he was prepared to give us a divorce provided that we arranged everything and paid all the costs. I hastened to meet him in the Salisbury and settle the details. I would be the co-respondent and admit adultery and the suit would be uncontested. Before we shook hands on the deal, he tapped me for ten pounds. Nineteen fifty-three was still a very good year.

twentyfour

Monica had a mind like a notebook that was always open. It jotted down every snippet of information it could pick up from scribblings on scraps of paper, past company records, one-on-ones with me and snatches of conversation overheard between any combination of Oliver, Hilary, myself and a telephone. By the end of her first month she knew enough to type out a detailed plan of action to cover most of the bases between then and opening night in Halifax. When I told her that the two of us would have to go to St. John's first to set up the advance box-office there, she was ahead of me. She'd already booked us a flight.

We were the two lone passengers to deplane at Gander. The shoulder flashes may have read CANADA CUSTOMS but the voice was pure Newfoundland: "And what would we be having in that little paper bag, sor?"

"Two bottles of Scotch," I said, "small ones."

"Ah. That's too much sor."

"Too much?"

"The limit's forty ounces, sor."

"How much have I got?"

"Fifty-two."

"Oh. Well – er – couldn't we drink the other twelve now?"

He spun on his heel and made a bee-line for a very official-looking door in the rear wall. I waited nervously for the gold braid to appear but it was himself who came out, with his hands behind him. He turned his back on me at the inspection table and dropped a coffee mug on it. I filled it. He went out and in seconds was back and repeated the process with a different mug.

"Me pal wants one too," he said, without moving his lips. Then he came back and marked our bags. He didn't waste a speck of chalk on Monica's new typewriter. It had been four years since New-

222

foundlanders had voted to join confederation, and it was going to take a while yet before they'd learn to live by the Canadian rule book.

In St. John's I gave Monica a quick tour of the London Theatre Company's nerve centres: the Balsam Hotel, the Crow's Nest, the scene shop, the box-office space at Bowrings and the liquor store. I knew the tiny office above the stage would be a bit of a comedown; so I saved it till last. It didn't faze Monica in the slightest, not even the six month's layer of dust. While she got busy with a duster, I went out to round up the programme advertisers. For the second straight year, the Bowring name was conspicuous by its absence. In fact, they never again took space in the programme they had totally monopolized the first year. But there were twenty-eight others who did and signing them all up without a car was quite a hustle. The A90 was still in Quebec, parked in a garage eight hundred miles away over what eastern Canada knew as roads in 1953. My first priority was to get it back. I told Monica to book me a ticket to Montreal and one for herself direct to Halifax to get things started there. When we got to the concourse at Torbay airport, she gave me the wrong ticket.

"This one's Halifax. You must have the one to Montreal."

"That's right," she said. "I'm going to pick up the car."

I told her she hadn't a clue what she'd be taking on: that an A90 was like driving a Churchill tank compared to her baby Austin in England; that maniacs rode the highways in Canada; that people drove on the wrong side of the road and that the mileage from Montreal to Halifax would be the same as driving from London to Edinburgh *and back*. Nothing I could say would stop her, so I just let her go and worried all the time she was gone. I insisted she stay the night in Montreal before setting out, have three stopovers on the way, and phone me at six o'clock every day to tell me where she was. She phoned me twice. On the third night she spoke to me in Halifax in person. From then on, I didn't worry any more about Monica.

While she was on the highway, I started the advertising and opened the box-office at Phinney's on Barrington Street. It was clear from day one that Halifax was delighted to see us back. And this time they didn't dicker over which production to choose, they bought the series. It had been designed to encourage them to do just that. They had told us plainly in box-office language the year before that they hated farce, didn't really care about drama, and adored sophisticated light comedy. We gave them two light comedies that they wouldn't want to miss, one classic that they'd be ashamed to, and a drama which they wouldn't care for but would come to see because they were Scots and it was free if you bought the series and paid for the other three.

Meantime, George Paddon-Foster and his new stage carpenter Joe Russell had been slogging away for three weeks in our scene shop in St. John's, augmenting our growing stock of scenery flats, doors, windows, pelmets, stairs, banisters, landings, fireplaces and built-in cupboards needed to mount all four productions on the massive Queen Elizabeth Auditorium stage. George and Joe saw every piece onto the Newfie Bullet for its rail and ferry trip to Halifax before boarding a plane to beat the arrival of the shipment by at least a couple of days.

George needed all that time. Our first production was to be Sheridan's classic comedy *The School for Scandal,* and George's immediate concern was to scour the second-hand stores for some suitable period furniture. Most dealers were happy to pick up a rental fee and put the items back into stock at the end of the week at the same price as before. But this time, our situation was different. In three months we would stop being a resident company and turn into a touring one. And there would be no time on the road to go shopping for set dressings en route from the railway station to the auditorium. The moment had come to start buying furniture of our own and travel it along with the scenery.

Our first purchase was a Victorian sofa closely followed by six brand-new dining room chairs, very basic with a thinly upholstered seat and a simple back that didn't tie them to any specific period in furniture history. They are still alive and well today, having outlived the London Theatre Company by nearly forty years and gathered quite a history on the way. They appeared countless times on the St. John's stage, always disguised with a new layer of paint or a change of seat cover. They travelled thousands of miles by train, truck and ferry, back and forth across Newfoundland, the Maritimes and Ontario and finally, ensconced in my basement in Toronto, they brought their stage careers quietly to an end – or so I thought. Pat Galloway, visiting on a day off from the Stratford Festival company, found them and offered to give them a good home in her new farmhouse in St. Mary's. It was in her kitchen in 1985 that Tanya Moiseiwitsch, Stratford's first and best-loved designer, discovered them and carted them off to Roy Brown at the Festival prop shop where they were exquisitely reconditioned, repainted with a beautiful floral pattern and given their Stratford debut on the Festival stage in the Mayor's parlour in *The Government Inspector.* It was an honourable finish to the career of the London Theatre Company chairs. They appeared in the last play

Tanya would design for the stage she had helped to create.

News of the unusual line-ups at Phinney's must have filtered down the street to the *Chronicle-Herald* office, because when the *Nova Scotia* docked, there was a photographer at the wharf to meet the cast and their picture made the front page the next morning. Until then, barely a drop of printer's ink had been devoted to the comings and goings of the London Theatre Company in Halifax.

As soon as the company was safely ashore, I was integrated into the cast of *School for Scandal* as Sir Oliver Surface, an old favourite of mine. Secure in the knowledge that Monica was successfully being me outside the theatre, I began to enjoy rehearsals again for the first time in a couple of years.

On our opening night in Halifax, a telegram arrived from St. John's: GOOD LUCK TONIGHT HURRY UP AND COME HOME. It bore thirty-nine signatures. We didn't break box-office records with *School* but we made a profit, which was a promising start to the longest and most ambitious year in our history. When the final curtain came down on Saturday, I took Monica through the mysteries of closing out a week: calculating the official box-office return, royalties, taxes, weekly getout, profit and loss statement, and just how much cash to place in the myriad hands always outstretched at the end of a run. Next morning, the A90 and I took off for Moncton and Saint John.

Oliver had deliberately left me out of the second Halifax production which kept my evenings free. And with only one scene to rehearse in play number three, *Camille*, Oliver could manage without me until the Friday. That gave me four days to drive four hundred miles, open two box-offices, stir up the media for our forthcoming mini-tour, and learn the part of Armand's father.

I returned to Halifax to find *Chiltern Hundreds* a roaring success, due in no small measure to Kevin Stoney's *tour de force* as the enchantingly vague Earl of Lister. While I was trying to catch up with the rest of the company in *Camille* rehearsals, a Charles Michael Turner called from Niagara Falls to know if we would be available to play a season at the Niagara Falls Summer Theatre which had fallen unexpectedly vacant. It could immediately follow our season at the Grand, London. I told him we wouldn't be the slightest bit interested if it involved any kind of financial risk. However, we might consider the idea for a weekly guarantee of two thousand dollars, we to be responsible for everything that went on backstage except for paying the crew, he to cover everything on the other side of the curtain including all the publicity. He thought that would be quite reasonable.

So did I. At that stage of the tour, we would have already amortized our transatlantic travel costs, and $2000 would give us a guaranteed profit of nearly $800 a week. I told him I would have to discuss it with my partners and the rest of the company, and he could call me back the next day.

I was stunned to find that Oliver didn't share the enthusiasm that was fairly bubbling over in Hilary and myself. In fact, all we got from him was his spaniel look, only a much sadder spaniel than we'd ever seen before. I really thought he was about to burst into tears.

"I'm – terribly sorry, old boy, I can't. It's er – it's er – cricket, you see."

At that precise moment I'm not sure who was made to feel the more wretched: he for being unwittingly cast as the spoiler, or I for being unable to imagine that any other form of life existed beyond the world of the London Theatre Company. Of course he couldn't go to Niagara Falls. The problem now was what did we have to do to go without him?

I didn't want to give up the Niagara connection. I needed the insurance. With a cast-iron guarantee, it would help us repair the financial damage if we ran into trouble on the road. Suppose we repeated our Grand Theatre playbill at Niagara? There wouldn't be much for a director to do except re-direct. And I could take over the parts that Oliver had played.

Unfortunately, it didn't turn out to be quite as simple as that. When I asked the company if they wanted a ten-week extension on their contracts to spend the summer in Niagara Falls, I had one non-taker. Kevin Stoney had married actress Rosalie Crutchley the day before the company had sailed from Liverpool and he still owed her a honeymoon. Add ten weeks in Niagara to his present contract and Rosalie would have to wait a full year to become the real Mrs Stoney. I don't know how he ever got her to agree to a nine-month separation in the first place, but he certainly hadn't the nerve to try to make it twelve.

Now short two actors, Kevin's "no" began to sound like the death knell for Charles Michael Turner. But I couldn't let a guaranteed income go without a struggle. I went through all the plays that would be in the repertoire by the time we got to Niagara and made a list of the ones we could do minus Oliver and Kevin. It looked awful. I slotted in a possible replacement actor from Toronto and it looked a lot better. With two fewer salaries to pay, we could afford him. But there was one big snag. To my mind, the ideal play in our repertoire to open the

Niagara season and show off an English company to what I anticipated would be a largely American audience would be *The Chiltern Hundreds*, already known to Broadway theatre-goers as *Yes M'Lord*. After Kevin's personal triumph at Halifax, how could I trust the Earl of Lister to an actor whose work I'd never seen? I couldn't play it myself: I would have to take over Oliver's huge part as the butler. I decided to have one last go at Kevin.

"Why don't you come to Niagara for just one week, play the Earl of Lister, and I'll fly you back to London from Toronto instead of that awful train trip to Halifax and the boat to Liverpool?" That did it. I phoned Charles Michael Turner.

Next day, I was standing in the bay window of our room at the Sword and Anchor Inn when Charles Michael Turner's taxi pulled up outside. As I watched him alight, I remember turning to Hilary and saying, "Oh dear, I think we've bought it."

Mr Turner just didn't look good casting for an impresario. He was altogether too precisely turned out: blue blazer with crossed oars and a Latin motto stitched in gold on his breast pocket, immaculate white ducks, old school tie, co-respondent's shoes and an ivory panama hat. And the briefcase was spanking new. That's what really bothered me. It lacked the wear and tear of experience. He was also very English which made me think of Harry Reynolds.

Nevertheless, I couldn't find a flaw in the contract: ten weeks at a flat fee of two thousand dollars to be paid two hours before the banks closed on Fridays. I signed, Monica drew up the riders to everybody's contract, Oliver was highly relieved to be let off the hook and gave us his blessing and we all went back to rehearsing *Camille*. Oliver's first job was to cure Barbara Bryne of a fit of the giggles in the ballroom scene. She would make a splendid entrance with Marguerite, stand at the top of the grand staircase, survey every actor we had been able to muster for the scene (all nine of them) and then say, "Isn't this wonderful! Half Paris is here!"

Hilary Vernon's moving performance as Marguerite drew the tears but not the masses, despite a rave review in the *Mail-Star* which began: "It is a long journey for us to London's West End but the London Theatre Company has brought it to our door." Unfortunately, good reviews don't always entice people into theatres in the same way that bad reviews drive them out. *Camille* barely squeaked its way into the profit column. But it kept up our winning streak, which was considerably enhanced by our final production, *Queen Elizabeth Slept Here*. We had played Halifax without a single losing week. I left Oliver to it and sent Monica off to St. John's where our opening was less than two weeks away and not an ad had been placed or a ticket sold. I drove to Saint John to await the company. We now had box-offices spread over a thousand miles and open in four cities, St. John's, Halifax, Moncton and Saint John, and only Monica and myself to service them.

The Saint John High School Auditorium had one of those bastardized stages designed to do dual service as a gymnasium by an architect who might have been nifty with a netball at school but had never been asked to play Hamlet. It had obviously not occurred to him that both dual purposes of his brainchild might be put to use at the same time: such was the misfortune that befell us in Saint John. While we were performing *School for Scandal* on one side of the sliding doors at the back of the stage, a basketball match was being played on the other, and Sheridan's witty barbs were punctuated with shrill blasts on a referee's whistle, more often than not at precisely the wrong moment. In addition, the school board had the audacity to charge $200 rent per performance which was twice as much as Halifax for a much inferior auditorium. That would be equivalent to $1400 today or $7000 for a five performance week!

Sheridan calls for nine stage settings in *School for Scandal.* These can be easily whittled down to three with a pair of centre curtains and a little imagination. *A room in Joseph Surface's House* can just as easily appear in the programme as *A corridor* or *An anteroom* or even *A corner of an anteroom,* with just a single sofa in view. The same sofa covered with a throw can also turn up in *A corridor in Sir Peter Teazle's house.* The main thing is to keep the action going in front of the mid-stage curtain while the set is being rapidly changed behind it, so that the audience never sees the stage crawling with human ants in black suits which seems to be the vogue today.

We did a special schools matinee on the Wednesday afternoon in Saint John. Barbara Bryne was having a sandwich later in a student hangout when she overheard the following conversations:

"What did you think of the play?"

"I didn't understand a word of it. The whole thing was in English."

And from another stool further down the counter:

" ... and that same old sofa kept coming on and going off and coming on and going off."

We gave *School* and *Chiltern Hundreds* three performances each in Saint John and one each in Moncton. We didn't break even in either town but we came close. Enough to prove that a thousand miles from home base they'd heard of the London Players. Could word have wafted another six hundred miles further west? We'd have to wait until February to find that out.

In 1953 we were doubly cruel to our most faithful followers. We not only rationed St. John's to a mere nine evenings of theatre to tide them over six long months of winter, we also gave them these nine productions in the deadliest period of the theatrical year, just before and just after Christmas, when box-offices the entertainment world over are invariably in deep mourning. The city responded by delivering us an astonishing run of four winning weeks out of four, even including the usually disastrous week but one before Christmas. And most satisfying of all, they proved they'd come of theatrical age by placing our only classic, *School for Scandal*, at the top of the money list, outdrawing *Laura, Spring Model* and *Queen Elizabeth Slept Here*.

Laura, with two showy parts for Hilary in the name part and Anthony Newlands as Waldo Lydecker, marked our fiftieth production in St. John's. On opening night, as the cast came on to take their final curtain calls, the head chefs of the city's two leading bakeries, Walsh's and Mammy's, wheeled on from each side of the stage gigantic birthday cakes with fifty candles, enough to provide a slice for everyone in the house. While the chefs cut the cakes and filled serving trays for the actors to hand round, the entire audience rose to its feet and sang "Happy Birthday." Next morning, the *Daily News* gave us a two-page spread. One page had photographs of all past and present company members surrounding a blow-up of cutting the cakes, and the other an honour roll of all fifty productions displayed in bold type within a framework of congratulatory messages from the city's leading advertisers. By contrast, the *Evening Telegram* left it to the critic to mark the occasion with a one-line intro to her review.

During the run of *Laura*, we received a telegram from Ernie Rawley, Manager of the Royal Alexandra Theatre in Toronto, offering us a three-week booking at the Alex from January 4th. Such short notice could only indicate an unexpected cancellation, but we weren't at all miffed to be a last-minute choice for Canada's number one theatre space. Nor did it do our reputation any harm to wire back: REGRET UNABLE ACCEPT DUE TO HEAVY SEASON TICKET COMMITMENTS HERE.

Our first year in St. John's had taught us that it was hopeless to play anything the week before Christmas, so we closed. We took the cost of the dead days and amortized it over the rest of the season, and used the extra time to rehearse our Christmas pantomime which even repertory actors couldn't do in a week. Oliver had finished his long-term commitment to Derek Salberg at the Birmingham Alexandra Theatre and was now able to add his considerable pantomime expertise to our own production of *Robinson Crusoe*. With his love for broad comedy, he also cast himself as my son Billy Crusoe, a perfect foil for me being outrageous in my second crack at a pantomime dame, Mrs Crusoe.

We opened on Christmas Eve to an invited audience of four hundred children from all the orphanages in St. John's. We persuaded Brookfields, the ice-cream makers, to hand out free cones in the intermission while Walsh's and Mammy's bakeries were once again to the fore with an unlimited supply of free cakes. On Christmas Day, a group of us went to the General Hospital in full costume and presented some short scenes to the patients and staff as part of the Rotarians' Christmas broadcast. This was the beginning of a tradition that would last as long as the London Theatre Company.

The strange things that go on in English pantomime are not restricted solely to casting a man as the dame and a sexy woman in long silk tights as the principal boy – in this case Honor Shepherd as Robinson Crusoe. I have a vivid recollection of Honor lying upside-down on my lap with myself stitching a patch on the seat of her well-curved red pants and singing *Mighty Lak a Rose* for no reason at all that I could think of. Believe it or not, it was quite moving.

Every panto has a running gag, and our *Robinson Crusoe* script called for a pair of kippers. This being St. John's and Brigitte Bardot having not yet found out that seals have puppies, inevitably the kippers became flippers which were a great local delicacy brought ashore as perks by the sealing crews at the end of the hunt. As I placed the pair of flippers on the side of the stage, I beseeched the audience to keep an eye on them for me as I was saving them up to make a flipper pie on Sunday. If anyone went near them, they were to scream out "Flippers!" and I would come running on to protect them. Every ten minutes or so, the stage manager, disguised as a pirate, would creep on and try to steal them. The kids would scream "Flippers!" and the longer I took to respond, the more frantically they'd scream.

In seven days, with just one Sunday intervening, *Robinson Crusoe* played to fourteen completely sold-out houses. With a performance every afternoon and evening and a *Camille* rehearsal every morning, the company ended the week exhausted. But they still found the energy to celebrate Christmas. With the orphans' matinee over by five o'clock on Christmas Eve, the Balsam Hotel annexe was jumping from six o'clock on, with Kevin Stoney the chief jumper. At one point, he zoomed to the top of the stairs with his arms outstretched like a plane and dropped Mary Facey's potted ferns one by one down the stairwell shouting "Bombs away!" as they hit the floor in the hall. He rounded out the evening by prancing naked in the snow and screaming like a banshee. The maiden ladies in the main building had never seen a Christmas like it. On Christmas morning, Kevin struggled up the darkened hill to the Basilica to confess his sins at the six o'clock mass and promptly fell asleep. He woke up at the same point in the service some three masses later, made his obeisances, and couldn't understand why it was broad daylight when he got outside.

Hilary's extraordinary drawing power in dramatic roles turned a traditionally quiet week following Christmas into the second-best box-office of the season with *Camille*. And Michael Ellis had never made her look more beautiful. He'd designed for her a ball gown and a cloak trimmed with a real sable collar. Michael, who adored Hilary, refused to rent this ensemble to anyone else at the end of our season, instead displaying it in a glass case in the middle of the Moss Bros store in London's theatre district for over a year. In the bottom of the case was a card that read:

WORN BY MISS HILARY VERNON
as MARGUERITE in CAMILLE
London Theatre Company tour of Canada – 1954

Our production of *Camille* had its own moment of drama that had nothing to do with Alexandre Dumas fils. Just as George Paddon-Foster was putting the finishing touches to the last of the three stage settings that the production demanded (all painted in a single week), he collapsed and was rushed off to hospital with acute appendicitis. And he barely gave the surgeon time to tie a knot in the last stitch before he was back in his paint shop, sitting in a wheelchair, directing the brushstrokes of our stage manager and our ingenue who had both volunteered to paint the set for our next show.

Although the crisis was quickly over, George had given my self-confidence a horrible jolt. His illness had uncovered a gaping hole in our defences – something over which I had absolutely no control and no contingency plans. Actors could go on for other actors; non-directors could sit in the director's chair and not muck up the play because the actors wouldn't let him, but no one could go on and be George. I shudder to think what might have happened had his appendix started to grumble three weeks earlier, with a full-scale pantomime to mount and touring sets to be painted. But, by the grace of God and George's good timing, the sets for the tour were all ready for the road because the plays we'd chosen had already been staged in St. John's.

Even without George's appendix, the pressure was intense, more than it had been at any time since the day we began. We were three weeks off the end of the St. John's season and the start of the tour. We had only one more play to go before the revue was upon us. As this demanded overlapping rehearsals for two weeks, we had three productions on the go at the same time. While we played *Separate Rooms* in the evenings, we rehearsed *The Deep Blue Sea* in the mornings and *Still More Screech* in the afternoons. And in between, Monica and I had to think touring and keep our chosen towns fed with press releases and small teaser ads as well as cope with the St. John's wrap-up.

When we were down to the last two weeks, I shipped the A90 by rail to Hamilton to await our arrival, and Monica off to Sydney to open the advance box-office there. I stayed in St. John's and finished writing a couple of sketches for the revue. One of these portrayed a colourful group of locals riding a city bus (a real rattler) over the pot-holes that notoriously peppered the roads during spring runoff. The set was simply six rows of two chairs, with a single seat in front for the driver. The opportunities for gossip were endless (and merciless) about the local nobs supposedly seen through the bus windows en route. And every time the bus came to a "pot-hole," the driver jumped two feet up off his seat followed by a ripple effect of each passenger doing the same all the way to the back of the bus. I don't know how many pot-holes we arranged for, but the more there were, the more hysterical the audience became. I called the skit "Bother on the Belt Line" (a circular city route).

Other hits I remember in our third end-of-season revue were Denny Spence and Barbara Bryne in a black light number as a couple of dancing skeletons, and Robert Dorning as the "Female Mountie who never got her man." But our biggest bonus in 1954 was the realization that Denny Spence, with a pair of horn-rimmed spectacles, was the dead spit of Premier Joey Smallwood. "The Cabinet Meeting

II" was wicked.

Still More Screech set a new revue box-office record, even outpacing its two successful predecessors. *The Deep Blue Sea* didn't quite make it and missed the break-even point by a mere $141. Every other production since we'd arrived in Halifax thirteen weeks earlier had made a profit and fattened up the treasury for our venture into touring. We were going to need it.

twentyfive

St. John's showed up in strength and its finery to see us onto the Port aux Basques train that snowy February morning in 1954. The platform was besieged and arms were reaching up to every window, dishing out goodies for the journey like prizes on speech day. And already stashed aboard was a full case of liquor, compliments of George Crosbie, President of the local Lever Bros. Almost as soon as the last waving hand had been withdrawn from the windows, the party began. It stopped just as abruptly when the conductor stalked in and announced: "No drinking in here. Only in the lavatory."

We had booked the drawing room at each end of a sleeper and most of the berths in between for the guarantee of a coach to ourselves, so I couldn't see how our social life could possibly corrupt any of the other passengers.

"Don't make no difference," said our conductor. But a couple of stiff rums did, and he left us with a glow he didn't have when he came in. So we set up the bar, put out the ashtrays, and in no time at all you couldn't read the NO SMOKING signs through the fog.

Until that trip, I had no idea just how many people it took to run a train, but we quickly found out. Long before we bedded down for the night we'd met them all, and most of them had come back for seconds. Next day the train stopped at Corner Brook where George Crosbie's local representative came aboard with another case of liquor. For the rest of the journey we practically ran a private social club for railway workers. At one point we even found ourselves pouring a drink for a large gentleman in overalls who said he was the one driving the train.

The Newfoundland Railway was narrow gauge so the train wasn't able to drive straight on to the ferry at Port aux Basques: the end of the line butted onto the wharf. One of my most vivid memories is of an entire train crew led by the engine driver, loaded down with our personal baggage, weaving dangerously from side to side along the full length of the narrow dock, leading the way to the waiting ferry and telling anyone who cared to listen that they'd never had another trip like it. In the early hours of the next morning, the company and six tons of equipment disembarked at North Sydney and we were on tour, bound for Sydney, Moncton, Saint John, Hamilton, St. Catharines, London, Kitchener, Ottawa, Peterborough, Kingston and Halifax.

It was a sweat for the stage management to hang the electrics, put up the set, dress it and light it for a performance that same evening. But they made it. And they would get faster as we went along. The actors were well rehearsed and would quickly learn to adjust to a stage that might be twice as wide and half as deep as the one they had played on the night before. George had painted extra flats for each set to extend them when needed. The plans we had laid so meticulously eight months earlier all bore fruit, though I had some second thoughts about our choice of the Guba Minto as our hotel in Sydney when Barbara Bryne came downstairs brandishing a couple of condoms she'd found prominently displayed on top of the pile of clean towels in her room.

Our only other problem was Kevin Stoney's black Homburg hat. He'd left it on the Newfie Bullet and didn't discover it until just before his first entrance in Terence Rattigan's *The Deep Blue Sea*. Oliver dashed out front to the checkroom, grabbed the first Homburg he could see and made it backstage in time to clap it on Kevin's head just before he went on. Oliver had to wait until the actors were taking their final bows before he could retrieve the hat, race out front and replace it on hook 63. The owner never knew he'd been watching his own hat onstage for most of the evening. The switch from weekly to daily rep was a bit of a shock to cast and crew as we performed *The Deep Blue Sea* the first night and *Spring Model* the next. We were spared the trauma of switching to our third touring production, *The School for Scandal,* on night number three because Sydney was only scheduled as a two-night stand.

Monica, meanwhile, was trying to light a few fires in another steel town thirteen hundred miles west. I leap-frogged the company by air to join her in Hamilton while the others spent the time seeing the landscapes of Upper Canada framed by a succession of railway carriage windows. I left Sydney in high spirits, buoyed by word from London that Hilary's divorce had gone through, but Monica's news put a quick damper on that. Hamilton was profoundly unmoved by the prospect of our arrival. Despite a prominent box-office at street level in the biggest department store on Main street, the sum total of advance bookings was nothing short of alarming.

Monica and I went into emergency session. How did one create a sudden thirst for theatre in a town that hadn't set eyes on a professional actor for over thirty years? Where "seeing a show" still meant going to the movies? Where no one could visualize an auditorium stage dressed for anything but a graduation ceremony, least of all "A ballroom in Paris in 1830." Where were we to begin? We couldn't afford to take half pages in the *Spectator* and they were being very grudging about editorial support. Entertainment editors were far less interested in what was afoot on their own patch than the latest exploits of Susie-what-the-hell's-er-name in Hollywood, California.

Monica and I did what we could. We plastered the town with flyers. We had student teams stuffing them under windshield wipers at every curbside, parking lot and private driveway that didn't have a DANGEROUS DOG sign. I bullied my way onto the radio. We tracked down secretaries of social clubs and offered special party rates at fire-sale prices. The box-office queue swelled from nothing to a trickle.

By this time, the company had arrived and the stage management was having its share of problems at the Delta Auditorium. For the first time, we encountered a school board that insisted we hire a union electrician. The one who arrived from the local must have been seventy-five but at least he was dressed for the part. He was wearing a huge leather belt with tools dangling from the entire perimeter of his very large stomach. Bernard Thompson, our stage manager, led him to our dimmer board and feeder cable, and assumed he would know where the auditorium main breaker was. He didn't, so Bernard took him there. Laden-belt stared at it for fully twenty minutes, scared stiff to touch anything, so Bernard finally did the hook-up himself. He then sat the man from the local on a chair well away from the prompt corner, pulled his morning paper out of his back pocket and told him to sit there, read it, keep quiet and not touch anything. Not a tool came out of his belt for a week, at the end of which I gave him a check that was twice as big as the leading actor's.

The day before opening night, we had such a pathetic house to offer the cast that Monica and I each took a handful of passes and waited outside the main gates of the Steel Company to catch the day shift coming off duty. We couldn't even give seats away. The *Spectator* said it best two mornings later:

> There is a certain group in Hamilton that is forever moaning the lack of theatre in the city. Where are all the plays, they

sigh bitterly. Why is Hamilton so devoid of culture? These people had an opportunity last night of seeing a first rate English company present "Camille" in the Delta Auditorium. The play was directed with integrity and skill. It was performed by a cast of good professional actors who know and obviously love their craft. Did our art-minded citizens turn out in their eager thousands to see the play? No, they did not.

They didn't come on the second and third nights either, and, after I had beseeched Marguerite not to marry Armand for the third and last time in Hamilton, I drove to St Catharines for an early start to our campaign there the following morning. I got back to Hamilton on the Saturday to find that the farce *Spring Model*, our second three-day offering, had warmed up a few empty seats but not enough to save us from an operating loss of more than two thousand dollars on the week. We had six more dates to go. I checked our liquidity with the Royal Bank in St. John's to make sure we could lay our hands on twelve thousand dollars in a hurry.

I had great hopes we wouldn't need to draw on it in London. The Grand was a real theatre with a trained theatre audience. If we couldn't drag them in there, we'd have to start looking for the blame in our own backyard. Monica skipped London and went direct to Kitchener. Somehow she and I had to strive to keep two weeks ahead of the company as well as run it and that meant the two of us trying to be in three places at the same time more often than not. The Grand, with its own box-office staff and PR machine, would give us a bit of a breather. It was about all they did give us. We played to bigger houses but it cost us more to get them and we ended the week minus another two thousand dollars. When St. Catharines followed the same dismal pattern, I had to do something to stop the bleeding and quickly.

I took a huge gamble. With thirteen actors under a watertight contract that I couldn't break, I phoned Ken Basquette at the Grand Theatre and told him that it very much looked as if we would have to cancel our summer season. I was banking on the probability that an empty theatre at this late stage would give him an even bigger headache than it would me. He made me sweat for a couple of days but finally called to say that the board had met and authorized him to cut the theatre rent in half for the summer. Based on our touring figures, that still wouldn't be enough to put us in the black but the shade of red would unquestionably become a lot paler. The rent was the only item to be cut: there would be no special deals struck with the crew or the ad-managers of the local media. But the rent would help. Now, if I could just find a way to get rid of one lone touring date and reassign it, I'd save us another two thousand dollars.

Logistically I had but one choice – Toronto. I had long ago taken it off the main tour list and used it to break the journey from Halifax back to London for the summer season. I drove in from St Catharines to see Jimmie Hozack at Hart House Theatre. Not only did he let me cancel the date, but he also gave me back my deposit. I could now "hold over" the company for an extra week in Halifax and fly them straight to London, Ontario.

Something strange happened in Kitchener. For the first time, there was a flicker of interest at the advance box-office. This could only have been sparked by an item in the Toronto *Globe and Mail* headed "Mystery Theatre" and written by Herbert Whittaker:

> One is beginning to consider the London Theatre Company as a mystery group which is a rare thing for a theatrical group to be you must admit. This company of players from England has been playing in Newfoundland for several seasons unnoticed by the rest of us and is now touring Upper Canada. No publicity has been circulated but it has leaked out that the company is doing *Camille* and a new farce *Spring Model* and there is also a report that *School for Scandal* is in the repertoire. A copy of the itinerary smuggled out reads ...

I had no idea then that the *Globe and Mail* was a national paper, and I was deliberately holding back our sequence of press releases until closer to the Toronto date. The effect of the unsolicited *Globe* plug was a twenty-five percent jump in our attendance and a corresponding drop in our loss for each remaining week of the tour.

We got a second boost in Kitchener. A man named Frank Hogg, a leading light in the local amateur dramatic society, was so impressed with *Camille* on the first night that he called his group together and they began a vigorous telephone campaign on our behalf. Sandy Black, another member of that telephone committee, told me something forty years later that almost made our money-losing tour worthwhile:

I don't think you have any idea what a tremendous impact the London Theatre Company had on the early growth of the theatre movement in Ontario. Here in Kitchener was a wildly enthusiastic bunch of young amateurs sitting around and dreaming of a career in the theatre and all at once you drop out of the sky. Most of us had never seen a professional actor before and suddenly there you were, twelve or thirteen of you that we could sit and watch and study and learn from and afterwards talk to and even touch! I don't know if you were aware of it but there wasn't a single night during your week in Kitchener without at least one member of your company in somebody's home after the show, pouring theatre tales into eager ears until the early hours of the morning.

I didn't know. Most of the time after a performance, I was driving on to the next town. Sandy Black is now chair of the Theatre School at Ryerson Polytechnic University. Frank Hogg is a veteran talent agent in Toronto. Several other members of the Kitchener group, like Ron Hastings, became successful professional actors.

Ottawa delivered our best box-office on the tour, but unhappily at the expense of the resident Canadian Repertory Theatre whose audience defected in large numbers to see us. Totally undaunted, Amelia Hall, the CRT producer, invited us all to their mid-week matinée of *The Mask and the Face* starring William Hutt and then threw a party in our honour backstage after their Saturday night performance. We responded by inviting her entire cast and crew to be our guests at a performance of *Camille* on the Monday night when their theatre was dark.

Ottawa was the only city to see our full repertoire of three plays. Unfortunately I had to perform in two of them, which made life almost impossible for advance scouting. Monica had to be two weeks ahead of us in Kingston, leaving Peterborough to fend for itself. To cope with that situation, I had to spend four of my performance days commuting from Ottawa to Peterborough, returning in time to go on at night. At six in the morning on the fourth day, I was so exhausted that I went to sleep at the wheel going round a bend somewhere beyond Smith's Falls, and I woke up climbing a bank so steep that it threw me back on to the road. I have never been more frightened in my life.

The move to Peterborough called for a tough set-up schedule for the stage management, and the only access to the stage for bulky items was over the orchestra pit. On the afternoon of our get-in, the school orchestra was having a full dress rehearsal of a forthcoming concert and the conductor flatly refused to stop playing. So in the middle of a concerto, we had no alternative but to pass the scenery over the heads of the strings section which slid off its chairs, knelt on the floor and continued sawing away as if nothing had happened.

In Kingston, the final week of the tour, the stage management filled in its only accident report. During the set-up, Bernard Thompson got in the way of a swinging scenery flat and gashed his head open. He was rushed off to emergency where they decided he needed stitches. As they prepared to cut off a chunk of his hair, he jumped to his feet and shouted "You can't do that! I have to go on as the Compte de Giray in *Camille* in forty-five minutes!" He looked at his watch, shouted "Oh my God," grabbed a handful of dressings and jumped in a cab. He made the stage just in time to portray his share of "half of Paris" in the ballroom scene.

Three days later we crossed the Ontario border into the sanctuary of the Maritimes. I felt like a missionary coming out of the jungle having just escaped being boiled for breakfast.

Our supply line was still open to the Royal Bank in St. John's despite the fact that $14,291 had poured along it into Ontario and stayed there. That would be nearly $100,000 in today's money. Most of it had only been paid into the account since the season opened, and it hadn't been there long enough for my three partners to realize that for a short time we'd been rich. I knew of course, and saw us getting poorer. But I also knew that the worst was over and we were still solvent, so I ceased to worry. In fact, I secretly felt a flicker of pride that a tiny company like ours, capitalized at only six thousand dollars, could lose over twice as much as that in eight weeks and still be solidly in business.

Although a second tour of Ontario wasn't on my list of burning ambitions, I felt impelled to give myself a report card on the first one. I put down an A for logistics and an F for artistic judgment. As Ontario had never heard of the London Theatre Company, they should at least have heard of the plays we brought them. *Spring Model* was an untried farce written by a friend of Oliver's in England. Why not play safe with *Rookery Nook* or *Thark?* I was solely to blame for *Camille*. It was not the greatest play in the world, but it was a vehicle for Hilary who had been our star attraction from day one. *School for Scandal*, our one good choice, had the fewest performances because the cast list called for every member of the company, including me, who was invariably a town ahead of them.

Others have wondered why we spent a whole week in each town instead of just a couple of nights. To them I would say that what we achieved in a one-week stand was nothing short of a miracle: a shorter turnaround would have been totally beyond us. We travelled without any backstage crew whatever, not even a stage carpenter or an electrician. Our stage management, aided solely by local schoolboys, hung the electrics, focussed them, put up a full stage set, lit it, dressed it, went on stage, played a part and between entrances operated the light cues on the switchboard. If ever there is a Canadian Theatre Hall of Fame, the names of Bernard Thompson, Denny Spence and Barbara Bryne should hang there in large letters.

We didn't make any money in Halifax this time around, but for the first time in eight weeks we didn't lose any either. About midway through the season, Hilary's *decree nisi* came through and the divorce papers arrived from London. As we were financially just marking time at the box-office, I suggested to Oliver that instead of holding over for an extra week in Halifax to make up for the Toronto cancellation, we could give the entire company a week's holiday while Hilary and I went off to New York and got married. Oliver thought it was a splendid idea and so did the company. We gave everybody a week's pay and per diems in advance with a train ticket to London allowing stopovers en route. We all agreed to rendezvous at the Grand Theatre at noon the following Sunday.

Desertion was the only legal way to get a Canadian divorce in 1954, which is why so many disenchanted housewives went to Reno to complain that their husbands ate biscuits in bed. It was also why Hilary and I went to New York where they weren't nearly so fussy. Or so we had been led to believe by all those Deanna Durbin movies where college kids routinely hopped into dad's coupe, drove across the state line, got a justice of the peace out of bed and tied the knot at two in the morning.

We began to have doubts that real life was not quite the same as in the movies when the clerk at New York City Hall asked us if we had medical clearance for marriage. When I asked clearance for what, he said "Syphilis." We could get it from a doctor (the clearance, not syphilis), and no he wasn't allowed to recommend one, but nonetheless his hand slid forward hiding a business card for which he would undoubtedly receive his commission later.

The doctor's receptionist took our blood and ten dollars and said we could have the result in two weeks. I told her that wouldn't do at all because we were leaving New York on Saturday.

"Well, I might be able to get it through for you in forty-eight hours for an extra twenty-five dollars each." For fifty dollars U.S. in 1954, you could practically take a hockey team to Sardi's for dinner. But I paid it. Two days later at City Hall, the clerk was all smiles.

"Good! Now, can I see the divorce papers?" Pause. "Oh dear, the grounds are adultery. You can't get married in New York State. You could try New Jersey across the bridge."

"What the hell's the point of that?" asked the businessman in me. "We get married in New Jersey and come back and live in New York and all you've done is lose yourself a five-dollar licence fee!" Hilary grabbed the papers and my arm and hustled me down the front steps to the nearest cab stand. We were lucky enough to find the only honest taxi-driver in New York city.

"City Hall New Jersey."

"If you guys are looking for a marriage licence, the bureau closes at four o'clock. I'll never make it."

We rushed to a phone and called New Jersey. Certainly we could get married there if the grounds were adultery. Of course, we knew about the two week residency clause?

I phoned every state within a day's drive of New York City. The shortest residency clause I could find anywhere was five days and it was already Wednesday. We drove back to Canada at the end of the week, still living in the same sin we'd been wallowing in since 1951.

After a long, tiring drive from New York, we arrived at the Grand Theatre to face a very fractious group of union stagehands who'd been waiting an hour to discuss our crew needs for the season. Discuss wasn't quite the word. As I entered the room, the business agent stood up, wagged his finger and said, "Now here's what you're going to do," at which point everybody started shouting at once. One of them had a large birthmark on his left cheek and looked positively dangerous. I tried a few polite "Excuse me's" and finally shouted "Shut up!" at the top of my lungs. They were immediately shocked into utter silence.

"As I will be the one paying your salaries, suppose I tell *you* what we're going to do," I said with a smile and a glint at the same time. They were stunned. I don't believe anyone had ever spoken to them like that before.

It took less time to win the stagehands over than it did the audience. Within days, the crew realized that our company's professionalism was on a par with their own, which was something they weren't accustomed to backstage. Good though they were, the

London Little Theatre, which owned the Grand, was an amateur group who worked sporadically and in their spare time, not regular theatre hours and every day like we did. By the end of our first week, the entire crew was enrolled in our fan club with "birthmark" the president. He was also by far the gentlest among the entire crew. I decided there and then that no stage villain I portrayed in the future would ever be made up with any kind of birth disfigurement.

With no front-of-house chores to worry about, I had time to think about other things, like getting married. We hadn't yet tried the State of Michigan for a licence, and the border was less than a two-hour drive from London. The first morning we weren't needed for a rehearsal, I grabbed Hilary and drove to Sarnia and across the bridge to Port Huron. I showed the clerk at City Hall the divorce papers. He said they were fine. He told me there was a two-week waiting period. I said that was fine. He then said we would need medical certificates and I said that was fine too because we already had two of those. He said, "Yes, but these are New York certificates. This is Michigan."

We gave up. Three times we drove anrgily across the bridge to Canada, and three times we weakened and turned back again. The Customs on both sides of the bridge began to think we were up to something sinister until we explained that all we wanted to do was get married. Finally we gave them our blood, we gave them our money and we gave them our waiting time. As we drove back into Canada for the last time, we gave customs the thumbs up and they rewarded us with a cheer. Two weeks later, we piled Oliver and the Dornings into the car and drove to Port Huron where we were married in a judge's kitchen with a sinkful of unwashed dishes, a baby screaming in the corner and dirty diapers on the floor. The ceremony took all of a minute and a half. We got outside as fast as we could and went looking for a drink. It was Sunday. Michigan was dry.

Back in London, we couldn't go public about our marriage because Paul Soles had already interviewed us as Mr and Mrs on CFPL-TV. About two weeks later, a large envelope arrived marked "Compliments of the City of Port Huron." If you pressed the thin manila wrapping paper down really hard you could just read the title of the book it contained: OUR WEDDING. Ken Basquette, the manager of The Grand, handed me my mail without even looking up. When I got back to our apartment, there was a gift-wrapped table lamp waiting with a card that said "Congratulations Ken."

Straight after the wedding, Oliver took off for England and the county cricket ground, and I quickly found out what I had let myself in for by adding his roles and directorial assignments to the ones I already had. In a twelve-year span of a consistent play-a-week routine, nothing came even close to the demands of that summer in 1954 in Central Ontario. In seventeen weeks in London and Niagara Falls, I directed or redirected seventeen plays and played in sixteen of them, often the lead. And there was still the little matter of running the company.

It took Londoners four weeks to decide that we might be worth seeing. They might never have found out if I hadn't stopped a few of them in the street and discovered that they all thought the London Theatre Company was just a summer name for the London Little Theatre whose shows were always sold out to subscribers. Next day an extra inch on top of our ads screamed: LIVE FROM LONDON, ENGLAND and the box-office woke up. The upturn in the last four weeks didn't quite make up for the loss on the first four, but we didn't miss by much. London was definitely worth another try. It hadn't helped us recoup any of our touring losses, but Niagara Falls with its guaranteed profit would soon deal with that.

We finished up our London season with a musical revue, lifting the pick of the items from the first three versions of *Screech* and giving the lyrics a local flavour. We called it *London Laughs*, and it easily outperformed all the other productions at the box-office. How we managed to play the closing night in London on the Saturday and open in Niagara Falls on the Monday, I'll never know, but we did. By this time, we weren't just touring three productions. It was more like eight. Even so, we couldn't save every set, and George had been busy painting and repainting scenery flats every week since we'd left St. John's. He was now in Niagara Falls ahead of us, having his third go at a set for *Yes M'Lord*.

I took over Oliver's magnificent role of the butler and Kevin Stoney was in top form as the Earl of Lister. Our reception was wildly enthusiastic on opening night, but audiences were a bit on the thin side through the week and needed time to build. At noon on Friday I walked into Charles Michael Turner's office to collect our two thousand dollars.

He said, "You're going to be awfully cross but I don't have the money."

I don't know how he expected me to react but it obviously wasn't the way I did. I frightened the life out of him. And my voice had never been calmer. I looked at my watch and said, "Well, you have just two hours to find it, in cash, or you won't have a show tonight." He went chalk white, grabbed his panama and literally ran out of the room.

I had my trauma after he'd gone. This was week one. We had ten more to go. I saw eleven cast paydays stretching into the penniless unknown and a vision of a WANTED poster on the wall of the Actors' Equity office with my picture underneath it and the dreaded words: DO NOT ACCEPT AN ENGAGEMENT WITH THIS MAN.

Two hours later, Charles Michael Turner handed me two thousand dollars in grubby used bills.

We replayed this scene every Friday for the next three weeks until the inevitable morning came when the well, wherever it was, ran dry. Then Monica and I moved into the box-office and took the money straight off the customers. After we had taken our legitimate share, we handed the rest over to Michael. After a week or two more, there was nothing left to hand him. The newspapers hadn't been paid and cut off his advertising. Nobody knew we were there.

The cast never had an inkling about the juggling act that went on week by week in the management office. They were all having fun which was rare in the world of weekly rep. They had paired off, not necessarily boy with boy and girl with girl, and had rented apartments. They were enjoying the summer sun that they only got in England once every seven years. They were repeating mostly plays they had already performed in St. John's, Halifax or London, and they often needed to rehearse no more than a couple of days a week. And on Sundays we brought them all to Niagara-on-the-Lake for a day-long barbecue in the rooftop garden of the apartment Hilary and I had rented for the season. All anybody was asked to bring was a corkscrew.

Sally Day, our ingenue, had rented a bike and almost every day rode across Rainbow Bridge to Niagara Falls, New York. She always had a few theatre comps for the Canadian Customs on the way over and always found a warm welcome waiting for her on the way back. After the performance each night she'd ask if anyone wanted anything brought back from the United States and invariably ended up with a long shopping list. She was a slim girl and constantly rode back wearing a couple of sweaters and two men's shirts and looked more like a character woman. The Customs would yell out, "Bought anything today Sally?" and before she could say "No," they'd all chorus it for her and wave her on.

We saw little of Charles Michael Turner socially, although every Monday on the opening night of the new play he had flowers handed up over the footlights for all the girls in the cast. I finally had to say,

"Michael, will you please stop spending my money on flowers for the ladies with your name on the card?" His reply was a classic.

"I'm not paying for them, old chap. They're being charged."

twentysix

When the final curtain came down on the summer of 1954, as well as on our touring aspirations, thirteen actors thousands of miles from home had been on the road for one week short of a full year. And I had gone through fifty-one Sundays without one of them off. I needed to rest my bones and put a brake on my mind, and I knew just where to go to do both. Hilary and I picked up Oliver in England and we all fled to Spain where nothing ever matters until tomorrow.

Under the same *sombre* where the summer before we had planned the conquest of Ontario, the three of us lay on the beach and held a gentle inquest on how we'd lost the battle. As chief tour booster, I held myself to blame. I knew if we didn't try it, I'd have gone through the rest of my days wondering whether I had let one of life's great opportunities pass me by. But there were no recriminations from the others. We were still solvent, St. John's still loved us and London Theatre Company Ltd had given us all another year of the good life.

The major casualty of our tour was not our bank balance but our schedule. We'd broken the pattern of an October start, an Easter finish and a summer in Spain. This time we couldn't possibly reopen in St. John's until Christmas. But we still needed twenty-six weeks to amortize transatlantic travel costs. That meant a June finish. We didn't fancy St. John's as a summer date, so we decided to give the Grand, London, one more try. Then the Niagara Falls School Board phoned to offer us a season under our own management, and we rashly added a further eight weeks to the schedule. But it was a tempting package to put before an actor. And if you could believe the résumés, there were plenty of them worth seeing and anxious to be seen within an easy drive from Redcliffe Square.

A particularly promising young actor was awaiting our visit to see him play in Ipswich, East Anglia, and I allowed Reggie Salberg, also out talent spotting, to take my place in the navigator's seat in

Oliver's battered old Volkswagen. With their attention concentrated more on the current Test Match than driving, and their vision somewhat impaired by a mist outside and the combined smoke from Oliver's pipe and Reggie's cigar inside, they were suddenly startled to find the windshield framing a panorama of the North Sea, particularly since Ipswich was an inland town. A poster told them they were in Frinton-on-Sea and that a small repertory company was playing in the Town Hall. As it was too late to backtrack to Ipswich, the Town Hall it was, which turned out to be a lucky day for a young actor named Joseph Shaw. He remembers Oliver arriving backstage after the show and saying, "Would you like to come to Canada, cock?"

Joseph Shaw spent three years with us and has stayed in Canada ever since, earning respect in all areas of the business, notably in Toronto as the first head of George Brown College Theatre School, which he ran for ten years.

Joining Joe as newcomers to the company were Victor Adams, Patricia Gould and my old flat-mate from the Penge days, Anthony Sagar. The other nine were all holdovers from the previous company who had only left us in September after a full year's work and opted for more of the same starting in December. Most of them used the cash in lieu of their return fare to England, to have a look at Vancouver, New York and even California. Charles Jarrott, who was not returning to the company, used his fare home to bring his wife to Canada. They settled in Toronto where Charles learned to direct television dramas at the CBC's expense and went on to become a director of feature films. Keeping so many familiar faces from the previous year promised to be a bonanza for the box-office, since repertory audiences tend to come to see their favourite players as much as the play.

The company complete, Oliver drove up to Birmingham to raid the Salberg warehouse for pantomime costumes. Hilary and I went looking for our first sticks of furniture as a married couple. A small unfurnished house was waiting for us in St. John's, nestling in the bend of the harbour with a picture window overlooking the Narrows. In an estate sale at a beautiful home near London, where buyers were only interested in antiques and old masters, we bought the entire soft furnishings of an elegant drawing-room for a mere sixty pounds, including brocade drapes and pelmets, lamp brackets and a three-seat sofa and two armchairs with down-filled cushions. These and other trophies were shipped to Newfoundland in time to furnish the house and welcome the new company for the first time on management turf instead of in the sitting room of the Balsam Hotel.

Monica, Hilary and I were the first to arrive and bask in the incredible warmth of a Newfoundland welcome. When we opened the box-office, we were all surprised at the sudden surge in downtown traffic until we discovered that they weren't heading for us but queuing up to try out Newfoundland's first set of traffic lights just installed at Rawlins Cross. Even so, the box-office lost no time in setting new records for advance bookings.

Being back in St. John's after touring was like coming home on leave. For the first time in months, we felt we were somebody. We were wanted. No more would anyone stop us in the street, like they sometimes did in small town Ontario, and say, "You can't be any good or you wouldn't be here."

Our season was to open with a flourish showcasing the entire company in the Christmas pantomime *The Babes in the Wood*. For the first time, we couldn't save money by rehearsing the opener in London since the two Babes, the ladies of the chorus and our new musical director, Eric Abbott, all lived in St. John's. And our student-staffed backstage crew needed time with the cast to learn how to fast-change George's six magnificent sets.

There is many a heartbreak for a repertory actor when he sees the new cast list go up. But for an actor-manager the torment is self-inflicted since he does the casting. It was very hard for me to relinquish the part of the dame in *Babes in the Wood*, but I knew that even with a Monica, I couldn't launch a new season and rehearse eight hours a day at the same time. My big consolation was to know that Dame Trot lay in good hands because Robert Dorning, like me, had served his time in the Music Halls.

We opened to the orphans on Christmas Eve, which was a Saturday. The following Monday we began to play two shows daily for six consecutive days with not a single seat empty all week. By Saturday night, we had played to over 5,000 theatre-goers in a city of 52,000 people. By Sunday, half the cast had lost their voices. They'd have a whole week to find them again since next on the playbill was *The Fourposter* with a cast of only two. *Babes in the Wood* was our most costly production ever, and it paid for itself in one week. And that one week's budget covered four weeks' salary for the actors: two non-producing rehearsal weeks and one twelve-performance playing week for which we paid everybody double salary because they had worked twice as hard.

The absence of twelve actors from the cast of *The Fourposter* didn't affect the box-office in the slightest, but the presence of one of the remaining two did: Hilary, sharing the lead with Victor Adams, kept up her ongoing reputation as our biggest drawing card. Victor gave a big boost to the company in more ways than one: he was unusually well-endowed and he was never shy about showing it off when the company needed some light entertainment. Barbara Bryne, who was a great giggler, had the job every night of visiting the dressing rooms to check that all the actors had their personal props for the performance – a notebook, matches, cigarettes and the like. Victor, who shared a room with Tony Sagar and Bob Dorning, would wait for Barbara to knock on the door and shout out, "I've come to check your personals" and when she opened the door, he'd have his in his hands ready for inspection. Barbara's screams of laughter could often be heard by the audience coming in. On one occasion, for a dare, Victor used it to bang the dinner gong at the Balsam Hotel.

With a farce, an Agatha Christie and the New York hit, *The Moon Is Blue,* in quick succession, the attendance graph kept climbing. By the end of the fourth play, we were turning people away four nights out of six and trying everything we knew to get the overflow to come on Mondays and Tuesdays.

For the first time I really felt that the city's heart would beat a little fainter without us. For another first, we were allotted a full page in the *Daily News* year-end supplement as one of the "thriving industries" in St. John's. We also made the official City Guide as a major attraction. Our name was up there on the list with all the big donors to the Flood Relief Fund, and Hilary and I were invited to represent the company at the opening of the Legislature. Even the *Telegram* chipped in with the headline LONDON THEATRE HUGE SUCCESS, until you read on and discovered that it didn't refer to us at all but to the phenomenal season in London's West End.

Outside St. John's our reputation was growing, too. The USO in New York wanted to book us to tour all the American bases in North East Asia Command but sadly we couldn't fit in the dates. A reporter/photographer team arrived from Toronto to record us at work and at play for a forthcoming article in the *Weekend Magazine,* a sixty-page colour supplement that was part of the Saturday editions of the leading newspapers all across Canada.

On a rare week when I didn't have to play or rehearse, I went to the other side of the island to scout Newfoundland's second-biggest city for a possible date in 1956. Corner Brook was a company town. The company owned the hotel, the movie theatre, the grocery store, many of the houses and most of the people. The company was

Bowaters and their product was paper.

Within an hour of registering at the Glynmill Inn, I received an invitation to dine with the mill manager and his senior staff that evening. The dress was formal. I phoned the RSVP number to say that I hadn't brought my tuxedo or my medal ribbons with me. The secretary was not amused. I gave him my vital statistics. Within the hour, a full outfit down to the black patent shoes was delivered to my room.

The manager's estate appeared to be a small forest planted in the centre of town. In a clearing stood a mansion surrounded by a moat. There was no drawbridge but there ought to have been because once across the moat you felt that you were totally cut off from the twentieth century. The atmosphere was friendly but rigidly formal and dinner was like playing a meal scene in an upper-crust British household in a period play, only this one was costumed by Bowaters instead of Moss Bros. Finally, at a signal from the host, the ladies meekly rose and withdrew to the withdrawing room while the men lit cigars and passed round the port on a miniature gun carriage, clockwise of course. Next day I was invited to see Sir Eric Bowater's country house, which was kept open and staffed year round for his annual visit of no more than two weeks. Through the huge bay window was a magnificent view of the Newfoundland countryside, somewhat limited by a large hill in the middle. The mill manager told me that they had once bulldozed the entire hill away as a surprise for Sir Eric. When the great man arrived and looked through his window, he said, "Where's my hill? Put it back!" And they did.

Corner Brook was beyond doubt a fiefdom. But I felt that if we could get the fief behind us, it might be a good stopover on our way to Halifax the following year.

Back at home base, the crowds refused to be daunted by a run of fierce blizzards. St. John's was determined to show us that we didn't need to go "over there" and lose "our" money.

Hilary and I put on our best frocks to sit in the VIP gallery for the opening of the Legislature. We were the guests of the Speaker of the House, Reg Sparkes, a keen theatre-goer. Joey Smallwood, the Premier, was hogging the limelight as usual. He had a habit of repeating a phrase three times, each time with a totally different intonation. It is a favourite trick of actors when they blow their lines and want time to think of the next one. As Joey droned on, I thought of all the chores waiting for me at the office and I got a bit restless. I saw the Speaker scribble a note, call a page and point to the gallery. The page walked right through the House during the Premier's speech, squeezed past the cream of St. John's society and held a silver tray out to me. I opened the letter, and read: "Don't get ants in your pants. I'll give him another five minutes, then I'll shut him up and we can all go and have a drink." It was written on official House notepaper and was my most treasured possession for years until a small flood in my basement reduced it to confetti.

About halfway through the season I received another note, an unusually formal one from Campbell Macpherson, Lieutenant Governor-in-waiting, suggesting I see him on a "matter of some importance." He and his wife Polly had been close friends of Hilary and myself since the Alexandra Company days, and neither of us could think of anything we had done to put a bee in His Honour-to-be's bonnet. He informed me very bluntly that one of my actors was "sniffing" round his daughter Heather, and I'd better put a stop to it and quickly or he'd make it very difficult for the London Theatre Company to continue operating in St. John's. As the actor in question, Tony Sagar, was currently outranking His Honour-to-be in the title role of a play called *His Excellency,* it wasn't easy to keep a straight face when I called Tony into my office, especially as he was already costumed for the evening performance. Nevertheless, I asked him to save up whatever it was he had until we got to the mainland. I didn't trust Campbell and I didn't want to do anything at this late stage to spoil what was shaping up to be our biggest-ever season. With only four weeks to go, the box-office was under siege.

One of the final quartet of plays was *Dial M for Murder,* and we were the first company to present it anywhere in North America outside Broadway. It cost us a special royalty fee – the highest we ever paid – but it was worth it. It held the season's top attendance honours for just one week before *Little Women* came along and broke the all-time box-office record held for nearly four years by *A Streetcar Named Desire.*

We were now down to our final production, the fourth edition of our annual revue, this time entitled *And Still More Screech*. It hadn't taken us long to discover that Oliver's detour to Frinton-on-Sea was not only Joseph Shaw's lucky day, but also ours: Joe could compose music and write lyrics. He was instantly given the portfolio of revue research-and-development. I had been in the habit of providing the broader comedy material; Joe had a more sophisticated touch and a good revue needs both. Joe could fit new lyrics to age-old Newfoundland sea shanties and milk all the local sacred cows. In one memorable number, he had two actors in oilskins in a dory that pitched and tossed on the stage as they rowed and sang their own version of "The Squid-Jiggin' Ground." Joe could take all the modern pop tunes and parody the lyrics for local enjoyment, just as I would do years later with the same success when I directed thirty large conventions for IBM and taught them to laugh at themselves.

I shamefully admit that I included in the revue a very funny sketch we had seen in the summer at the Adelphi Theatre in London, starring Jimmie Edwards. The rights were not available until the run finished, so we paid Oliver's brother to sit in the stalls at the Adelphi for three nights in a row and write down the entire script and all the comic business. I regret to say that I wasn't nearly as funny as Jimmie Edwards.

The revue sold out for ten days and brought to an end the most astonishing run we would ever have in St. John's. Through all kinds of plays and weather, St. John's playgoers had filled a staggering 82.7 percent of the seats available over the entire season and had yielded us a net profit of almost a thousand a week in 1955 dollars. Halifax would probably have followed suit had we not let the school board talk us into moving our season to St Patrick's High School to christen their brand new auditorium. It took one performance and a lot of complaints to discover that there were serious problems with the acoustics.

At our opening play, *Mountain Air*, the people who sat in rows G to L heard every line twice but, unfortunately, a nanosecond apart, which made them totally unintelligible. I was anything but unintelligible at the school board offices the next morning. At a hastily convened gathering of their worthies, they reduced the rent by one third for the entire season. This resolution was duly reported in the *Chronicle-Herald,* which brought the architect storming to the theatre, threatening to sue me for libel. I calmed him down, sat him in the front row and got two of the actors to play him a short scene.

"Can you hear that?" I asked him. "Every word," he replied. I moved him to the back row and the actors repeated the scene. He could hear that too. Then I sat him in the afflicted zone. In the middle of the same scene, I stopped the actors and said to the architect, "What was that he just said?" He couldn't tell me. Fortunately the seating capacity at St Pat's was huge and we simply roped off the offending rows. But as they were in a prime position, we gave ourselves a crashing headache dealing with the season-ticket holders.

Our second production in St Pat's was *Little Women,* which, having just broken the all-time attendance record in St. John's, proceeded to set another record in Halifax for driving the most people away. But when *The Moon Is Blue* and *The Fourposter* came to the rescue in a big way, Halifax joined the club with its most profitable season to date. The success of *The Fourposter* was doubly valuable because, with a cast of only two, we were able to fly the rest of the company and half the stage management to London and open *Mountain Air* there simultaneously, playing to two different audiences twelve hundred miles apart in the same week.

Our old friend Ken Basquette threw a great party to welcome us back to the Grand Theatre, London. We'd left an audience full of promise at the end of the previous summer. We returned to find our fans being lured away by a new messiah named Tyrone Guthrie, who was working miracles in a tent with the cream of Canada's actors and William Shakespeare at Stratford, only forty minutes down the road. To add to our disappointment, we searched in vain every Saturday for the three-page article that could give us such a boost in the *Weekend Magazine* supplement to the *London Free Press*. But it waited until our last week to appear and was totally wasted. Business hovered tantalizingly close to the break-even point but only took us over the top once, and that was for *Little Women*. But the big worry in London was not the box-office but the fact that Hilary, now pregnant, nearly lost our baby. She had just finished playing Patty in the last performance on the Saturday night of *The Moon Is Blue* when she was rushed off to the London General. She fortunately had no part in the next week's play and neither had I; so I spent the weekend at the hospital with her. The gynecologist told me privately on Sunday that if she were still carrying a baby on Monday it would be a miracle. Monday came and went and so did Hilary, still pregnant, back to the theatre. But that problem was not yet over.

We finished up the London season with a localized version of *Screech,* and I'm glad to report that the Jimmie Edwards sketch was a riot. I waited for the first big laugh to cover my voice and hissed to the company on stage: "I told you it was funny you faithless sods!" Our London losses ate a little into our Halifax gains but left our new-found wealth from St. John's intact. I'd have been very happy if Niagara Falls had done the same, but it turned out to be an absolute disaster.

I had convinced myself that it shouldn't be too difficult to run a summer season better than Charles Michael Turner did. I totally overlooked the fact that Maude Franchot, aunt of film actor Franchot Tone, had also tried and failed in the same theatre, and she'd had famous film stars as headliners. But the biggest star of them all was in nature's theatre just down the road, and their floodlights came on about the same time as ours did and were much brighter. Only two of the eight plays we presented attracted any real attention: *The Moon Is Blue* came within a whisker of breaking even, and the fail-safe weepie *Little Women* looked finally set to take us over the top when master Jamie-Yeo-in-waiting chose the Saturday night to put his foot down. For the first time in two summers in Niagara Falls, we were heading for a capacity house, enough to cover our running expenses for the entire week. Had our emergency call been answered by a real theatre doctor, who would acknowledge but never understand that the show must go on, he might have given us three hours before carting Hilary off to the hospital, particularly because there was absolutely no other female left in the company who could even go on and read her part. But when he challenged me point blank with, "Do you want to have this child or not?" I knew I had no choice. It was the only time in my fifty-seven years in the theatre that I found out what it meant to cancel a performance. Children were crying all over the lobby. Parents who had driven them from Buffalo and even beyond were trying to console them and wondering at the same time how they were going to get their money back. Monica and I were frantically wrestling with the logistics of that problem behind the scenes. Joseph Shaw remembers that night. His description of me, standing at the box-office window, buying back sixteen hundred tickets with tears pouring down my face, is of course totally untrue. But our take for that one night would have been in the neighbourhood of $20,000 in today's money. If my son ever becomes a millionaire, I'll send him a bill.

twentyseven

Nineteen fifty-five was the year the London Theatre Company came home. We had flirted with the mainland at great expense and we'd found ourselves ahead of our reputation. Not a whisper had filtered west of our prowess in the far east and we were now coming back to the womb. The seventy productions and four years we had invested in St. John's had built up a following as solid as the rock it sat on and it was payback time, to the citizens for their loyalty and to us for our perseverance. So when we returned in December to pick up the near-capacity audience we had left behind in March, it came as something of a shock to find that we would now have to share it with a newcomer to the entertainment scene, a television set, which clamoured for instant attention without having done any of the spadework.

I had no way of knowing what harm this might do to us but Don Jamieson and Geoff Stirling had. When they landed the licence for CJON-TV, they'd seen the statistics and knew how TV gobbled up live audiences in its early days. And that made them worried about their adverse effects on us and consequently on their own local image. So they dashed off a letter to us in England warning of the dangers ahead and reassuring us that they would do what they could to counteract it. "We feel you have done so much for St. John's," they wrote, "and we hate to think that TV will harm your theatre season. We shall do everything in our power to promote you and keep the crowds besieging the box-office."

By this time it was too late to think about shortening the St. John's season even if we wanted to. Actors were contracted, tickets printed and performing rights cleared for firm dates for twenty-five productions, eighteen of them in St.John's, three in Corner Brook (in a single week) and five in Halifax. To compound our difficulties, there would be a host of new faces in the company this time around and repertory audiences hated that. Denny Spence and Barbara Bryne had gone to Halifax to work in television. The same medium was luring actors away from us in Britain, making it difficult to hang on to them for more than one season. Most serious of all, our biggest drawing card would be out of the line-up except for her one-woman show for the staff of the maternity ward at the Grace Hospital some time in December. And I wouldn't be able to play so often either because I'd lost Monica and I would have a sister-in-law, Marion Pagniez, to break in as my new admin assistant. On the plus side, we still had the huge popularity of Avis Lennard back for a fourth season and Joseph Shaw returning for his second. But the rest of the company would have to play their way into people's hearts still aching for the favourites who had not returned.

When TCA declined to bring Hilary back to Canada so late in her pregnancy, we put the clock back five years and booked a berth on our old friend the *Nova Scotia*. They didn't mind a bit about Hilary's condition because they had a doctor on board. They treated us like royalty, upgrading us to the ship's only suite and an automatic seat at the captain's table because our company had been such good customers for the past five years.

Our first discovery on landing in St. John's was that Geoff Stirling was already making good on his promise to us. He had found two firms who were willing to sponsor a transfer of our radio show *Keep Talking* to television. This would be invaluable exposure and would effectively mean double salary for each of our actors every second week. *Keep Talking* quickly became popular and made a Canadian Press cross-Canada release as "one of a handful of live television shows east of Montreal."

Since I had allowed Niagara Falls a second chance to muck up our balance sheet and our schedule, once again we had to delay our Newfoundland season opener until December and that meant pantomime. We had chosen *Dick Whittington* and this time nobody was going to play the dame except me. I would be Sarah the cook supported by Oliver as my sidekick Idle Jack. The orphans gave the two of us their hearty approval at their special preview on Saturday December 23rd, and with the rare prospect of a full day and a half to relax before our official opening on Boxing Day, Hilary went into labour. She was dead set on a natural childbirth, which meant a leading part for me in the delivery scene, but they told me at the hospital that I'd better go home and get some sleep because nothing was going to happen for several hours. They would call me in plenty of time.

Hilary was never one to hold up a production and by the time I got the phone call I was already a father. Grace Sparkes, our reviewer and tireless promoter, was at the hospital with a photographer almost as soon as I was. And Jamie Yeo, one day old, upstaged both his parents in a three-shot on the front page of the *Daily News.* Of the many congratulations and gifts that showered in upon us on that day forty years ago, I remember only one. It was a bottle of rum with a card attached on which there was a phone number and a message which read: FOR GOD'S SAKE GIVE ME THE FORMULA. I'VE TRIED SIX TIMES AND I KEEP COMING UP WITH GIRLS. When Jamie Yeo finally came home, he found, as an enchanting surprise for both him and his mother, his nursery walls painted from floor to ceiling with giant toys and nursery-rhyme characters by George Paddon-Foster.

Based on our twelve sell-out houses all in the same week the previous year with *Babes in the Wood,* I felt certain *Dick Whittington* could run to four more, and to make life easier for the company I had scheduled two weeks of eight performances each. The first week sold out but the second one died. Television had already picked the lock on our gold mine. The first four plays after panto confirmed this deadly discovery. They came in at a profit but nothing like the thousand a week of a few months before. And when for the first time in our history we actually lost money with a farce, *One Wild Oat,* I knew we were in trouble.

The maddening thing about the new medium was that it didn't start until six in the evening. Then the entire city, it seemed, would dash home from work, clap a tray on its knees and not move until the last black and white flicker on the screen turned into snow at midnight. St. John's had invented the TV dinner.

My most effective weapon in emergencies had always been my programme editorials and I immediately went to work. Gentle warnings had no effect whatsoever. Even a veiled hint that the city might be in danger of losing its theatre failed to have an impact. So I lifted the veil. On February 25th, the Monday night audience at Agatha Christie's *The Hollow* was stunned to read in the programme that it looked very much as if this would have to be our last season in St. John's. This time the repercussions went through the town with the force of an Atlantic gale.

CJON-TV declared the following Monday the start of "London Theatre Company Appreciation Week," and the city poured out its affection for us with a huge community effort. CJON pounded out the message on television and radio for the next twelve days. We made the leading editorial in the *Evening Telegram* on two successive days, and we were also the subject of one of Werther's best cartoons. In the *Daily News*, Wayfarer devoted his entire column to the company twice in the same week. The Lions Club booked seats for sixty members and their wives for the following Monday and the Business Women's Association took a big block on the Tuesday. Glen Burn Nursery offered free flowers as stage dressings every week for the rest of the season. Students of Memorial University sent a deputation to ask how it could help and promised us unlimited free advertising space in their own newspaper, *The Muse*. Appreciation Week was sold out before the first performance. The play was J.B. Priestley's *When We Are Married.*

While we could keep up the pace of a play a week, the audience apparently couldn't, not with a movie star in every sitting room, and one you could see without even having to put on your snowboots. But just as the sinking box-office graph was once again about to cross the break-even line, we brought out our own star, Hilary Vernon, in her only appearance of the season. As Eliza Doolittle in *Pygmalion* she gave us another sellout as she so often did and the following letter helps to explain why. It was typical of the many messages we received during Appreciation Week:

> Just a little note to say my friend and I haven't missed a Monday night for the past five years. It is the one night we look forward to with the greatest pleasure. We are eagerly awaiting Pygmalion as Mrs. Yeo is sadly missed. You have a wonderful troupe and we have grown to love them all.

How could we walk out on people who felt compelled to sit down and write letters like these? I felt guilty every time I read one because the true picture was never as black as I painted it in my programme notes. Like one who plays the stock market, I was factoring in the future as I saw it six months down the road. Television sets were still coming in by the shipload, every one of them with tentacles waiting to wrap around the most ardent theatre-goers and yank them off to the sitting-room. But sooner or later the defection curve had to flatten out. The question was when.

With one week to go and *Even More Screech* already a sell-out, I was able to tell Oliver, Hilary and George that despite the advent of television we would end up the season with a profit. It wouldn't be as big as the one we started out with in 1951, but we shouldn't forget that we were now paying ourselves four times the salary we earned in 1951 and we had a company car and lived rent-free. Under those conditions we could still live well with a box-office that just broke even. Besides, we couldn't just slink out of town after five glorious fighting years. We must come back at least one more time and make a proper exit.

At the first hint of a further season, George Paddon-Foster went white. My programme editorials had so convinced him that we were about to close, he'd got himself another job. He hadn't worked in England for five years, and I'd so worried him about his future that he had accepted a commission to organize a display department for a new string of supermarkets to be opened by Ayre's, the downtown department store. A season without George? It was unthinkable. He had star billing in our book, in letters far bigger than any actor since the day we began. Unlike the rest of us, he had played a leading part in *every* production, week in, week out. In St. John's alone, he had single-handedly designed and painted 157 different stage settings. Two summers in London and Niagara Falls had bumped that total to well over 200. The name of George Paddon-Foster made almost every review, often ahead of the lead actors. He never missed a personal mention in the end-of-season laurels usually handed out by the two local newspapers. Like this 1955 leader in the *Evening Telegram*:

> The best tribute paid to the London Theatre Company playing for the fourth season in St. John's has been the well-filled houses that have greeted the performances. It has presented a splendid repertoire, the acting has been of the highest order and the stage settings by George Paddon-Foster have displayed the skill of a master-craftsman.

In 1991, forty years almost to the day that our first company came ashore, I took a nostalgia trip back to St. John's. I climbed the hill to Bishop Feild Hall and I stood on the terrazzo floor and looked at the tiny proscenium arch that had been George's picture frame for five years. And I remembered the magic he had mounted behind it week after week: a Paris ballroom complete with grand staircase for *Camille*, the transformation scene in *Cinderella*, the grandeur of Manderley in *Rebecca*, the seediness of New Orleans in *A Streetcar Named Desire* with an alleyway, a split-level apartment and the side of the house next door, all squeezed into a stage opening that was only thirty feet wide. George was a genius. But he already knew that his kind of genius didn't fit into the theatre he saw ahead where wood and canvas scenery flats would give way to solid plywood. It would no longer require a master-craftsman who could paint mouldings you'd swear were real from two feet away, since designers would learn to pour plastic over a real moulding, peel it off and staple it to the scenery. A house-painter could do the rest. George had come to the end of an era. Ours had still one year to go as we took off for Corner Brook and announced we would return to St. John's for one last season.

The fief had done his work in providing a capacity audience for us. But he took his danegeld at the checkout desk of his Glynmill Inn, where the company lived in great comfort for the week in return for nearly forty percent of our total box-office receipts. The result was a small net loss on the engagement.

We never again took the gamble of an overnight move to Halifax but gave ourselves a comfortable four days for the get-in. The absence of the usual line-up at the Phinney's box-office was our first indication that *Dragnet* and *Monday Night Wrestling* were siphoning away our audience here too. Our first two plays failed to show a profit.

Since TV was causing the damage, I felt strongly that it should help with the repairs, but my overtures for a TV interview with me or any member of the company got nowhere. This prompted a Yeo special to the editor of the *Chronicle-Herald* in which I accused the CBC of maintaining a strict television silence on the rather important subject of our arrival in their city:

> The reason put forward by CBH-T is that TV appearances by the London Players is "against policy." It is a very interesting policy, this, for the same policy permitted television interviews for no less than four members of the recent visiting Ice Revue and also devoted eight minutes of screen time a few days ago to the blatant publicizing of a local amateur production of *Harvey.*

I was very quickly summoned to the CBC to meet the big boss Captain Briggs who was furious at my letter. I stood for fifteen minutes on his quarterdeck listening to what he thought of me in seafaring language, before he grudgingly told me I could have my interview that evening with the famous Max Ferguson of radio fame, now on television. Max was polite but obviously not best pleased to be made to do something that was against CBC policy.

My persistence paid off and the advance bookings picked up for *Pygmalion.* But on the Thursday before we were due to open, I received a devastating telegram from Samuel French Ltd in Toronto:

YOU ARE FORBIDDEN OPEN PYGMALION MONDAY STOP RIGHTS WITHDRAWN WORLDWIDE BY NEW YORK PRODUCERS OF MY FAIR LADY. In a rare moment of panic, I rang Mona Coxwell, doyenne of the Toronto branch of the world-renowned play publishers. I told her that the play was in our repertoire and we had already performed it in St. John's. We had cleared the rights long ago. Wrong. We had cleared St. John's but had made no mention of Halifax. I gave her my desperate performance and I didn't have to act it: we had nothing else to take the place of *Pygmalion* at such short notice, and we would have to close for a week and pay back thousands of dollars in advance bookings. I also took care to remind her of how much Samuel French had collected from us in performing rights over the past five years in a country where there wasn't much professional theatre going on. She finally consented to call the producer Herman Levin personally in New York but didn't really hold out much hope. After an agonizing afternoon of waiting, she finally rang to say that Herman Levin had conceded that he didn't think the London Theatre Company production in a school hall in Halifax would seriously impact his box-office receipts in New York. He probably hadn't the faintest idea where Halifax was.

Pygmalion made a profit. It was the only play in Halifax that did. And that meant that St. John's would have to stand alone next season just as it had the year we first began: twenty-six plays in twenty-six weeks.

The 1955-56 company spawned three marriages, breaking its own previous record. When we interviewed Paddy Drysdale and Olwen Rasbridge in London as potential assistant stage managers, they told us they intended to get married if they got the job. That was marriage number one. Norman Welsh swept Dawn Lesley off her unmarried feet and tied the knot in Toronto, and Bernard Thompson, our stage manager for three years, stole our beloved Avis Lennard, married her in Halifax and took off for a look at Hollywood. He later ended up as a TV producer for the BBC in London. The Drysdales stayed on in St. John's with Paddy as assistant professor of English at Memorial University. Dawn and Norman joined the burgeoning community of professional actors in Toronto.

twentyeight

It was not by design that we chose to open our make-or-break season with *For Better or Worse*. Nor were we being intentionally pessimistic when we followed it up with *Rain*. Box-office receipts for both productions were down on the previous year but at least they showed a profit. And so did the farce that came after them. But when Hilary, in her first major appearance of the season as Elizabeth Barrett-Browning in *The Barretts of Wimpole Street*, did well but didn't sell out, we knew that television had eaten deep into our loyal fan base. Small winning weeks had turned into small losing ones by the time we closed the theatre to rehearse the Christmas pantomime. But at least we knew we could bet on the crowds being back for that.

Although we were fighting for our survival, we hadn't stinted on the company. We actually brought out one more actor than in our very first year when there were twelve plus George Paddon-Foster. This time we were thirteen plus a new scenic designer named Stanley Rixon. He knew his job but also proved that if a George Paddon-Foster II was in the marketplace, we hadn't found him. As for the company, Hilary and I for the first time played no part in its selection. We thought people might like it if we spent a summer in Newfoundland, so we left the choosing to Oliver. Our mistake became immediately apparent when we saw the company for the first time, lined up along the rail of the *RMS Newfoundland* and my eyes lit upon Ronald Fraser.

"Oliver," I asked, "how many parts do we have this season for an ex-pugilist?" Ronnie Fraser has since become very successful in films where craggy features are much sought-after. Unfortunately, on the stage, while handsome young juveniles can acquire them with a good make-up box, the reverse process isn't so easy. Ronnie was very hard to cast twenty-five times in a season.

Oliver was by no means a poor judge of talent, but in a crucial year when his Volkswagen should have been driven harder and further in search of it, the battered old wreck probably spent most of its time in the parking lot of some cricket ground. As a result, we ended up with the weakest company in our history just when we needed the strongest. Had it not been for the presence of Moya and Gillie Fenwick, Bill Glover and, for the third time, Joseph Shaw, we'd never have been able to hide our decline in standard. Hilary, with a nine-month-old child just becoming mobile, would not be able to play every week and I'd scarcely be able to appear at all. This was one of the sad disadvantages of being an actor-manager.

I doubt there were any financial short cuts to the bottom line that I hadn't already discovered, but I still looked for some new ones. For a secretary, I saved a transatlantic fare and hired Heather Macpherson, daughter of the Lieutenant-Governor-to-be-still-in-waiting. The first production to feel the pruning shears was the Christmas pantomime. It was agonizing to restrict a lavish production like *Aladdin* to eight performances, but eight full houses was the maximum we'd been able to muster for *Dick Whittington* the previous year. Since Boxing Day disobligingly fell on a Wednesday, we had no alternative but to play twice daily for four days and leave it at that, unquestionably the shortest pantomime run anywhere in the world.

Of all the British pantos, *Aladdin* has the dame that every famous comedian wants to play. She is Widow Twankey and she runs the Emperor of China's laundry. In the part, I made the most of my last trip back in time into the wonderful world of the Music Halls. St. John's will remember *Aladdin* for another reason. As in the past, Oliver was my sidekick and played Wishee-Washee, my laundryman. He could be extraordinarily clumsy for one who could make such spectacular catches on the cricket field. In one scene he was supposed to trip accidentally, grab my waist to break his fall and at the same time pull off my skirt to reveal a long pair of bright red lace-trimmed knickers underneath. In one performance, he pulled down not only my skirt but everything else underneath it and I gave St. John's more than a passing glimpse of a full moon.

One other memory lingers of *Aladdin*. "Rick" Rixon had painted some colourful sets, but he was no George Paddon-Foster when it came to engineering. In the dress rehearsal, during the blackout when the big transformation scene was supposed to take place, half the set fell down. And the lights came up on Gillie Fenwick as the evil Abanazar, sitting cross-legged and smoking a hookah with one arm still in Widow Twankey's laundry and the other in the middle of the Arabian desert.

After *Aladdin,* box-office rot set in and my editorials took on a more pointed tone. I learned afterwards that some members of the company were embarrassed at my constant nagging in print. It wasn't that we needed the money; it was a matter of pride. I'd always been very conservative about doling out dividends, and the balance sheet was showing a handsome undistributed surplus that was six times our original investment. We'd worked very hard for six years to accumulate it. I didn't see the point in paying it all back while waiting for someone to find a miracle cure for televisionitis.

At this gloomy moment in our history, I received a visit from Bob Furlong, then a Q.C. and later the Lord Chief Justice of Newfoundland. He told me that the Federal government had just established a new body called the Canada Council, and it was expressly designed to come to the aid of companies like ours. He was the official Council member for Newfoundland, and he was quite certain he would be able to get us a grant to carry on. I told him I wanted people not money. I didn't want subsidies sitting on the seats; I wanted bums. Furthermore, I was strictly a child of the commercial theatre. After six years of independence, I didn't want some bureaucrat in a bowler hat telling me what plays to put on and what actors to hire. I didn't, of course, put it all quite as bluntly as that but he went away a very disappointed man. And having been possibly the first person to be offered a Canada Council theatre grant and unquestionably the first to refuse one, I went back to the problem of trying to work out how to get through the rest of the season without a loss. Back in October, one good week had covered four losing ones. Now it barely managed to cover three and pretty soon it might not be enough to cover two. The message was clear. The fight against television was a battle we could not win. I turned to the schedule and tried to pick out the possible winners and the probable losers of the ten productions remaining. I thought we might just make it, and with the sixth and farewell version of SCREECH as our final bow we could go out in style. But that was before, suddenly and without warning, we came under attack from the *Evening Telegram.*

I say "without warning" but I would have to confess that I was the one who unwittingly struck the match that started the fire by my reaction to the *Telegram* drama critic, Sylvia Wigh. She, you may remember, was for a short time an employee of ours as assistant stage manager with our first company in 1951. She had been our critic for two or three years in the immediate past and had for the most part reviewed our productions quite favourably. I don't know what happened to stir her up in 1957, but for the first time, she started to pan us. I could have understood it if she had begun by slaughtering *Dragnet*, a dreadful stage version of the famous television cop show, but she liked it. *Dragnet* was our attempt to lure TV addicts away from their sets but instead almost certainly succeeded in driving people back to them. It was by far the worst show we did in six years. The production wasn't helped by Mary Williams who had inherited Avis Lennard's roles but not her memory. On opening night she addressed Sergeant Joe Friday as Mr Sunday. But Sylvia still liked it. The trouble was she didn't like *Anastasia* and that was our season blockbuster. Besides being Hilary's last starring role in St. John's, it was also our hundredth production and should have been an occasion for some rejoicing. The *Daily News* devoted two full pages to the event; the *Telegram* gave an inch in the leader. But this time there were no birthday cakes. The aura surrounding the company just wasn't the same.

One week later, on the first night of *Anne of Green Gables*, with the final curtain barely down, our Sylvia stumped grimly out of the theatre and telegraphed to everyone in the audience over the age of five that she was going to give us a real blast. And she did. *Anastasia* had merely "reduced the audience to shuffling boredom." In *Anne*, she saw "some of the very worst attempts at acting that I have ever seen from the London Theatre at any time in its long history." I'm afraid I did something that could have got me drummed out of the Actor-Managers Club: I went down to the *Telegram* office and told them we would not be requiring any more reviews for the rest of the season. I didn't see the point of paying for an ad on page five urging people to come to the theatre when a space twice as big on page six clearly told them not to.

For a couple of weeks there was an ominous silence from the *Telegram* building. Then Sylvia came forth with a two-column page-long glorification of the amateur theatre, stressing how much harder their members had to work than we did to put on a play. And how much better they were at taking criticism than the professionals (no mention of drama festival adjudicators who'd been run out of town, of course!). Then the real vitriol came out of the inkwell. A pro-Sylvia letter to the editor next day spearheaded a string of them so vindictive that they had some members of our company in tears. I went down to see Hubert Herder, the publisher. He gave me a homily on the danger of trying to muzzle the press and a lot of similar claptrap that might have been lifted from a comic cartoon about the Daily Planet in the

1920s. When I left his office, I came face to face with Harold Horwood, the city editor, and it became immediately apparent who was the real pot-stirrer-in-chief.

"Why are you doing this to us Harold?" I asked.

"You haven't seen anything yet. You wait until tomorrow," he replied. It wasn't what he said so much as the way he said it. It was dripping with pure venom.

Tomorrow brought a letter that was plainly offensive. It was signed by a Mary Alice Maher and said about us: "They are the worst group that has ever been seen on a local stage and I include all amateurs, even the beginners."

That we could laugh at, but not Harold Horwood's Editor's Note at the end which read:

> *The Telegram thought Miss Wigh was doing an excellent job. But since the London Theatre Company was dying anyway, and since Mr. Yeo thought our reviews were making the disaster more complete, we decided that it might be as well to let them die in peace. Miss Wigh fully concurs in this policy.*

The voice of the gutter press? No, I think this one came from halfway down the pipe to the main sewer.

I hope they've updated our file in the morgue at the *Evening Telegram* because the London Theatre Company never did die. In a last-minute show of strength, it ended its six-year run with its record intact of *never having had a single losing season in St John's.*

There is a moral to this tale for all young actors. If you get a bad review, and you will, put it aside and look at it again tomorrow. You won't think it nearly as bad as you did the day before. And if you look at it forty years later, you'll probably wonder what the hell you were so upset about.

Another lesson, one which has been taught many times before: publicity is publicity be it good or be it bad. *Anne of Green Gables* and *Anastasia,* top of Sylvia Wigh's hit list, were the only two plays in the last half of our season that made a profit.

Harold Horwood's premature obituary of the London Theatre Company marked the last of the nasty letters. From then on they came from the converted. Our fans had been a little slow off the mark in coming to our support, or perhaps the *Telegram* had been slow to publish them. One lady wanted to know why the paper was "conducting a hate campaign against Mr Yeo," and concluded with, "I am ashamed to be a Newfoundlander." Geoff Stirling, head of CJON-TV, rang up and wanted to know why the hell I was still taking advertising space in the *Telegram*. He offered us ten free TV spots a day instead. So I pulled the ad for the rest of the season but it didn't really make any difference. The subject slowly staled into yesterday's news and stayed there until our end of season revue when it got one last very special mention.

Two months before the time came to say farewell to Newfoundland, I attended a ceremony to receive my certificate of Canadian citizenship. I also received an offer from a New York impresario to take the company for two weeks to Williamsburg, Virginia, as part of that city's centennial celebrations. In view of the city's history, they specifically wanted an English company and asked for *Anastasia* and *The Barretts of Wimpole Street*, so they had obviously been following our programme. Unfortunately the Williamsburg theatre would not be available until May. Under normal circumstances I would have extended the St. John's season for an extra four weeks as a fill-in. But at current box-office figures, our fill-in days were over and to my undying regret I had to say no.

But we went out with all the flags flying. Our final revue outdrew all five of its predecessors, and the number of theatre-goers who came to say goodbye were almost double those who had turned out to welcome us at *Rookery Nook* in 1951.

We should have called the last in the series *The End of the Bottle* but I felt the word Screech must be in the title as it had been in all the others. So we settled on *Screech – The Last Drop*. But the minute I saw it in print, I knew we'd made a mistake. It looked so final, almost reproachful, a gust of cold air to all those regulars who had supported us so warmly through six tough winters. Five of them came forward who had not missed a single week and I listed their names in our farewell programme. They had seen a hundred and seven different productions, all mounted without subsidy or sponsorship or a donation of any kind. Except one. In December 1953 we received an unsigned card postmarked St Anthony, an outport in northern Newfoundland, which read:

> Christmas greetings from one who enjoyed every play in 1951/2 and 1952/3. I enclose ten dollars, the amount I would have spent this season had I been in St. John's.

The success of our farewell revue was helped in no small measure by Joseph Shaw. He was not only the fountain of our material – some of it borrowed and massaged but much of it original – but also the director. He knew all the closets in the city where the skeletons were and he rattled them mercilessly in his lyrics. I specifically remember his "Calypso of St. John's" and his magnificent closing number. My contribution was a skit entitled "Breakfast with the Yeos in 2000 AD," which I wrote especially for Hilary and myself as a couple of nonagenarians in St. John's looking back on all the boondoggles of government in the six years we'd spent with the company – items we'd made people laugh at before and were able to do so again in a different guise. Like the story of the *William Carson*, a lavish ferryboat which was the Centennial gift of the Federal government to Newfoundland and was found to be too big to get into port. Our version in 1957:

> SHE: (*in a quavering voice*): Whatever happened to the *William Carson?* Did they ever get her into port?
>
> HE: (*also quavering*): Oh yes dear, they got her in but they couldn't get her out. They've turned her into a floating hostel for fallen women in Port aux Basques.

In the same sketch, I asked Hilary to hand me a copy of today's *Daily News,* and she staggered across the stage with a paper about six inches thick. When she got to me, I said, "Would you like to read today's *Evening Telegram?*" And I handed her a large blanket pin holding four pages of newsprint cut to small notebook size. The roof fell in and we got a huge round of applause to the embarrassment of publisher Hubert Herder and five members of his family who were sitting in the front row. That didn't quite close the account with the *Telegram.* A day came when the leading article began with a very warm tribute to the London Theatre Company and all that it had meant to St. John's. Unfortunately the cast had left by the time it appeared and they didn't see it.

Once the revue opened and we had no more rehearsals, we set about winding up the company. For two successive Sundays, Hilary, Oliver and I held a reception for all those who had invited us or a member of the company to their homes during the previous six years. To every school with a stage, we presented a window, a pelmet, a door and door frame, a fireplace, some stairs and enough scenery flats to build a complete stage set. Our stage lighting instruments and dimmer board went at a token price to the Holy Heart of Mary school auditorium. Our sound equipment ended up at the Crest Theatre in Toronto. During our final week we held a rummage sale in the Bishop Feild School gymnasium with the actors as our sales staff. We sold props, costumes, furniture and office equipment. There were over sixty sets of curtains that had graced the settings of George Paddon-Foster. There was a mountain of production photographs that we sold for a nickel each and from which I was foolish enough not to put some aside for myself.

At the end of the season, Gillie and Moya Fenwick would go west and become one of the best-known theatrical couples in Toronto. Bill Glover would do a couple of seasons at Stratford before heading for Hollywood. You already know what the future held for Joseph Shaw. Hilary and I had enough to put down sixty percent on a house in Rosedale in Toronto. Not bad for six years work. Hard, but joyous too. And all achieved with a total capital outlay of two thousand pounds ($5,600 in 1951, $39,200 today).

During the run of *Screech – The Last Drop*, we made no curtain speech after the performance because there was no play to announce for the following week. But I knew that I would have to say something on the very last night and I had prepared myself. Joe had written a real tear-jerker for our finale. This was the last stanza:

> *The time has come to stop pretending*
> *The closing of our season nears*
> *From many far away places*
> *We'll think of all your friendly faces*
> *And our grateful thanks we're now extending*
> *For all those truly happy years*
> *As we regretfully break the tie*
> *We wish that au revoir could be our cry*
> *But now we know that we must say goodbye*

We reprised the last stanza and the actors began to link arms and slowly drift offstage in pairs until Hilary and I were left standing alone. As the two of us sang the last line, we too strolled towards the wings, then stopped, turned and simply spoke the final word "Goodbye." The stage behind us, with its minimal set, looked almost as bare as the day we first saw it in 1951. As we walked off, we let the lights dwell on its nakedness for a few seconds before slowly fading to black. The audience was stunned.

As we took our final curtain call the tears began pouring down my face. At the bottom of the fifth or sixth bow I whispered to Hilary under the applause "I can't do it".

"I will" she said.

I have a cassette of her speech together with some excerpts of our farewell revue. It is the only recording I have of the London Theatre Company. I play it sometimes and have a little cry.

postscript

This story belongs to the people of St. John's who welcomed us, nurtured us and sustained us in tough theatre-going weather for six winter seasons. With a top ticket price that started out and remained at two dollars, they paid $277,197 (almost two million in 1998 dollars) to see a hundred and seven different productions, thirty-nine of them in period costume, all of them staged in one week. We did six major classics including two Shakespeares, five full-length British panto-mimes and six musical revues. We brought ninety-eight actors to Canada at a transatlantic travel cost of $44,492 (over $300,000 today). Twenty-three of them stayed and joined Canada's fast growing entertainment community. We spawned nine marriages and changed many lives.

my thanks

To Reggie Salberg in England who played such an important part in the story and was my most valuable source of information in recording it.

To John Holmes in Newfoundland who has kept me posted with all the happenings in St. John's since I left him there forty years ago.

To Elsa Franklin in Toronto who garnered me the nicest rejection letters from the biggest publishing houses.

To my memory-joggers Barbara Bryne, Denny Spence, Moya and Gillie Fenwick, and Joseph Shaw (with a special thank-you to Joe for the use of his lyric, *The Party's Over.*)

To Heather McCallum who lovingly took my jumble of press clippings, programmes, box-office returns, salary lists and other financial data and, with the help of Joseph Tatarnic and Anne Sutherland, turned them into The London Theatre Company file among the Special Collections at Metro Toronto Reference Library.

To Erica Fischer and David Harrison, from across the street, who answered all my questions and never failed to give me my daily shot of encouragement.

To my first-draft guinea pigs Herbert Whittaker, Laurie Freeman, Sandy Robinson, Eric House, Pat Galloway, Joan Gleadall, Erica Fischer, Michael Bawtree, my son Jamie, and my memory-joggers above, who all gave me such valuable feedback (sometimes conflicting) and will now know if I made the right choices.

To Denis Johnston and Michael Power, my editors, who so cleverly trimmed my excesses and camouflaged my shortcomings.

To my wife Grete who, for two years, was made to share my devotion with a word-processor.

To everyone, everywhere, who speaks with a Newfoundland accent.

Leslie Yeo – A Theatrical Chronology

1939   First professional stage role: Gerald in *When Irish Eyes Are Smiling* at Woolwich Empire, south London

1940   First feature film – one line in *Night Train to Munich* with Rex Harrison and Margaret Lockwood

1940-41   Repertory seasons at Chatham, Bath, Dundee

           Toured the Music Halls in *The Best of Everything;* toured the playhouses in *High Temperature* with Henry Kendall

1941-6   Spare-time revue producer and stand-up comic for the RAF when not on a morse key in United Kingdom, India and Burma.

1946-7   Two repertory seasons (84 plays) at Wolverhampton

1947-8   Tour to St. John's, Newfoundland, with the Alexandra Company.

1948-9   Two repertory seasons at Penge Empire, south London; wrote and played lead in *And the Whistle Blew*

1950   Only West End appearance: Rudge in *Madame Tic-Tac* with Françoise Rosay

           Tour of *On Monday Next* with Terence de Marney; repertory seasons at Richmond Theatre and Eastbourne

1951   Repertory season at Richmond Theatre

1951-7   Actor-manager London Theatre Company, St. John's, Newfoundland

1957-9   Canadian agent for Strand Electric Stage Lighting (U.K.)

           Radio and TV roles in Toronto

1959-61   Opened in Toronto first North American branch of Strand Electric (U.K.) and served as Vice-President and CEO

1962   Stage design consultant and first general manager of Bayview Playhouse

1963   Radio, TV and film roles

Co-producer of revue *Suddenly Last Summer* at Toronto's Theatre-in-the-Dell.

1964   Manitoba Theatre Centre: played Stanley in *Five Finger Exercise*.

Played Stan Mountain in Canada's first full-length feature film *The Luck of Ginger Coffey*.

Co-produced two more revues at Theatre-in-the-Dell: *Surprisingly This Spring* and *Actually This Autumn*.

1965-89   Directed over 50 high-budget Industrial Dealer shows, musicals and conventions across Canada and the United States and in Mexico, Bermuda, The Bahamas, Jamaica, Britain, Holland and Japan: IBM (30 conventions), Chrysler (9 major musicals), Toyota (2), Molson's (3), Esso (3),ASTA, and two for Rootes Group (U.K.)

1966   Shaw Festival: played Tarleton in *Misalliance* with Zoe Caldwell

1967   Shaw Festival: played Lord Porteous in *The Circle* with Kate Reid

1968   Royal Alexandra Theatre, Toronto: Alan-Brooke in world-premiere of *The Soldiers*

1969   Manitoba Theatre Centre: Duke of Norfolk in *Man for All Seasons*

1970   Meadow Brook Theatre, Detroit: Doolittle in *Pygmalion*

1973	Vancouver Playhouse: Jacob in *Leaving Home*
1974	Theatre Plus, Toronto: Ben in *The Little Foxes*
	Vancouver Playhouse: Elwood P. Dowd in *Harvey*
1975	Stratford Festival: Toby Belch in *Twelfth Night*, Earl of Warwick in *Saint Joan*, Provost in *Measure for Measure*, Justice Balance in *Trumpets and Drums*
	Theatre Aquarius, Hamilton: Jacob in *Of the Fields Lately*
1976	Shaw Festival: directed Kate Reid in *Mrs Warren's Profession*. Played Boanerges in *The Apple Cart* and Petkoff in *Arms and the Man*
	Alley Theatre, Houston: played William in *You Never Can Tell*, Captain Boyle in *Juno and the Paycock*
1977	Stratford Festival: Lafew in *All's Well that Ends Well*, Capulet in *Romeo and Juliet* and Duke Senior in *As You Like It*
	Alley Theatre, Houston: directed *The Corn is Green* and *The Importance of Being Earnest*
1978	Shaw Festival: Boss Mangan in *Heartbreak House*
	Alley Theatre, Houston: directed *The Happy Time*
	Citadel, Edmonton: Toby Belch in *Twelfth Night*
1979	Shaw Festival: Artistic Director; played William in *You Never Can Tell*. Directed *The Corn Is Green* and *Blithe Spirit*
1980-3	Three summers as instructor at Banff centre. Directed student productions at Ryerson, Dalhousie and Alberta universities

1980	Neptune Theatre, Halifax: directed *How the Other Half Loves*
1981	Neptune Theatre, Halifax: directed *Absurd Person Singular*
1983	Citadel Theatre, Edmonton: Gloucester in *King Lear*
	Magnus,Thunder Bay: Willard in *The Gin Game*
1985	Vancouver Playhouse: directed *Noises Off*
	Gryphon Theatre, Barrie: Hobson in *Hobson's Choice*
1986	Royal Alexandra, Toronto: directed *The Foreigner.*
1988	Citadel, Edmonton: directed *Major Barbara*
1990	Theatre Aquarius, Hamilton: directed *The Diary of Anne Frank.*

FEATURED ROLES IN FILMS:

Chief Justice Daly in *Scales of Justice* (1993)
Eddy in *L'Automne Sauvage* (1991)
Arthur in *Bye Bye Blues* (1988)
Stephan in *Dreams Beyond Memory* (1987)
Fred in *Improper Channels* (1980)

London Theatre Company: performance calendar

A. In St. John's, 1951-57

First Season 1951-1952

Company: Michael Atkinson, Oliver Gordon, John Holmes, Sheila Huntington, Geoffrey Lumsden, George Paddon-Foster, Gladys Richards, Rosemary Rogers, Dorothea Rundle, Hilary Vernon, Paul Williamson, John Woodnutt, Leslie Yeo

Date	Production	Dramatist	Author's Role
Oct 8-13	Rookery Nook	B. Travers	Gerald
Oct 15-20	Born Yesterday	G. Kanin	Harry Brock
Oct 22-27	The Heiress	R. & A. Goetz	Dr Sloper
Oct 29-Nov 3	The Chiltern Hundreds	W.D. Home	
Nov 5-10	Ten Little Indians	A. Christie	Blore
Nov 12-17	High Temperature	A. Hopwood	*Director*
Nov 19-24	Wuthering Heights	J. Davison	Edgar Linton
Nov 26-Dec 1	Private Lives	N. Coward	
Dec 3-8	Tons of Money	Evans/Valentine	Aubrey
Dec 10-15	Whiteoaks	M. de la Roche	*Director*
Dec 17-22	Black Chiffon	L. Storm	*Director*
Dec 24-29	Charley's Aunt	B. Thomas	Fancourt-Babberley
Dec 31-Jan 5	Worm's Eye View	R.F. Delderfield	Porter
Jan 7-12	Grand National Night	D. & C. Christie	Morton

279

Jan 14-19	Present Laughter	N. Coward	Gary Essendine
Jan 21-26	The Perfect Woman	Geoffrey/Mitchell	Freddie
Jan 28-Feb 2	Jane Eyre	H. Jerome	
Feb 4-9	Harvey	M. Chase	Elwood P. Dowd
Feb 11-16	White Cargo	L. Gordon	
Feb 18-23	A Streetcar Named Desire	T. Williams	Kowalski
Feb 25-Mar 1	Claudia	R. Franken	
Mar 3-8	A Lady Mislaid	K. Horne	Bullock
Mar 10-15	The Taming of the Shrew	W. Shakespeare	Grumio
Mar 17-22	Smilin' Through	A.L. Martin	
Mar 24-29	The Ghost Train	A. Ridley	Teddie
Mar 31-Apr 5	Screech (*musical revue*)	various	various
Apr 14-19	The Voice of the Turtle	J. van Druten	Bill

Second Season 1952-1953

Company: Richard Eastham, Rae Ellison, Oliver Gordon, Roma Haycock, Jacqueline Lacey, Avis Lennard, Charles Mardel, David Morell, Anthony Newlands, George Paddon-Foster, Ruth Perkins, Hilary Vernon, John Woodnutt, Leslie Yeo

Oct 6-11	Pink String and Sealing Wax	R. Pertwee	
Oct 13-18	This Happy Breed	N. Coward	Frank
Oct 20-25	She Stoops to Conquer	O. Goldsmith	Hardcastle
Oct 27-Nov 1	Jane Steps Out	K. Horne	
Nov 3-8	Johnny Belinda	E. Harris	

— interrupted by tour to Halifax—

Dec 26-Jan 3	Cinderella (*pantomime*)	H. Marshall	Ugly Sister
Jan 5-10	The Holly and the Ivy	W. Browne	
Jan 12-17	See How They Run	P. King	Clive

Jan 19-24	Random Harvest	J. Hilton	
Jan 26-31	Duet for Two Hands	M.H. Bell	
Feb 2-7	Love's a Luxury	Paxton/Hoile	*Director*
Feb 9-14	The Seventh Veil	M. & S. Box	Dr Kendal
Feb 16-21	Menace	C. Laurence	Inspector Field
Feb 23-28	Someone at the Door	D. & C. Christie	Ronnie Martin
Mar 2-7	To Dorothy a Son	R. MacDougall	Dr Cameron
Mar 9-14	The Merchant of Venice	W. Shakespeare	Launcelot Gobbo
Mar 16-21	Spring Meeting	Farrell/Perry	Johnny
Mar 23-28	Rebecca	D. du Maurier	Tabb
Mar 30-Apr 4	The Vigil	L. Fodor	Joseph/Peter
Apr 6-11	The Mating Season	Cameron/Boehm	
Apr 13-20	More Screech (*musical revue*)	various	various

Third Season 1953-1954

Company: Barbara Bryne, Sally Day, Robert Dorning, Oliver Gordon, Charles Jarrott, Avis Lennard, Anthony Newlands, George Paddon-Foster, Honor Shepherd, Denny Spence, Kevin Stoney, Bernard Thompson, Hilary Vernon, Monica Wilkinson, Leslie Yeo

Nov 16-21	Queen Elizabeth Slept Here	T. Rothwell	
Nov 23-28	Laura	Caspary/Sklar	Mark
Nov 30-Dec 5	The School for Scandal	R.B. Sheridan	Sir Oliver
Dec 7-12	Spring Model	A. Atkinson	Charlie
Dec 26-Jan 2	Robinson Crusoe (*pantomime*)	H. Marshall	Mrs Crusoe
Jan 4-9	Camille	Storm/Morgan	M. Duval
Jan 11-16	Separate Rooms	Carole/Dinehart	
Jan 18-23	The Deep Blue Sea	T. Rattigan	
Jan 25-30	Still More Screech (*musical revue*)	various	various

Fourth Season 1954-1955

Company: Victor Adams, Barbara Bryne, Robert Dorning, Oliver Gordon, Patricia Gould, Avis Lennard, George Paddon-Foster, Anthony Sagar, Joseph Shaw, Honor Shepherd, Denny Spence, Bernard Thompson, Hilary Vernon, Monica Wilkinson, Leslie Yeo

Dec 27-Jan 1	Babes in the Wood (*pantomime*)	H. Marshall	
Jan 3-8	The Fourposter	J. de Hartog	
Jan 10-15	Murder at the Vicarage	A. Christie	
Jan 17-22	The Moon Is Blue	F.H. Herbert	
Jan 24-29	Will Any Gentleman?	V. Sylvaine	Charlie
Jan 31-Feb 5	The Importance of Being Earnest	O. Wilde	
Feb 7-12	Bell, Book and Candle	J. van Druten	
Feb 14-19	Come Back Little Sheba	W. Inge	Doc
Feb 21-26	His Excellency	D. & C. Christie	Colonel Dobrieda
Feb 28-Mar 5	Mountain Air	R. Wilkinson	
Mar 7-12	Dial M for Murder	F. Knott	
Mar 14-19	Little Women	M. de Forest	
Mar 21-26	And Still More Screech (*musical revue*)	various	various

Fifth Season 1955-1956

Company: Patrick Drysdale, Oliver Gordon, Valerie Hermanni, Michael Lees, Avis Lennard, Dawn Lesley, George Paddon-Foster, Marion Pagniez, Olwen Rasbridge, David Ryder, Joseph Shaw, Bernard Thompson, Hilary Vernon, Norman Welsh, Leslie Yeo

Dec 26-Jan 7	Dick Whittington (*pantomime*)	H. Marshall	Sarah the Cook
Jan 9-14	I Killed the Count	A. Coppel	Diamond
Jan 16-21	The First Year	F. Craven	

Jan 23-28	My Three Angels	S. & B. Spewack	Joseph
Jan 30-Feb 4	The Country Girl	C. Odets	
Feb 6-11	One Wild Oat	V. Sylvaine	Alfred
Feb 13-18	Sabrina Fair	S. Taylor	
Feb 20-25	The Hollow	A. Christie	
Feb 27-Mar 3	When We Are Married	J.B. Priestley	Parker
Mar 5-10	Fair and Warmer	A. Hopwood	George
Mar 12-17	The Caine Mutiny Court-Martial	H. Wouk	Dr Lundeen
Mar 19-24	Pygmalion	G.B. Shaw	
Mar 26-31	Outward Bound	S. Vane	
Apr 2-7	George and Margaret	G. Savory	
Apr 9-14	Lo and Behold	J. Patrick	
Apr 16-21	Even More Screech (*musical revue*)	various	

Sixth Season 1956-1957

Company: Fred Davies, Moya Fenwick, Gillie Fenwick, Ronald Fraser, Bill Glover, Oliver Gordon, Nancie Herrod, Jack Hine, Elizabeth Howe, Heather Macpherson, Ruth Perkins, Stanley Rixon, Joseph Shaw, Hilary Vernon, Mary Williams, Leslie Yeo

Oct 22-27	For Better or Worse	A. Watkyn	
Oct 29-Nov 3	Rain	Colton/Randolph	Joe Horn
Nov 5-10	For Pete's Sake	L. Sands	
Nov 12-17	The Barretts of Wimpole Street	R. Besier	
Nov 19-24	Young Wives' Tale	R. Jeans	
Nov 26-Dec 1	Seagulls over Sorrento	H. Hastings	P/O Herbert
Dec 3-8	Murder on the Nile	A. Christie	
Dec 26-29	Aladdin (*pantomime*)	H. Marshall	Widow Twankey
Dec 31-Jan 5	Life with Father	Lindsay/Crouse	
Jan 7-12	The Tender Trap	Shulman/Smith	

Jan 14-19	The Bishop Misbehaves	F. Jackson	
Jan 21-26	Dragnet	J. Reach	
Jan 28-Feb 2	Running Wild	P. Powell	Roddy Will
Feb 4-9	Anastasia	G. Bolton	Dr Syrensky
Feb 11-16	Anne of Green Gables	A. Chadwicke	
Feb 18-23	The Magic Cupboard	P. Walsh	Bill
Feb 25-Mar 2	The Seven Year Itch	G. Axelrod	
Mar 4-9	The Little Foxes	L. Hellman	
Mar 11-16	The Girl Who Couldn't Quite	L. Marks	
Mar 18-23	The Far-Off Hills	L. Robinson	
Mar 25-Apr 3	Screech – The Last Drop (*musical revue*)	various	various

B.   On tour, 1952-56

1952   Halifax, Nov 10 - Dec 13
> The Perfect Woman, Johnny Belinda, Harvey,
> She Stoops to Conquer, See How They Run

1953   Halifax, Oct 5 - 31
> The School for Scandal, The Chiltern Hundreds,
> Camille, Queen Elizabeth Slept Here

Saint John, Nov 3 - 7
> The School for Scandal, The Chiltern Hundreds

Moncton, Nov 9 - 10
> The School for Scandal, The Chiltern Hundreds

1954   Sydney, Hamilton, London, St. Catharines,
Kitchener, Ottawa, Peterborough, Kingston,
Feb 2 - Mar 27
> The School for Scandal, Camille, Spring Model

Halifax, Mar 30 - Apr 24
> Spring Model, Laura, High Temperature,
> Robinson Crusoe

London (Grand Theatre), May 3 - June 26

High Temperature, The School for Scandal, The Perfect
Woman, Johnny Belinda, Queen Elizabeth Slept Here,
Laura, Present Laughter, London Laughs *(revue)*

Niagara Falls Summer Theatre, June 28 - July 3

The Chiltern Hundreds, Johnny Belinda, The Perfect
Woman, Laura, Queen Elizabeth Slept Here, Harvey,
High Temperature, Present Laughter, Love in a Mist,
Jane Steps Out, See How They Run

1955 Halifax, Apr 4 - May 7

Mountain Air, Little Women, Dial M for Murder,
The Moon Is Blue, The Fourposter

London (Grand Theatre), May 2 - July 2

Mountain Air, The Moon Is Blue, His Excellency,
See How They Run, The Importance of Being Earnest,
Dial M for Murder, Little Women, Murder at the
Vicarage, London Laughs Again *(revue)*

Niagara Falls Summer Theatre, July 4 - Aug 27

Murder at the Vicarage, The Moon Is Blue, Little
Women, French without Tears, The Importance of
Being Earnest, Dial M for Murder, My Three Angels,
Bell Book and Candle

1956 Corner Brook, Apr 30 - May 5

George and Margaret, The Country Girl, Lo and Behold

Halifax, May 7 - June 9

I Killed the Count, My Three Angels, Pygmalion,
Sabrina Fair, Lo and Behold

index

AGMV
MARQUIS
Québec, Canada
1998